STEP ON A CRACK—BREAK THE UNIVERSE'S BACK!

Don't step on the cracks—everyone knew the sense of that. One of the first things you learned as a child. But too many people forgot. Or didn't care.

Graham Smith cared. He knew that paving stones set the cadence of a street; that cracks regulated the stride length and set the resonance that kept everything stable and harmonious. Step on the cracks and the street slipped out of kilter.

Imperceptibly at first. Minute changes around the edges, a new person living at number thirty-three, a strange car outside number five. Step on the cracks too often and . . . well, anything could happen.

He'd seen houses turned into blocks of flats overnight. Parades of shops come and go. Terraces demolished, office blocks erected. All overnight when no one was looking. The world was a far more fragile place than people realized.

And every now and then a thread would work loose and something or someone would unravel. . . .

Baen Books by
Chris Dolley

Resonance

Shift

RESONANCE

CHRIS DOLLEY

RESONANCE

A Baen Book

Baen Publishing Enterprises
P.O. Box 1403
Riverdale, NY 10471
www.baen.com

ISBN 10: 1-4165-2134-8
ISBN 13: 978-1-4165-2134-1

Cover art by Alan Pollack

First Baen paperback printing, June 2007

Distributed by Simon & Schuster
1230 Avenue of the Americas
New York, NY 10020

Library of Congress Cataloging-in-Publication Data:
2005022403

Printed in the United States of America

10 9 8 7 6 5 4 3 2 1

*I'd like to thank Kat Mancos,
Elizabeth McGlothlin, N.R. Simpson,
Shawn Thompson and
Derrick Barnsdale for their helpful
advice and comments.*

ONE

Graham Smith locked the Post Room door, turning the key clockwise as far as it would go. He paused, counting his breaths—one, two—then turned the key counterclockwise. Another pause, more breaths, it had to be four this time, four was good, all even numbers were but four especially so. He repeated the procedure, action for action, breath for breath. Lock, unlock; breathe and count. Twice with the right hand and twice with the left. Only then could he leave work, satisfied that the door was indeed locked and all was well with the world.

Not that it would be for long. You can't create a world in seven days without cutting corners.

"Are you going to the Princess Louise tonight?"

A woman's voice. Anne from Small Businesses? He didn't turn to find out, he knew the question wasn't for him. People didn't talk to Graham Smith unless they had to. Or they were new. Before someone took them aside for a friendly chat, thinking themselves out of earshot, thinking that just because someone was quiet they must be deaf as well. But he'd heard them, heard the whispered warnings by the coffee machine. *Don't bother with Graham, he'll never answer. I've worked here fifteen years and never got a word out of him. Don't get me wrong, he's not dangerous or anything. Just weird. Weird but harmless.*

The woman brushed past, not giving Graham a second look as he turned and dropped the Post Room key into his jacket pocket. He'd been right. It had been Anne, now deep in conversation with the new girl from personnel, planning their night out, eyes flashing, words dancing between them. Conversation came so easily to some people. A tap they could turn on and off without ever worrying what would come spewing out.

Something Graham Smith had never mastered. He'd barely spoken since his ninth birthday and that was twenty-four years ago.

He followed them into the lobby, watched as they waved to Andy at the door, barely breaking sentence as they wished him a good night and pushed through onto the pavement outside.

Graham carefully placed the Post Room key on the reception desk with his right hand—Mondays were always right-handed days—and smiled towards the guard's left shoulder. Eye contact was unlucky whatever the day.

He stepped outside, blinking into the early summer evening. London on a sunny day in June—bright summer clothes, red buses and black taxis. Noise and bustle all around.

He turned right, striding out along the pavement, matching his step to the paving stones, assiduously avoiding the cracks.

Don't step on the cracks—everyone knew the sense of that. One of the first things you learned as a child. But too many people forgot. Or didn't care. Graham Smith cared. He knew that paving stones set the cadence of a street; that cracks regulated the stride length and set the resonance that kept everything stable and harmonious. Step on the cracks and the street slipped out of kilter. Imperceptibly at first. Minute changes around the edges, a new person living at number thirty-three, a strange car outside number five. Step on the cracks too often and . . . well, anything could happen. He'd seen houses turned into blocks of flats overnight. Parades of shops come and go. Terraces demolished, office blocks erected. All overnight when no one was looking.

The world was a far more fragile place than people realized. And every now and then a thread would work loose and something or someone would unravel.

A cloud of diesel smoke spilled out from a bus revving away from its stop. Graham stepped diagonally to avoid it, stretching three pavers over. A few steps more and he had to change lanes again, the pavement filling with commuters and tourists. He sidestepped, jumped and picked his way through the crowd. One eye on his feet and one a few paving stones ahead, searching out the next obstacle.

Which was when he saw her.

She was walking in front of him—four paving stones ahead. Four paving stones exactly, her feet studiously avoiding the cracks, just like Graham. Except that she didn't have to dart back and forth to avoid the other pedestrians—they moved aside for her. He watched, fascinated, as a group of men split apart to let her pass, turning as they did so, their eyes scanning every inch of her, their attention wandering so much that Graham had to sidestep quickly to avoid a collision.

The young woman walked on, indifferent, not looking left nor right.

Graham was fascinated. She flowed along the road, catlike, not walking so much as dancing with the street, her feet matching perfectly the rhythm of the pavement.

Who was she?

And why hadn't he seen her before? He walked this road every day, always at the same time. Was she a tourist? He could see no telltale sign. No camera, no map, not even a bag. Her hands swung loose by her side. Elegant hands, long and slim, like her. Everything about her resonated elegance . . . except . . . except now that he looked closer he could see that her clothes were dirty—her short brown dress looked like it had been slept in for weeks. Or was that the fashion these days? And her hair was badly dyed, a metallic red streaked with black . . . or was that dirt?

He followed her, couldn't take his eyes off her, as she cut a swath through the packed pavement. He watched her from her long, bare legs to her streaky, tousled top. She was like a sinuous metronome, clicking out an unchanging beat, looking straight ahead and not deviating an inch.

Something else caught his eye. What was that above her right ankle? A bruise? No, a tattoo. Something in blue. He quickened his pace, he had to know everything about this girl. He closed the distance between them to three paving slabs, two. He could almost make it out. A bird? Yes, a bird. A tattoo of a blue bird.

He was so engrossed he almost missed his tube station. The entrance loomed on his right like a deep, dark tunnel. The girl walked on. Graham hovered by the entrance, hoping she'd stop or turn.

She didn't.

He had a choice. To take the tube like every other day . . . or follow the girl. Curiosity begged him to follow, instinct said no—he had a routine, routines had to be followed, not girls.

He looked one way and then the other. He couldn't decide. He watched her bobbing head disappearing into the crowd, he peered into the shadow of the foyer; the turnstiles, the ticket machines. He looked back.

She'd gone.

Forty minutes later, Graham was counting the paces as he walked between the post box on the corner to the near gatepost of his home at number thirty-three. A ritual he'd started four years ago when he'd first moved to Oakhurst Drive. A ritual that demanded he arrive exactly on the sixty-sixth step. Sixty-sixth step, left foot, no room for error or bad things were certain to follow.

Fifty-five, fifty-six, he passed next door's laburnum dead on schedule, his feet rising and falling on the dusty grey tarmac. A light wind kept him company, swirling eddies of sweet wrappers around his feet.

He arrived at the gate exactly on the sixty-sixth step, his left toe precisely in line with the inner edge of the gatepost. He turned, swivelling on the ball of his left foot, unlatched the gate with his right hand and walked through.

Two steps and turn, breathe and reach, he took the gate in his left hand and swung it gently back and forth—once, twice, three times—then let it close.

He listened for the latch to click shut then gave it a gentle tug to check with his right hand—it was a Monday—then, satisfied, turned, relaxed and ambled— not even bothering to count the steps—to the door of his prewar pebble-dashed semidetached house.

He was home.

Another day safely negotiated.

He took out his key and pushed it into the lock.

It wouldn't turn.

He tried again.

It still wouldn't turn.

He tried with his left hand, both hands. He took the key out, counted to four and tried again.

Nothing.

Was it stuck? Was it . . .

A sudden intake of breath. Not again. Not so soon. He'd been so careful this time!

A muffled sound came from inside the house. Foot-steps on the stairs, someone coming down, someone inside his house, the house he shared with no one, the house no one ever visited.

A shape appeared, distorted by the frosted glass door. A woman's voice on the other side, nervous, uncertain.

"Is that you, Rob?"

Graham froze, his hand still clutching the key in the lock. It was happening again.

The shape filled the glass door, he could make out a hand moving towards the latch.

"Who's there?" The voice was louder this time, a hint

of panic. Graham withdrew the key, trying to be quiet, trying to keep calm while he backed away from the door. It began to open, he turned, ran, fumbled with the gate, forced himself through.

A voice came from the doorstep. "Who are you? What do you want?"

He ran, flying along the pavement, his breaths coming short and fast, his lungs burning, his eyes watering with the strain. And this time he didn't count or care where he stepped. It was too late for that.

Bad things had already happened.

TWO

He turned right at the corner, dropping down to a fast walk, turning his head every few seconds to check he wasn't being followed, praying that the woman had given up and gone back inside.

It seemed she had.

But what if she'd called the police?

He crossed over, waited for a gap in traffic then hurried across to take the next turning left. He had to get out of the area, stick to the back roads and not look suspicious.

And he had to find his way home. Wherever that was.

His hand reached instinctively into his jacket pocket, searching for the piece of paper he knew it must contain, his lifeline whenever the world and his memory became detached.

He took it out slowly and unfolded the note.

9

Graham Smith
Home Address: 47 Wealdstone Lane

Wealdstone Lane? He couldn't believe it! He'd left there six years ago! He remembered packing, he remembered waiting all morning for the movers to turn up. He'd moved to the flat in Pierrepoint Street . . . until that had unravelled four years ago and he'd found himself at Oakhurst Drive.

Had the last six years unwound?

He read the rest of the note.

Job: Office Messenger
Work Address: Post Room (Room 001),
12 Westminster Street

At least his job hadn't changed. He'd worked at the Department of Trade and Industry since he'd left school at sixteen.

He stared at the note, rereading every line, hoping the words might magically alter in front of his eyes and give him back the life he remembered.

They didn't.

A group of children pushed by, running out into the road to pass, laughing and shouting and seemingly unaware of the fragility of the world they were growing up in. A lawnmower engine started up a few doors down, a car cruised by. Normality all around, seeping in to cover the cracks.

Graham slipped the note back into his pocket and took a deep breath. Wealdstone Lane was about three quarters of a mile back the way he'd come. Back through Oakhurst Drive if he wanted the shortest route.

He didn't.

He took the circuitous route instead, settling back into his walking ritual, looking for landmarks when the streets weren't paved, markers he could use to pace between, counting the strides and making sure he always finished on an even step. Finding comfort in the simple ritual and the hope that, somehow, he was helping the world bed down and the healing process begin.

It was nearly seven o'clock by the time he turned into Wealdstone Lane. The street looked much the same as he remembered it. The house on the corner had a new drive. Number thirty-five had been repainted. But beneath the trimmings the structure of the street remained unchanged. The same red-brick semis, tightly packed. The same undulating pavement of cracked and badly laid paving stones.

And there was his home, number forty-seven, just coming into view. He'd been born in that house. He knew every inch of it. Nothing had changed.

Except the wrought iron gate.

It was black. The old gate had been silver. He'd thought about painting it black but had never gotten around to it.

He unlatched the gate and stepped through, keeping his feet cleanly positioned in the center of the patio paving stones—one, two and turn, breathe and reach, switch hands and swing—once, twice, three times, release and click. He smiled, he couldn't help it. The beauty of ritual and the unexpected joy of seeing an old friend. The gate could have performed the ritual by itself, all those thousands of times it had swung back and forth to his touch.

Every caress, every motion, ingrained into its fabric.

He took a deep breath and felt for his key as he walked the few yards to his front door. Would the key fit? He counted to four then slowly slipped the key into the lock.

The key turned, smooth and unchecked. He counted to two, relaxed his grip and let the pressure of the lock slowly force the key back to its original position. Another count, another turn, left, right and push.

The door swung open.

Inside, it was like stepping back six years. The carpets, the stairs, the furniture—all exactly as he remembered. Only his face in the hall mirror had aged, everything else looked straight out of a time capsule.

He walked from room to room, picking up familiar objects, opening cupboard doors, fingering ornaments. He recognized them all.

Even the ones that shouldn't be there. Like the sofa he'd sold when he moved to Pierrepoint Street. And the electric kettle he'd bought only six months ago.

He walked upstairs, slowly taking in his surroundings. Everything familiar, everything clean and orderly. He crossed the landing into his bedroom at the back. Again, everything was present and in its place. His small pine bed, his blue quilt, his dressing table, lamp and clock.

And his notice board. Covered as usual in yellow Post-it notes. Everything he needed to know would be recorded there. The name of his doctor, his dentist, any appointments he had or addresses he needed to know. Everything he'd need for times like this, when the world slipped a thread and became detached from his memory.

He read them one by one. All were written in his hand-writing and yet he had no recollection of writing any of them—even the one dated yesterday.

He crossed the room to his bookshelf and ran a hand along the spines, checking the titles. A few he didn't recognize, a few that should have been there weren't. A story repeated with his clothes. The new jacket he'd bought last week was missing and there was a pair of black jeans he'd never seen before.

Another thought hit him. How far had this thread unravelled?

He stepped uneasily onto the landing. His parents' bedroom door was closed. But then it always had been. At least, since the last time, the time his mother had disappeared.

He stopped in front of the door, unsure, his hand hovering over the door handle. Should he knock? Call out?

He knocked tentatively, the word "mum" lodged in his throat.

No answer.

He closed his fingers around the knob, twisting and ever so slowly easing the door open. The door creaked. He peered in. Not sure what to expect. Would he see his mother, his father, an empty room?

He could barely breathe. His hand began to shake. He pushed the door wider. Their double bed came into view; the pink bedspread, the fluffed pillows, the two bedside tables.

His hopes fell. Both tables were empty; no book, no glass of water, no open box of tissues. No sign of occupation.

He forced himself further into the room and checked behind the door. His mother's dressing gown was still there. He opened the wardrobe. It was full: dresses and suits, skirts and jackets. All their clothes were there, wrapped in the smell of mothballs. He wondered if he should call out. Was there a chance they'd hear? Was there a chance they were still alive? Somewhere?

Silence.

He didn't call and no one answered. The story of Graham Smith's life.

The next day he set off for work at his usual time, walking to the tube station at Harrow-on-the-Hill, waiting on the platform for the Baker Street train. The train came and he jumped on, quickly moving inside to take one of the few remaining seats. He liked to sit and gaze out the window on the opposite side. To wile away his journey by looking out for landmarks. He'd tick them off as they flew by: that school, the big fir tree, the funny-shaped tower. They gave meaning to his journey. He wasn't just travelling from A to B; he was helping preserve the fabric of the world.

A fabric in need of constant reinforcement. The more something's observed the stronger it becomes. Its edges become sharper, its colors brighter. But ignore something long enough and it always goes away. That's the nature of the world. One day you ride by and it's gone.

The train pulled into and out of stations; people got up, sat down, walked by, hung from straps, the train filling with every stop. A large man carrying a suitcase shuffled in front of Graham and grabbed a strap. Graham shifted in his seat, looking for another unobstructed view of the window. A girl stared back at him. He looked away, gazing hurriedly at someone's back while watching the girl out of the corner of his eye. She was still looking at him, her eyes fixed. Had he left some remnant of breakfast on his face?

He moved his tongue in a wide sweep around his mouth, checking for crumbs. The girl did the same and smiled.

Graham reddened and slid along his seat as far to the right as he could, away from her line of sight.

The train entered a tunnel; there was a sudden whoosh of noise and a momentary blackness followed by the stutter of the carriage lights.

Graham leaned even further to the right, trying to catch his reflection in the blackness of the window opposite. Was there something strange about him today? Had he cut himself shaving? He strained his eyes, peering at the badly focused image. He ran a hand through his hair, over his face. He found nothing. No breakfast, no blood, no enormous spot.

He looked down at his clothes. Had he misbuttoned his shirt? Was there a stain?

There was nothing, nothing that he could see.

He checked the other passengers, was anyone else looking at him? He slowly scanned the carriage, watching people's faces in his peripheral vision, never looking at anyone directly, never giving anyone a chance to take offense.

No one appeared to be watching him.

Except the man by the doorway! He *was* looking. Wasn't he?

The man looked away.

The train lurched and swung, tunnels came and went in quick succession.

Graham was confused. He was anonymous. People

didn't look at him. Ever. Even if the man by the door was a coincidence there was still the girl. She'd smiled at him. No one ever smiles on the tube.

He glanced back towards the girl, with her face hidden behind the ample body of the man with the suitcase he could watch her in safety. She was wearing jeans, her legs crossed, her right foot bouncing up and down with the motion of the train, her shoe loose and flapping, her . . .

No, it couldn't be!

She had a tattoo, just above the right ankle, just below the hem of her jeans. A tattoo of a blue bird.

Graham's mind raced. Was it the same girl? Her hair wasn't red, was it? It was more orange from the brief glimpse he'd had. But that didn't mean anything these days. It might have been dyed. Or a wig.

And if it *was* the same girl . . .

He was intrigued. And panicked at the same time. Intrigued by the possibility that here was someone who saw the world as he did. Who appreciated the danger of stepping on cracks. And panicked by the fear that she didn't; that it was all an act, a joke primed to explode in his face. He'd been the butt of too many jokes to trust the first stranger that smiled at him on a train.

And even if it wasn't a joke what could he do about it? He wasn't like other people. Any attempt at casual conversation would end in disaster. He'd learned that lesson a long time ago. The rest of the world was on a different wavelength to him, anything he said would either be laughed at or cause offense.

The train began to brake hard. Graham looked up, was it Baker Street already? The train continued its long deceleration, commuters grabbed hold of straps and hand rails, newspapers were folded, bags picked up.

The train stopped. Graham stayed in his seat, watching for the girl as an endless stream of people filed between them. He caught glimpses of her between the bodies. She smiled, he looked at his shoes. She was attractive in a street urchin sort of way, her features angular, her hair bright orange and unbrushed. What was she; twenty, twenty-two? A few more people filed past. He looked for her again. She'd gone.

He was still thinking of the girl on the tube as he performed his morning unlocking ritual on the Post Room door. He'd looked for her on the platform, he'd looked for her on the Bakerloo train, he'd half-expected to see her walking ahead of him on Westminster Street. But he hadn't.

He pushed open the door and switched on the lights. The Post Room flickered into life. He walked over to the terminal in the near corner and switched it on, waited for the screen to come to life so he could log in and print off the staff list.

"Morning, Graham." A young Indian girl came through the door. Graham smiled and nodded in her direction. Sharmila smiled back and hung up her coat.

"Oh, I nearly forgot. Mr. Anton was in the lobby. He wants you to call round at three this afternoon. Something about a large batch of documents that need to go out on the afternoon van."

Graham picked up a Post-it pad on the desk and searched for a pen. Which room was Mr. Anton in these days? Three hundred thirty-six? He browsed the staff list on the screen to make sure. There it was, U.S. desk, room 336. He carefully wrote out the details and stuck the note to the side of his in-tray. A dozen other Post-its ringed his in-tray like an early Christmas decoration. Another twenty adorned the notice board above. They were his memory made tangible. Whatever happened to the world outside, however dislocated his memory became, he knew that here was one place he could trust. One place that kept pace with an everchanging world.

He didn't know how other people coped. He used to ask—his parents, other kids—but they'd look at him as though he was stupid or swiftly change the subject.

His father had taken him aside one night just before his eighth birthday. "Sit down, Graham," he'd said. "We need to talk." Graham had sat down, shuffling along his bed to sit back against the headboard.

"Children can be cruel," his father had said, smiling and making room for himself on the edge of the bed. "They pick on kids who are different. They'll pick on you if you keep asking these questions. See?"

Graham had nodded, bouncing his head up and down in exaggerated agreement, his arms clenched tightly around his bear.

"Good," his father had said, looking relieved. "We'll never talk about this again. Right?"

"Right, Dad."

And he hadn't, though it hadn't stopped him thinking about it. It was obvious people didn't want to talk about unravelling. He understood that now. It made them uneasy. So they pretended it never happened. And hoped to God they were somewhere else, safe and untouched, whenever the next thread worked loose.

❀   ❀   ❀

Graham pushed the mail trolley along the short corridor back into the Post Room.

"Well, if it isn't Mr. Post-it."

Graham's heart sank. Surely it had gone eleven. He always timed his rounds to be out of the Post Room whenever Ray was driving the midmorning van. He glanced at the clock on the far wall, just the slightest of glances, enough to confirm the time—eleven-fifteen—and then quickly turned the glance into a deferential nod towards Ray.

And added a smile, his shield against the world.

"Shut up, Ray, you know he doesn't like it."

That was Sharmila, undoubtedly the reason Ray was still hanging around the Post Room. She sat at her desk, probably trying to work, while Ray hovered behind her, looking down her dress.

"Of course he does," said Ray. "Look at him, he's smiling."

Graham turned away, retracting his smile and pushing the trolley over to the sorting stacks. If only he could push Ray away so easily.

"I'm surprised he hasn't stuck one of those notes on you, Shar."

Ray laughed. Sharmila hissed something inaudible. Graham started sorting the mail from the trolley. He picked up the first envelope and looked for the name: G. Stevens, 5th floor. He didn't recognize the name, not that that in itself was unusual. People had a habit of coming and going.

He checked the list for G. Stevens, and found her in

room 510. She must have taken Jerzy's old job. He checked the list again. What had happened to Jerzy? He wasn't anywhere on the list and he hadn't heard anyone talking about Jerzy leaving. There'd been no collection or leaving card. At least not that he remembered.

But then that's what often happened. Sometimes people just disappeared. Their name would be removed from the staff list and all record of them having worked in the building would be erased. They'd never existed, never worked for the department and no one would ever talk about them again. The office taboo; you don't talk about the unravelled.

Even when they came back.

Which Graham couldn't understand at all. How could you not talk to an old friend who'd disappeared for six months? But it happened so many times. They disappear, they come back and everyone treats them as strangers. Even close friends, people they'd gone drinking with every lunchtime, would pass them by in the corridor without a second look.

It was like they'd broken some unwritten rule. They'd come back. They'd made people face up to something they preferred not to. So they had to be punished, made to start over as though it was their first day and everyone was a stranger.

Laughter broke out behind him. Ray again. He had an unpleasant laugh, more sneer than humor.

"Shush!" hissed Sharmila. "He'll hear."

Graham tried to block Ray out of his mind as he filed the first envelope in 510's pigeonhole. Not that he understood why Ray was still employed by the department. He'd been arrested last year for abducting little girls. Even used the department's van. Or so Graham had heard. You hear a lot when you keep your mouth closed and your ears open.

Though he'd never heard what had happened to the charges against Ray. Dropped most likely. The legal system was in a mess. Everyone said so. You only had to read the papers.

"Well, nice talking to you, Graham."

Ray's departing shot, loaded with sarcasm and fired in Graham's direction. Graham ignored it, as he always did, lifting a hand in acknowledgement and keeping his eyes on his work.

"See you tomorrow, Shar."

Ray whistled into the distance, the delivery bay doors swinging shut behind him.

"He's all right really. Once you get to know him," said Sharmila, looking almost wistfully towards the door.

Graham had known many Rays over the years. None of them had improved with acquaintance.

The cloakroom door swung closed behind him as Graham stepped out into the second floor lobby. He liked to use the men's room on the second floor on Tuesdays—it was part of his rota; five men's toilets, five working days. Visit them in turn and keep them all functioning. So easy for a room to lose cohesion without regular use. Once you took people out of a room anything could happen. Storerooms were notoriously fragile.

He pressed the button for the lift and waited. The seconds ticked by, he checked his watch, rocked back and forth on his heels and counted the first row of ceiling tiles.

The lift bell rang as he counted the twelfth tile—always a good sign. Lifts that arrive on an odd number never feel right. They're either packed or stop at every floor or there's someone inside you don't want to meet.

The lift doors opened and Graham walked in, carefully avoiding eye contact and turning to face the doors as soon as he could.

"Hello, Graham, haven't seen you today."

Graham beamed. He hadn't noticed Brenda in the corner. He turned and grinned and gave her his "maybe this afternoon" sign—a shrug and a fist rotated clockwise, one of the half dozen or so signs he'd developed over the years.

"I'll look forward to it."

He liked Brenda—always had—they'd joined the department at the same time, Brenda as a clerical officer, Graham as a messenger. She made him feel almost normal. She didn't treat him as deaf or stupid, she didn't slow down her speech or raise her voice or talk about him as though he wasn't there. She wasn't brusque or patronizing. She made him feel visible, something that Graham Smith appreciated more than most.

He waved goodbye to Brenda on the ground floor and slipped back into the Post Room to pick up his jacket and sandwiches.

And found something unexpected.

There was a second note in his jacket pocket.

Do it now. They're on to you.

He read it again, shocked. What did it mean? He flipped it over—blank—flipped it back. *Do it now. They're on to you*. Do what now? Who was on to him?

And who had written it? He didn't recognize the hand-writing. Which was odd. He was used to finding strange notes in his pocket but they were always in the same handwriting. And it was always the same note—even if he never remembered writing it—it always contained the same basic information—name, address, job, place of work. All the information he'd need to get home or find his way to work. But this?

Had someone slipped it into his jacket while he'd been out of the room? Or maybe before that—on the street or on the tube? It hadn't been there when he'd left this morning, had it?

Not that he could trust his memory.

Best to ignore it, he decided. Ignore it and it will go away. It'll be a joke, probably Ray. He stopped at the curb and waited for the lights to change. People milled all around him; the noise of lunchtime traffic and conversation, music spilling out from the shops and passing cars.

The lights changed and a wall of people surged over the road. Graham hung back and let them flow around him. Then he was back on the pavement, his mind free of strange notes and soothed instead by the calming mantra of ritual. Left and right, back and forth, one foot after the other, each step preordained and symbiotic. Streets were like pets—they loved to be stroked. They loved the repetition, the constancy, the daily caress of a well-measured stride.

He noticed her shoes first, walking alongside him, matching his stride and avoiding the cracks. Her blue bird tattoo rising and falling to the amplitude of the street.

Then she spoke. Her voice low, soft and, unexpectedly, American.

"Don't look around. Look straight ahead. They're watching."

Graham wobbled momentarily, his eyes swivelling nervously from the girl on his left to whoever might be lurking in the shop doorways to his right.

"Pretend I'm asking for money."

She walked a little ahead of him, her body half turned towards him, her face boring into his. He kept on walking, not sure what he was supposed to do.

"Did you get my note? Look, I don't know what it is you do but whatever it is you better do it soon. They're on to you and they're gonna stop you. Any way they can. You know what I mean?"

He shook his head. He didn't have a clue what she was talking about.

"It's all right, you can talk to me. I'm a friend. Probably the only friend you've got at the moment. Trust me, there is some way serious shit going down and you're right in the middle of it. People want you dead. Important people with a lot of money and a lot of friends."

Graham swallowed hard and kept walking. This had to be a joke. He was invisible to the world. No one could possibly have any interest in him.

"Trust me, it's for real. You don't have much time. And burn that note I gave you, they go through your garbage."

She peeled off and immediately latched onto a middle-aged couple walking in the other direction.

"Spare some change, lady?"

THREE

Graham spent the rest of the afternoon in turmoil. What the hell was going on? Was the girl insane or part of some elaborate joke?

He couldn't fathom it. If it was a joke, what was the point? To frighten him, to make him do something stupid? He could imagine Ray setting him up, he could imagine Ray persuading a girlfriend to play along. But he couldn't imagine Ray not being there to watch. That wasn't Ray. He'd have to be there and he'd make sure he was seen to be there.

But if it wasn't Ray?

It had to be mistaken identity. The girl had mixed him up with someone else. That or she really was insane.

He looked out for her on his journey home that evening. Once or twice he thought he caught a glimpse but either he was mistaken or she didn't want to be seen.

Gradually he pushed her out of his mind, burying himself instead in ritual and extra counting. Nothing like monotonous exercise to cleanse the mind.

Graham performed his ten o'clock door-locking ritual: lock, unlock, breathe and count, right-handed for the front door, left-handed for the back. He latched the chain on the front door and bolted the back. And then did it all again.

Twice.

You can't be too careful about home security.

Or overlook the fragility of memory.

He scribbled "Tuesday" on a Post-it note and pressed it firmly to the front door, burning the image into his memory—*front door locked, Tuesday*. He repeated the process at the back door. He knew only too well the fear of lying awake in the middle of the night, unable to remember if he'd locked the doors, unsure if a memory came from last night or the night before.

Peace of mind was always worth the extra effort.

Which made him remember the girl's warning about the note. He stood for a moment at the foot of the stairs, wondering. What if she was right? What if people were going through his rubbish?

He went back to the kitchen, picked up a box of matches and set the note alight, holding it between his finger and thumb before letting it fall into the ash tray by the cooker. He watched the note crinkle and blacken, then took the ash tray into the cloakroom under the stairs and flushed its contents down the toilet. Let someone try and piece that back together.

❋ ❋ ❋

He awoke suddenly in the night. Everything black except for a grey veil of light at the bedroom window. Something had woken him. He wasn't sure what. A noise, a voice—something—nearby.

The girl's warning flew into his head—*people want you dead.*

He froze. Listening. Everything quiet. Everything except the thud of his heart in his chest.

There it was again! A scraping noise coming from his back garden! He threw off his covers and fell out of bed, landing on the carpet on all fours. He stayed there for a second, ears pricked like a dog. Unsure what to do.

The noise returned, not so loud this time. What was it? Was someone trying to break in? Or was it a cat?

He inched towards the window, fighting his fear. The curtain rippled slowly in the cool night air. His window was open. Just an inch, he liked the fresh air. Had that been a mistake? Should he have heeded the girl's warning and kept it locked? Maybe he should close it now, pull down the sash and lock it tight? Or would that draw the killer's attention?

Calm down, Graham. Why does it have to be a killer? It could be a burglar, a twelve-year-old kid on a dare, a scavenging dog.

He rose to a crouch and crept towards the window. Everything seemed lighter as his eyes gradually became accustomed to the dark. He moved to the side of the curtain and stretched up on tiptoe. Slowly he pulled the edge of the curtain back, an inch—no more—just enough to peer down at the garden.

Nothing. The small back lawn, the flower beds—everything grey and empty.

He eased the curtain wider and leaned further in. Still nothing. No movement, no noise. He could see all the back garden now, all except the area immediately below the window.

He stepped gingerly across the room and out into the corridor, the carpet cold and soft against his bare feet. He'd check the front: the storeroom curtains were open; he'd have a good view from there.

He tiptoed towards the window. The houses across the street stared back, grey and silent, not a single light in any window.

He edged closer. He could see the street now, two lines of parked cars, his front wall . . .

His gate! It was open. He never left it open. And no one had come to the house last night, no one had knocked at the door or pushed anything through the letter box. He'd have heard, he'd have seen.

Someone had to be out there, now. They'd left the gate open for a quick getaway. They were around the back trying the windows. That's how they worked, wasn't it?

He flew back to his bedroom. He had to find some clothes, he had to get dressed, he had to get out.

People want you dead, her words wouldn't go away. He threw off his pajamas, searched the darkness for whatever clothes he could find.

Click!

He froze, one leg in a pair of trousers. The sound came from his back door, he was certain of it. The sound of a lock being turned. He had bolted the back door, hadn't he? *Back door locked, Tuesday*. The memory came flooding back. But what day was it now? Wednesday? Thursday?

He hopped and pulled at his trousers, one leg was stuck and the other was cramping. Shit! Shit! Shit! He fell over, still pulling and stretching. He had to get out. He had to get out now!

A low thud came from downstairs. Then another. Graham swept the floor with his hands, frantically searching for his shoes. He found them, struggled with the laces, grabbed his jacket, his keys, his wallet.

He flew downstairs. *People want you dead.* He had to get out. It was his only hope. There was no telephone. He wouldn't have one in the house. He was alone, totally alone.

His hands closed on the chain at the front door. He held his breath as he slipped the chain and slowly, noiselessly, opened the door.

A window smashed behind him. The kitchen! He pulled the front door towards him and squeezed through, easing it closed behind him—no ritual, no counting, barely a breath.

Had he been seen? He prayed not, he prayed that whoever was breaking in had been too busy working on the kitchen window to notice him slip out the front.

He stepped lightly toward the open gate, slipped through, glanced back towards the house. A circle of light flitted alone in the darkness—a torchlight—ascending the stairs.

He turned away, head down, walking fast, trying to suppress the noise of his feet on the paving stones. The night was so quiet. If he ran they'd hear him for miles.

The moon shone through dappled clouds, its light

haloed in a giant circle. In the distance, the orange glow from a line of streetlights bled into the sky. He walked on, stepping through the moonlight. Was the man alone, was there a lookout in a car?

He felt like he was wading through treacle, would the corner never come? *People want you dead.* Was this what it was like to be at the epicenter of an unravelling? Had all the others he experienced been mere aftershocks? Was he about to disappear like his father?

A noise from behind. A door closing—his door—running feet. He ran, no point being quiet now. A car door slammed, an engine started. Graham ducked around the corner, tires screeched behind him. He ran out between two parked cars, racing across the road in the darkness. More tire screeching, the car had reached the corner and was turning, its headlights swung round, light bouncing off the curving avenue of trees and parked cars. Graham ran ahead of the beam, keeping low, the path ahead alive with light and bouncing shadows. Trees loomed out of the night, twisted branches dancing between grey and black.

The car was catching up. Seconds away. Graham ducked lower, keeping to the shadows, praying he was hidden by the line of parked cars. There was an alley up ahead, a footpath between the houses, too narrow for cars. If he reached it the car couldn't follow. By the time the car had driven around the block Graham would be gone.

Unless the driver stopped.

And followed on foot.

Graham ducked into the alley, praying his exit had been obscured in the shadows, praying never to hear the squeal of brakes. The car flew past. Graham ran. A deep darkness descended as the alley curved between high wooden fences. It snaked left then right. Light appeared, the distant glow of shops from the High Street about two hundred yards up ahead.

Still no sound of brakes.

A moment's optimism soon smothered. *People want you dead.*

He ran faster. The lights of the High Street drawing him onward. He'd be safe there. There'd be people: witnesses, passing traffic, police cars. The alley opened onto a cul-de-sac; more lines of cars and houses in darkness. He pounded along the pavement, the lights of the High Street bouncing closer, he could see them through the film of water that covered his eyes. Pain was everywhere: his lungs, his chest, his legs. His nose ran and his head hurt. But he kept running.

People want you dead. The High Street grew ahead of him, the shops, the lights, the faint noise of traffic. He was nearly there. A girl sat in a shop doorway opposite, a girl with bright orange hair. He was running towards her. She stood up, waved. He was crossing the road, barely glancing right or left.

"In here!"

She pointed to a huge cardboard box at the back of the doorway. Her hands began to fold back the flaps at the mouth of the box.

"Come on! Inside."

He could see the darkness within, bright lights all around, safety beckoning; could he trust her, was it a trap? Before he could answer he was diving, full length, hitting the marble tiles of the doorway on his hands and knees and sliding, scurrying across the cardboard flaps and into the blackness beyond. The flaps closed behind him, darkness descended and all around was the lingering smell of stale sweat.

FOUR

Blackness, breaths coming fast, chest heaving, hands shaking, leg tapping. His world contracted into a few cubic meters, he sat, hunched over, knees drawn up, hands locked around them, head bowed, hair brushing against the roof of the box.

Fear.

Stark and raw.

People want you dead.

Words whispered in the black of night. *People . . . Dead . . . Want you.*

The words wouldn't go away. He rocked back and forth, closed his ears, pulled his world in tighter and tighter. No one else existed. Just him, the box and the night.

And the sound of a car coming closer and closer.

No! He clamped his hands to his ears and rocked faster,

his hair swishing against the cardboard roof.

The car kept coming, its engine whining through the gears—first, second, third—louder and louder. A roar, a squeal of brakes, the car thrown into reverse, another squeal of brakes.

"You see a man run this way?"

"Yeah," said the girl. "He ran down there."

The car pulled away, screeching, whining, roaring into the distance. Graham held his breath—three, four, five seconds—the car kept going, quieter and quieter. Breathe and pray, count and hope. Six, seven, another squeal. Brakes? Panic welling. The car accelerating again, its sound muffling. It must have turned a corner, taken the left fork at the top of the High Street. Eleven, twelve . . .

"He's gone," said the girl. "You're safe now."

A scrabbling noise came from the far end of the box. Graham looked up and blinked at the sudden influx of light as the girl drew back the flaps. Her face appeared, tilted to one side, framed in light from the shops, her hair falling over one cheek. She smiled and held out a hand.

"Hi, I'm Annalise, Annalise Mercado, and you'd better be Graham Smith."

He took her hand nervously, forced a smile and nodded a thank you.

"I know about the not-talking thing, that's cool."

A car engine roared in the distance. She turned and listened. Graham rocked gently back and forth, praying for the car to go away, praying for the night to end and for everything to return to normal.

The car was coming closer.

Annalise ducked her head back in the box, "I'd better close this up. Can't be too careful."

Darkness descended once more. The car, the night, the endless chase, the fear. He closed his eyes and swallowed hard. He couldn't handle this, he couldn't handle this at all. He rocked, he shook, he pulled his arms tighter around his knees. Make it go away, make it all go away.

The car raced by closely followed by another. Time dragged, Graham counted, the sound of the two cars taking forever to die. The flaps opened on eleven.

"All clear," she said, smiling. "Wasn't him."

Graham tried to return the smile but couldn't.

"You know, you're a difficult person to meet. You don't go out, your house is watched, people like follow you everywhere. I bet they even open your mail. And I've been like trying to get your attention for days without anyone noticing. You know, the walk and the eye contact thing? And now here you are. How'd you know I was gonna be here?"

Graham shrugged, his shoulders still hunched from gripping his knees. He felt cold and his throat was dry.

"Just lucky I guess," the girl continued. "I'm only here so that I could catch you on your way to work. I was going to slip this note into your pocket. Here." She dug into her jeans and pulled out a folded scrap of paper. "You might as well have it now. You're lucky I'm a light sleeper. Not that you were exactly quiet. You are *no* stealthy fugitive."

He took the note, glancing at it briefly as it shook in his hand. What would it say? Even more people want you dead? He found his jacket pocket with difficulty and stuffed it inside.

"Anyway," said the girl. "It's all in the note. What I've managed to figure out anyway. It's all linked to ParaDim. Don't know where you fit in but they are way interested in you. And me. Though no one wants to kill me. Which is a big plus. And they give me money—I'm a kinda consultant. Yeah, I know the kind that lives in a box but, hey, a box is bigger than a suitcase, right? Anyway, it saved your ass."

Her words flowed right over him. It was like she was talking to him down a long dark tunnel. Her words echoed and ran into each other. He felt light-headed and tired and cold and wanted everything to stop. This wasn't happening. This couldn't be happening.

He rocked back and forth, wringing his hands, repeating the same phrase over and over to himself. *This can't be happening, this can't be happening.*

Arms enfolded him. Warmth pressed into his cold, dark world.

"Everything'll be okay," whispered someone very close.

And for a while he believed her.

He awoke with a start. The ground vibrating, the roar of an engine—a truck—passing within feet of his head.

He panicked, thrashing in the dark, his feet hitting cardboard. He was . . .

In a box?

Fragments of the previous night drifted back into memory. The chase, the girl, the cardboard box.

Where was she? He reached out, hesitantly, his hand ready to draw back the instant it encountered anything soft.

It didn't.

He was alone.

He turned and pushed at the end flaps of the box. It was light outside, traffic was building up, a few pedestrians walked by on the other side of the road.

He crawled out, feeling conspicuous, confused and dishevelled. He brushed himself off and stepped out onto the pavement.

Where was she?

He looked up and down the street. There were about a dozen people but no Annalise. Where had she gone? Had she stepped out for breakfast or a call of nature?

He didn't know what to do. Was he still in danger? Should he look for her, hide, go home?

His little voice told him to go home. Go home, keep out of other peoples' way and they'll keep out of yours.

But he couldn't. She might be in trouble. She might need money for food. He couldn't abandon her. She'd helped him. He owed her.

He ran along the High Street, first in one direction then the other, quartering the area, looking inside the handful of shops that were open—the sandwich bars, the newspaper shops. He couldn't find her anywhere. The girl had disappeared.

He lingered in the last sandwich bar, overpowered by the smell of bacon. He glanced at the clock above the counter—six forty-five. He'd be having breakfast now. If he hadn't been chased from his home in the middle of the night.

He ordered a bacon sandwich and wondered what he should do next. Could he go home? Should he contact the police? Would they believe him this time?

He doubted it; there was probably a file on him several inches thick. *Come to report another missing person have you, sir?*

He wasn't going through that again.

He'd give the High Street one more go. Maybe the

girl had returned, maybe she was back in the doorway
wondering what had happened to him.

She wasn't.

And neither was the box.

FIVE

Had someone moved it?

The shop owner? Road sweepers? The girl? Had she come back and taken it away, hidden it somewhere so she could use it again tonight?

Or had it unravelled?

He prayed for the unravelling. If ever there was a time for a thread of reality to be pulled, this was it. He'd welcome the uncertainty—anything—to have a line drawn under the last twenty-four hours.

He felt for his note, pulled it out, unfolded it. Maybe he wouldn't have to go back to Wealdstone Lane after all.

He read the note, nothing had changed. He was still living at Wealdstone Lane, still working at the DTI. He put the note back. And froze. Shouldn't there have been a second note? The note from the girl, the one that explained everything?

He searched his pockets. Twice. The note had gone.

Or had peeled away in the unravelling.

A church bell tolled seven. Graham instinctively looked at his watch. It was a minute fast. He stopped dead. When had he put his watch on? Not last night. He'd had enough trouble finding his shoes let alone locating his watch. It shouldn't be here.

And yet it was.

Another thought; he felt his chin. It was smooth. He'd shaved. There *had* been an unravelling! There must have been.

He grinned. He couldn't help it. Let the rest of the world think him strange, what did that matter? At least no one was trying to kill him any more.

For two days Graham Smith's life settled back into its normal routine. There were the usual aftershocks that followed an unravelling—a few more colleagues at work disappeared than was usual, a new road appeared where people's gardens used to be and two tube stations changed their names. But that was only to be expected. You can't remove a thread without affecting those close by.

He tried to forget everything that had happened. It had unravelled, gone. All part of the flawed nature of existence. Threads worked loose and there was nothing anyone could do about it. You endured and it went away. End of story.

And then came Friday.

He was on the fifth floor counting ceiling tiles while waiting for the lift. The lift arrived on the thirteenth tile.

Any other day and he'd have swung his trolley into a quick one-eighty and tried the lifts on the far side of the building. But, today, he was in a hurry.

So he took the lift, pressed the button for the ground floor and hoped no one else would get in. The lift stopped on the third floor. Two men strolled in. He vaguely recognized them, senior managers—assistant secretaries, under secretaries—something like that. Neither of them acknowledged Graham. The older of the two selected the first floor and turned to his companion.

"Don't forget, Brian, I want those ParaDim tenders prioritized."

Graham's ears pricked. Paradigm?

"Ring round all the major software houses and impress upon them the importance of getting in on the ground floor. The universities too. I don't care how sceptical they pretend to be—ParaDim is going to be massive and no one can afford to miss out."

The lift doors opened on the first floor and they left. Graham remained rooted to the back of the lift, he couldn't even reach out and close the lift doors. Annalise had talked about Paradigm. "It's all linked to Paradigm," she'd said. "People want you dead."

It was starting again.

The rest of the morning and all through lunch he couldn't stop thinking about Paradigm and what it might mean. Was it coincidence or just the inevitable result of boarding a lift after a count of thirteen?

He sat down at his terminal as soon as he returned from lunch. He logged in and navigated around the DTI site, trying to remember where the search page was located. Sharmila had shown him once but he hadn't been that interested. It wasn't something he'd thought he'd ever use.

Until today.

He found something called search, waited for the page to load, then typed in PARADIGM.

No matches.

Perhaps he'd spelt it wrong? He deleted the "g," it didn't look right anyway, and pressed send. He waited, wondering if the "m" was wrong too.

The result came back. One hit. *ParaDim: General project overview and tender information.*

He clicked on the entry and watched as a new screen appeared. It read:

> *ParaDim: the future today.*
>
> *ParaDim is a vast data collection and analysis project designed to revolutionize the advancement of knowledge. By collating data across all subjects and disciplines and applying groundbreaking artificial intelligence algorithms, ParaDim accelerates scientific discovery. What would have taken decades to accomplish is now achievable in months.*
>
> *Imagine bringing ten thousand of the world's premier experts together in one room and allowing a spontaneous cross-fertilization of ideas. Now imagine a hundred thousand, a million, ten million. ParaDim makes that possible. It sifts, collates and interprets, using the collected experiences and knowledge of the world to bring a fresh eye onto old problems. No preconception, prejudice or personality. No subject too complex or task too large.*

ParaDim seeks partner organizations to help in the collection, storage and processing of data. Partner organizations will be allocated shares in ParaDim Inc. ensuring that everyone benefits from the patents, franchises and new business opportunities that are certain to be generated. The pilot project produced five patents that are widely predicted to revolutionize the electronics and manufacturing industries.

The amount of data to be processed is vast, as is the amount generated by the AI process in its intermediate scans. ParaDim envisages approximately five hundred partner organizations in ParaDim Phase One, increasing to three thousand by ParaDim Phase Three. Exact specifications are detailed in the appendices.

Knowledge has always been power, now it can be profitable too. Be a part of the new technological revolution: ParaDim.

Graham clicked on the appendices but soon got lost in a mass of figures and technical specifications. How many bytes were there in a terabyte? And just how big was an octillion?

He returned to the previous page and reread the overview. And wondered how any of it could have anything to do with him?

SIX

Graham left work that evening determined to put ParaDim out of his head for the entire weekend. He'd dig out his hardest jigsaw—The Quarrel of Oberon and Titania—the one with all the faces, five thousand pieces of obscure fairy parts and water lilies. Guaranteed to tie up anyone's mind for two days.

The thought pleased him, he loved jigsaw puzzles, he loved to lose himself in the pursuit of a puzzle that, however complex, never had more than one answer. The cover picture never changed, the pieces never altered shape or disappeared. Everything stayed as it should.

If only life could be that constant.

He paced between the flagstones, imprinting his brand of stability into the fabric of the street. The usual Friday evening rush milled discordantly around him. Up ahead a subway opened in the pavement like a giant mouth. Graham migrated into the center of the pavement to pass by and stopped dead.

She was there. The girl, Annalise, standing by the railing at the mouth of the subway, two suitcases by her feet and an A to Z guide in her hand. She was blonde this time but it was definitely her. She was staring straight at him, looking as though she'd seen a ghost.

He walked towards her, not sure what to do. Instinct told him to look down at his feet and walk past. The girl was trouble, all people were. But she'd helped him, saved his life maybe. And he hadn't even thanked her.

He wobbled in midstride, unable to make up his mind. She looked older than he remembered, her clothes were less shabby too—no rips or weeks of ground-in dirt. She also looked lost. Lost and shocked. As though seeing Graham was the last thing she'd expected.

Graham slowed as he approached. Should he walk past? Wait for her to make the first move?

Her hand shot out as he drew level and closed tight around his forearm.

"You're real?" she said, answering her own question with a squeal of delight. "You really exist!"

Graham didn't know what to do. Whatever he'd expected this hadn't been it. Was Annalise playing another role for the benefit of some unknown observer?

She withdrew her hand. "Sorry, you must think me a total flake but you don't know what this means to me."

Her voice broke, a tear spilled down her cheek, she smoothed it away with a hand then grabbed his arm again. "We can't talk here," she said, sniffing loudly. "Don't ask me how I know, I just do. Trust me. We've got to get you off this street. Now!"

He hesitated, not wanting to be deflected from his routine but . . . He did trust her. She'd helped him when he'd needed it most.

She handed him one of her cases and led him down a side street. She seemed different somehow, her voice was the same but . . . Could she be Annalise's sister?

He sneaked a look at the address tag flapping from the suitcase handle. *Annalise Mercado, 17 Fairchild Street, Boston, Mass.*

Annalise caught him looking at her luggage and smiled. "I flew in today. Came straight here from the airport. I had to see if this place was real or not." Her expression hardened. "I didn't dream it would be this real."

They walked on, past lines of meters and parked cars. The street curved gradually to the right, a green awning came into view, a few tables clustered beneath it on the pavement.

"In here!" Annalise wove her way through pavement tables towards the door of a small cafe. Graham hesitated. He hadn't been inside a cafe for years.

"Come on," said Annalise, beckoning him from the doorway. "I'm buying."

He followed, reluctantly. They found a table at the back, slid the suitcases to the side and sat down.

"My name's Annalise, Annalise Mercado," she said, holding her hand out across the table towards Graham. Her voice started to quiver, "And I'm not crazy." Graham shook her hand; Annalise closed her eyes and took a deep breath. "You cannot believe how good it is to be able to say that."

A waitress appeared. "Can I take your order?"

"What? Oh, sure, I'll have coffee. And you?"

Graham nodded and began lining up his cutlery—knife, fork, spoon—making sure they were all parallel and equidistantly spaced. Annalise turned back to the waitress. "Make that two coffees."

As soon as the waitress left Annalise reached out and placed her hand on top of Graham's. He flinched but Annalise didn't seem to notice. "Tell me," she took a deep breath, "is your name Graham Smith?"

He nodded, keeping his eyes well down, looking at Annalise's plate and wondering if she'd mind if he took his hand back and rearranged her cutlery.

"I knew it!" She clapped her hands in delight. Graham took the opportunity to retrieve his hand.

"This is *so* amazing! Like, all my life I've known that there was something I was supposed to do, but no one would ever tell me what it was. And now I know. I'm here to save you."

Graham looked up.

"I know it sounds weird but it's true."

The coffee arrived. Annalise leaned back in her chair, grinning broadly, her eyes sparkling.

"All my life I've been the odd one out," she leaned forward conspiratorially, lowering her voice as she did so. "I hear voices. Always have. Even as a kid. There's this girl inside my head who keeps calling my name. She won't go away. She's always asking me where I am, what I'm doing, who I'm with. But whenever I answer she doesn't seem to hear. I thought I was going insane."

Graham knew the feeling. Being different, not being able to trust your eyes, ears or memory. Living in a world where no one understands you.

"I've done analysis, I've done drugs. Nothing ever worked. But that's all changed now, I can feel it. I've been given a purpose in life. Can you believe that?" Her eyes filled with tears. "I got this message on Monday. From the girl in my head. 'We've got to go to London, England,' she said. 'There's a man there. Graham Smith. He's in danger. They're going to kill him. We're the only ones who can save him.'•"

She dabbed at her eyes with her serviette. Graham braced himself for another people-want-you-dead story.

"I didn't know what to do. I didn't know any Graham Smith. I'd never been to London. And then on Monday night I started having this dream—a real vivid dream— that I was over here. There was this plaque, high on a wall. Westminster Street, it said. And I was following this man. You." She jabbed a finger in Graham's direction. "Now you can see why I freaked out back there. You walked straight out of my dream!"

She smiled, looking down at the table, her right hand absent-mindedly playing with her spoon. "You had this weird game you played on the sidewalk—the not-stepping-on-the-cracks thing. And I'd follow you and do the same and I'd feel like a kid again."

She stopped smiling and looked up.

"But then this big black car pulls up, two men get out and walk behind you, they glance over their shoulder then run forward, grab you from behind, the car pulls alongside, a door opens and they bundle you inside. I'm too far back to do anything. I can't even scream, I'm skipping between the cracks, powerless to do anything but watch. The car speeds off and, suddenly, I start screaming. Then I wake up."

She put the spoon down and shook her head.

"That dream really freaked me out. It was so real. And then I had it again the next night and the next. More like a memory than a dream. I thought maybe I had a past life over here in England. That maybe I'd tapped into a past memory of a time when I'd known someone called Graham Smith. Maybe I felt guilty that I hadn't been able to save him. Or maybe it was a vision of the future. Something I had to prevent. What do you think? Has any of this already happened?"

She drew back and rolled her eyes. "Listen to me, I sound certifiable. I'm in a cafe with a man I've never met, asking him if he's ever been dragged into the back of a car at gunpoint."

Graham wanted to tell her that they'd already met. That she'd saved his life in the early hours of Wednesday morning. But he couldn't. He'd learned too many hard lessons over the years. Open your mouth and people change towards you. They laugh at you, run away or hit you.

And he liked Annalise, she spoke to him as though he was normal—more than normal—she treated him as though he was someone special. Someone worth saving. He couldn't ruin that by opening his mouth and sending her away.

He still remembered the look on Robbie Osborne's face. And how long ago had that been? Twenty-six, twenty-seven years? Robbie had been his best friend. They'd been inseparable for an entire summer.

Until the day the stranger arrived and unlatched Robbie's gate.

The two children had been playing in the front garden,

sitting on the grass with two armies of toy soldiers between them. Graham had seen the man first.

"Who's that?" he'd asked, nudging his friend.

Robbie had swivelled round. "Dad! You're back," he'd shouted, jumping up and wrapping his arms around the man's legs.

The man had ruffled Robbie's hair then grabbed him under the arms and swung him up over his head. "More! More!" Robbie had shouted.

"Later," said the man, setting Robbie down. "I've got to see your mother first. You play with Graham."

Graham had watched the man trot up the steps and disappear inside the house. He couldn't understand it.

"Why did you call that man 'dad'?" he'd asked.

"What do you call yours—papa?" Robbie had replied, putting on a posh accent and dissolving into giggles at his cleverness.

"But he's not your dad. Your dad's dead."

Robbie's smile had vanished in an instant. Graham could see it still. The shock in his eyes, the quiver in his lower lip.

The two boys never spoke again.

"Why do you say such hurtful things?" His mother had asked him the next day. And many other days after that. Every time Graham opened his mouth he either offended someone or convinced them of his stupidity. So one day he stopped talking. It wasn't worth the pain.

"You don't say much, do you?" asked Annalise.

Graham looked up from his plate. Annalise was looking at him expectantly. Graham smiled and shook his head.

He had so many questions he wanted to ask her. Did she have any memory of saving him on Wednesday morning? Did she know anything about ParaDim, about why people were after him, who they were and what they wanted?

"Don't you like talking?"

He felt awkward, torn between his need to know and his fear of making things worse. How would she react if he asked her if she'd ever spent the night in a cardboard box? Would she laugh, get upset, change the subject? He hadn't the slightest inkling. Conversation was a complete mystery to him. Normal people understood the rules, he didn't.

He closed his mouth and looked down.

"You know, I used to be shy. About a gazillion years ago. Not now, though. Want to know how?"

Graham shrugged and rotated his coffee cup, bringing the handle around until it was at right angles to his knife and fork.

"Someone told me to imagine that everyone else in the room was in their underwear."

Graham went bright red, he couldn't think of anything less helpful.

"Can you imagine that?" Annalise laughed and peered around the side of the table, looking at Graham's hips. "Why, Mr. Smith." She clapped her hands to her face in mock surprise. "Not the purple boxers with the yellow elephants . . . again!"

Graham giggled, he couldn't help it.

"You try. You can't be intimidated by a roomful of people who can't even dress themselves, can you?"

"I can," he whispered, head bowed, surprised at the sound of his voice, so thin, so fragile. He cleared his throat and swallowed hard.

"Why? Look at me. I'm the only other person at this table. And I'm a wreck! I hear voices. I quit my job yesterday and flew four thousand miles to save someone I met in a dream. I'm the last person you should feel intimidated by."

She was right.

"I've seen you before," he said, his head still bowed.

Annalise's lower jaw dropped. "In a dream?"

Graham shook his head and told her what had happened on Wednesday morning. Annalise listened, her eyes widening in amazement.

"You're sure it was me?"

He nodded. "Your hair was orange, but it was you."

Annalise gasped. "The girl in my dream had orange hair! That was one of the reasons I thought it must be a past life. I've never had orange hair. That is *so* spooky."

Graham took several gulps of coffee. His mouth felt dry and his throat sore.

"Do you think I might have a doppelganger out there? Or a twin?" She took another sip of coffee and then almost dropped the cup. "The girl in my head! I bet it's her! She needs help so she contacts me. What do you think?"

Graham shrugged. He couldn't tell her what he really thought: that the orange-haired Annalise had unravelled into non-existence, that her life had peeled away just as another was brought to the surface—the blonde-haired girl from Boston. He might not know much about the art of conversation but he knew enough to recognize that unravelling was a topic no one wanted to talk about.

"So, what next? Do we wait for this other Annalise to contact us or do we check out this ParaDim company? Whatever we do I'm going to have to stay real close to you. Is there some place I could stay near where you live?"

Graham tried to remember the name of the guesthouse at the end of his road. Dunedin? Or was that the one that had unravelled into a block of flats a few years back?

Then he had a better idea.

"Do you like jigsaws?"

Graham and Annalise sat together, their backs to the window, as the train rattled and swung from side to side. Every now and then the carriage was thrown into darkness and every time the lights flickered back on, Graham turned to see if she was still there.

He wondered what would happen if he kept his hand tightly closed around the handle of her suitcase. Would that anchor her to him? Would it stop her from unravelling or would it pull him along with it?

She smiled every time he looked at her, unaware of his motives or the fragility of the world in which she lived. Should he tell her? Or was that too cruel a burden to place on anyone's shoulders.

And in between the smiles, she talked. She talked about her life in Boston, about how she'd always wanted to visit London. But mostly she talked about her dream.

"It's got to be something that's going to happen. Something I'm meant to stop."

Graham was unconvinced. The orange-haired Annalise had unravelled. The chances were she'd taken her future with her.

"Maybe I can find out when it's supposed to happen? It's got to be summer because everyone's wearing summer clothes. Maybe there are other clues? Like maybe there's a clock somewhere in the dream or some guy reading a newspaper with a date on it. Or, I know!" She nudged Graham hard in the ribs. "The license plate! Next time I have the dream I'll try and get the black car's license plate. Then we'll know who's after you."

Graham didn't say anything. A new world had formed over the skin of the old. The black car could have disappeared with the unravelling thread. Maybe the men too. Or maybe on this new thread of reality they hired a different car, or hunted a different target.

Who could tell in a shifting world?

The endless tail-chasing tired him. And he had something else to worry about. He had a visitor. He'd never had a visitor before. Ever. Where was she going to sleep? She couldn't have his parent's room. She'd have to have his, he'd sleep downstairs on the sofa. And what did she eat? Did he have enough food in; should they stop off at the supermarket?

Graham turned the key counterclockwise for the final time and pushed his front door open.

"Wow," said Annalise, "that's some lock you've got there."

Graham pushed through into the hallway and set Annalise's case down by the hall table. Annalise followed and closed the door behind her.

"Can I use your bathroom?" she asked, setting her case down beside the other.

"Up the stairs and first door on the right."

Graham dropped his keys on the hall table and walked towards the kitchen. He'd put a kettle on, she was certain to want a cup of something. Wasn't that the first thing a host provided for a guest? Or would she want something stronger? Did he still have that bottle of whisky in the lounge?

He dithered by the lounge door before deciding against the whisky. And noticed a small pile of dust on the carpet. Barely a quarter of a teaspoon but where had it come from? He was meticulous about cleaning. The house was hoovered every day.

He stepped into the hall closet, fumbled in the darkness for the Hoover and lifted it out. He was just unwinding the electrical lead when he looked towards the front door.

Both suitcases had gone.

SEVEN

He pulled open the front door and looked outside.
Nothing.

He ran to the gate. No Annalise. No car racing off into the distance. No person struggling with heavy luggage.

He ran back inside.

"Annalise?"

Silence. He ran upstairs, wondering if he was over-reacting, what would she think if he knocked on the bathroom door?

He didn't have to knock.

The bathroom door was open.

No one was inside.

He felt the towels—they were dry. He checked the sink, looking for something—anything—a lipstick, a tooth-brush, a hairbrush. She couldn't have unravelled. Not again. Not so soon.

He looked behind the door, he ran onto the landing. "Annalise!"

Silence.

He checked his bedroom, the storage room. He hovered by his parents' door, his hand fluttering a few inches above the handle, hope and foreboding mixed in equal measures.

He grabbed the handle, turned and pushed. He had to find out. An empty room stared back. No Annalise, no mother, no father.

He was alone.

Again.

He checked his jacket pocket, pulled out the note and read it.

Nothing had changed.

Same job, same room, same address.

Only Annalise had disappeared. Though he wondered for how long? Was she out there somewhere now? Sitting in a shop doorway, or boarding a flight for Heathrow?

And what of ParaDim and the men in the black car? Were they waiting for him on Westminster Street or lying forgotten on a discarded thread of possibility, never to return?

Graham did not want to think about it.

He walked slowly around the house, proceeding from room to room, cataloguing what he found, checking what had changed this time.

Very little had. A few books, a few items of clothes, a vase that his mother had broken ten years earlier had reappeared—pristine and filled with flowers.

He checked the kitchen window, looking for signs that it had been broken.

It hadn't.

He rummaged through his drawers, looking for any notes he might have written to himself. Anything that mentioned ParaDim or Annalise or expressed concern about his safety.

Nothing.

He ate his evening meal in silence, broken by the muffled sound of next door's TV and the hum of passing traffic. Occasionally, he looked up when he thought he heard someone walking past. But it was never her.

By eight o'clock he'd lifted his jigsaw down from the top shelf and had started sorting out the edge pieces. By nine he'd forgotten about everything except fairy wings and the jagged silhouette of a woodland glade.

The next day saw him back inside his fairy glade— kneeling on the lounge floor, the huge frame of the jigsaw in front of him, pieces scattered around him; sorted by color and shape.

Late Saturday afternoon he dragged himself away, there was shopping to do, housework and the garden needed attention.

He mowed the back lawn, dead-headed the roses, tied back the shrubs that were flopping over, weeded the patio. He vacuumed, he dusted, he . . . stopped.

The brass candlesticks on the lounge mantelpiece were not where they should have been. They'd been switched. The one on the left had a slight scratch. It should have been on the right-hand side, a thumb's width in from the edge.

He switched them back, carefully aligning them with his thumb. He looked at the clock in between. It was centered correctly but it was too close to the wall. He should have been able to push his index finger between the clock and the chimney breast.

He checked the other ornaments in the lounge: the vases, his mother's figurines, the holiday souvenirs. They were all slightly out. An inch here, a quarter inch there. But they should have been placed exactly. Every ornament had a home. He measured them precisely, using fingers and thumbs and reference points; the edge of a tile, the tip of a leaf on a wallpaper pattern, a knot in the wood.

Had the last unravelling knocked everything askew? Or had someone searched his house?

He put all the ornaments back, carefully sliding them into position. And wondered what else had changed? If someone had been inside his house, would they have taken things away? Maybe removed any notes he'd written to himself?

He checked the other rooms. A similar picture; items slightly out of place or rotated. Even the freezer compartment of his fridge wasn't immune. Someone had put frozen peas on top of the beef burgers. Something he'd never do. He always kept his vegetables on the left and meat on the right.

Why would anyone want to search his fridge?

And should he care? The rate the world was unravelling at the moment it was unlikely that anything would last more than a few days. All he had to do was sit out the weekend and everything would change. Once these ParaDim threads worked themselves loose, the world would settle down—a thought that kept him content all the way through to late Sunday night.

He yawned, stretched and staggered to his feet. His knees were killing him and he was starting to see fairies in the wallpaper.

He picked up his cup and carried it to the kitchen, stopping by the light switch to flick it on. The fluorescent light flickered once before humming into life.

She sat on the floor between the fridge and the back door—Annalise, with long black hair this time—leaning back against the side of the fridge, her knees drawn up. She grinned, placed a finger to her lips and held out a slip of paper.

"Don't say a word," it read. "Your house is bugged."

EIGHT

Graham stared at the note and then at the girl. She was wearing a long, pale green dress. And she looked younger again. Or was that the hair? Long, straight and fringed at the front.

She rummaged in an embroidered canvas bag on her lap and brought something out, something black, the size of a small radio. She extended the aerial and switched it on, a red light pulsed slowly. She pointed it at the door and then slowly brought it around until it pointed at Graham. The pulse changed frequency. She handed the detector to Graham along with another note.

Red light = bug. Fast pulse hot, slow pulse cold.
Find bugs, stomp them. All bugs dead, make coffee.

He looked at the detector slowly flashing in his hand and then at Annalise. Maybe he was tired and seeing too many fairies but he couldn't understand why Annalise was sitting on the floor behind the fridge.

Annalise must have noticed his confusion; she took the note from his hand and scrawled two words on the back—*hidden cameras!*

Graham immediately swung round, looking up at the ceiling above his kitchen cabinets, wondering what he should be looking for—a black dot, a video camera, a strange box that shouldn't be there?

And then he remembered the detector in his hand and felt foolish. The red light pulsed slowly. He slipped the note into his pocket and took hold of the detector with both hands, sweeping the room in a slow deliberate arc. The pulse increased when he pointed it towards the kitchen table. He moved the detector over its surface, the light flashing fastest over the far left-hand corner. He set it down and felt underneath where the leg met the top. There was something there, shaped like a bolt.

He swung down and peered under the table. There was a piece of metal, the size of a small button, attached to the wooden corner brace. He tugged at it, dug his fingernails between the metal and the wood and pulled. It came away. A small button of metal with three tiny spikes protruding beneath.

He placed it on top of the detector and the red light flashed continuously. Someone had bugged his house. He stared at the transmitter in his palm, wondering how long it had been there, trying to remember what it might have recorded. The sound of water running in the sink, the clink of glass and plates. Was someone really recording all that?

Annalise waved at him and tapped at her watch. He looked back at the transmitter and rolled it between his finger and thumb. It didn't look that easy to crush.

Annalise beckoned him over and held out her hand. Graham gave her the transmitter and stepped back.

She rolled it around in her hand for a few seconds before placing it carefully on the floor beside her. She took a stick of chewing gum out of her bag, unwrapped it and folded it into her mouth. Graham watched transfixed. Was she going to soundproof the bug with chewing gum?

Annalise tapped her watch again and pointed at the kitchen door. His work hadn't finished.

Graham checked the rest of the house. Every room had at least one bug, even the closet under the stairs. Some were like the one he'd found in the kitchen, spiked and pushed into crevices in the woodwork. Others were concealed inside electrical sockets. He had to turn the electricity off at the mains and unscrew the sockets by torchlight.

And then there were the cameras. One in the lounge, masquerading as an electrical junction box. And one in the hallway, in the light fitting, directly above the spot he'd found the small pile of dust on Friday night. The instant before Annalise had disappeared.

Or had it been the instant after?

He carried everything back to the kitchen, taking extra care with the cameras, placing a finger firmly over each lens.

Annalise covered both lenses with chewing gum and then took everything out into the back garden.

Graham watched from the doorway, the light from the kitchen spilling out across the lawn. Annalise stood in the shadows by the back fence, tossing bugs into the night. Some to the left, some to the right, some into the gardens of the houses in back. A few must have hit stone, Graham heard the slight crack and skittle as they bounced.

"How did you know the house was bugged?" asked Graham as he filled the kettle under the tap.

"A spirit told me," said Annalise, sitting on the kitchen table, swinging her legs back and forth. "I'm a medium."

Graham turned off the tap, he must have misheard with the noise of the running water.

"A medium?"

"With two hundred spirit guides all called Annalise. Go figure."

He knew he had his mouth open but he couldn't help it. Annalise was a medium? He turned his head to see if she was joking.

"What?" she said. "Is there something in my teeth?"

"No, sorry," he looked away hurriedly, swung the kettle over to the stove and switched on the gas.

"Ever heard of the De Santos case?" asked Annalise. "Teenage heiress goes missing? Big news last year, all over the Midwest."

He shook his head. He never watched TV, never read a newspaper. The only news he ever picked up was second-hand—snatches of conversation he overheard at work or travelling on the tube.

"September last year, Des Moines, Iowa. My home town. Kimberly De Santos, aged twenty, went to a party, never came home. Headline news everywhere. Police didn't have a clue. No ransom, no witnesses, no clues, no motive."

Graham took two clean cups from the near cupboard.

"Anyway, one night I'm communing with my spirit girls and I ask if anyone knew what had happened to Kimberly. One answers. 'You mean the girl who got shot in the bungled kidnapping?'•"

She paused for effect, looking directly at Graham.

"Her exact words, *the girl who got shot in the bungled kidnapping*. Spooky, right?"

Graham nodded as he spooned coffee into the two cups.

"•'What bungled kidnapping?' I asked. 'The one outside the Park Hotel,' she said, 'the one where the off-duty cop shot the ringleader.'•"

Annalise stopped swinging her legs and leaned forward. "Now, I knew the Park Hotel was where Kimberley was last seen. But no one said anything about a shooting or one of the kidnappers being shot.

"Now this is where it gets really spooky. I asked this spirit Annalise if she knew the name of the guy who got shot. She didn't, but she said she'd get back to me. And when she did, she gave me the names of the whole gang. The one who'd been shot and the two who'd got away but were arrested later."

"How did she know?" asked Graham, leaning against the sink.

Annalise smiled and tapped the side of her nose. "The dead know more than you think. They don't spend all their time on the astral plane, you know. They come back and visit. They're drawn."

Graham nodded. That was very true. Dead people came back a lot.

"So, public spirited medium that I am I gave the names

to the police. Told them it was a kidnapping. They didn't want to know so I phoned her father. And kept phoning until someone put me through. 'These are the guys that took your daughter,' I said and gave him their names. 'Have you told the police,' he said. 'Sure,' I said, 'but they're not interested.' Daddy was not impressed. 'We'll see about that,' he said and slammed down the phone.

"Next day it's all over the papers. *Kimberly freed, kidnappers caught.* The day after that I'm hauled down the police station to explain myself. How did I know so much? Was I a witness who should have come forward earlier or an accomplice looking for a piece of the reward? 'Neither,' said I, 'I'm a medium.'"

Annalise grinned and started swinging her legs back and forth again. "Which went down like shit at a picnic. Then the press picked up the story and suddenly I'm famous. For three whole weeks. I even had my own show on cable. Didn't last though—couldn't contact enough dead people." She put her hands on her hips. "You'd think two hundred spirit guides could dig up enough stiffs to fill a fifteen-minute daily show. I know I did."

The kettle began to whistle.

"So, they cut my show. I drifted back into roach-infested obscurity and Kimberly De Santos inherited a new beach house. Life's a big fat bitch."

Graham stirred the coffee and thought about the blonde-haired Annalise and the voice in her head. The one that told her to come to England. Was that a spirit guide? Maybe the one that had told this Annalise about the kidnapping?

"Is that how you found out about me?" he asked. "Did a spirit tell you to come to England to find me?"

"No way, I found out about you through Kevin Alexander."

"Who's Kevin Alexander?"

"The Canadian guy I came here to tell you about."

NINE

They moved through to the lounge. Graham sat in an armchair, nursing his coffee, while Annalise flitted about the room—picking up ornaments and photos, examining them, putting them back down. Graham watched her progress—realizing he'd have to realign everything before he could face going to bed.

"So, last month," said Annalise, waving a candlestick to emphasise her words, "I got this phone call from the cable network. This guy was trying to contact me, he'd seen the show last year and wanted to meet—real urgent. He was like leaving ten messages a day and the network weren't sure if he was for real or some whacko stalker. So they passed his number on to me. I called him up and we arranged to meet."

Annalise inverted the candlestick and scrutinized the

base for a few seconds before putting it back on the mantelpiece.

"Needless to say I chose a very public place. Big coffee house downtown. Turns out he was on the level. Kevin Alexander, a Canadian guy working for ParaDim."

"ParaDim?"

Annalise moved over to the sofa and sat down on the arm, a few feet away from Graham.

"I see you've heard of it. Anyway, he was real interested in the De Santos case. Real interested I said the ringleader had been shot by an off-duty cop. 'How'd you know that?' he said. 'My spirit guide, Annalise, told me.'•"

Annalise's head moved from side to side and her voice changed as she reenacted the conversation. "•'Your spirit guide's called Annalise?' he said. 'They all are,' I said.

"At which point he starts looking at me real excited. He had these big hands which he held out in front of him, fingers spread wide." Annalise mimicked the encounter. "And he like pumped them up and down as he spoke. 'How many Annalises are there?' he asked. 'Two hundred at the last count. Spooky, ain't it? Must be a real common name on the astral plane.'•"

Graham sat back and listened, mesmerized by her performance. She had such an easy way about her. She didn't seem to weigh up her words or wonder what anyone might think. She just launched into her story and out it all came.

"Anyway, he's sitting there, mouth open and big hands stuck out in front like some kinda freaky Canadian lobster guy and he wants to know how I can possibly have two hundred spirit guides all with the same name. How can I tell them apart?"

Annalise rolled her eyes. "•'We have a code,' I said.

'I'm Annalise One. Then there's Annalise Two. Get the drift? We've all got numbers. And those that fight over the same number agree on a letter—eventually—so there's Annalise 9a and 9b.'•"

Annalise stopped and looked round. "Where did I put my coffee?"

Graham pointed at the cup on the coffee table behind her. She leaned back, reached out and scooped it up in one flowing motion. Graham held his breath as the full coffee cup teetered precariously over his clean carpet.

"So, this guy—still excited, still pointing those enormous hands at me—asks if I do private consultations. He'd pay, money no problem. He needs to contact some friends on the other side. 'No problemo,' says I, 'but I'll need a hundred up front. Some of these dead guys don't like to be found.'•"

Annalise took a sip of coffee and gradually brought the cup into the conversation. Graham watched the liquid lap from side to side.

"•'Not a problem', he says and hands me two fifty-dollar bills, just like that. Then he says how important it is that his friend gets his message word for word. 'Verbatim,' he says, 'exactly as I dictate or it's no good.'•" She rolled her eyes. "These scientist guys. Anyway, I agreed and then he says something really spooky. 'Tell your spirit Annalise that she **has** to speak to my friend in person—no phones, no faxes, no emails.'•"

"They have faxes on the astral plane?"

"Believe me, they have everything on the astral plane. Just 'cause you're dead don't mean you can't live."

She paused and took another sip.

"As I see it, they're dead, but they don't know it. So

they go around doing everything they did before. They live in houses, they drive cars, they shop, they make out. Makes sense to me."

It suddenly made sense to Graham too. An epiphany. He'd never understood why people who came back from the dead never talked about their experiences. He'd put it down to embarrassment, shame maybe, some social taboo that said you don't talk about death or unravelment. But maybe they just didn't realize where they'd been.

Wouldn't that explain his father's reaction? That first time he'd come back from the dead. Graham still remembered every moment of that morning. Getting up, going downstairs, walking towards the kitchen expecting to see the tear-stained face of his mother still grieving three months after her husband's passing. But hearing laughter instead. A man's laugh. He'd slowed in the passageway, not knowing what to think. The kitchen door ajar, unable to see all the way in, he'd hovered outside for an age. And then the man spoke. It was his father! His father had come back!

He'd raced into the kitchen, thrown the door back against its hinges and jumped on his father's back. The sheer joy of finding him alive!

"Dad, it's really you!" he'd said, his voice breaking.

"Of course it's me, who'd you expect? The milkman?"

His mother had laughed. "How come I don't get a hug like that?" she'd asked.

"Because you weren't dead," he'd replied and, suddenly, all the world went very quiet.

But now, looking at that scene again, he could see it had been shock on his father's face. Not embarrassment. All those years Graham had thought he'd broken some unwritten taboo and dared to tell one of the returned that he'd been dead. But it hadn't been that at all. His father hadn't been embarrassed at his son's outburst, he'd been mystified. *Because he hadn't known he'd been dead.*

"Earth to Graham." Graham returned to find Annalise waving a hand in front of his face. "Where'd you go just then?"

"Sorry, I was thinking about what you said about dead people."

Annalise shrugged. "That's cool. Now where was I?"

"You had to send a message to your spirit Annalise."

"That was it. And I had to learn it by heart. I wanted to write it down but lobster guy didn't want any of that. 'Nothing on paper,' he said. 'Can you memorize a twelve-digit number?' he asked. 'For another hundred bucks, I can.'"

"The message was a twelve-digit number?"

"Part of it. He wanted me to get in touch with the same Annalise that told me about the bungled De Santos kidnapping. Very insistent. It had to be her and no one else and she had to contact Gary Mitchison, some doctor who worked at the Queen Alexandra College over here in London. 'Resonance wave,' she had to say. 'I have a message for you from Kevin Alexander on 015 498 226 373.' "

"Was that his telephone number?"

"No, I checked. And it wasn't a URL or anything internetty. I double-checked. Probably some code the two of them had worked out before the guy passed over."

"Why would anyone do that?"

"To prove they were who they said they were. Houdini started it all. It's a way of checking the medium's for real. If the medium comes back with the wrong code then she's a fake."

Annalise drained the last of her coffee.

"Anyway, that was supposed to get this spirit guy's attention. Then came the rest of the message. 'Danger, be careful what you broadcast, remember everything's monitored. Resonance project teams are being closed. No longer safe. Take research off line. The girl can be trusted. Pay her. She's the only secure line of communication. Resonance wave intensifying, repeat, resonance wave intensifying.'•"

"What's a resonance wave?"

"You don't know?"

Graham shook his head. He hadn't a clue.

Annalise tilted her head to one side and looked closely at Graham. "Lobster guy and his dead pals sure seem to think you do." She paused. "They think you're the key."

Graham swallowed hard and looked at his feet.

"Anyway, there's more of the message. 'Access the Census logs,' it went on. 'Look for traffic on Graham Smith and cross-reference with disbanded Resonance projects. Can't be coincidence. Why the interest in him and why were the projects closed soon after? End message.'•"

Annalise paused to deposit her empty cup on the coffee table.

"Spooky, right? What kinda census logs would a dead guy look at? Some kinda dead guy inventory? Or is there something a dead guy can do that a live one can't? Like pass through locked doors and check out classified files?"

"But what could any of that have to do with me?"

He was totally confused. Why would anyone in Canada or anywhere else for that matter have the slightest interest in him? He was as near to a nobody as you could get. He could disappear tomorrow and no one would notice.

He had no family, no friends, no . . .

And then it came to him. It was obvious.

"They've got me mixed up with another Graham Smith, haven't they? It's a very common name."

"Urrrr!" Annalise pressed an air buzzer with her finger. "Wrong answer, Graham. You haven't heard the dead guy's reply."

TEN

Annalise retrieved her coffee cup and held it out to him. "This is definitely a two-cup story."

Graham took it from her and made a fresh cup. Just the one this time; he knew he'd be up all night if he drank any more.

Annalise was standing over his jigsaw when he returned.

"I still can't get over this jigsaw of yours. It's gotta be like—wow—the biggest jigsaw I've ever seen. You must be a real patient kinda guy."

Graham held out her coffee.

"You're not having one?"

"No."

"This is definitely not how I pictured it," she said, swinging her coffee cup to point around the room. "Your house, I mean. It's not a guy house. It's like normal in a

79

spooky old-fashioned kinda way. Were you married?'

Graham shook his head.

"And no TV. Or do you like have one of those home entertainment rooms?"

Graham shook his head again. "My parents had a TV but . . ." He let the sentence end in a shrug.

"But what?"

"I never really liked TV."

"Wow, you really are weird."

"You were about to tell me what happened next," said Graham, changing the subject.

Annalise stared blankly.

"The dead guy's reply?"

"Oh, right!" She looked around for somewhere to rest her cup and found the sideboard. Graham fought the impulse to rush over with a coaster.

"It was a long one, can't remember it all but it went something like, Census logs checked. Can't see link but agree there must be one. Cross-reference Crime and . . ." She paused, tapping her forehead. "Medical. That was it. Crime and Medical logs. Someone wants Graham Smith dead. Possibly same person behind Resonance project closures. Graham Smith under surveillance. Wealdstone Lane house searched, nothing found. Message out. 015 blah blah blah."

"They searched my house?"

"Everyone's searched your house. Good guys, bad guys and dead guys. Did you see how many different types of listening devices you uncovered? Bet they weren't all planted by the same people."

He shook his head in disbelief. "Why would the good guys want to bug my house?"

"To find out what you know. You're the key to this big mystery of theirs. This resonance thingy. Way I see it, they're all working on these Resonance projects—some secret offshoot from ParaDim—but someone doesn't want them to succeed."

"Who?"

"That's what these guys are trying to find out. They don't know either. All they know is that it's gotta be someone high up in ParaDim or someone with real heavy connections. As soon as anyone gets close to an answer about this resonance wave—zap—the project gets closed down. So, lobster guy sneaks a peak at their logs and finds you. You're like the last entry in all these dead guys' diaries."

"They're dead?"

Annalise shrugged. "No one's said. But if they're not, why doesn't lobster guy just ask them. Way I see it, they're either dead or locked up somewhere."

Graham felt the need to sit down. His head was swimming. How could his be the last name in the diaries of people he'd never met?

He settled back on the arm of the sofa. Annalise scooped up her cup and bounced down into the armchair opposite.

"But why me?" asked Graham. "I don't know anything about resonance waves or ParaDim. I've never met any scientists."

"The dead guy thinks it must be something you know. He reckons you gotta be the key. Why else were all these people interested in you, why did it get them closed down and why's someone trying to kill you?"

Why did it always come back to that? *People want you*

dead. Wasn't there an Annalise with some good news?

"And the more these guys uncover, the worse it looks for you. I've been channelling messages back and forth for three weeks now. But instead of protecting you, they're way more interested in studying you. Crazy, ain't it?"

He couldn't disagree with that.

Annalise set her cup down on the hearth and bounced forward onto the edge of the seat. "Which is where I come in. Lobster guy flew me over here—he works in London now and needed me close. I *am* the house medium, after all." She smiled. "Naturally a girl can't help being curious. I was in London, you were in London. You were like key guy and all alone.

"So, I tracked you down. They said you lived in Wealdstone Lane. I bought an A to Z street guide. There was only one Wealdstone Lane, so how many Graham Smiths could there be? Swung by early one morning and asked the mailman. Pointed me right to you. Then it was just a matter of keeping tabs. Believe me," she smiled, "you are *way* easy to follow. You have a routine you could set a clock by."

She slid back in the armchair and brought her legs up beneath her. "Then I called in the girls. They're not all here yet. But they're coming. You're gonna be the safest guy on the planet."

Two hundred Annalises. He tried to remember how many he'd already met. And then froze. How could he have met them? They were all dead. Unless . . .

"Are any of your Annalises from Boston?"

"Let me see." She put her head on one side and screwed up her eyes. "Two of them are. Why?"

"Any of them ever live at . . ." He couldn't remember

the address. "Fairburn or Fairchild Street?"

"Not as far as I know. Though that's not saying much. A lot of the girls think they live with me."

"They do?"

"Spooky, right? Way I see it, when you die your memory gets wiped. But it doesn't always work. Some memories stick. Others start to resurface after a time. But the mind can't wait so it starts filling in the gaps by borrowing stuff from wherever it can.

"My girls fastened onto me. Probably because I'm a medium. They liked my name so they took it. They liked my house so they took that as well. And they borrowed other stuff. Like chunks from my life. I say I had an Uncle Louie in Minneapolis and some of the girls say, 'Hey, I had an Uncle Louie in Minneapolis too.' But not all the girls, some still had memories of their real families so they didn't need mine. That's cool," she shrugged, "I'm a sharing person."

Graham could see another possibility. Something he'd never dreamed of. Something he could barely imagine.

What happened to all those threads that unravelled? Could they still exist somewhere, independent of the world they'd been pulled from but somehow still coherent, still able to support life?

And was that where Annalise's spirit guides lived? Were the dead and the unravelled somehow mixed together?

His mind felt heavy and slow. So much was happening all around him. The dead, the unravelled, two hundred Annalises popping in and out like Cheshire cats. Why hadn't fate picked someone brighter? Someone used to thinking on their feet? Not someone mired in inactivity, someone who took five minutes to lock a door and couldn't sleep if he thought a picture was hanging crooked.

Here was a chance to discover so much and yet he could feel the opportunity slipping through his fingers. He wanted everything written down. Something solid he could put down and come back to, like a jigsaw puzzle, something he could walk around and study for days or weeks, dipping into and out of whenever he felt like it. Not something he had to react to immediately. The spoken word was like water cascading through his fingers—he was drowning one minute and dry the next.

"Of course, you could stop this any time you like," said Annalise.

"What?"

"You're the key. Somehow you can stop this resonance wave. So, go ahead and do it. Once you do, it's over. No resonance wave, no reason to kill you, right?"

Graham shook his head. If only it could be that simple. "How can I stop something I don't understand?"

"Beats me," Annalise shrugged. "I'm a medium, not a psychic."

She looked at her watch. "Time to go. My B and B locks its doors at eleven thirty. Can you believe that?"

"You're going?"

"Why, Graham." She put her hands on her hips. "What kinda girl do you think I am?"

Graham reddened and hurriedly looked away. Annalise grinned and punched him playfully on the shoulder.

"But what about the people who planted the bugs? What if they send someone round tonight to find out what's happened?"

"No problemo. Annalise Twelve's outside watching the front door. If anyone starts anything she'll stop them."

Graham glanced towards the drawn curtains and wondered what on earth was on the other side.

"How?" he asked, turning back to Annalise.

"She's got it worked out real good. Anyone so much as walks though your gate, she's gonna start heaving bricks through your neighbor's windows. The street'll be crawling in neighbors and cops within a minute flat. Who's gonna dare touch you with that many witnesses?"

"She can do that?"

"You ever see *Poltergeist*?"

ELEVEN

Graham set off for work the next morning, wondering if Annalise Twelve was watching. Was she floating, invisible, above the trees or crouched down between the parked cars? And who else was watching him? Was that Kevin Alexander who sat in the parked car over the road?

He tried to settle back into his old routine of counting paces between the landmarks but found it hard to concentrate. Part of his mind was analyzing faces—was that woman familiar, hadn't that man passed by on the other side of the road ten minutes earlier?

It was the same on the tube—anyone getting on or pushing through into the carriage or hanging back by the doors. What would they do if he jumped off at Finchley Road, ran across the platform and took the next northbound train back to Harrow?

Finchley Road came and went. He'd toyed with the idea of jumping off just as the doors were closing. He'd even edged forward onto the balls of his feet, ready to spring. But something had held him back. His fear of attracting attention, his fear of upsetting his daily routine.

He walked into the Post Room thirty minutes later, glanced over towards Sharmila's desk and stopped.

Sharmila wasn't there.

Michael was. Michael hadn't worked at Westminster Street for six months, not since he'd been transferred to Greenwich.

Michael raised a well-muscled arm in acknowledgement and carried on talking. He was on the phone as usual. He spent most of the day on the phone— organizing his social life, keeping his girlfriends in line, checking all the players were available for the match on Saturday, booking squash courts, restaurants, arranging nights out. Michael lived enough lives for four people— all of them busy.

Graham waved back. And almost said hello. His mouth started to form the word but his brain kicked in and promptly closed it. He wasn't ready. Not yet. Talking to Annalise had been fun but it had been unsettling too. There was a warm protective feeling about silence. Silence couldn't hurt you. Whereas words could tear your life apart.

Graham's phone rang. A sound as frightening to Graham as the low drone of a wasp. He swung round, Michael was still on the other phone, he must have switched calls through to Graham's extension.

The phone kept ringing. Graham hovered close by,

praying it would stop, wondering if he could pretend he hadn't heard it and walk out the door.

The phone rang on. Michael laughed and chatted. Graham's insides churned. He hated phone calls. All he could say was mmm for yes and uh-uh for no. And even that was a strain. His throat would invariably tighten or the person on the other end would shout at him.

But what if it was urgent? What if in five minutes' time someone came storming into the Post Room demanding to know why the phone hadn't been answered?

He lifted the receiver.

"Michael, you were supposed to be here five minutes ago. What's keeping you?"

It couldn't have been worse. Frank Gledwood. Graham didn't know what to say. A thin voice attempted a cross between a mmm and a uh-uh.

"Shit!" said Frank. "Shenaz, go and fetch Michael. There's only that moron in the Post Room and I haven't time to play twenty questions."

Graham listened, knowing that Frank hadn't even thought to hold his hand over the mouthpiece while talking to his assistant.

The phone clicked and the ringing tone purred. Shenaz would be on her way down.

Graham hated telephones.

Lunchtime came and Graham couldn't leave the building quick enough. He didn't unwind until he reached St. James's Park, found an empty seat by a stand of bushes, sat down and started to unwrap his sandwiches.

"Don't look around," said Annalise from somewhere behind him. "We have to talk. I'll be here tonight at seven.

Make sure you're not followed. Take the subway as usual, lose your tail in the crowd, then double back. Scratch your head if you understand."

Graham scratched his head and fought the desire to turn around. Had Annalise received another message?

He waited to find out. Hardly daring to breathe in case he missed a word. Five seconds passed, ten, twenty.

No answer came. She'd gone.

TWELVE

Back in the office, Graham thought about Annalise and what she might have discovered. He felt so useless. All he ever did was wait for Annalise to bring him news. Wasn't there anything he could do? Something to convince the people at ParaDim that he was no threat to them, that he wasn't the key or anything remotely deserving of interest?

Maybe there was.

He switched on his terminal and quickly navigated through the DTI screens until he found the search page. He typed in "ParaDim" and waited. Would it be different this time? Would it show entries for resonance projects, maybe an explanation of what a resonance wave was?

It didn't.
But it did show two hits:

ParaDim Phase Two: General project overview and tender information.
ParaDim: Census Project.

Census Project? Graham stared at the screen. He'd heard that name before. In one of Annalise's messages. *Access the Census logs.*

He clicked on the Census Project and shuffled closer. A new screen appeared. A project overview and several sections of technical specifications.

The Census Project, jointly funded by ParaDim and Her Majesty's Government and based in London, is seeking partner organizations to help expand its highly successful and recently completed pilot project into a fully operational global model.

The Census Project is part of ParaDim Phase Two. Information on family and medical history will be gathered, collated and fed into the ParaDim model. The Census Project seeks to identify people with natural immunities to various diseases and conditions.

Information gathered will also be invaluable to the many other linked ParaDim research projects. As in Phase One, partner organizations will benefit through the distribution of shares in ParaDim Inc., details of which can be found on page 4 of the tender document.

Graham read the overview again. What could any of that have to do with him? There was nothing in his family or medical background that could possibly interest any-one. He'd had all the usual childhood diseases and had never been exposed to anything exotic.

It didn't make any sense.

He returned to the search results page and clicked on ParaDim Phase Two.

ParaDim Inc. is seeking partner organizations to help in the collection, collation and processing of data for ParaDim Phase Two. After the phenomenal success of Phase One, ParaDim is expanding its model into Health and the Humanities.

Data collected during Phase Two will be used to create the data reservoir required to power ParaDim Phase Three.

Many of the Phase Two projects are joint sponsored by national governments. Appendix H gives details of countries offering grants and tax incentives for ParaDim partner organizations.

As with Phase One, partner organizations will share in the success of the project by the allocation of shares in ParaDim Inc. This will be at a reduced level, reflecting the lower profitability of the Phase Two work. However, significant breakthroughs in the areas of health and insurance are forecast and Phase Two partners will be given special consideration when assessing candidates for Phase Three.

Pages and pages of technical specifications followed. Graham scrolled back to the top and logged out.

❋   ❋   ❋

By four o'clock, Graham was having second thoughts. He'd meet Annalise another time. He wasn't cut out for clandestine meetings and even less for giving people the slip.

But she'd told him to be there. And doing what other people told him was one of the tenets that paved his path of least resistance through life.

He was torn and becoming more so by the minute. Why couldn't Annalise slip him a note? Why all the cloak and dagger?

He paced the fifth floor, tried to bury himself in work and in-trays but it wouldn't go away. The fear, the foreboding, the certainty that something bad was going to happen. Didn't she realize what she was asking him to do?

Even if he didn't make a scene at the tube station—which he was certain he would—she was asking him to break his journey home. A journey that had become a ritual. Seventeen years of treading the same path at the same time.

Ignore ritual and bad things were certain to follow.

He'd broken his journey home on Friday and, within an hour, a girl had unravelled in his hallway.

What would happen tonight? He wasn't just breaking his journey, he was going to change trains, run, hide, make a scene.

The world was unstable, evolving. Its fabric wafer-thin and in need of constant reinforcement. Streets had to be walked, buildings observed, rituals honored. Without that, the fabric failed and strands worked loose.

A tree falling, unobserved, deep in the forest makes no sound. He'd read that years ago. It was so true. A tree like that would have lost all coherence, it would have faded as it fell, its timber eaten away by neglect. There'd be nothing left *to* make a sound.

And it was worse today. You only had to read the newspaper headlines. Alaskan wilderness in danger, rain forests shrinking, ice caps melting. Take away the observer and the world unravels. Without observation there can be no substance and without ritual there can be no cement.

Even the cities weren't immune. So many people detached from their surroundings, walking by without looking. Was it coincidence that the oldest buildings were always the ones surrounded by tourists? Their walls thickened by centuries of observation and held together by the ritual of guided tours.

And if he turned his back on his usual train who was to say if it would be there tomorrow? His defection might be the last straw. His use, his eyes, his belief might be the only thing keeping the train from fading away. It could be cancelled, rerouted, the entire line might unravel and reappear several miles to the west.

Strange things happen. That was the nature of the world.

But if he ignored Annalise?

Wouldn't that be worse? Wasn't he caught up in a prolonged aftershock? Caught up in a thread where people broke into his home and threatened his life?

And if he didn't meet her tonight, mightn't he miss forever the opportunity to break free? Annalise and her message unravelling away into dust?

By the time he left work he was terrified. Terrified of drawing attention to himself at the tube station and terrified of missing his only chance to escape.

The lights changed and he followed the crowd across the road. He gazed at the shop on the corner and let his eyes trace its outline. He could feel the building strengthen under his gaze. The bricks looked darker, the cement more solid.

His inner voice agreed. Forget about the girl and celebrate the real world, observe and record. Who was he—an amateur—to think he could give professionals the slip? He'd only make things worse. Forget. Go home. Ignore. The girl was trouble.

But why were people following him? Why were they bugging his house? How could he ignore people who broke into his home?

He walked, he argued, he counted. He handed decision making over to fate. If the next set of lights changed on an odd number he'd go to the park—even, he'd go home.

They changed on fifteen.

A little voice in his head whispered, *best of three*.

By the time he reached the station, it was screaming, *best of eleven*.

He followed the stream of people onto the crowded eastbound platform and joined the small line of people snaking their way along the back wall.

His little voice pleaded. *Forget. Go home. Ignore.*

Graham pushed further along, stopping by an access tunnel to the westbound platform. He sneaked a sideways glance down the tunnel; the far platform was packed too. A train couldn't be that far off.

It won't work. They'll see you.

He felt terrible; the anticipation, the fear, the nausea, the rush of stale air against his face, the cold sweat, clammy hands, the feeling that a thousand eyes were watching his every move. The eastbound train arrived, roaring and rattling, lights flashing from the passing carriages.

He thought he was going to faint. Train doors opened, people surged forward. He moved with them. Every fiber of his being screamed at him to get on that train, *forget, go home, ignore.*

He closed his eyes, counted, dug in his heels. He had to meet Annalise. He had to!

People all around—milling and shoving. He hunched down and turned, saw the tunnel and pushed, squeezed, elbowed his way towards it.

He fell forward into the tunnel, stumbled, regained his balance and flew the twenty yards to the westbound platform. He ducked left and pushed along the back wall. Another roar, another rush of air, another squeal of metal on metal as the westbound train roared in. He reached the end of the platform, the crowd thinning, the train stopping. He felt himself move forward—a strange disembodied feeling—he pushed and squirmed his way to the far side of the carriage, grabbed the metal upright by the door and gripped as hard as he could.

Eleven, twelve—he'd been counting forever—the train stationary, the doors still open. No one else getting on, the platform emptying. What were they waiting for!

The doors closed on fifteen. The train lurched forward. Graham swayed against the pole, braced himself and tucked his head down as far as it would go, praying that he'd got away, praying that his watchers were speeding away on the eastbound train.

He clung to the metal pole for three long minutes, his knuckles white from the pressure. He jumped out at the next station. He wanted to run, he wanted to get out, he wanted to push past. Why was everyone moving so slowly!

He reached the ticket barrier, the lobby . . .

Daylight! He blinked into the sun, took a deep breath, found his bearings, and started to run, glancing back every twenty yards or so, taking sudden lefts and rights though the maze of tiny side streets.

Gradually, he calmed down. He wasn't being followed. He slowed to a walk and adjusted his stride to the cadence of the street.

He looked round as he approached the park bench. A final check that he wasn't being followed. He glimpsed Annalise out of the corner of his eye, strolling across the grass to his right. Her long black hair had been bleached honey blonde and braided but it had to be her. Even from this distance, her walk was unmistakable. The way she floated over the grass, sinuous and effortless.

He watched her approach. She looked distracted. No smile of recognition or friendly wave. Didn't she recognize him? Was she a different Annalise?

"Thank God, you came," she said. "My name's Annalise, Annalise Mercado, and I'm here to help. Anyway I can. What do you need?"

Graham didn't know what to say. He'd expected to meet Annalise One, to hear what Kevin Alexander had to say. Not to start all over from the beginning again with another girl.

He shook his head. He'd risked so much. And for what?

"But you're the key," the girl said, grabbing his arm.

"The key to what? I wish someone would tell me."

"The key to getting us out of here! Look, you can talk freely in front of me. It's okay. I know what's really happening. I know about the VR worlds."

THIRTEEN

"What VR worlds?"

"You know," said Annalise. "Artificial worlds created by computers. That's where we are now—trapped in a VR world."

Graham frowned. He'd heard people talking about virtual reality, he'd even skimmed through a book about it once, but it wasn't a subject that held his interest.

"It's obvious, really," Annalise continued. "I can't understand why I didn't work it out earlier. Guess I was too busy listening to the others." She paused and tilted her head to one side. "The other Annalises? You know about the others, right?"

He nodded. "All two hundred of them."

"Exactly! That's my point. There's two hundred Annalise Mercados, some of us even live in the same city and yet we've never met. Now you tell me how that's possible if we all live in the same world?"

He could . . . up to a point. He could explain how the world was unstable and threads were forever unravelling. How, most likely, there was just the one Annalise whose life unravelled from time to time. But how she communicated with her other selves or how she had even learned of their existence . . . that was beyond him.

Maybe something unusual had happened during an unravelling. Maybe a thread had broken somehow and a fragment had been left behind. A fragment of Annalise's life forever snagged in the fabric of the world, not part of the world and yet not fully disconnected either. A loose thread caught between layers of reality. A loose thread around which two hundred others had gathered.

"It's not that we haven't tried to see each other. Last month two of us sat at the same table in the same coffee bar at the same time. Never caught a glimpse. We sat there, talking to each other in our heads, describing what we saw, who was sitting where and what was on the menu." She paused for breath. "It was like we were in different places! Can you believe that? Similar but not the same. The menu was the same, the decor too, even some of the waitresses, but the customers . . . they were all different."

"You talked to each other while this was happening?"

"All the time. And last week there were six of us. The full Des Moines chapter—except for Annalise One. We all met up at Rosie's Bar but none of us saw each other. It's like we all arrived on different nights. We took turns describing what we saw. One of the guys behind the bar—Sergio, I think his name was—five of us saw him and five of us described him wearing different clothes. Annalise

Nineteen even said he had a beard. Now that's spooky."

Graham agreed, very spooky.

And, suddenly, very worrying. What would Annalise Twelve have seen last night if anyone had tried to break into his house?

"Of course, Annalise One thinks we're all dead—except for her—and that's why we can't see each other. We're all spirits on the astral plane, living in imaginary worlds, constructing imaginary Rosie's and describing imaginary barmen." She shook her head. "Doesn't work, does it? She can't have it both ways. She can't accept what we tell her when it suits her and dismiss it when it doesn't. You heard about her TV show?"

Graham nodded.

"That's what got me started. People would ring in to Annalise's show with the names of loved ones they wanted to contact. There were like ten or so a day and she'd pass them to us and we'd flip through our phone directories looking for them all. Most of the people we couldn't find or we contacted the wrong person. But I was interested and kept a list of all the names. Checked them out later. Found most of them too. But *not* in the phone book."

She stopped and looked right at him, daring him to guess.

"Where?" he said.

"Obituaries column of the local paper. Now you tell me how you can die when you're already dead?"

He couldn't.

"But the real clincher's what happened last Wednesday. Annalise One had a message for me from Kevin Alexander. Guess who he wanted to contact?"

"Who?"

Annalise looked disappointed. "You're supposed to guess."

Graham considered it for a while, hoping Annalise would relent and tell him the answer. Guessing was not something he was good at.

Annalise continued to look at him. "Well?" she said, carving winding motions through the air with her hand.

"Gary Mitchison?"

"Wrong! He wanted to contact Kevin Alexander. Now you tell me why Kevin Alexander's sending messages to himself? There's only one answer. He's not using the Annalises to contact the dead, he's using them to bridge the VR worlds. It's the only thing that makes sense."

"What was the message?"

"Exactly the same message he sent to Gary Mitchison the first time. You know—danger, resonance projects disbanded, Census logs, Graham Smith, resonance wave?"

Graham nodded.

"Except this time he gave us a telephone number to try. Annalise One said it was a test, just for a few of the girls, we had to ring this number and ask for Kevin Alexander. We had to phone from a call box and hang up the moment we found out if he was working there or not."

"Working where?"

"ParaDim, of course. Over here in London. I was the only one who got through. So I was asked to come to London and give Kevin Alexander the message from himself. Now why does anyone do that?"

A very good question. Was Kevin Alexander looking for a way to talk to the unravelled? But for what end? Pure research? Something to do with resonance waves?

"It has to be VR worlds, doesn't it? Two hundred of

them and we're all strapped inside these VR chambers with strange helmets on our heads and wires going everywhere. And then one day some wire gets crossed and suddenly all the Annalises can talk to each other. That's it, isn't it?"

She looked at him expectantly. He looked away.

"Come on, it's gotta be!" She grabbed him by the elbow and tried to turn him back to face her. "And there's more proof. Think about all those alien abductions." She shook her head slowly from side to side. "No one was ever abducted. That was just a cover-up to hide the real truth. Equipment malfunction."

"Equipment malfunction?"

"Damned right! The VR hookup fails now and then and people have to be taken off-line but sometimes they wake up during the process and see all these wires and probes and stuff and freak out. It's not alien experimentation, it's scientist guys fixing the VR hookup. Think about it. What would all that VR equipment look like? We're all strapped into chambers somewhere with wires poking in and out of us, there'll be guys standing over us with bright lights shining in our faces."

Annalise was animated. Too animated for Graham's liking. He glanced nervously to his left, was anyone looking at them? Was Annalise drawing unwelcome attention?

Annalise tugged at his elbow again.

"Do you know how many people go missing each year? Tens of thousands and that's just the U.S. Now, you can't tell me they're all living on the streets. And if they're all dead—where's the bodies? No, they're gone. Real gone. Program malfunction." She crossed her throat with her finger. "Zap. One minute they're walking around, the next minute they're history. Erased from the system never to return."

Graham thought about all the people he'd seen disappear. The way people vanished and then returned as though nothing had ever happened. Had Sharmila been switched off? Had Michael really been transferred to Greenwich six months ago or had he been off-line since January?

And where were his parents?

And did that explain the changes to his surroundings? The houses that became shops overnight, the roads that were built in a day, the offices that migrated across London?

Was the program slowly breaking down? Not an unravelling thread but a program slowly degrading?

Graham found himself nodding. Annalise was right. People *were* disappearing. More than usual recently. The world was becoming less stable.

"And how else can we talk to each other? The Annalises, I mean. We're not crazy and we're not mediums. But we can communicate. We know there's something else beyond this existence.

"And Kevin Alexander knows it too. He's gotta be some kind of resistance leader, him and Gary Mitchison and the others. They're working through the Annalises to talk to each other and organize some kinda rebellion. A way to free us from this prison and you're the key. Which is why your life's in danger. You can get us out."

Her phone rang. "Shit!" she said, fumbling with her handbag and extracting her mobile.

"Hello."

"Dinner tonight. Usual place. Eight o'clock."

The line went dead, Annalise switched off the phone and turned towards Graham.

"I've gotta go. It's Kevin. He's got another message to send. Look, I'll meet you here tomorrow at one."

"I can't. I go to Green Park on Tuesdays."

She looked at him incredulously.

"If I changed my routine they'd get suspicious. They'll be suspicious enough after tonight."

"Okay, makes sense. Is that the park you went to on Friday?"

He nodded.

"Okay, you sit on your usual bench and I'll be the girl behind you, sunbathing on the grass."

"Won't they recognize you?"

"Trust me, no one will be looking at my face."

FOURTEEN

Graham watched her leave, standing rooted to the path as she cut across the grass. His meetings with Annalise always left him feeling slow and laden with questions that he knew he should have asked but had never found the opportunity. She never gave him a chance. He'd have a question ready and she'd knock it out of his head by saying something completely unexpected. And while he was still grappling with the ramifications of what she'd said, she'd be several sentences into the next story.

He'd never get the hang of conversation.

He sighed and watched a child run in front of Annalise, stumble and fall down. Annalise stopped and helped the little girl to her feet. The girl ran off, tottering on unsteady legs back to her mother.

There was something so natural about that scene and

yet . . . if Annalise was right, none of that had actually happened. The girl, the mother, Annalise—all computer generated.

How could anyone tell?

Was the little girl strapped inside one of Annalise's VR chambers being forced to live out her life in a fictional world of someone else's making? Or was she a fabrication, a prop, a slice of background color generated by a computer subroutine to make the park more believable?

Was there enough room inside Annalise's VR chambers to house the entire population of the world? Surely not. Which meant that most of the people he saw—people he'd worked with for years—were nothing more than computer-generated fabrications.

Was there a way of telling who had a mind and who was controlled by a line of code? Would they think differently, act differently?

Or was Annalise wrong? Was everything around him real? The lake, the trees, the people?

How could anyone possibly tell?

He walked back to the station confused. Everything suddenly looked so artificial, the people, the cars, the buildings. Could he really have missed so much? A man who spent his life observing his surroundings, who ticked off landmarks and counted the paces between lamp-posts?

He boarded his train. Could he have been wrong all this time? Was his life of ritual and repetition having no effect on the fabric of the world?

He shook his head. He *had* made a difference. He was sure of it. He remembered what it had been like before.

But could he trust his memory? Were the horrors of his childhood real?

He leaned back in his seat and rubbed his eyes. He used to be so sure of everything. His view of the world had barely changed in twenty-five years. The world was an unstable place—imperfectly formed and still evolving—old threads unravelling to make room for the new. A subject so complex to understand and so unsettling to contemplate that people looked the other way.

Had he been wrong all this time? Should he have questioned more?

And what would have come of those questions? More ridicule, more anger, more isolation?

He shook his head. This was getting him nowhere. There were probably people waiting for him at Harrow, wondering where he'd been for the last hour.

A thought that worried him for the rest of the journey. He'd look guilty, he knew he would. The moment he stepped off the train, he'd have "clandestine meeting" written all over his face. They'd see it, push him into the back of a big black car and torture him. Real or virtual, the pain would be the same.

He had to have a story, a reason for the missing hour. Something to make him feel less guilty.

Shopping! He could have gone shopping! Maybe broke his journey at Oxford Circus, walked around the shops, bought something small, something that would fit inside his pocket, no need for a bag.

He thought himself into the part. He could almost feel the imaginary object in his pocket.

The train braked hard and a platform streaked by the carriage windows, streaks of color gradually forming into people and kiosks, waste bins and brick.

Graham stepped out, patting at his pocket. He was pleased with his purchase. It was something he'd been planning for weeks. A facade he maintained all the way to his front gate.

When it hit him. Even if they bought the story about the missing hour, there were still the bugs. He'd removed them from his house. The two cameras would have shown it all.

His imaginary object dissolved in his pocket.

He latched the gate and hurried towards his door. His key danced on the metal scratch plate of the lock. Nerves. His hand wouldn't stay still. Even Annalise Twelve had been taken away from him. Which house would she be watching? His house? Or would it be like Rosie's Bar, would she see another house altogether?

He clasped his right hand with his left, steadied, found the lock, turned—left, right, left, right, breathe and count, turn and push. The door shuddered and flew back. Graham followed, reached for the edge of the door and swung it shut behind him.

He fell back against the door, closed his eyes and tried not to think.

Seconds passed, he listened to the slow tick-tock of his lounge clock. He counted each beat, then every other beat, synchronizing his breathing to the clock, lengthening the interval as his breathing slowed.

He opened his eyes.

He'd check each room, see if anyone had been inside. Maybe he could leave them a note, explain how it had all been a terrible mistake, he wasn't a key, he didn't need to be watched. He was Graham Smith. That was all.

He stepped into the lounge.

And stopped.

His jigsaw had gone. He stared down at the bare stretch of carpet. Had it unravelled? He *had* met a different Annalise today. Did his home change every time she did? Had their lives become so inextricably linked that they shared the same thread? Were they unravelling together, snagged in a long succession of aftershocks? Or did they share the same corrupt segment of program memory, a segment that was forever being reset?

His eyes strayed to where the camera had been. It was back. Same place, same disguise.

He looked away quickly.

Maybe on this new thread, he hadn't found the bugs. A thought which took him into the kitchen and the far left-hand corner of the kitchen table. He swung down to take a look. It was back. A small metal button pressed into the wooden corner brace of the table.

He closed his eyes and exhaled deeply. Sunday's bug hunt had unravelled away. No one would plant identical bugs in identical places the day after they'd all been discovered. He was free again! In this new reality he hadn't removed any devices. The only thing he was guilty of was disappearing for an hour on the way home from work.

And if he left all the recording devices where they were, they'd soon realize he was no threat. They'd leave him alone. They were bound to, he was harmless.

He put the kettle on while he made a cursory inspection of the rest of the house, opening windows in every room while taking note of anything that had changed. Little had, other than every ornament being misaligned.

He hovered as usual by his parent's door. Tapping on

the door just in case. Waiting those extra few seconds for
an answer that, deep down, he knew would never come.

It didn't.

He leaned over his mother's dresser to open the window and wondered if knocking on the door had been a
mistake. The room was bugged, what would people make
of him knocking on a door to a room that was supposedly
empty? Would they think he was harboring someone?

He looked down at the dresser, his mother's hairbrush
was half an inch further to the right than it should have
been. He nudged it back into position and shook his head.
What possible interest could his mother's hairbrush hold?

He felt angry. The thought of a stranger picking
through his mother's things, looking through her wardrobe, touching her clothes. He shivered. He'd have to
spring-clean the whole house—every room, top to bottom. He wouldn't be able to settle down otherwise.

FIFTEEN

Graham was back at work the next day, pushing the mail trolley along the rear corridor of the fifth floor. He was alone. The corridor empty, the office doors all closed. No muffled sounds of conversation, no tap of a keyboard or hum of a printer. The only sound an intermittent squeak from one of the trolley wheels.

Strange, he thought. To be surrounded by so many people and yet to hear so little. Was it always this quiet? Or had he become oversensitized since yesterday's meeting with Annalise?

He stopped by a door and listened.

Nothing. Absolute silence. Not even the hum of traffic from the road outside.

His fingers rested lightly on the door handle. He turned it slowly, easing the door open. A phone rang on the desk in the near corner. Graham didn't recognize the man who answered it. He smiled in Graham's direction. Graham forced a smile back and quickly cleared the out-tray.

As he closed the door everything went quiet again. Were the doors soundproof? He was sure they weren't. Had the phone conversation ended the moment Graham closed the door? A phone that hadn't rung until the moment he'd opened the door?

Was this what it was like being inside a virtual world? Were all the rooms empty? Were they voids that only became real the moment he looked inside? Voids that suddenly had to be furnished and populated? Was it all like that? Westminster Street, London, the world— theatre scenery to be pulled out when needed?

His hand closed around the door handle again. If he threw it open now, would the program have time to react?

Slowly, he turned the handle . . . and then let go. He jumped over to the door opposite and threw that one open instead. The door flew back, further and faster than he'd intended. It banged against the wall and shuddered. He stared inside. The room was full of packing crates, empty desks and boxes. A phone sat on the floor. It hadn't been like this on Friday. All the rooms on this floor were occupied. Had he beaten the program? Had it been unable to flesh out the room in time? Forced to resort to this half measure?

"Excuse me," snapped a voice from behind.

Graham jumped. Frank Gledwood stood in the doorway, his arms full of files and his usual sneer on his lips. Graham stepped aside, pressing himself back against the open door.

"You can always help if you've nothing better to do."

Graham swallowed. Was this the program's revenge? Cross me and I'll make your life hell?

Frank let the files fall with a clatter on the nearest empty desk.

"Well, speak up, I haven't got all day."

Graham nodded reluctantly. Shenaz arrived, her arms weighed down by two bulging plastic bags. She rolled her eyes conspiratorially towards Graham before dumping them in the far corner. Kathy wasn't far behind, carrying a plastic crate overflowing with files and assorted stationery.

"So, this is our new room," Kathy said as she slid the crate into the center of the near desk. She turned to Frank who was hitching up his trousers while looking out the window at his new domain. "I thought you said this new job was important."

"It is," he said, still looking out the window, flexing his shoulders and stretching his neck from side to side. "Believe me, this is just the start. From what I've heard this ParaDim section is going to be massive."

SIXTEEN

Graham checked his watch as he entered Green Park. Five past one—he was late. Twenty-five minutes helping Frank Gledwood had disrupted his morning schedule.

He hurried along the wide avenue of massive plane trees, peering ahead trying to catch sight of Annalise. He couldn't see her. His usual bench was empty and no one was on the grass nearby. He scanned the lawns beyond the trees: a few sunbathers, a few people sprawled in groups, some men playing football. No obvious sign of Annalise.

But now he got closer he could see there *was* something on the bench. He couldn't quite make it out, something flat. He walked faster. There were two things— a folded newspaper and a notice.

Wet paint, the notice read. He looked at the newspaper; was there a message inside? He bent down to pick it up.

"Don't look around. It's me."

Graham froze, his hand outstretched over the bench. Where was she this time? He could have sworn the voice came from behind the bench but that was impossible— no one was there.

"Pick up the 'wet paint' sign and sit down."

Graham obeyed, sweeping the park with his eyes as he did so. The only people nearby were three people on the path—a middle-aged couple and a young girl with a Walkman. He stared at the girl. She didn't look like Annalise.

"Pick up the paper and pretend to read, it'll mask your lips when you talk."

The girl's lips never moved. And the voice seemed to be coming up from the ground.

The young girl passed by to his right, the older couple to his left. Graham picked up the newspaper and carefully unfolded it, looking for some kind of microphone or loudspeaker. Nothing fell out.

"In case you're wondering—there's a baby monitor under the seat. Neat, huh? It's got a range of 150 feet. I'm sunning myself out here on the grass, talking into my very large hat."

"Can you hear me?" Graham pitched his voice just above a whisper.

"Hang on, I'll adjust the volume . . . try again."

"Can you hear me?"

"Loud and clear. Sorry about last night but I had to fly. Kevin's found something important. Something to do with October 16, 1966."

"That's my birthday."

"October the sixteenth?"

He nodded.

"Are you still there?" she asked.

Graham remembered the baby monitor and felt stupid.

"Yes, I was born on October the sixteenth, 1966."

He was even more confused. What had his date of birth to do with anything?

"You think that might be the date when all this was created?" said Annalise. "And you're the key 'cause you were the first to be plugged in?"

Graham shrugged, "Did they have VR in the sixties?"

"Roswell was '47 and—" She broke off. "Best be quiet for a minute. There's a man walking towards you. Doesn't look like a tourist."

Graham turned a page of his newspaper and glanced to his right. The man looked like a businessman—smart suit, tie, shoes that shone. Graham slipped back behind the newspaper and waited.

"He's gone," said Annalise. "Didn't look like a spy but can't be too careful. Who can tell what the bad guys look like in a virtual world."

"Do you think everyone we see is trapped somewhere inside a VR chamber?"

"Doubt it. Maybe a few dozen per program. You, me, Kevin, Gary, a few others we haven't met yet."

"But why? And how?" He had so many questions— each fighting to be aired first. He shook his head, blinked and tried to order his thoughts. What baffled him the most? What didn't baffle him? It all seemed so improbable. Virtual worlds, keys, resonance waves, two hundred Annalises . . .

"Why are there two hundred of you?" he asked. "If Annalise Mercado's such an unusual name, how come there's two hundred of you strapped inside a VR chamber?"

"Good question. Way I see it, we're two hundred different people all playing the part of Annalise Mercado. And for some reason we can't access our real memories. I might not even be female. But when I'm in here—I'm Annalise One Eight Seven. It's the only thing that makes sense. Some of us have identical pasts—up to a point. We all have the same parents but Annalise Nineteen and me— we have the same aunts, uncles and cousins too. We lived in the same house, went to the same schools, had the same friends, the same experiences. Right up to the age of fourteen and then—*wham*—our lives diverged. I think that's when we were plugged into the system—Nineteen and me—we were given identical memories up to the age of fourteen and then let loose in the world."

"To what end?"

"No idea. I'm not even sure Kevin knows. But it has to be some kind of experiment. Maybe the CIA are using VR worlds for interrogation purposes. Maybe they're testing two hundred simulators to find the best way to break someone down."

"We're spies?"

"Or test subjects. Trust me, governments don't care about using their citizens when they're short of guinea pigs."

Was that why his home was bugged? Had he been a guinea pig all his life, people observing his every move?

"Or it might be aliens," continued Annalise, "setting up a VR lab so they can study us, tweak our environment and watch how we react to different situations. Gotta make more sense than those ridiculous medical probes."

"So, I might not be Graham Smith?"

"Exactly. That's your persona in here. But you're also the key—someone important—who they've imprisoned in here."

"For thirty-three years?"

"Not necessarily. Just 'cause your character's been here for thirty-three years doesn't mean you have. And even if you have, who's to say how much time has elapsed in the real world? One year in here might be the same as a minute out there."

He paused. Was that possible? Then he had another idea.

"Are there two hundred Graham Smiths as well?"

"I think so. We've met about ten. Every time an Annalise has looked for a Graham they've found one."

"So the key could be one of the other Grahams?"

There was a pause. "I hadn't thought of that. Maybe you should talk to the other Grahams? Compare notes. I can send a message now, if you want."

"I'm not sure that would work."

"Why not?"

"When we first met, you asked me if I knew about the Annalises."

"Yeah."

"But you never asked me how."

"Didn't need to, you were the key, that's the kind of thing you'd know."

"But I'm not the key. I knew about the Annalises because I'd met them. Annalise One has long black hair, I met her Sunday. And last week I was saved by an Annalise with bright orange hair who lives in a cardboard box."

"You met Annalise Seven!"

"She didn't say. And I've met an Annalise from Boston . . ."

"You actually saw them and talked to them?"

"Yes, Annalise One came to my house on Sunday and helped clear the bugs."

"That was you!"

"That was me."

"So you think there's just the one of you and you flip between programs?"

"I don't know."

"I'll find out. Won't be long."

Graham waited, wondering what Annalise was doing, wondering if it would be so bad if he casually glanced behind to find out.

He didn't. He turned another page of the newspaper instead, his stomach rumbling as he did so. Maybe he should take the opportunity to have his sandwich? He checked his watch. He'd give her five minutes and then he'd eat.

Two minutes later Annalise returned.

"Just got through to four of the girls. The others are elsewhere. But there's at least five Graham Smiths sitting in Green Park at the moment. And you're the only one reading a newspaper."

Graham didn't have time to reply.

"There's a woman coming towards you on your left. She's looking right at you."

He glanced furtively to the left, lowering the newspaper a touch and quickly pulling it back up. She *was* looking at him. A young woman, mid twenties, short hair.

He waited, his hands tightening around the newspaper. She sat down at the far end of the seat, rummaged in one of her two voluminous bags, brought out a book and started to read.

Graham observed her as he pretended to read. She showed no signs of leaving any time soon, nor signs of any interest in Graham. She just sat there, her head bowed over her book.

Graham folded the newspaper, placed it back on the bench and took out his sandwich.

No doubt he'd find another wet paint sign in St. James's Park tomorrow.

He was unsettled for the rest of the lunch hour. The idea of there being other Graham Smiths hit him more than he'd expected.

He didn't like it. He didn't like it at all.

And the possibility that he wasn't Graham Smith but someone else entirely was even worse. Admittedly his life wasn't great. As a child he'd have given anything to be someone else. But not now. Now, he was used to being who he was. He'd adapted. And he wasn't sure he could do that again. Especially given the choice of new identities—an abductee at the heart of an alien experiment or a guinea pig in a brainwashing project.

Annalise must have got it wrong. And there were other explanations. His old theory for one: the unstable world shedding threads of existence. That's where the other Annalises were living—on unravelled strands of reality that had been discarded and were slowly fading away. His was the only true reality, all the others were transient, ephemeral memories of what used to be and could never be again.

The planet was alive, an imperfect unstable sphere that evolved by shedding its outer layers. Layers of reality detaching every now and then, part of the natural evolution of the planet. Wafers of existence shed like dead skin and replaced from beneath. Something similar but never identical. The planet slowly evolving, sloughing off its outer layers.

And some of those outer layers could still harbor life—for a time. While they drifted aimlessly, slowly decomposing, unaware of their impending disintegration.

And, somehow, Annalise had learned to bridge those strands of existence. She could talk to her other selves and those other selves could talk back, tell her something of their lives, of what they did and saw on their slowly degrading threads. Where his other selves, the shadow Graham Smiths, sat and ate and slowly unravelled into nothingness.

By the time he returned to work, he'd pushed all thoughts of virtual worlds deep into the recesses of his mind. The world was real—imperfect and unstable, but real.

SEVENTEEN

Later that afternoon, Graham was waiting by the coffee machine on the second floor lobby. He wasn't sure why, but the coffee always tasted better from the second floor machine. Brenda said it was because they cleaned it more often, though he couldn't see why that would be so. Why would anyone clean one machine more often than the others?

Stephen Leyland was ahead of him in the queue, talking quietly to someone Graham couldn't quite place. Brian, was it? Roger? The name escaped him but it was someone from the fifth floor.

"How long's he been missing this time?" asked the unknown man.

Graham tensed. Had someone else noticed that people were going missing?

"Four weeks," mumbled Stephen, so softly that Graham had to strain to make it out.

"How's Janie taking it?" continued the man, extracting his fifth cup from the machine and placing it precariously on a small tray.

"Bad."

Janie? Wasn't that Stephen's wife?

"Haven't the police got any leads?"

Stephen shook his head and turned away from the conversation while another plastic cup clattered into position, the machine whirred and a dark brown liquid streamed out.

Had someone in Stephen's family gone missing? Someone close?

"They say he'll probably get in touch when he needs money. And that the best we can do is check the answerphone every day and wait."

"They told you that?"

Stephen nodded. "It's no way to live, is it?"

"Can't you hire a private detective to go round the shelters?"

"The police say they've done that already. All the shelters have Jason's picture."

Now Graham understood. Jason was Stephen's son. Fourteen, fifteen? Something like that. Stephen had a picture on his desk. Always had, ever since Graham had known him.

The lift bell rang. Graham watched the doors slide back. No one got out. And no one was waiting in the lobby either. Graham looked harder, expecting someone to suddenly remember it was their floor and rush forward from the back of the lift. No one moved.

A tall, gaunt man stared back at Graham. Graham

looked away. Seconds passed, the man continued to stare. Shouldn't the lift doors have closed by now? Stephen's friend loaded the last drink onto his tray, made his farewells and headed off towards the back corridor. Still the lift doors remained open. Were they stuck? Was the man holding them open on purpose?

Graham edged along the lobby wall, following Stephen towards the head of the queue. He glanced back towards the lift. The doors were closing at last.

David Fotheringale, Her Majesty's Minister of Trade, strode into Conference Room C. He'd been looking forward to meeting Adam Sylvestrus for two reasons. One, anything to deepen the working relationship with ParaDim was good for the country. And, two, it wasn't that bad for David Fotheringale either. If he could keep in with Sylvestrus, maybe there'd be a directorship— something lucrative to step into when his political career started to wane.

Formalities exchanged, the two deputations sat. Three men on each side of the table. Fotheringale watched how Sylvestrus let his two American associates do most of the talking and how often they glanced towards him—as though seeking approval. And when Sylvestrus spoke— in that still recognizably English accent—people listened.

He was a very impressive figure—Sylvestrus—tall, gaunt, eyes that missed nothing. And he had a reputation to match. He had turned ParaDim from a little-known research project into the world's fastest growing company. A company with the true Midas touch. Everything they undertook succeeded. So many patents, so many discoveries. It was staggering.

And incredibly profitable too. Every major country had vied for the Census project, they knew the money that would be generated from the spin-offs and the benefits of being in bed with ParaDim. It had been one of Fotheringale's proudest moments—the day Sylvestrus announced that Census was coming to Britain.

As the meeting progressed, he wondered if this might be another of those days. The first results from the Census project were coming through. Several exciting medical discoveries had been made.

"In fact, Minister," said the younger of the two ParaDim aides, "one of your employees was flagged in our latest medical sweep. Very interesting family history. Potential breakthrough."

"Indeed?"

"Yes, a Mister—" he glanced at his notes "—Graham Smith. He works in this building."

"This building?" The minister sat up. "Are you sure?"

"Positive. It says here he's a messenger based at 12 Westminster Street."

"Would you like to see him?"

Both ParaDim aides looked towards Sylvestrus.

He leaned forward, placed his elbows firmly on the table, brought his finger tips slowly together in a triangle ending at his chin and looked directly at Fotheringale.

"Yes," he said. "That would be most agreeable."

"Graham, where you been, man?" asked Michael as Graham walked into the Post Room. "We been looking everywhere for you. They want you in Conference Room C right away."

Graham was surprised. Why would anyone ask for him?

Did they want the furniture moved?

He took the stairs to the third floor—no point waiting for the lift if people wanted him in a hurry—and arrived outside the conference room, out of breath and sweating slightly.

"Graham Smith?" asked an impeccably dressed young man whom Graham had never seen before.

Graham nodded nervously and forced a smile.

"If you'll wait here, I'll enquire if the minister is ready to see you."

Graham's eyes widened. Minister?

The young man disappeared inside, closing the door quietly behind him.

Graham smoothed down his hair with a clammy hand and flapped at some dust on his right trouser leg.

And waited.

The young man returned and opened the door wide. "The minister will see you now," he said, standing back to allow Graham room to pass.

Graham felt even more self-conscious, walking through that huge door into that long rectangular room. He'd never been inside before. Not this room. He'd helped move the furniture a couple of times in the other conference rooms but never this one.

"Take a seat, Mr. Smith."

Graham wasn't sure who'd said it, he was still taking in his surroundings—the huge conference table, the panelling, the paintings, all those important people looking at him. All of them in shirtsleeves, showing the new relaxed attitude—we're powerful men but, deep down, we're just like you, see how we dress down to make you feel comfortable.

It didn't.

The choice of seats didn't help either—there were about twenty of them and only six were taken. Should he sit by the door, well away from everyone else? Or sit closer? And how close? Or should he take one of the chairs by the wall, like that man taking notes?

Graham hovered by the foot of the table, smiling nervously. The impeccably dressed young man appeared at his elbow and gestured that he join the others at the head of the table.

Graham obeyed. A chair was pulled out for him, next to a man whose face he dimly recognized—a deputy secretary? Permanent secretary? Someone like that. Whoever it was, he smiled at Graham and held out a hand. Graham wiped his right hand down his trouser leg and shook hands.

"I expect you're wondering what you're doing here?" asked the minister.

Graham nodded, his fixed smile widening to a death rictus grin.

"I'll explain. These gentlemen here are from ParaDim. You may have heard that name before."

Graham swallowed hard. The minister was still speaking but it was as though he'd suddenly stepped back twenty feet and started talking through water. All the words were squeaking and smothered. Except one. ParaDim. Which broke against his ears like a crashing wave. ParaDim. *They've come for you. They're sitting opposite. They're here!*

He swallowed again, trying to unblock his ears. He looked down at his hands and clenched them firmly in his lap.

"Mr. Smith?"

Graham looked up, forced another nervous smile and swallowed.

"You'd be making an important contribution to the advancement of medical science," continued the minister. "A contribution that would not go unnoticed."

"Indeed," said the man next to him. "I'm sure the gentlemen opposite will recompense you handsomely for the two days they require of you."

"That we will," said one of the Americans. "Five hundred dollars a day plus expenses."

"Pounds," said a voice—English, well-spoken, assured. "Make that five hundred pounds per day." Graham looked up. The man was staring at him—more than staring—he was dissecting him with his eyes. The same eyes that had watched him by the coffee machine. The tall, gaunt man.

"We have access to one of the world's premier medical facilities," broke in the American opposite. "We'd pick you up from your home in the morning and take you back at night. Or we could put you up at a top London hotel, if you'd prefer."

Everyone was looking at Graham. He could feel the entire room willing him to say "yes."

"There'd be nothing invasive. All the tests are state of the art. We'd need a small blood sample but that would be all. If you'd prefer we could take a DNA sample from your saliva instead?"

"Or your hair," suggested the other American.

"Whatever you want. We can show you a complete list of the tests involved and talk you through everything they entail. You can choose the two days which are the most convenient for you."

Again the wall of faces turned on Graham. Again he

stared back blankly, waiting for everyone to give up and let him go.

"If there's any test you're unhappy with, we'll cancel it."

"You really would be helping medical science. Lives could be saved."

They all looked at Graham. Well-meaning smiles, encouraging nods. Waiting for the "yes" that had to come.

Graham was torn. He was terrified of ParaDim and he was terrified of saying "no." He'd spent his life agreeing with people, pursuing the line of least resistance through life with his nods and smiles. *Do what people say and they'll stop bothering you. Life's hard for people like you. Don't make it any worse.* His mother's advice. Advice that had served him well.

The minister broke in. "You wouldn't lose any holiday entitlement, if that's what you're worried about. You'd be on full pay for the duration of the tests and we'd offer you time off in lieu as well."

More smiles, more encouragement. Should he tell the minister he didn't trust ParaDim? That once they had him, they'd likely keep him? No one at the department would care if the two days turned into a week and then a month. And then what—an accident? A tragic unforeseen event? A car crash, a fatal allergic reaction, a mystery illness?

How could he say anything without sounding paranoid?

People are out to get me. They follow me everywhere. Annalise told me. She hears voices.

Smiling faces turned quizzical. He recognized the look—surprise and pity rolled into one. The look before people changed the subject or walked away.

Would these people walk away? Would ParaDim ever give up?

Graham looked away. His skin burned so much, he was certain his face was bright red. His hands knotted together in his lap. His mouth opened and closed like a fish—struggling to speak, struggling not to speak. Constrained and impelled in equal measures.

"Perhaps you need time to consider?" asked the tall, gaunt man.

Graham looked up, eager, smiling, nodding. A way out!

"Here's our card," he said, pushing a black and gold business card across the table. "Contact us when you've had sufficient time."

Graham nodded again and reached out eagerly to take it. The man didn't let go, he kept his index finger pressed down hard on the card.

"If you have any questions," he continued, looking directly into Graham's eyes. "Don't hesitate to ring. There will always be someone to take your call."

He raised his index finger a fraction and released the card.

Graham took it and almost tripped over the chair leg in his haste to get to his feet. He smiled, grasped the card to his chest with both hands and nodded deferentially several times as he backed away from the table. Then turned and almost ran to the door.

He grasped the ornate handle, pushing and pulling, rattling the door until it flew open. And then he was flying, down the stairs and away.

Graham kept on the move for the next hour. He didn't feel comfortable at his desk—they'd called down for him once, they could do it again. He took over Michael's rounds—except for the third floor. Michael didn't mind. Michael was always flexible.

Just after five, Graham was walking through the ground floor lobby on his way to the stairwell when he was called over to reception.

"Could you take this up to 515?" the receptionist asked, holding out a small parcel the size of a book. "I've tried ringing through but it's engaged. The courier said it was urgent."

She managed to smile and look pleadingly at the same time. Graham smiled back and took the package.

Five minutes later, the parcel delivered, he pressed the lift button and stood back to wait for it to arrive. He rocked gently back and forth on his toes and heels and counted the first row of ceiling tiles. They were all there. A good even number to finish on.

The lift arrived. He got in, pressed "ground" and walked to the back. He liked to stand at the back—dead center, heels against the wall. He stretched his arms out against the back wall, judged the distance between the corners and the tips of his fingers and shuffled a few inches to his right. Perfect. Lifts appreciated equilibrium—all machines did. He watched the lights descend, five, four . . .

The lift stuttered as it braked for the third floor. A muffled bell tolled in the lobby and then the doors slid back.

Three people were waiting.

All of them from ParaDim.

The tall, gaunt one spoke.

"Such a small world, isn't it, Mr. Smith?"

EIGHTEEN

The ParaDim deputation stepped inside. Graham watched as they filed in, one to his right, one to his left and one by the doors—the man with the eyes. Graham looked beyond him into the lobby. Wasn't anyone else getting in? All he needed was one more person, a witness.

The lobby was empty except for one girl at the coffee machine, her back to the lift. The doors began to close. Graham could feel the shoulders of the two Americans touch his own. Why were they standing so close? He felt paralyzed, hemmed in, trapped.

Ignore them and they'll go away. More advice from his mother. Applicable to bullies, wasps and men from ParaDim.

The lift began to descend. The tall, gaunt man was

staring again, an amused expression on his face. Graham swallowed hard, fixed his eyes to the control panel, watched the floor numbers light and dim, willing them to move faster, watching for any movement out of the corner of his eye, his hand ready to spring for the emergency button the moment anyone moved.

Should he press a floor button and get out? Or would that force their hand? The moment his finger hit the button, a hand would fly round his neck and a needle would find its way into his body. They'd carry him out of the lift, security wouldn't stop them. The man's had a seizure, they'd say. No need for an ambulance. Our car's outside, we'll take him to the hospital. We're doctors.

The lift began to brake. The light flashed on "one." Graham waited for it to flip over to "ground." It didn't. He heard the muffled sound of the lift bell on the first floor lobby. He had a chance. The lift doors slowly opened. He could see one, two, three people standing back from the doors waiting for people to get out. He delayed until the last second and then surged forward, squeezing sideways past the tall, gaunt man and stumbling into the lobby. A nervous smile, a nod of apology to the girl he'd nearly collided with and he was away, half walking, half running down the rear corridor.

He looked over his shoulder several times. No one appeared to be following. He heard two girls giggling and the lift door close. And then nothing.

He stayed on the first floor for ten minutes—mostly in the far lobby, looking out the window onto Westminster Street, straining to catch sight of the three men from ParaDim.

He didn't see them.

They could have kept to the near side of the pavement, they could have walked off in the other direction.

Or they might not have left the building.

He tried the windows above the main exit, plucking up courage to return to the scene of his escape from the lift. There were a few people at the coffee machine, which made him feel safer. He stretched up on tiptoe and peered down at the pavement. Plenty of people walking by but not one of them from the ParaDim delegation.

They must have gone by now. Important people wouldn't hang around, would they?

He tried the stairs, descending slowly, pressing himself against the wall, peering around corners. The door to the ground floor lobby had a glazed panel, he looked through, twisting his face to the left and right.

He couldn't see them anywhere. He opened the door a crack and looked along the wall to the lifts. Nothing. Four people waiting for the lift, all of them people he recognized.

He left work, convinced they were waiting for him somewhere. Maybe in that big black car from Annalise's dream.

He kept away from the curb, hugging the near side of the pavement, up against the shops and offices— stop-starting all the way down Westminster Street as streams of people flowed in and out of doorways. No one was going to bundle *him* into any slow-moving car.

He buried himself in the crowds at the tube station, kept away from the platform edge, kept away from any nook or passageway where someone could hide or sneak up on him. He pushed inside the carriages as far as he could, far from the doors where someone could force him off the train against his will. The stations flew by, light and dark, the ebb and flow of people, the noise, the rock and roll of the carriage.

And gradually, ever so gradually, his fear began to fade. Maybe, just maybe, he was safe. ParaDim had come for him, he'd said "no" and they'd gone away. Twice, if you counted the lift. Twice they'd had him and twice they'd let him go. Did that sound like people who wished him harm?

Maybe these were the good guys at ParaDim? Maybe the medical tests were for real? Something to do with Kevin Alexander and his friends? He'd ask Annalise tomorrow when they met in the park. Even if Kevin wasn't behind the tests, he'd be able to find out who was.

He felt relieved as he walked home from the station. An enormous weight had been plucked from his shoulders. Maybe the tests would convince everyone that he wasn't the key?

He closed the front door behind him, dropped his keys onto the hall table and rushed upstairs to his room. He'd jot down a note to himself— have AM ask KA about medical—and pin it to his message board while the idea was still fresh in his mind.

He stopped by his bedroom door.

His room was different. Very different. His bed was covered in a green bedspread. There was no quilt. The pillows were white. As was his wardrobe—white, laminated and modern. Not the solid oak antique he'd grown up with.

He opened the wardrobe door and looked inside. He'd

never seen so many ties. He touched them, let them cascade over his fingers. So many, so colorful. And the clothes—he hardly recognized any of them.

He moved quickly around the room, dipping into drawers, running a finger along the spines of his books—at least most of those he recognized.

He crossed onto the landing. Nothing there had changed. The same carpet, the same wallpaper, the same color paint on the doors and skirting boards.

Was it just his bedroom that had changed?

He lingered outside his parents' room. A few deep breaths to steel himself, a pause and then he knocked—ever so gently. Tap. His hand moved towards the handle, closed around it and turned. Click. He pushed the door open a crack.

There was a book on his mother's bedside table.

He swallowed and stepped inside the room—slowly—his eyes drawn to the book. He walked over, reached out and picked it up.

"You're home early, Graham."

He dropped the book and turned towards the window. His mother was seated at the dresser, combing her hair. She was back! Alive! After all these years!

He ran towards her, tears welling in his eyes. His mother was alive!

And then he caught sight of the face in the dresser mirror.

And stopped dead.

It wasn't his mother.

NINETEEN

"You look like you've seen a ghost," she said, looking at him quizzically in the mirror while she patted at her hair. "You're not starting all that nonsense again, are you? I've already told you it's not funny."

Graham stood rooted at the woman's shoulder, unable to take his eyes from her reflection. She didn't look anything like his mother. His mother's nose had been longer, her eyes bluer, her face fuller. Even seven years couldn't have sculpted those changes. The woman was an impostor. Sitting at his mother's dresser, using his mother's things. It wasn't right. It wasn't. . . .

His eyes fell on the picture. The one on the dresser. The wedding photograph. His father's face smiling up at him. His father's face pressed up against a younger version of the woman at the dresser. Not his mother. Though

it should have been. It was practically the same wedding
picture he'd grown up with. The same church, the same
smiling, youthful dad.

Something was wrong, very wrong. His mother couldn't
have unravelled away completely. Without his mother, he
couldn't exist. He wouldn't have been born. He shook his
head and stepped back from the dresser. No, this could
not be happening. It had to be a trick or . . .

Or what? Virtual reality? Was this part of the brainwashing technique? Mess with his mind until he had
nothing left to trust or cling to?

He couldn't believe that either. The world was real,
solid and unforgiving. Imperfect—yes. Unstable—
definitely. But it obeyed rules. And one of those rules
was that when people unravelled completely they took
everything with them—including their children.

It had to be a trick. And if it was a trick, how thorough
had they been? They'd doctored the wedding photograph
but what about the others?

He raced downstairs to the lounge. The sideboard had
three photograph albums in the bottom drawer—family
snaps from every holiday they'd ever had, every outing,
every family occasion captured forever on film. He took
them out and flipped through the pages. Not one picture
of his mother. *She* was there instead—the impostor, the
woman upstairs—smiling and posing and wrapping her
arms around Graham and his father.

It wasn't right! It wasn't right at all!

How could anyone think that this woman was his
mother? He didn't look anything like her. There wasn't
the slightest hint of a family resemblance. Not around
the eyes, the nose or the shape of the head.

He looked again at the picture of his father—a portrait from about twenty years ago. He traced the outline of his face, the curve of his jaw, the nose, the slightly hooded look to his eyes.

And realized.

He didn't look anything like his father either.

He prized his father's portrait out of the album and looked for a mirror. There was one on the chimney breast, above the mantelpiece. He walked over, picture in hand. What would he see? Would his face have unravelled along with his mother? Would he find a stranger staring back at him, a stranger with this other woman's features?

He stared deep into the mirror. A familiar face stared back. He hadn't changed one bit. He placed his father's picture against the mirror and compared the two—photo and reflection—scanning every line and feature. There was no family resemblance. None at all.

He summoned back a picture of his mother. The one from the shelf where the TV used to be. He knew it by heart, he'd picked it up so many times since her disappearance. And he tried to see it in the face in the mirror. Just one feature would do—eyes, nose, mouth, chin, forehead. Something!

He saw nothing. No similarity, no resemblance.

How was that possible?

Had he been adopted? Was that the significance of 16/10/66?

Who could he ask? Not the woman upstairs. And there were no close relatives. All the old neighbors had moved away. And as for family friends—the few that might remember that far back—he'd lost touch with them many years ago.

There was no one.

Except for her. The stranger in the bedroom.

And he could hear her coming down the stairs. He turned towards the door and waited for it to open. It didn't. He heard the click-clack of her shoes on the kitchen floor. The opening and closing of cupboards.

And then her voice.

"Graham, where did you put the shopping I asked you to get? I can't see it anywhere."

He replaced the picture of his father, slammed the albums shut and stuffed them back into the sideboard.

"Graham? Where are you?"

The lounge door opened. The woman came in.

"There you are. Did you get the shopping like I asked you?"

Graham shrugged, not sure what to do. Should he confront the woman or play dumb?

The woman shook her head. "I despair of you sometimes, Graham. I really do. Did you get the shopping or not?"

Graham shook his head. The woman rolled her eyes.

"Have you still got the list?"

He checked his pockets. He found a shopping list in the same pocket as his note.

But no black and gold business card.

He searched his pockets again.

"It's there in your hands," the woman said impatiently, pointing at the small strip of light blue note paper. "I can see it from here."

Graham stopped looking for the business card and held out the shopping list.

"I don't want it," she snapped. "You know perfectly

well you do the shopping on Tuesdays. It's all the heavy stuff." She looked at her watch. "There's still time if you leave now. They're open to half past."

Graham nodded, folded the list into his pocket and hurriedly left. He was glad to get out of the house.

Graham shook his head as he walked along Wealdstone Lane. What was happening to this world? Every day there was something new, some new twist that, if ignored, changed tack and came back twice as scary the next day.

There must have been a major unravelling. It was the only thing that made sense. Something enormous. Something that reverberated through the outer layers of the planet, fracturing reality and generating host after host of aftershocks.

He'd just have to ride them out.

After all, he'd done it before. He'd been through far worse as a kid. Twice he'd woken up to find his father had died in the night. Twice he'd watched his mother grieve, unable to comfort her. "He'll come back," he'd told her the second time, rubbing her back, trying to console her. "He came back last time, didn't he?"

Not a pleasant memory; his mother's head spinning round, the look in her eyes, the anger so intense she couldn't speak.

But he'd been right. His father had come back. Appearing out of the blue one morning as though nothing had happened. Only to vanish again within the year.

He'd lost his mother twice as well. The first to a heart attack, the second . . .

He never knew what happened the second time. He woke up one morning and she just wasn't there. Her bed hadn't been slept in, no note. She'd just unravelled away, leaving a room full of clothes and a house full of memories.

But he'd endured. Survived. Moved on.

This too would pass.

He turned the corner, lined up his right foot with the back edge of that big cherry tree, and started to count.

Graham looked at the shopping list as he manoeuvred the shopping trolley towards the supermarket door. He liked everything arranged in supermarket aisle order so that he could walk along the aisles and go down his list one by one. But this list wasn't in any order. Unless they'd changed the shelf layout again.

They hadn't.

He wheeled the shopping trolley down the first aisle. Music blared out from an unseen speaker, a few last-minute shoppers darted purposefully back and forth between the shelves. He took another look at the list. What was the woman buying? All those processed foods, products he'd never touch. He liked his food fresh and home-made. He liked a strict order to his meals. Roasts on Sunday, pie on Monday, fish on Friday.

The week had an order to it. His stomach expected it.

God knows what he was going to have to eat tonight.

He rearranged the list in his head and started loading the trolley—tins of soup, baked beans, ravioli. Up and down the aisles, more tins, more ready meals.

He stopped by the frozen food display and leaned over to rummage through the packs of frozen fish. He liked to take the ones from the middle, they felt more . . .

A hand reached in and touched his. A woman's.

"Graham Smith?" she whispered.

Graham glanced to his side. He knew who it would be but had to check just the same. His eyes widened in surprise. It was Annalise but . . .

"I know," she said. "I have a slight weight problem. But the way I see it, if I'm VR girl then all diets are off."

She grinned and waited. Graham blinked and quickly looked around to see if anyone was watching.

"You're supposed to laugh," she said. "That was my ice-breaking joke. I spent hours on the plane thinking that one up."

"Sorry. It's just . . ."

"You do know who I am, don't you?" she said anxiously. "I'm Annalise Mercado. The other Annas were sure you'd know."

Graham nodded and straightened up. He could hardly take his eyes off her. She was so familiar and yet so different. It was like seeing a close friend who had gained fifty pounds in a day. The friend was still there but all her features had softened.

"You forgot your fish," said Annalise, handing it over to him and looking at him quizzically.

He checked the aisle again—still empty. But for how much longer?

"I need you to get in touch with Kevin Alexander," he said. "It's urgent. Three men from ParaDim came to see me this afternoon. They want me to go for two days of medical tests. I need to know if it's safe."

"Three men from ParaDim, two days of medical tests," she repeated. "Is it okay to ask Gary Mitchison? He's my contact in this world."

Graham wasn't sure. A trolley appeared at the far end of the aisle, a woman ambling by the meat counter. Graham backed away from Annalise and pretended to be interested in hamburgers. The woman continued on her way.

"You really think people would follow you in here?"

Graham shrugged. "I didn't think people from ParaDim would show up at work. And—" he looked over his shoulder, one more check up and down the shelves "—I didn't expect to come home and find someone pretending to be my mother."

"Someone's pretending to be your mother!" Annalise said in a voice much louder than Graham would have wished.

"Ask Gary Mitchison about that as well."

He looked at his watch, five minutes to go before the shop closed. He'd have to hurry.

"Sorry," he said, "I've got to go. The shop closes in five minutes."

"Wait! I don't understand. Why don't you throw this woman out?"

"I . . ." He couldn't finish the sentence. Throw this woman out? The thought had never occurred to him. He'd never thrown anyone out of anywhere in his life. He adapted, avoided, ignored. He never confronted.

He'd found a strange woman in his house and accepted it. The idea of asking her to leave or who she was or what she was doing there hadn't crossed his mind once. Should it have? Should he go back and ask her to leave?

Could he?

"Look, here's my number." She handed him a card. "Give me a ring if you need help. I'm staying nearby."

He took the card, his mind already elsewhere, wondering what he was going to do when he returned home.

"I'll meet you in the park tomorrow," she said. "Anything you want to know, write it down and we'll swap notes."

❀   ❀   ❀

It didn't take Graham long to bury the idea of confronting his new house guest. He'd run a few scenarios—what he'd say to her, what she'd say to him. They all ended with her saying "no" and storming off upstairs.

He'd wait, maybe she'd go away?

He put two of the plastic shopping bags down on the floor as he closed the front door. Music filtered through from the lounge, followed by voices and explosions. She had to be watching TV.

He went through to the kitchen and set the groceries down on the table. Another room that had changed. The cabinets, the fridge, the sink, the lino—all different. There was even a phone on the wall. Only the kitchen table was the same.

He started unpacking the bags. The lounge door opened.

"Is that you, Graham?"

Graham nodded and continued unpacking. The woman walked in, pulled back the lip of the nearest bag and peered inside.

"I thought I'd do sausages tonight, what do you think?"

Graham shrugged. He usually had sausages on Thursdays with macaroni and cheese and baked beans—the way his mother used to make it. His real mother.

"I'll take that as a yes. Did you remember to get the oven chips?"

Graham nodded and moved on to the next bag. More tins. He stacked them in a pile on the table; he'd find out which cabinet they belonged in later.

An orange escaped from a string bag and rolled off the table onto the floor by Graham's foot. He swung down to pick it up. And remembered another time—one hand resting on the tabletop, one hand swinging down to locate a bug. Was it still there?

It was.

He folded the last of the shopping bags and placed it with the others. He'd check the hall next. He left the kitchen while the woman's back was turned and drifted into the hallway, quiet and casual, making sure he never looked directly at the hall light fitting. The camera was there. Same place as before, same model probably.

He pushed open the lounge door, the television flashed and blared. He walked over to the armchair by the fireplace and sat down. The rogue junction box was there too. He caught it out of the corner of his eye, nestling up against the ceiling directly over the door.

Everything was as it was.

Except for the woman passing herself off as his mother. Why was *she* here? Was she an extra pair of eyes? Someone sent to confuse him, drive him mad? Was this part of that interrogation program Annalise had talked about? Was the program degrading so fast it had lost all data concerning his mother and had had to construct a new one? Or didn't they care any more? Just throw in any old woman—he was too far gone to notice?

He got up. It was impossible to think clearly with the television so loud. He'd go to his room.

The woman stopped him in the hallway.

"Don't forget about that medical tomorrow. The car's coming to pick us up at seven."

TWENTY

Graham was stunned. Not *that* medical?

"And don't forget—we're not supposed to eat anything after ten."

She turned and left him, one foot on the stairs and one hanging, like his life, in midair.

How had this happened? They'd agreed to wait! Had that thread been pulled? Had it been replaced by one where they'd convinced him to accept?

Or had *she* accepted on his behalf? Was that her purpose in this reality? Graham Smith wouldn't agree so send for his mother. Any mother.

There had to be a letter, a card, something. Something to tell them where to go and when. A letter with a signature, a name that he could give to Gary or Kevin to check.

He tried the hallway first, searching the hall table,

flicking through postcards and circulars, looking for anything remotely official or medical. Wouldn't ParaDim have
preprinted stationery with a logo?

He found a card. A business card. Black and gold.

Adam Sylvestrus, Chief Executive Officer, ParaDim.

Was that the man with the eyes?

He turned the card over. It was blank. No mention of
a medical tomorrow or a car picking them up at seven.

And why *them*?

She'd said the car was picking *them* up, that *we're* not
supposed to eat anything. Was she undergoing tests too?

He flicked through the pile of envelopes again. Still
no letter. Maybe the lounge? He checked the sideboard,
the mantelpiece . . .

There was a letter propped up against the clock.

It was signed by Wayne Freeman, vice president of
Census-Medical. It confirmed the dates of the medical—
Wednesday and Thursday, eight 'til four—to be conducted
at the Cavendish Clinic, Knightsbridge. For two people—
Graham Smith and Eileen Susan Smith. Her name was
Eileen? His mother's name was Rebecca.

He read further. A car would pick them up at seven
both mornings and take them home. Meals would be provided. And money too. Two thousand pounds—a thousand
each—to be presented on completion of the tests.

He barely tasted his dinner; all he could think of was
tomorrow and what he should do. He helped with the
washing up. He sat in front of the television. He panicked. Internally. His mind on fire behind a straight-faced
facade of unruffled calm.

Every plan he devised, a little voice shot down.

Should I run away? *Where to?* Annalise would know. I'll call her now, there's a phone in the kitchen. *The phone'll be tapped.* I'll call from a phone booth. *They'll see you leave the house.* I'll climb over the back wall and get out through the garden at the back. *The woman'll notice. She'll tell them.* I'll go at night, when she's asleep. *They'll see you come down the stairs on the hall camera, they'll hear the back door open. They'll send someone round to check.*

On and on it raged until he could stand it no longer. There had to be a way. There had to!

He left his new mother to her TV and walked through the kitchen to the patio at the back. It was still light outside, a tinge of red in the western sky. He could be over that back fence and away before anyone could react. He stood poised, rocking ever so gently back and forth, unsure whether he had the courage to suddenly spring across the lawn. He stayed there, rocking, heel and toe for five minutes.

He couldn't do it.

That little voice again. *Not now, try again later.* Delay, put off, postpone. *Why risk everything when it might just go away?*

But what if it didn't? The more he ignored ParaDim the stronger they became. A week ago they'd been a small start-up company he'd never heard of. Now they had the ear of ministers and bought people for a thousand pounds.

Back came the voice. *What if the tests prove you're harmless? This could be your way out—your way back to a normal life.*

He had to contact Annalise. If he could be certain the tests were on the level . . .

And if he could only find a way of leaving the house without being seen by the hall camera.

He looked up at his bedroom window. Could he climb down from there?

The ladder! He kept one in the gap between the shrubs and the side fence.

He ran over to look, praying it hadn't unravelled along with his mother.

It hadn't. It was still there, nestling at the foot of the fence behind the shrub bed. He slid it out and propped it up against his bedroom window, then went inside, pulled down the kitchen blind and locked the back door.

He'd wait until everyone was asleep, then . . .

A click from the hallway made him turn. *She* was there. By the lounge door, stifling a yawn. Had she been there long?

"•'Night, Graham," she said sleepily. "I've set my alarm for six."

She turned towards the stairs.

"And don't put any of those silly yellow stickers on the doors. I do know what day it is."

Graham lay on his bed, fully clothed, anxious, waiting for the last light to be extinguished in the house at the back. He checked every five minutes, peering out the open window—a single light in the kitchen, then a light in the hallway, a light in the bedroom. And then nothing. The house in darkness.

He raised one knee onto the window sill and slowly shifted his weight forward, ducking his head under the open window. Onto all fours, tiny adjustments of hand and knee as he turned and swivelled, his right leg searching for a rung, his hands grasping onto the inside of the sill. He found a rung, then another, both legs on the ladder, then hands. One rung at a time, he descended, slow and silent, hardly daring to breathe.

Everything was still, not a breath of wind, a night when you could hear for miles. A thin blanket of cloud lay across the sky, the hint of a moon low in the eastern sky. He crept across the lawn, keeping low and listening. Music, television, sporadic shouts and traffic—distant noises from the two rows of houses and beyond. But nothing from the house beyond the fence.

He placed his hands on the top of the wooden lap fence and pushed off, locking his elbows, leaning forward, one leg over, two. He dropped down, followed the light-grey stepping stones across the black expanse of lawn. The house loomed, grey and silent. There was a motor bike in the drive. He squeezed past, scraping up against the rough brick of the house.

A toilet flushed. He froze. Water cascaded down a drainpipe a few feet away, gurgling into the ground. He looked up. A pale light at a frosted first-floor window, more water, a trickle, then silence. The light flicked off.

Graham breathed again, ten steps to the front gate, another heart-stopping few seconds as he struggled with the latch and he was through—onto the street and striding towards the corner.

He found a phone box a couple of blocks away. A drowsy voice answered.

"Hello?"

"I need to see you now, it's me, Graham."

The voice at the other end woke up instantly. "What's happened?"

"Did you find anything out about the medical?"

"Not yet. I'm meeting Gary at eight tomorrow morning. Why? Has something happened?"

"They're coming for me at seven. I need you to ring Gary now."

"Wait! Slow down. Who's coming for you at seven? No! Don't tell me. Don't say another word. Do you know the Belle Vue? It's a B and B on Headstone Avenue. I'll be waiting outside."

A girl stood on the corner, her breath rising on the cold air. It had to be Annalise.

Graham hurried along the pavement. The girl turned, peered for a few seconds then waved. It was Annalise, wrapped in an enormous coat.

"Sorry to wake you," he said in a voice just above a whisper.

"No problem, I'm still on Minnesota time. Who's coming for you at seven? ParaDim?"

Graham nodded. "They arranged it through the woman pretending to be my mother. A car's coming round at seven to take us both for tests."

"Whoa," she said, holding up a hand. "The woman pretending to be your mother set you up?"

"Not only that but *she's* going for tests as well."

"They want to test both of you?"

"That's what this letter says."

He passed the letter to Annalise. She struggled with it for a few seconds before taking it over to the streetlight on the main road to read.

"Wait, let me get this straight," she said. "This woman's name is Smith and she says she's your mother?"

"Not in so many words. But I've seen the pictures. All our family snaps have been changed. My real mother's been erased and *she's* there instead."

"They've doctored all your pictures?"

"Every one. There's even pictures I've never seen before. From holidays I don't remember going on."

"So, in this world you've got a different mother?"

He shook his head. "She's not my mother. I don't look a bit like . . ."

He stopped dead and looked down at his feet, too embarrassed to continue. He didn't look a bit like anyone.

"What's the matter?"

He sighed. He might as well tell her.

"I don't look like anyone," he said slowly. "Not my father, not my real mother, not . . . not her. I must have been adopted."

"And no one ever told you?"

"No."

"Do you think that's why everyone's interested in your date of birth? They're trying to trace your real parents?"

Graham looked up. His *real* parents. Why hadn't he thought of that? Was that why he hadn't unravelled along with his mother? Because he wasn't hers? Had he been tied to a different thread all these years?

"But if that's so," she continued, "and ParaDim's testing families . . . why would they want to carry out tests on the woman who adopted you?"

A question that Graham's little voice could answer. *Because there are no tests. It's a ruse. Once they get you inside that clinic you're never coming out.*

"I'll call Gary," said Annalise. "Can you hold this while I dial?"

She handed the letter back to Graham. Two cars came by in quick succession, racing along the main road towards the High Street. Annalise put the phone to one ear and a hand to the other. Graham watched, anxiously tapping his toes on the pavement.

"Sorry to wake you but this an emergency. Kevin's waiting for an immediate answer. Do you know anything about GS being invited to two days of medical tests?"

Graham listened for a reply but heard only a muffled buzz. Annalise looked at him and shook her head.

"They start tomorrow. He's being picked up at seven. Should he be worried? Kevin, that is."

Graham tried to read her face. A feat made more difficult as she had her back to the streetlight. Her hair and hands shone in the spectral glow.

"So you don't know anything about it? It's not something you'd organize?"

Another shake of the head and then another question.

"Is GS in any danger from these tests? Kevin wants to know if he should pull him out or not. What would you do?"

A long silence. Graham inched closer. Annalise shrugged and then held her hand out for Graham's letter.

"The invitation comes from a . . . Wayne Freeman, a VP at C-M."

Annalise pressed a button on her mobile and whispered, "He knows him," to Graham before pressing the button again.

"Uh-huh," she continued. "So you think it's safe?"

Another long wait.

"Unless what? Sorry, could you repeat that?"

She turned away. Graham followed her around as she spun to face the road.

"Right," she said. "But there were no medicals prior to any of those incidents, were there?" She paused. "Good, that's what Kevin thought."

A car accelerated from the High Street, Annalise handed the letter back to Graham and put her hand to her ear again.

"Uh-huh, and Kevin will know what that means, will he?"

The car raced by, leaving a smell of exhaust.

"Right. I'll tell him. Oh, and he also wanted to know if there'd been any moves to close the RP here?"

"RP?" Graham mouthed.

"Resonance project," Annalise mouthed back.

"Good, I'll tell him. Thanks for your help."

She closed the mobile and tilted her head to one side.

"Well?" asked Graham.

"Good news and bad news. He thinks it's safe to take the tests. He was going to suggest something similar himself. Something about testing for anomalies."

"And the bad news?"

"He said all the attacks came the day after the RPs were closed down."

"Attacks?"

"Do you want to sit down, Graham? There's a wall over there."

"No." He shook his head impatiently. "What attacks?"

Annalise took a deep breath.

"Reading between the lines, it looks like the day after a resonance project is closed, they find you unconscious in the street."

TWENTY-ONE

Graham could feel the blood draining from his face. "Unconscious?"

"But the resonance project here hasn't closed—I asked—so you're safe."

"There's two days of tests. What if they close the resonance project tomorrow?"

"I'll call Gary tomorrow. I'll call him every day. If I can't get through or he says the resonance project's been closed then we'll get the hell out. We'll have a day's notice."

Graham wasn't convinced. "What if they've changed their plans? What if they don't wait a day any more?"

"Maybe if you take the tests they won't need to hurt you?"

And maybe hurting was part of the tests. The final part. Just before his body was dumped on the street. He wanted

161

to kick something—the lamppost, the front wall of the guest house. Anything!

"Wait!" Annalise held up a hand, a smile breaking out across her face. "I just had an idea." She grabbed him by the shoulders. "What if those other Graham Smiths weren't really in a coma? What if they'd escaped? Have you thought about that? They found you unconscious because you'd got the hell out—your counterpart, that is—he'd unhooked himself from the VR and left his virtual body lifeless on the street.

"And that's why everyone's so interested in you—you found a way out. And no one has a clue how."

They adjourned to the low wall at the front of the guest house. Graham needed to sit down. His head was spinning. One minute she was telling him he'd been found unconscious in the street, the next that it was a good thing.

"I bet it's something to do with your ability to move between the VR worlds?"

He shook his head. He felt drained. "I don't move between VR worlds," he said emotionlessly.

"But you must. You've met other Annas, haven't you?"

He nodded, not looking at Annalise but looking straight ahead towards the Headstone Avenue sign on the other side of the road.

"So how do you do it? Is there a portal you've discovered or some kinda machine?"

He shrugged. "I don't *do* anything. Things unravel from time to time. People disappear, change."

"So you're just thrown from world to world?"

"It's all one world to me."

"You don't notice any flashing lights or solid objects

shimmering just before you flip?"

He shook his head. "Yesterday I was talking to Annalise One Eight Seven and today I'm talking to you. That's all I notice."

"But you have a different mother."

He nodded. "And different furniture."

"But you never know the exact moment that things change?"

He started to shake his head then stopped. There was that one time. He turned his face halfway towards her.

"Last Friday, I was talking to an Annalise from Boston. She went upstairs to the bathroom, I looked around and her suitcases were gone. She'd disappeared."

"Annalise Eighty-Five?"

"She didn't say. I don't think she had a number. She heard voices, and she had a recurring dream about me being bundled into the back of a black car."

"That happened to Annalise Twelve! She was right behind you when they grabbed you outside your office. That's when we decided to warn you. Gary and Kevin didn't seem to care—they were more interested in finding out why than warning anyone."

She held out a hand and touched his arm.

"She still visits, you know? At the hospital. She says you look peaceful."

Annalise withdrew her hand and looked away. Graham rearranged the letters in the Headstone Avenue road sign.

And wondered.

How could he be in a coma? It wasn't something that had happened to him and then unravelled. He'd never been bundled into the back of a car. It must have happened to another Graham Smith on another thread of reality.

And it must have happened after that thread had been pulled from the fabric of the world.

How long did these threads last? Were there whole lifetimes being lived out on these discarded remnants of existence? Were hundreds of Graham Smiths out there at this moment? Seated on walls, asleep in bed, running for their lives?

Or was it all illusion? An experiment? A series of VR worlds created for God knows what?

Annalise's voice broke into his thoughts.

"So you could be like sitting there on the wall next to me and then the next second you turn around and I'm gone?"

He nodded.

"And you get no warning at all?"

"No."

Annalise shook her head. "How long has this been going on?"

Graham shrugged. "As long as I can remember. The world's always been an unstable place. Things changing around the edges, things you'd hardly notice. But it's getting worse. Once I'd go a whole year without anything major changing. Now it's every other day."

He turned towards her. "Hasn't it ever happened to you? Haven't you ever gone round to a friend's house and had the door opened by a father who'd died the year before?"

Annalise looked shocked. "You've had that happen?"

Graham nodded. He remembered every face, he remembered every door. It wasn't something you easily forgot. "You've never had anyone close to you come back from the dead?"

"Never."

"My father died three times." His lower lip trembled. He looked away, surprised and embarrassed. His eyes pricked.

Annalise placed a hand on his shoulder and squeezed. "Do *you* change too?" she said softly, changing the subject. "Physically, I mean?"

"No," he paused and sniffed. "Not really. Sometimes I might touch my face and find that I've shaved—though I can't remember having shaved. And my hair—sometimes it's long even though I went to the barber the day before."

"How do you cope? How do you know where you're supposed to be or who you might have planned to see?"

He shrugged.

"I write things down. I keep a note in my pocket at all times." He reached into his jacket and brought it out to show her.

"It's got my name and address and where I work—so I know where to go. I keep notice boards at both places. Anything important, I jot down and stick on the board. Doctor's appointments, holidays, collection times."

"So it's like you wake up in a different body but with all your old memories intact?"

He nodded.

"I thought we had it tough, but you . . ." She shook her head. "How was that girl from Boston doing? The other Annalise you met. Was she having a hard time?"

"She thought she was crazy. She wasn't sure if she was picking up visions from a past life or a premonition of the future. So she quit her job and came over to find out."

He wondered where she was now. Would she have stepped out of the bathroom to find an empty house? Or a bewildered Graham Smith—one with no idea who she was or how she'd got there?

He hoped she was okay.

"We all handle the voices differently," said Annalise. "Annalise One became a medium, Annalise Sixteen discovered religion and I discovered chocolate." She laughed. "I think I made the best choice. What d'you think?"

Graham forced a smile.

"Did you say you were with One Eight Seven yesterday?"

Graham nodded.

Annalise shook her head. "She's another having problems adjusting. The voices came late for her. She was a college girl, life all mapped out, doing well at school. Then—*wham*—along came the voices and she freaked. Couldn't handle it. Dropped out of college, joined a cult, ran away and then decided to blame everyone she could. She's slowly coming out of it but she still sees conspiracies everywhere. Last month it was aliens, this month we're all prisoners in VR worlds."

"You don't believe we're in a VR world?"

"Sometimes I do, sometimes I don't. But I do know it's time we found out. I've lived with these voices for three years. There were thirty-one of us when I joined, now there's two hundred. Soon to be two hundred and one if your friend from Boston makes it through the next stage. I don't want to be still guessing in three years time. I want to know who I am and where I'm living. We all do."

They agreed to meet the next night—same time, same place. Graham borrowed a pen from Annalise and wrote the details—*Belle Vue, Headstone Ave., 1:00 a.m.*—on the back of his note.

Just in case.

Who could tell what world the sun would rise above tomorrow?

He hurried back home, retracing his steps, squeezing past the motor bike, scaling the back fence, silently climbing the ladder.

His bed felt cold as he slipped between the sheets. He shivered and then remembered his alarm. He flung out an arm and felt around for his clock radio. He set the alarm for 5:50, plenty of time to put the ladder away before his mother came down for breakfast.

And to remove the Post-its from the two outside doors.

A car horn sounded from the street outside.

"It's here, Graham," Eileen Smith said, peeling back the lounge curtain.

Graham hung back in the hallway, fiddling with his jacket.

"Come on, Graham. The man's waiting."

He followed her outside, pausing on the step to complete his locking ritual. A large car—maroon, shiny and expensive—hung in the middle of the road, double-parked and blocking the street. A chauffeur climbed out and opened the near-side rear door. Eileen Smith climbed in and slid across to make room for Graham.

Graham studied the chauffeur closely before sliding in. Had he seen the man before? On the tube, in the park, standing in a doorway?

He couldn't tell. The door slammed shut behind him. The journey proceeded smooth and wordless. A radio played softly, the car's engine purred. Graham felt small against the vastness of the back seat. He was so used to sitting on trains, wedged up against his neighbor, not knowing where to put his elbows, that the space unsettled him. His mother—that woman—was so far away a third person could have sat between them.

He looked out of the window, ticking off the landmarks—a curiously shaped tree, a brightly colored building. Comforting signs in an ever-shifting world.

The car wallowed around a bend, Graham felt himself moving against his will—sliding across the shiny leather seat towards his mother.

"Put your seat belt on, Graham," she said as he pressed up against her.

Graham straightened himself up and fumbled with the straps.

The seat belt snapped home.

Half an hour later, the car pulled up outside the Cavendish Clinic. Graham peered up at the Georgian façade; it looked more like a hotel than a hospital.

A man was waiting for them on the pavement. He was young, tall and immaculately dressed. He ushered them through the clinic's revolving doors into an ornate lobby—plush chairs, polished marble, fountain. More people came forward to fawn over his mother, who basked in the attention, refining her voice as she joined in the small talk. Graham sank further within himself. Wanting to be somewhere else but resigned to his fate. If he didn't submit to the tests today they'd only hound him until he did.

They took the lift to the first floor. Graham clung to the back wall as music played and people smiled.

The lift doors opened. More luxury, more opulence—paintings on the wall, decorative mouldings on the ceiling, thick blue carpet on the floor. Graham hung back as his mother and her two new friends walked along the wide central corridor. He looked down at the carpet, felt the lush pile spring beneath his feet. And wondered. Why was a hospital floor carpeted? Wasn't that asking for trouble? All the hospitals he'd seen had floors you could wash easily.

Maybe it wasn't a hospital?

They were shown into a room on the left—more smiles, more handshakes, more observations about the weather.

They sat down, they filled in forms—all of them on differently colored pieces of paper. Graham signed everything automatically, not bothering to read a single line. He just wanted everything over with as soon as possible.

More smiles ushered them back into the corridor.

"Jasmine, could you show Mrs. Smith to her changing room?"

Jasmine could. The two women walked companionably towards the lift.

"And now, Mr. Smith, if you would follow me."

Graham followed, wondering why they were walking away from the lift. Were the male and female changing rooms at opposite ends of the corridor?

Graham was shown into a room at the far end.

"A nurse will be along shortly. If, in the meantime, you would be so good as to remove your clothing?" He smiled and pointed to a coat stand with a sweep of his hand. "There's a dressing gown provided."

The man left, clicking the door closed while Graham stared at the coat stand.

He sat down on the chair provided and started to untie his shoe laces. And stopped. Why did he have to take off his clothes? Couldn't they test him fully clothed? What kind of tests were they going to do? They'd said earlier he didn't have to undergo anything he didn't want to.

And he did *not* want to take off his clothes.

He opened the door a crack and looked out. Perhaps he could have a word with someone?

His mother was in the corridor about twenty yards away. Fully clothed. Why wasn't she in her changing room? And who was that she was talking to? He looked familiar.

Recognition hit him an instant later—the tall, gaunt man. Even in profile, he was unmistakable. But what was he doing talking to Eileen Smith?

Had it all been a ruse? She'd delivered him to ParaDim and now she was being congratulated?

Graham drew back inside the room. He had to get out. He had to get out now. This wasn't a hospital, this was a trap.

He knelt down and quickly tied his shoes. His mind raced. There was no window in the room. The only way out was back through the corridor.

He pressed up against the door and opened it a crack. The two of them were still there—his mother and the man with the eyes—still talking amiably. Someone else—a nurse by her uniform—was waiting by the lift.

He opened the door further. There was a door to the stairs opposite. Ten feet away. He could be through it before anyone could react.

He hesitated, rocking back and forth on the balls of his feet. To go or not to go? Fear on both sides. He had to decide. He had to decide quickly.

He threw himself across the corridor, his right hand

outstretched, praying that the door was a push and not a pull. The door gave way, swinging back behind him. He was on the stairs and running, his ears closed to any possible pursuit. He didn't want to know if he'd been seen. He just wanted out.

The stairs took him to the ground floor. He pushed through, slowing to a brisk walk, trying to look as though he belonged. The corridor was wide and empty, his shoes squeaked faintly on the polished black marble.

He kept walking. Double swing doors came off to his left and right. None of them looked like potential exits. He could see the entrance lobby, the fountain, the lift. Everything empty. Maybe he could slip out unnoticed? Thirty yards, twenty. Still no one had seen him.

A phone rang in reception. A male voice answered.

"No, Mr. Cross, no one has left the building in the last ten minutes."

Graham hung back out of sight. The reception desk was set back against the wall opposite the entrance. Whoever sat there couldn't see down the corridor.

A light above the lift doors flashed. The lift had left the first floor. It was on its way down.

Graham ran for the exit, his footsteps echoing on the marble.

"Excuse me!" shouted a voice from reception. Graham kept going, across the lobby towards the doors.

"Stop!" A shout this time, the scrape of a chair pushed back against the hard marble floor. The lift bell rang.

Graham continued, his hand outstretched towards the door, a silent world, just him and a glass door, everything else pushed far away into a peripheral world of slow-motion inconsequence.

The revolving door gave way with a stutter. Graham pushed harder, the doors began to fly, Graham chased after them, his feet dancing in small staccato steps.

He lurched through onto the pavement, almost toppling over. Everything quiet, just the groaning of the doors and his feet bouncing off the paving stones. He skidded into a turn and ran blindly towards the corner. The pavement empty, the—

"Stop!"

A shout from behind. Graham kept going. A strange whine split the air, increasing in volume and then . . . an explosion. A few yards above his head. Shards of stone and brick dust fell like rain, hitting his head and shoulders. He flinched and ducked but kept running, blinking through the cloud of dust. There was a left turn, a side street up ahead. He was almost there. A few yards to go. Another whine, he could feel the air crackle, his hair felt like it was standing on end.

He ducked and threw himself into the side street, lost his footing and tumbled onto the trunk of a car parked on the corner.

An explosion rent the air. Masonry tumbled from the first floor of the building opposite. And glass. He looked up. Two windows had blown out. There was a hole in the building the size of a football.

He pushed himself off the car trunk. The car was damaged too. The roof was crumpled and the rear window stoved in. But not from the explosion. This was old damage.

He glanced around. The whole street was damaged— debris everywhere, buildings pock-marked, windows missing, blinds sucked through shattered panes.

"Stop!"

That voice again, nearer this time. He ran, his feet crunching over glass and chips of stone and brick. Everything so empty—no people, no traffic—nothing moving except him and his pursuer.

And there was a burning smell in the air. Why hadn't he smelled it before? And a distant roar—like passing within a mile of a football stadium on a Saturday afternoon.

And a whine.

That whine.

The one that split the air, shrill and growing in volume.

There was a doorway on his left—recessed into the building. An office. He leapt sideways. He could feel the air burn as he did so. A car ten feet away exploded. Its roof jumped fifteen feet in the air. A cloud of black smoke, the sound of debris falling like hail on the pavement.

The office door was locked. He rattled the handle. The sound of running feet was coming closer. There was a slab of masonry on the floor. He picked it up, heaved it through the glass door, kicked the remaining shards free and climbed through. If there was only one man he could lose him in the building. There'd be a fire exit, a back door, a place he could hide.

He raced up the stairs, swung around the landing, glanced back to the door, no one there.

Yet.

He took the next flight. Everything was dark but no hint of the carnage that had wrecked the street. He cut across the first floor, following a corridor that snaked between rooms. White walls, blue carpet, natural wood doors. He reached the end, not the lobby and back staircase he'd been hoping for but a large open-plan office with windows on three sides.

"Where are ya, ya bastard!"

The words came—fast and angry—from the stairs behind him. Graham slipped away from the door, looking left and right, desperately searching for somewhere to hide, a fire exit, a back door, anything!

Crash! Graham jumped. It sounded like a door being kicked in back down the corridor. Graham wove in and out of the clusters of desks towards the back of the building. There were some screens in the near corner, he squeezed through. There was a desk and a large array of filing cabinets. He found a gap between them and the wall and wedged himself into it.

Another door flew back against its hinges.

"Bastard!"

It was more a scream than a shout. A man losing control. Graham pressed himself further back against the wall.

More doors, more shouts, the man sounded close to tears.

Crash! Another door, much closer this time. Maybe too close. The man might be in the same room as Graham.

"Andy? Are you in here?" A second voice—male, authoritative, further away.

"Come on out, ya bastard! I can smell you." The first voice again, getting higher and higher pitched.

A click. A low whine. That weapon, it must be charging again. Graham squeezed his eyes shut and tried to dissolve into the fabric of the wall.

Footsteps along the corridor, fast and heavy.

"Andy!"

The whining continued, building up.

"Andy!" The second man was in the room now. "Are you mad? Andy? Listen to me! Put that weapon down."

There was no reply. Graham swallowed hard.

"Come on, Andy. Don't be stupid. Put the gun down." The voice calm and authoritative.

"That's an order, constable. Put the gun on the desk. Now!"

There was a click and the whining stopped.

Then there was a crash. Graham could feel the internal wall at his back vibrate. One of the men must have been thrown against it.

"What are you playing at, lad? Are you stupid? You could get put away for using one of those. Where'd you get it?"

Another crash, another vibration in the wall.

"Answer me! Where'd you get it?"

"From one of the smellies," Andy said, his voice quiet and subdued at first, then becoming more animated. "You saw what it was like out there, Sarge. They're better armed than we are."

"That's as maybe but . . ."

"They were killing us out there. And laughing at us. That looter must have been one of them. I couldn't let him get away. I couldn't."

There was a burst of static followed by a metallic voice. "All units report to Brompton Road immediately. Repeat. All units fall back to Brompton Road."

"Come on, we'd better go," said the sergeant.

"What about the looter?"

"He'll keep."

❀   ❀   ❀

Graham listened to them leave, following their feet along the corridor and trying to catch the sound of their boots crunching on the broken glass in the foyer. Only then did he feel safe to come out of hiding and brush himself off.

His hands hit an unexpected pocket. He looked down. His jacket was different—more pockets, lots of zips. He hadn't noticed before. Though he should have expected something like it. He must have unravelled leaving the clinic.

He checked his pockets, searching for his note. He found a computer disk in an inside pocket and stared at it—surprised—why would he carry a computer disk? He flipped it over, but there was nothing written on either side. He put it back and continued his search. He found his note in the next pocket.

> *Graham Smith*
> *Home Address: 47 Wealdstone Lane (but staying at 12 Westminster Street until it's safe)*

He reread the last line. *Staying at 12 Westminster Street until it's safe.* He was sleeping at work? What could have happened to make his home unsafe?

TWENTY-TWO

Graham looked out the window on his left, hanging back so that he couldn't be seen from the street. The buildings opposite looked undamaged—no pockmarked facade, no broken panes. Had the street at the back of the building somehow escaped? He leaned a little closer. The parked cars looked undamaged too. And there was no debris on the street. Everything looked normal.

Except there were no people and no traffic.

And it was the middle of the morning rush hour.

Where was everybody? Had there been a riot? Was there some kind of curfew in place and he'd been mistaken for a looter?

And what kind of weapon had that been?

He noticed a newspaper in a waste bin by the desk and

retrieved it. It was dated Tuesday, June 20, 2000. Yesterday.

He glanced at the headline. *Monopolies row spills over into trade talks.*

He read further.

The proposed breakup of ParaDim and Sylvestrus Industries took another turn yesterday when Adam Sylvestrus, CEO of ParaDim, confirmed that plans to relocate all their operations to "friendly" countries were in an advanced stage.

"ParaDim and Sylvestrus Industries will not be broken up," he asserted. "We will move all our operations to countries that still believe in a free market economy."

Only North America, Europe and Australasia still back the antitrust legislation that, if ratified, will break ParaDim into thirty separate companies and Sylvestrus Industries—the manufacturing arm of ParaDim—into five.

The most controversial aspect of the proposed breakup is the placement of ParaDim Defense under American military control. A Pentagon spokesman reiterated yesterday that "The catastrophic weapons proliferation of the past two years had to be brought to an end."

Sylvestrus, addressing a meeting of the Latin American and Asian trade delegations in London last night, declared the antitrust legislation to be politically motivated. "The Pentagon has wanted to get their hands on ParaDim from its inception. Not to share information as we have, but to keep the information for themselves."

Trade delegates had earlier been told that America would use sanctions against any country that worked to undermine the antitrust legislation. "ParaDim has to be broken up. It's too big and too powerful. Power has to reside with the people and their elected governments, not big business."

The London trade talks were further hit by threats from the Japanese and ASEAN delegations to walk out. "The new tariffs are biased against New Technology products and particularly ParaDim-generated New Technology."

The one piece of good news for the trade talks came late last night. After protracted talks with the police, antiglobalization protestors have agreed to move this afternoon's rally from Trafalgar Square to Hyde Park. Organizers expect thirty thousand people to attend. Police are confident they can now keep protestors away from the trade talks.

Graham looked up. Hyde Park was just to the north, less than half a mile away. Had yesterday afternoon's rally turned into a riot?

He walked over to the windows along the northern wall. Smoke rose between gaps in the buildings, the horizon dotted by fire and columns of thick black smoke. The building opposite was pitted with damage, there was a car slewed sideways in the middle of the street.

And yet some buildings were untouched. In fact, looking to the left, the whole street seemed untouched. It was like throwing open a window after a tornado had passed. Some buildings, some streets, were unaffected. Others were wrecked. Destruction at its most random.

Lights suddenly flickered on. The whole room awash with light. Graham turned towards the door. Had someone flicked a switch?

No one was there.

Screens flashed into life, computers hummed, printers clicked. The power had come back on. Had it been turned on at the mains? Was someone downstairs?

And was that a voice? He could hear someone talking nearby. He dropped down behind a desk. Was it the police? Looters? The owners of the building?

Music played. A snatch of a song, more voices. A television?

He moved towards the door, listening intently. No sound of footsteps on the stairs. Everything quiet except for that one voice, calm and matter-of-fact—a woman.

" . . . thirty-six people dead and another eighty-seven critically injured. Eleven policemen lost their lives. Two looters shot dead."

Graham followed the voice along the corridor, listening to the tale of destruction, the individual acts of heroism, the unthinking acts of violence, the statistics.

Another voice took over by the time he reached the room and looked inside. A television was hanging on the wall like a picture. A terrifying picture of London at night—ablaze with fear and hatred.

The picture flashed back to Hyde Park the previous afternoon.

"Fifty thousand people had attended the largely peaceful rally. It was only when the crowd were asked to disperse that a heavily armed splinter group opened fire."

Graham watched. The firing was indiscriminate. Arcs of flame poured down on the lines of police. Explosions, that eerie whining sound, screams, panic, people running, people falling. People lying very still.

Graham looked away.

"Police are advising everyone not to travel. Bands of heavily armed rioters are still at large in many parts of West and Central London. Residents are advised to stay at home and keep away from windows."

Graham closed the door and tried to shut out the sounds of terror and dissent. Muffled screams and sirens followed him down the corridor as he walked blindly away. What should he do? Wait in the building like the police advised or leave while it was still quiet?

He paused by the stairs and listened. What if that policeman came back—the one with the gun? He was in a strange building without the owner's permission. He'd smashed a door to get inside. Did that make him a looter? Could he be shot on suspicion?

He hurried over to the lobby windows and glanced outside. It looked quiet enough. He peered up and down the street. Still no sign of movement. He held his breath and listened. Maybe a dull murmur in the distance, that was all. Surely he'd hear a rioting mob if they were close?

And Westminster Street was only a mile away. He could be there in fifteen minutes, less if he ran.

There was a crash followed by an explosion. Not loud but not far away either. He pressed his face against the glass and peered to the left as far as he could. There was movement—difficult to make out—windows shimmering from upper floors at the northern end of the street. Nothing distinct, reflections maybe, ripples of changing light and dark.

And noise.

He heard it that time. People shouting. People coming this way.

He ran down the stairs, crunched over the glass at the

bottom and threw himself flat against the northern wall of the covered doorway. The sounds were louder, distinct voices amongst the background roar, shrieks amidst the sound of smashing glass.

He inched along the wall and peered around the corner. They were about two hundred yards away. A mob, spilling across the street, into and out of buildings. Debris rained down as large objects—monitors, chairs, cabinets—were dropped from upper storey windows. Cars bounced up and down in the street, people climbing all over them, jumping, shrieking, yelling.

And that strange whining sound, a group of hooded youths at the back, firing volleys into top-floor windows. Explosion after explosion. And then the flames. A building on the far corner caught alight.

He had to get away.

He slipped out of the doorway and walked briskly along the pavement, keeping close up against the buildings, his right shoulder brushing along the stone and brick. He followed the contours of the street, pushing into every recess and doorway, counting his way to safety with every step and praying that whoever was behind him was too caught up in their own amusement to notice one stray pedestrian.

Eighteen, nineteen. A railing pushed him away from the building. The wall eight feet away, he felt exposed. Twenty-one, twenty-two. A large explosion. Another. A huge cheer. Twenty-five, twenty-six. Broken glass everywhere, he picked a path through the debris, trying to make as little noise as possible. Thirty-three, thirty-four. A smooth white stone wall brushed against his shoulder. Almost there.

He broke into a run for the last few strides and threw himself around the corner. Nothing else moved. Even the clouds seemed frozen in the sky; there wasn't a breath of wind.

He flattened himself against the wall of the building. Where to next? He needed to go east but that would mean crossing the road in full view of the mob. Should he go west for a block and then work his way south and east?

He looked to the west. The Cavendish Clinic was less than a hundred yards away. What would happen if he went back through the revolving doors? Would he step back into a world of medicals and bogus mothers? Or had that thread unravelled away for good, unloosed from reality to float forever in some twilight realm?

An explosion brought his head spinning back around. That sounded very close. A cheer, a chant, a series of crashes.

He ran away from the noise, heading west then crossing over to the south. He reached a side street, turned south, everything so still, no people, no signs of life. He kept going, turning east at the bottom. He passed a row of shops—boards hastily nailed to where the windows used to be. A dog barked. Four security men stared out from behind the glass wall of an office foyer. All of them armed. He'd never seen armed security men before. He'd never even seen armed police before.

He hurried past. He could feel their eyes upon him. One wrong move and he was sure they'd open fire.

A noise up ahead. A car, several cars. Graham froze. A convoy of white police vans raced past him—no sirens, no flashing lights. Van after van went by, the occupants all looking at him, grim determination written on every face.

He kept going, heading east and south and east again. Gunfire crackled in the distance, punctuated by explosions and screams.

He entered a residential area—expensive houses, white columns, black railings. And cameras. Cameras everywhere—on top of the porches, halfway up the lampposts. All of them swivelling to track his progress.

And all of them had a tiny red light that pulsed just as he was about to pass by. Three short flashes then nothing. He was fascinated, fascinated by the regularity. He watched the cameras turn as he approached and then—one, two, three—

He . . . stopped. He'd noticed another flash of red light. Not from a camera. He'd caught the rapid flash of light out of the corner of his eye.

It had come from him.

He took a step back. The camera on the lamppost swung back with him. He stepped forward. Three flashes from the camera. And two flashes from his left wrist.

He stared at his watch. It looked like an ordinary watch. It looked very much like *his* ordinary watch. But it wasn't. He could see the manufacturer's name on the dial.

ParaDim.

TWENTY-THREE

His first thought was to take the watch off and fling it into the nearest bin. And then he remembered the cameras. He'd do it later, when he was alone and unobserved.

He hurried along the street, wondering what information was passing between his watch and the cameras on the street. Was he being tracked or was it something more sinister?

Movement at the far end of the street caught his eye. Something small and fast was flying along the center of the road at roof height. It looked—Graham rubbed his eyes in disbelief—like a tiny UFO.

It stopped and hovered noiselessly some fifty feet above Graham's head. A grey disk stationary against a blue sky. It swooped down and slowly circled him. It was almost within reach. Graham turned with it, swivelling on the spot. It looked like a large metal discus—one foot in diameter with a black band around its rim.

And a red light that flashed three times.

Graham looked at his watch. It flashed twice.

The disc rose and accelerated in one smooth movement, levelling off at roof height before continuing its journey along the street. Graham watched as it swung north at the next intersection and disappeared.

What had happened to this world? It was as though he'd stepped out of the clinic into a future world. A world where disks flew silently through the air. And strange weapons whined and exploded. Nothing like this had ever happened before. Was this the resonance wave that Kevin Alexander was so worried about? A wave so powerful that it made the biggest unravelling seem nothing more than the weakest aftershock?

He had to get to Westminster Street quick. He was sure to have something written down on his notice board or hidden away in his desk. Some explanation as to what the hell was going on.

He started to run. Expensive homes, squares, offices, hotels and shops—all came and went. All looked deserted. Occasional signs of damage—abandoned cars, smashed windows, smoking holes where houses used to be. Occasional glimpses of a face at a window, or the sound of child crying or a dog barking behind a locked door. And over everything hung the distant sound of destruction and hate.

Where was everybody? Were they really all hiding inside their homes? Or had most been evacuated? And if so, where to? The desolation stretched for miles. It was like running through a ghost town.

There was a sudden squeal of tires and a car turned the corner up ahead. It was going so fast it mounted the pavement in front of Graham before swinging back onto the road and zigzagging away at breakneck speed.

A red disk flew around the corner and set off in pursuit. Graham watched it flash past, ten feet off the ground, a colored version of the grey disk he'd seen earlier.

Graham turned into Westminster Street. There was a roadblock up ahead. Dark green army trucks and . . . was that a tank?

He slowed to a walk. It was a tank; there were two of them. And behind them a host of other vehicles and people.

A voice came from low to his right. "Keep going, Mr. Smith."

Graham jumped and swung round. There was a soldier crouched in a doorway, cradling a rifle in one arm and signalling with the other.

"They're waiting for you at the checkpoint," he continued.

Graham walked on, wondering how the soldier knew his name. People called to him from behind the roadblock.

"What's your name?" they shouted. *Who are you? What are you doing? Seen any bodies?*

Police and soldiers held them back. A green and red disk hovered over the police lines.

A gap appeared and he walked through, microphones were thrust in his face, reporters everywhere.

"You okay, Mr. Smith?" asked a heavily armored policeman grabbing hold of Graham's left arm.

Graham nodded.

"We'll soon get you through this rabble, sir. Don't worry."

Two more policemen cleared a way though the fifty yards to the DTI's main entrance. So many people. After the desolation of the past hour Graham felt claustrophobic. Reporters were everywhere, and those disks—there were dozens of them, hovering just above head height. They had to be some kind of flying camera, reporters were talking to them, disks of all colors, some with logos—NBC, BBC, RTL.

The door swung open just as he climbed the last step. Two armed men in full riot gear came out and escorted Graham inside.

"You'd better go straight up, Graham," said Andy on reception. "They're waiting for you in Conference Room C."

His first, second, and third thoughts were ParaDim, ParaDim and ParaDim. They'd come for him. It was happening the same as last time. *Ignore ParaDim and they only get stronger.*

What did they want with him now?

Graham climbed the stairs hesitatingly, trying to push back the moment of his arrival. A security guard stood motionless outside the conference room door. He watched Graham's approach for a few seconds before leaning to the side and pushing open the door.

Graham walked through. The room was as impressive as he'd remembered it. The huge table, the panelling, the paintings—but this time the room had a more lived-in feel. Jackets were strewn on the backs of chairs, cups and plates and papers were lying haphazardly about. And the people—he counted five of them—looked as though they'd been up all night.

Graham hovered by the door.

"Come straight in, Mr. Smith," said a tall man Graham vaguely recognized. "Don't stand on ceremony. Did you get the disk?"

Graham was about to shrug when he remembered the computer disk he'd found in his pocket. He took it out and handed it over.

"Good man. We thought we'd lost you during the power cut." He took the disk and handed it to someone Graham hadn't seen for two years—Roger Tyler, used to work on the fourth floor, very small handwriting.

"Have you had breakfast?"

Graham shook his head. He didn't think so, he felt hungry.

"There's plenty over there," the tall man said, pointing to a table against the wall. "Help yourself. You deserve it."

Graham sidled over to the table. There was a pot of coffee, milk, plates of croissants and bread rolls, a rack of cold toast, butter. Graham stood over the table, wondering whether he was meant to grab a handful and leave or stay, silently, in the background and eat.

The disk was slid into the computer in the corner, a few taps on the keyboard, a long pause, more taps and then a long, relieved sigh.

"It's all here," said Roger. "The Japanese have accepted the amendments to the energy proposals and suggested a rewording to the section on patent extension."

"Excellent. To recap, gentlemen. I want the updated tariff proposals evaluated, changes noted and the draft ministerial briefing revised for discussion at nine. I'll be leaving for the trade talks at nine-thirty."

The tall man picked up his jacket and walked towards the door. Graham poured himself half a cup of coffee and prepared to drink it very quickly.

"You think they'll still go ahead with the talks?" asked a short, middle-aged man.

"Until we hear different, the assumption is the talks start as planned."

"Even with the Japanese delegation stuck in Knightsbridge?"

The tall man stood by the door and shrugged. "It's not our decision."

The door clicked closed. Graham quietly buttered a piece of toast and listened to the conversation behind him, hoping to discover how a Japanese disk had found its way into his pocket. Had he been sent to Knightsbridge to collect it? Was that part of a messenger's duties in this thread of reality?

"I still don't understand why the army hasn't been sent in." A different voice this time, Graham couldn't tell who. "It seems madness to sit back and let a few hundred rioters have the run of London. Have you seen the TV pictures? They're laughing at us."

"That may be what they want," said Roger. "I was talking to the captain outside. He thinks they're trying to lure the army into a trap."

"How?"

"You've seen the pictures. That's no random mob. A mob would take out all the cameras and street detectors. But this lot don't. They want to be seen. They rampage through a small area, then disappear and another group springs up in front of the cameras a mile away. It's organized. They want to provoke a reaction. The army think they may have planted several large devices around the city—ready to detonate if they can get the security forces to take the bait."

"They'd do that?" Graham could hear the shock and incredulity in the man's voice.

"The army reckons they have a hardcore who will. And you don't have to be a rocket scientist to use New Tech weapons."

"Then why haven't they cancelled the trade talks?"

"Haven't you heard? They've set up a New Tech defensive perimeter all around the talks and Westminster. Nothing can get through."

"Are we inside the perimeter?"

"I didn't ask."

Graham stuffed two extra bread rolls into his jacket pocket—stepping out for lunch might not be an option today. He slipped out of the conference room unnoticed and made his way back downstairs to the Post Room.

A television was on, the screen flashing with images of riots and mayhem. He'd never seen a television in the Post Room before. And this one was large and hung like a picture on the wall—exactly the same as the one he'd seen earlier.

Three people were perched on desks watching, their heads swung round guiltily as Graham walked in.

"Relax, it's only Mr. Post-it," said Ray to the other two men—security guards from the look of their uniforms.

Graham groaned inwardly and forced a smile. Could the day get any worse?

Ray's smirk told him it could. It followed Graham across the room. The television and the riots forsaken in favor of more immediate entertainment.

"You found your desk all right then?"

Graham didn't bother to turn round. It would only prolong the ordeal. He'd check his desk, see what he could find, then leave.

"You don't want to walk around the room a couple of times to get your bearings?"

Graham pushed Ray's words to the back of his mind and opened the top drawer. There were several notes inside—reminders of jobs he'd agreed to do, procedures he should know about, his tube route home.

"This is the bloke I was telling you about. You know, the one on TV a half hour back? All he had to do was pick up a disk from a hotel in Knightsbridge and the muppet gets lost."

A reporter reeled off another list of statistics and Graham continued reading his notes. It looked like he worked on the van deliveries as well as in the office. There was a schedule of deliveries and routes and a list of contacts at the other buildings.

"You can't blame the bloke for walking into a riot," said one of the security guards.

"*I* didn't walk into a riot," said Ray indignantly. "*I* had to go all the way to Earl's Court for my pickup but you didn't see me get caught up in any riot, did you?" He paused, calming down. "You get in quick and you get out quick. And you keep your ears open. Course, it doesn't help if you're deaf as well as stupid."

Graham closed the drawer and leaned forward to check the array of Post-it notes on his notice board.

"What do they want with disks, anyway?" asked the other security guard. "I thought everything was sent electronically these days."

"You haven't heard?"

"Heard what?"

Ray lowered his voice in a conspiratorial way. Graham stopped reading and listened.

"You know that New Tech phone system? The one that was going to revolutionize everyone's lives?"

"The ParaDim NG?"

"That's the one. Infinite bandwidth, infinite capacity. A friend of mine overheard some of the IT guys talking last week. They reckon ParaDim scan every call."

"I thought that was impossible."

"It is. To everyone but ParaDim. You got to admire the bastards. They practically give away their system to make sure everyone uses it. They show everyone this amazing code that no one can crack and all the time they have the program to do just that."

"But they can't scan every call, can they?"

"What's the matter? Guilty conscience?" Ray laughed. "Those buggers have technology that can do anything they frigging want."

Graham wondered if Ray was telling the truth. Was this another of his stories to impress people? Or was it true? And was that why Gary and Kevin were so circumspect whenever they called Annalise? Because they knew all calls were routinely scanned?

He checked the last of his Post-its—nothing to say why he was sleeping at work or for how long. Presumably it was something to do with the riots and the trade talks rather than a specific danger to him at Wealdstone Lane.

If only he could find Annalise.

Gunfire blared out from the television as Graham walked over to the trolley and swung it around towards the door.

"Where do you think you're going?" asked Ray.

Graham tapped his watch and pointed towards the door.

"You'll be lucky. There's no post and no one to deliver it to. Essential staff only since yesterday afternoon. Well," he paused, "essential staff and you."

Graham went to the cloakroom instead. Choosing the fifth floor even though it wasn't a Friday—anything to put the greatest distance between him and Ray.

He wandered empty corridors, checked empty out-trays in empty offices and gazed out windows over an empty London.

What the hell was happening out there? It all seemed so unreal.

Maybe that was the problem—it wasn't real. Maybe he was trapped inside a decaying virtual world—the program degrading so fast it could no longer populate the streets. The riot no more than a device to cover the fact that the world was collapsing in on itself.

He stared towards the horizon. Was it getting closer? Was that why he had to sleep at work—because Wealdstone Lane no longer existed? The world having shrunk to a few square miles?

He shook his head. So much was happening. Every time the world shifted, ParaDim became more prominent. It was like he was moving into the future watching ParaDim grow from concept to company to threat to the world's stability. And yet the year never altered. Time flowed as normal. Yesterday was June 20, tomorrow would be June 22. But tomorrow for ParaDim? It could be the equivalent of years in the future. Was that the resonance wave? Something that ParaDim used to extricate itself from the constraints of time?

And where would it end? Would ParaDim grow and grow or collapse? What would this world be like in another year? More riots, more advanced weapons, more chaos?

He closed his eyes and tried to blink the world away. Maybe if he refused to believe in its existence . . .

The same world stared back. Real or not, it wasn't going anywhere.

Yet.

TWENTY-FOUR

Graham took the long way back to the Post Room, walking every floor and corridor, peering into offices and seeing who was about. There was a strange mix of noise and silence, calm and bustle. Some people scurried from room to room with papers and briefcases while others sat staring blankly into space, or at the televisions on the wall.

Graham hovered outside the Post Room door and listened. He couldn't hear Ray. He took a deep breath and walked inside. The room was empty. The television flashed and boomed in the corner of his vision. A reporter broke in occasionally with background information and statistics but mostly let the pictures do the talking. And the screaming, and the wailing.

Suddenly a voice broke Graham's concentration. A

voice he recognized. He turned. The man was there, on the wall, talking to the camera—the tall, gaunt man. A caption came up with his name. *Adam Sylvestrus, CEO ParaDim.*

"The world is not the same place it was three years ago," he said. "The pace of change has been unprecedented. Yes, established industries have become obsolete. Yes, this has caused problems. But the gains far outweigh the losses. We have synthetic food processing plants that can alleviate famine and drugs that can enhance and prolong life. For the first time in history, disease and famine have been tamed. How can that be bad for the world?"

The camera cut immediately to a close-up of a young male reporter. His question fired back at Sylvestrus almost before the older man had stopped speaking.

"Isn't it true that Sylvestrus Industries has released untested drugs into the Third World?"

Sylvestrus smiled and shook his head as though dismissing a child.

"Every one of our drugs is thoroughly tested. Why waste four years testing products by outdated means when new technology can carry out those tests in days? We have saved millions of lives by getting our products into hospitals *when* they are needed and *where* they are needed."

The camera cut back and forth, Sylvestrus taking his time, calm and assured. The reporter trying to unsettle him, interrupting, sneering and shaking his head to camera whenever Sylvestrus made a point.

"Isn't it more truthful to say that, so far, you've been lucky and that Sylvestrus Industries is a disaster waiting to happen?"

"Luck has nothing to do with it. The world has moved

on. We have models and simulations that can compress centuries of study into a handful of hours. It's the Western World who are endangering their people by clinging to outdated methodologies and refusing to accept the benefits that New Technology can bring. Death rates in what you call the Third World will soon be lower than in the Developed World."

"But what about weapons proliferation? You can't deny that ParaDim has been responsible for making weapons of mass destruction freely available."

"As I have said many times before, neither ParaDim nor Sylvestrus Industries deal in weapons of mass destruction. For every new offensive weapon we bring to market, we introduce twice as many defensive products."

"But people don't buy the defensive products, do they? They buy the weapons. Last year, you sold twenty offensive weapons for every countermeasure sold."

"That will change."

"Don't you feel any responsibility for the riots in London? They're your weapons being used against the police."

"And they are our weapons being used to protect the trade talks. A more pertinent question would be to ask the British government why the New Tech shields are only in place around selected government buildings and not the whole of London."

"Do you think that ParaDim is above the law? You don't like the antitrust legislation so you pick up your ball and leave."

"What I don't like is politically motivated legislation. Do you really think that breaking up ParaDim will stimulate competition and help the consumer?" He shook his head and smiled warmly into the camera. "It's a thinly disguised attempt to nationalize ParaDim Defense and gain control of our artificial intelligence system."

"So you ship all your assets out of the country? Take jobs away from the countries that back the breakup of ParaDim and open new factories in countries that support you?"

Sylvestrus shrugged. "It's a natural progression. New jobs go to the areas with the greatest prospect for growth. If America and Europe are bent on protectionism and the suppression of New Technology, then what else can we do?"

"But isn't it financial suicide to take on the regulators of the world's biggest market?"

"America and Europe are no longer the world's biggest market. Things have changed. The West has to realize that it can't dictate to the rest of the world any more. Money will follow the new economy wherever we decide to locate it. ParaDim isn't about bricks and mortar—it never has been—it's about ideas. And ideas are mobile. As is money. If America and Europe don't recognize that, then in ten years time they'll be nothing more than a backwater . . ."

The interview ended abruptly as a new picture flashed across the screen—a bird's eye view of London, shot from roof height. Two helicopters were flying ahead, skimming low over rooftops. They began to open fire on the streets below, the target out of camera shot. The camera swooped down and to the left. There were people on the streets. Smoke, fire, a sudden flash, two flashes coming up from ground level. The lead helicopter exploded, the other pulled hard to the right and out of shot. A second explosion. A blur of cloud as the camera swung violently through 180 degrees.

"These pictures were taken a few minutes ago," a breathless female voice reported. "Two military helicopters have been shot down over Knightsbridge."

The picture changed again. An office block, the camera zooming in and out, panning wildly, windows coming into and out of focus. A flash. The camera swept back, zoomed in, a window, the outline of a face, another flash.

"He's over there!" A shout off camera. The sound of heavy breathing, running feet and a microphone rubbing against fabric.

The shot changed again. A woman—young, worried, breathless—talking to the camera. "A sniper has opened fire from the top floor of—"

An explosion. The woman ducked. The camera panned to the smoking remains of a vehicle.

The picture changed again. An aerial shot, looking down on the southern tip of Hyde Park. A convoy of military vehicles spread out along a road. One was on fire, then another. Beams of light arrowed down on the convoy from the tops of office buildings. Every vehicle they hit glowed for an instant before exploding in a shimmering ball of flame.

Graham stood transfixed. He'd never seen anything like it.

Another explosion, louder this time and not from the television. The Post Room windows rattled, the floor shook, glass shattered somewhere in the building. Graham clung to his desk and looked back towards the door.

"Help! Somebody!" A cry from the foyer. More voices. "We've got wounded here!" Confusion, smoke, screams. Graham ran into the foyer. People everywhere—soldiers, reporters, wounded. Bodies lying on the ground by the lift, by the door, being carried in from the street. More people arriving from the stairs, from outside. Everyone shocked. So much blood, so many burns. And the noise, everyone talking at once. *Where's a doctor? Help me! There's more outside!*

Graham stood at the back, unable to help, not knowing what to do.

Another explosion. A rush of air from outside, a cloud of smoke blew past the door. Screams, engines revving, panic and flight.

Someone shouted from the main entrance. "They got the second tank!"

"Stand away from the door, you idiot!"

Another explosion, smaller, further away this time.

"Jesus, it's a weapons drone. The bastards have got a weapons drone out there! It's taking out everything that moves."

A soldier ran to the door. "Can't be! They're not supposed to have anything like that."

"It's firing again!"

Graham winced automatically and turned his body away from the door. A small explosion, a stifled scream from a woman hunched up against the wall next to him.

"What's a weapons drone?" someone asked in a quiet voice.

"A modified surveillance drone."

"Like our flying cameras?"

"That's right. But modified to carry a pulse weapon."

"Shit."

There was a sudden cry from the door and a shout of "Get down!"

Graham glanced towards the door. A red disk hovered

in the doorway. People were scattering. Shots rang out—four, five, in quick succession, the noise deafening in the confines of the lobby. The disk wobbled for a second, then dropped and clattered to the floor.

Everything went silent.

A man stepped out from behind the reception desk and leaned over the smoking disk.

"Congratulations, Corporal, you've just shot down CNN."

"It looks worse than it is. Mostly cuts, burns, flesh wounds."

One of the senior civil servants was being briefed in the corridor as Graham brought the last of the first aid kits into the lobby. Already some journalists were reporting in, interviewing the wounded while multicolored camera disks floated just above head height.

A hand settled on Graham's shoulder. "You're wanted in the Post Room."

Graham put the first aid kit with the others and made his way back through the crowded lobby towards the rear corridor. He stopped outside the Post Room door and listened. Ray was having an argument with someone.

"Look, Ray, if I needed something delivered fast, I'd pick you every time."

Graham recognized the voice—Jack Kingston. Jack had been Graham's boss for three years before he'd transferred out eight, nine years back.

"But," Jack continued, "if my life depended on that package getting through, I'd choose Graham. It's as simple as that. He may not be quick but give him a job and he does it. He doesn't ask questions, doesn't take risks and he doesn't get sidetracked."

"I don't believe this," shouted Ray. "I do *not* believe this."

There was a crash—it sounded like a filing cabinet being kicked—then Ray appeared at the door, his face contorted in a scowl.

"What you lookin' at?" he snapped at Graham before barging past.

Jack Kingston smiled apologetically as Graham walked into the room. "He'll grow up one of these days."

Graham smiled nervously.

"We have a problem," said Jack. "Our masters, in their infinite wisdom, have decided that the trade talks have to go on. They're not sure if they'd ever get the buggers in the same room again. And after the sixteen hours we've just had, can't say I blame 'em. Can't see many countries volunteering to host the next meeting, can you?"

Graham shook his head in agreement.

"So," he said, holding up a black computer disk, "this is the briefing document for the UK delegation to the trade talks. All the details're there—facts, figures and projections. I don't need to tell you how important this is. Or what's happening out there on the streets. If there was another way, we'd take it. But there isn't. All the comm lines are compromised. Someone's got to take this to St. James's Palace. And that someone is you."

Graham swallowed hard.

"I wouldn't be sending you out there if I didn't think it safe. I'm not going to kid you that there's no risk. But it's been quiet out there for the last twenty minutes. Intelligence reports say they've pulled back. The army has pulled back too, so there shouldn't be any reason for anyone to open fire. We reckon that a lone civilian on foot stands the best chance of getting through unscathed."

Jack paused and looked hard at Graham.

"It's less than a ten-minute walk if you go through the park. There'll be someone waiting for you at the main gate. Once you get within fifty yards of the Palace, you're safe. They've got New Tech shielding, missiles, the lot.

"And don't take any risks. If things change, find somewhere to hole up and try again later. The riots can't go on forever."

He handed the disk to Graham.

"Now slip out the back way and keep your head down."

Graham circled around the block, crossing Westminster Street a few hundred yards to the west of the DTI building and the still smoldering wreckage of the tanks and news vans. Everything was quiet. The streets were deserted and a faint burning smell hung on the air.

He walked briskly, hugging the walls of a side street heading north towards the park. He turned left and right again, zigzagging along the undamaged back streets. No hint of danger anywhere. No far-off shouts, no bangs, no rubble in the street. Not even a flying camera to dog his progress.

He paused opposite the entrance to the park. As soon as he crossed the road he'd lose the protection of the buildings. He'd be out in the open. He looked left and right. Still no sign of anyone. He had four hundred yards of trees and open lawns to cross.

He took his note out of his pocket and wrote six words on the back. *Take disk to St. James's Palace.*

He took a deep breath and stepped out into the open.

❋   ❋   ❋

Graham followed the path as it curved right to bypass a stand of trees. A stand of trees that hadn't existed two days earlier.

The path swung back and Graham stopped. There were people on the path up ahead. About fifty of them standing quietly in a group about one hundred yards away. There was a car there too—a police Land Rover.

Graham walked closer. Everything open now—rolling lawns to his left and right. A few stands of trees around the long thin lake that ran east to west across the center of the park. The lake bisected by a single footbridge, sixty yards long. St. James's Palace on the other side, a mere two hundred yards from the far side of the bridge.

He was almost there.

He counted three police Land Rovers, he could see them clearly now. A handful of burly policemen walked amongst the crowd, talking and leaning over to examine people sitting on the ground—or were they children? He couldn't quite see.

Some of the people on the edge of the group had blankets wrapped around their shoulders, some stared blankly into space, others walked aimlessly. They looked shell-shocked.

Graham stepped out onto the grass to walk past. People stared right through him, not saying a word. A police radio crackled.

"Say again, how many do you have there?"

"There's about fifty of them," a deep Welsh voice responded. "Mostly from flats attacked in Buckingham Gate. They're pretty shook up but no major injuries. What do you want us to do? There's another group coming over the park from the Buckingham Palace end. About a hundred or so. Do you want us to wait for them or start ferrying this lot over to you?"

Graham glanced to the left and saw another group in the distance walking slowly across the grass towards him.

There was a rush of static as the radio switched over.

"Can they all walk?"

"There's a couple of young kids who look completely out of it. We could load them and their families into one of the Rovers and send them up first."

"Roger that. We'll divert some of the drones to search for other groups."

Graham moved further out from the path to walk past a bed of shrubs and small trees. A girl sat, leaning against the trunk of a small flowering cherry. For one second he thought it was Annalise. But it wasn't. She was only a child.

He looked again—harder this time. Could it be a young Annalise? The nose looked wrong, and the eyes, but the mouth?

The girl never moved. She sat there, lifeless, blank, no hint of anyone home.

Graham shook his head. It couldn't be her. The line of the face was all wrong and . . .

He heard the whining sound first.

Then the explosions.

The group coming across the lawns were not evacuees. They were rioters.

A Land Rover went up in a ball of flame. People were screaming, running. Graham threw himself flat on the ground and rolled over. He could see a hundred people charging across the grass firing indiscriminately, whooping, arcs of light emanating from their center, the air rent with whines and bangs and screams and . . .

He had to get out. The footbridge was only fifty yards away, he could get there ahead of the mob. There were trees on the far bank—cover to hide behind, to protect his back as he ran the last two hundred yards to the trade talks and safety.

He started to run. A tree by the near end of the footbridge went up in flame. Were they shooting at him? Most of the fire was arcing over his head back towards the police.

And the girl.

The girl sitting in the bushes.

He stopped and turned. She was still there, she hadn't moved an inch. No sign of emotion or knowledge that her life was in danger. And the police didn't know she was there either.

Two of the Land Rovers were moving, people clinging onto the back and sides, people running alongside, people falling over. Everywhere panic, confusion, noise and smoke. Everyone heading east and away from the advancing mob.

Except the girl, forgotten in the chaos.

Graham had a choice—complete the mission or save the child. Jack Kingston's words came back to him. *He doesn't get sidetracked. Give him a job and he does it.*

He looked back towards the bridge. He could still get there ahead of the mob. But not with the girl. If he went back for her the moment would be lost.

His eyes were drawn back to the girl. She couldn't have been more than twelve years old. The shrieks grew louder, whining, flashing, explosions, the air filled with smoke and static. He had to leave. Now!

He looked at her again. If she asked for help, he'd give it. All he needed were those two words—*help me*—and he would. Two words and it would be her choice, not his.

They never came. He turned and ran towards the bridge. Three steps, four. The trees by the bridge were enveloped in flame, black smoke rising and billowing. He could still make it. They might not even see him behind all that smoke.

The girl.

She was behind him but he could still see her, imprinted on his memory, the vacant gaze, the despair. He couldn't leave her. *He doesn't get sidetracked. Give him a job and he does it.*

But not today.

He turned and ran back, grabbing the girl, whisking her to her feet in one easy movement, clutching her to him as he turned and skirted the shrub bed, his feet pounding in time to his breaths. The Land Rovers were up ahead, people spread out behind, everyone running for their lives between the smoke and the craters.

There was a police line in the distance, a long line of blue, two hundred yards away. The first Land Rover drove through a gap, then the second. The gap immediately closed, officers gesticulating wildly at the fleeing stragglers—about a dozen of them, caught in no-man's-land and running for their lives.

"Come on! Hurry up!" Desperation in the officer's words. Some were running out from the lines towards the stragglers. Graham and the girl were at the back, way behind everyone else. He was struggling, her extra weight and . . . the pain! A sudden stabbing pain behind the eyes.

His hands wanted to fly to his head but he couldn't take them from the girl.

He slowed, his legs buckling. And his eyes—the park shimmered, all color drained, features blurred and blended and starting to spin. He wouldn't let go. Had to run, had to see her safe. Not far.

A wave of pain hit him and dropped him like a brick. The girl fell out of his arms and tumbled somewhere in front of him. He rolled over, reached out, blind and desperate. He felt her hand, her fingers closed around his. He looked towards her. The world a blur and receding. He could feel himself being pulled backwards, the world in front of his eyes receding like a tunnel. Was he unravelling?

No!

He fought through the pain and pulled the world back. Like hurtling through a tunnel on a runaway train, the park flashed from black to dazzling white to greens and . . .

He could see the girl. She was smiling at him, her arm outstretched. If only he could get up.

The girl flickered before him. Three, four times. She was there, she wasn't there. There was smoke, there wasn't smoke. He was leaving her against his will.

No!

He was not going to unravel. Not now. The world could unravel later—as many times as it wanted—but not now!

He fought through the pain, the nausea, the disorientation, and staggered to his feet, all the time keeping hold of that tiny fragile hand. Noise everywhere—fire, smoke, screams, whines and explosions. The police lines lit up like a World War One trench.

But no one was falling down. The police lines were

holding, the explosions hit an invisible wall. The New Tech shield?

He started to run again, jerky, doubled over, the girl running beside him. Eighty yards to go. He could hear people behind him, close. Some of the explosions started to drop short of the police lines.

More shouts of encouragement from the police, frantic gesticulation. Two, three people reached the police lines, were grabbed, blankets thrown over them and enveloped. Others weren't so lucky. A woman fell twenty feet short and didn't get up. A man rose up on a ball of flame and split apart.

Graham didn't want to see any more. He knew where he was running. He squeezed the little girl's hand and she squeezed back. And they both ran blindly through the smoke.

TWENTY-FIVE

"Are you all right?"

A girl's voice. American? Annalise? He tried to focus but he thought his head was about to explode. Lights, shooting pain, he was falling.

A hand dug into the top of his arm, pulling him back. Another wave of nausea, he lurched forward to retch.

"Graham, what's happened? What have they done to you?"

She was standing to one side, her arms wrapped around his shoulders, a look of horror on her face. Annalise, with bright orange hair.

"Is that you?" he asked, his face breaking into a smile. "Annalise Seven? You've come back?"

"No. I'm Fifteen. We met last night, remember?"

He didn't. Everything was so fuzzy. The last thing he remembered . . .

"The girl? Where's the girl?" He struggled, twisting and turning in Annalise's arms. "Where is she!"

"Who? There's no girl here. Only me."

He was in St. James's Park. He recognized the sweep of the lawns and the layout of the paths. The same view he'd seen a few minutes earlier but without the confusion and running people. All was peaceful now. No sound of explosions or screaming women. And the traffic was moving again! He could hear it rumbling in the distance.

"There's no riot?"

Annalise's eyes widened. "You've just flipped worlds, haven't you? Oh, my God! Is it always this bad? I saw you from over there." She flapped an arm in a direction too fast for Graham to take in. "You were walking along the path and then suddenly you kinda pitched forward. I thought you'd tripped but then you started acting real weird and people started moving out of your way. You looked drunk and kinda crazy."

She stopped and gave him a long hard look. "You're not drunk, are you?" She leaned closer and sniffed his breath. Then stopped. "They didn't drug you, did they?"

"No." He tried to clear his head; everything was so fuzzy, he couldn't think straight. "It's," he took a deep breath, "it's never been like this before. I . . . I had to get the girl to safety. You haven't seen a girl, have you?" He held out his hand. "About this tall, black hair. She was holding my hand."

Annalise shook her head. "There was no one with you."

He wondered if he'd held on long enough. Had he got her to safety? He'd tried his best, but the pain . . . he'd had to let her go. He'd had to! Surely someone had seen them and ran out to help.

"What happened to the riot?" he asked.

"There's been no riot here. Were you caught up in a riot?"

"What about the trade talks? And ParaDim, what happened to ParaDim?"

"Wait, slow down. What trade talks?"

"The London trade talks. Maybe it happened here about a year ago. There were riots and they were threatening to break up ParaDim."

Annalise shook her head. "I don't remember anything about riots in London. And no one's threatened to break up ParaDim. Everyone loves ParaDim."

"What year is this?"

"Two thousand. Why?"

"And the date? Is it June . . ." He couldn't remember the date. Twenty something but twenty what? He felt so stupid.

"It's June twenty-first. Why?" Her eyes widened once more. "Have you been back in time?"

"No, I . . . I don't know. Do reporters here have cameras that fly? Like little flying saucers."

Annalise gave him a long sideways glance. "You saw flying cameras in this other world?"

Graham nodded. "And they could be modified to fire weapons."

"You've been to the future! I knew it! I knew this had something to do with the future."

"What?"

"These VR worlds or whatever they are, they're like simulations. I think these resonance projects are some kinda vast scheme to predict the future."

"How?"

"I don't know. Maybe someone plays with all these variables and 'what ifs' and then sits back and watches how the simulations play out. And we're like the guinea pigs caught up inside it all."

Simulations. He'd heard the word recently—someone talking about simulations—but he couldn't remember who or in what context. Would his head ever clear?

"And it ties in with what Kevin Alexander's been doing."

"What's Kevin Alexander been doing?"

She started to speak then paused, a brief look of uncertainty clouded her face.

"I'm not sure if Kevin Alexander's on the level," she continued, her voice slow and measured. "I know a lot of the girls think he's some kind of hero and all, but if Kevin Alexander's a freedom fighter, why's he suddenly so interested in lottery numbers?"

"Lottery numbers?"

"Exactly!" said Annalise, her natural animation returning. "He's had all us girls hunting down U.S. lottery numbers from Saturday's draw. Thirty-seven states I had to surf through! Why'd he suddenly want that?"

Graham couldn't imagine.

"And all that money he's throwing around—where'd he get it? And why's he more interested in the Annalises than in you? You're supposed to be the key but he hasn't done anything to help you, has he?"

Annalise released her grip on his shoulders and brought her arms into the conversation. Graham swayed slightly.

"What if he's found something more lucrative?" she said. "What if he's discovered that these VR worlds can predict the future and he's using the girls to collect winning lottery numbers? He could make a fortune if it works."

Graham's head spun. What kind of fortune could you make in a VR world?

"Or maybe he's got gambling debts and someone's putting the squeeze on him? Or . . . are you okay? Graham?"

Graham wasn't sure. The ground seemed to be moving away from him and he felt light-headed and . . .

Annalise grabbed his arm. "You better sit down before you fall down. Come on, there's a bench over there."

Graham felt better closer to the ground, the world stopped spinning and his head began to clear. He told Annalise about the medical, his escape, the riots, the rise of ParaDim, the trade talks and the little girl. He pointed out where the police lines had been, which trees had caught fire, the line of bushes where he'd first seen the girl. It still seemed so real. Barely old enough to be called a memory, he could hear every shout and bang. If he closed his eyes he was sure he'd be able to see every face.

"You realize what this might mean?" said Annalise.

"What?"

"Think about it. There's this simulation of a future where ParaDim's about to be broken up. There's these real important trade talks going on. Maybe the future of ParaDim's riding on the outcome. And you're the guy chosen to deliver the disk."

She paused.

"What if the success or failure of the talks hinges on you delivering that disk? What if the future of ParaDim depends on you delivering that disk? And what if someone at ParaDim has run this simulation before?"

Graham didn't need to hear any more. ParaDim ran simulations. *That's* where he'd heard the word recently—Adam Sylvestrus—ParaDim tested their products by running simulations. Was that what these VR worlds were? Part of ParaDim's product research to condense years of testing into a few hours of simulation? And in the course of their research had they stumbled upon something else, something unexpected—the demise of ParaDim?

And if they found that the trade talks could be sabotaged by the elimination of one expendable little man?

"Come on," said Annalise, rising up from the bench, "it's after ten, we've got some surfing to do."

"Surfing?"

"The Internet. We talked about it last night." She stopped. "You don't remember anything about our meeting last night, do you?"

Graham shook his head.

"Well, today is the day we find everything out. We're meeting Kevin Alexander at eleven thirty and we're not letting him go until he tells us all he knows."

"I can't . . ."

"Because you gotta be at work," interrupted Annalise. "I know, you told me last night. But we worked that one out. You're on sick leave."

"I'm sick?"

"That's the cover. We came up with a plan. You go to work as normal, walk through the front door, march into the Post Room, drop the sick note on Sharmila's desk and duck out the back through the delivery bay door. Anyone watching's left stranded on Westminster Street while you circle round to meet me here. And no one'll be looking for you until six tonight when you miraculously reappear outside your office. Neat, huh?"

It was. And it explained why he was in St. James's Park at ten o'clock in the morning. Would he have written it down? His hand reached instinctively for his jacket pocket and found his note.

It was written on the back—*take sick leave, meet A at SJP 9:30 a.m.*

He flipped it over. He was still living at Wealdstone Lane. He wondered if he was living there alone.

"Anyway"—she looked at her watch—"it's getting late. We've gotta be in Victoria in twenty-five minutes. You show me the way and I'll tell you why we're going there."

"You gotta remember," said Annalise, "I've been stuck at home listening to this story unfold for the past month. It's been driving me crazy. All you guys out there detecting. I've had my bags packed for two weeks."

They walked back through the park towards Buckingham Palace. Graham found himself eyeing suspiciously any large group of people, wondering if they had concealed New Tech weapons, wondering if at any moment they'd turn and charge across the grass.

"So, I started doing what I could—using the net to search for dirt on ParaDim. I mean, they come out of nowhere and in two years they're one of the top ten companies in the world. How'd they do that?

"Anyway, I was getting nowhere—there were so many hits and so much crap to wade through that I thought I'd try something different and started looking for entries under artificial intelligence. Guess what I found?"

Graham shrugged.

Annalise waited, looking as though she was going to

pounce as soon as he opened his mouth.

"Come on! ParaDim—big company, made its name with its revolutionary AI engine. What am I gonna find under ParaDim and AI?"

"Details of ParaDim's AI engine?" he hazarded without any confidence.

"Urrrr!" Annalise smiled as she pressed her imaginary air buzzer. "Wrong answer, Graham. I didn't find a thing.

"Which is seriously weird. I mean, ParaDim have gotta be *the* guys when it comes to AI, don't they? I searched through pages and pages of articles on AI and Ph.D. research papers and came up with nothing. No mention of any research using AI the way ParaDim claim they do. Don't you find that strange? I mean, did the ParaDim algorithm come out of the blue? There had to be some initial research, didn't there? An idea, a theory, some mention of work that went before."

"Perhaps they kept their research secret?"

"But how? And who? ParaDim wasn't even incorporated until two years ago. The algorithm and the company appeared at the same time. So who kept the research secret?"

"The government?"

"Not according to your flip to the future. The U.S. government was trying everything to get hold of the ParaDim algorithm, weren't they?"

They left the park and walked down Buckingham Palace Road towards Victoria. The traffic was heavy as usual, the pavements filled with people.

"Anyway, last night it came to me. Maybe I was looking in the wrong place. Maybe I shouldn't have been looking under AI but VR."

"Which is why we're looking for this Internet cafe in Redfern Street?" asked Graham.

"Exactly. Kevin couldn't see us 'til late morning, we had an hour to kill, there was a cyber cafe nearby. Made sense to use the time constructively. The more dirt we have on ParaDim, the more serious Kevin Alexander's gotta take us. I don't want him using the 'you don't understand' line and bailing on us."

They found the Internet cafe—a small converted shop with nine computers laid out in three rows. Five heads looked up as they opened the door. Annalise folded away her *Cyber Cafe Guide* and walked over to the assistant.

She handed over four pounds for an hour and was directed to the computer in the middle of the back row. Graham pulled up an extra chair and Annalise took the keyboard.

They searched in vain using ParaDim and VR, scrolling through pages and pages of hits with only passing references to ParaDim or VR. Time ticked on. Annalise scrolled faster and Graham's eyes hurt as he tried to keep up with the moving text.

"How about looking for rumors about ParaDim?" suggested Graham.

"Search on 'ParaDim' and 'rumor', you mean?"

"Yes, if you can do that?"

She tapped in the words and waited. Another mass of hits scrolled onto the screen.

"Welcome to the web," she said sarcastically. "We could be here for hours wading though this crap."

"Try adding 'AI.'"

"Okay." She tapped in the new search criteria. Fewer

hits than before but still several hundred. Annalise scrolled through them, moving so fast that Graham had to look away.

"This one sounds marginally less whacko than the rest." She clicked on the site and a new screen appeared. *The Truth about ParaDim.* They read the text as a picture loaded.

It started by casting doubt on ParaDim's use of artificial intelligence. *How can an AI algorithm come up with over three hundred patents in two years? Isn't it more likely that ParaDim is a front for a government-backed alien resettlement program? The aliens giving their technology in return for a homeland on Antarctica?*

"See what I mean?" said Annalise. "Every whacko with an opinion and access to a computer can upload their two cents."

She hit the back button, scrolled through the other entries and stopped.

"What's the matter?" asked Graham.

She hit the forward button and returned to the previous screen—*The Truth about ParaDim.*

"Look," she pointed to the words on the screen. "ParaDim and AI. My old search engine should have flagged this site."

"Are you sure it didn't?"

"I think I would have remembered an alien resettlement program in Antarctica."

Graham agreed; it did have a certain ring to it.

"Search engines only look at a small subset of the web," said a male voice at the station to Graham's left. "Sorry, couldn't help overhearing," apologized the young man, not taking his eyes from the screen in front of him. "But what you want is a meta search engine—like this one." He pointed to the address line on his screen. "It calls fifteen other search engines to make sure you get the widest coverage."

Annalise leaned over and copied down the address. "Thanks," she said, smiling. "No problem," replied the young man.

Graham watched the exchange in silence, discomforted by the sudden intervention of a stranger and feeling, irrationally, that somehow, it should have been him—Graham—and not the outsider who had furnished Annalise with the solution to her problem.

Annalise called up the new engine and retyped the search criteria. The number of hits multiplied. Everyone seemed to have an opinion on ParaDim. They were too big, too fast and there had to be a catch. Some thought they bugged the universities and stole ideas, some thought they had a mind-reading device or a time machine or access to the UFO that crashed at Roswell.

They waded through hundreds of pages. They followed links, going back and forth, refining the search, trying to find some common credible theme amidst the paranoia.

And then they found a site that made them sit up and look at each other.

It was a simple, plain text site with a minimum of color or artwork. But it raised a question that neither Graham nor Annalise had heard before.

How come no one at ParaDim has a background in artificial intelligence?

They read further. It published the names of the original ParaDim research team along with their specialities. Every one was a theoretical physicist or a mathematician.

"Can we find out if that's true?" asked Graham.

Annalise thought for a while. "We could search on those names but there'd be no guarantee that any information we found would be true. We don't even know if this list *is* the original ParaDim research team."

"What about Kevin Alexander? We know he works for ParaDim. What's his speciality?"

Annalise typed in Kevin's name and paged through the entries. The young man on Graham's left gathered his papers together and left. He looked like a student—young, undoubtedly bright, confident. Graham watched him walk down the aisle towards the door and noticed Annalise watching him too. The young man turned and smiled at Annalise as he lingered by the door. Annalise quickly looked down and started tapping at the keyboard while Graham hoped the door would suck the young man out onto the street.

The young man left leaving Graham feeling stupid and ridiculous. His life was in danger, his world unravelling and, suddenly, he starts feeling proprietorial about a girl that, arguably, he'd met less than an hour ago. Ridiculous!

"Maybe we should type in Canada?"

"What?" Graham's thoughts were still elsewhere.

Annalise pointed at the screen. "All these Kevins and Alexanders. If we added Canada to the search criteria it'd cut down on all this lot."

Graham agreed. Annalise typed in the new query and out came another long list of sites. They found one with a link to Toronto University which looked promising and clicked on it.

Kevin Alexander's details came up. He'd been a fellow

at the University of Toronto. He was another theoretical physicist. A picture gradually downloaded. A broad, smiling, open face.

"That's him," said Annalise as soon as the picture sharpened.

A list of published books and papers gradually formed on the right-hand side of the screen.

The title at the bottom of the list stood out from all the rest.

Parallel Dimensions: The Science of Alternate Realities.

"Parallel dimensions?" said Annalise, thinking out loud.

The connection hit them both at the same time.

"ParaDim!" they exclaimed in unison.

TWENTY-SIX

"That is *so* cool!" said Annalise, staring wide-eyed at the screen.

Graham wasn't so sure. "What does it actually mean?"

"It means we don't need VR worlds any more. The girls are real. We all are. It explains everything—Rosie's Bar, the six Sergios, the different versions of the De Santos kidnapping."

"The resonance wave?"

Annalise stopped. "Okay, so it doesn't explain every-thing. But it explains enough. I've gotta tell the girls."

She closed her eyes and leaned back in her chair. Graham watched, fascinated as her face seemed to drain of all emotion. Her muscles relaxed, her breathing slowed. And then she smiled, a warm smile which came and went, as though she was listening to a play inside her head, a play that only she could hear. One minute, she was laughing to herself—excited, bubbling—the next she was quiet, her head tilted to one side, listening intently to a hidden voice that played somewhere deep inside her head.

Graham looked nervously around the room to see if anyone else was watching. No one was. Every head was buried in a screen or a paper.

Annalise giggled to herself. Graham watched the way her face lit up and wondered why he couldn't feel the same elation. It was *his* life in danger, shouldn't he feel something now that they'd made such a major discovery?

Or wasn't it such a major discovery? Why should this theory last any longer than VR or Annalise One's astral plane? And what was wrong with his theory of an unravelling world? Wasn't that just as likely as a universe made up of two hundred parallel worlds?

He ruminated for several minutes. Wondering which was preferable—to have your life fragmented over two hundred parallel worlds or disrupted by the one, very unstable, unravelling world?

And was there a way of determining which was true?

"We've gotta go," said Annalise, bursting into life. "Best not give Kevin a reason to bail on us. Not now we've got some real questions to ask him."

"Where are we meeting him?" asked Graham as they crossed the road.

"Here," said Annalise, handing Graham a piece of paper with a roughly drawn map on it. "It's ParaDim's new offices. Don't panic—they haven't moved in yet. It's still being refurbished. Kevin said all the doors are unlocked and workmen are wandering about all the time so it's an ideal place to meet. No one'll notice a couple of extra people walk in unannounced. And if anyone asks who we are, we're with ParaDim—checking office accommodation."

"You've been there before?"

"No, we met at his office the first time. After he'd calmed down. I had to call him twice before he'd agree to meet. He slammed the phone down on me the first time."

"You know ParaDim scans all calls?"

Annalise tilted her head to one side. "Do they?"

"That's why I had to take a disk to the trade talks. ParaDim was scanning all electronic traffic."

Annalise nodded her head. "Which explains why all the Kevins insist we talk in code over the phone. Neat, huh? This is the day when everything begins to make sense."

They zigzagged across Victoria, running out between the gaps in the traffic, waiting on windswept islands, buffeted by the wash from passing lorries, the swirl of dust and the stench of diesel. Gradually the roads became smaller and quieter and the pavements less busy. The two of them fell into step, walking side by side, avoiding the cracks and stretching to the cadence of the street.

"This is *so* cool," beamed Annalise. "I've been practicing at home. You know, the walk thing? And here I am doing it with the man."

Graham smiled back. It did feel good. But then it always had.

"Why does Kevin Alexander suddenly want to see me?" he asked. "I thought he wasn't supposed to know that you talked to me?"

"Who said he knows you're coming?"

❀   ❀   ❀

ParaDim's new offices were in an old Georgian grey-bricked terrace—four storeys high, black railings, a columned entrance with steps up to an ornately panelled door. Part of Graham hoped that the door would be locked. He dwelt on the lower steps, looking down into the basement windows, while Annalise turned the door-knob.

It opened. The sound of an electric drill rang through the hallway.

Annalise led the way inside. The hallway was cluttered with boxes and paint tins. An electric wire trailed down the stairwell like a vine. The smell of fresh paint hung in the air. And from upstairs came the sound of hammering and drilling and the occasional shout.

"We're meeting in the basement," whispered Annalise. "Room four."

They followed the stairs down, stepping over the wires at the bottom and squeezing past the tables and chairs stacked in the lower corridor. The door to room four was open. They went inside.

The room had been freshly redecorated, a faint smell of paint could still be discerned. Some of the furniture had been positioned—a desk, a table, a pair of filing cabinets—others were still stacked in the corner—the chairs, another table, a bookcase. Packing crates and boxes filled another corner—some had been opened and pieces of white polystyrene jutted out from inside.

But no Kevin Alexander.

Graham checked his watch—11:29—they were early. Annalise tried to open one of the filing cabinets. It was locked. She moved over to the desk and opened one drawer after another.

"What are you doing?" hissed Graham. He glanced towards the door; what if Kevin Alexander suddenly walked in?

"Looking for a key to those cabinets. Might as well make full use of our time. Why don't you try those boxes over there? See what you can find."

Graham did as he was told, glancing up at the window from time to time, in case anyone was looking in from outside. The sky stared back through a line of black railings. Only the top quarter of the window was aboveground, the rest looked out on a dingy concrete well.

A man's voice boomed from the doorway. "What are you doing? Who's he?"

Graham jumped. He hadn't heard the man's approach. He swivelled round. Kevin Alexander filled the doorway. He was enormous, thick-set, huge hands.

"You don't recognize him?" Annalise asked the newcomer, sounding surprised. "This is Graham Smith."

Kevin Alexander seemed to crumple in the doorway, his face whitened. "What's he doing here?" He took one step back, glanced left, right, up the stairs. "Has anyone seen you? You've got to get him out now!"

"Why?" said Annalise.

"Because it's dangerous." He slipped back inside the room and carefully closed the door.

"Dangerous to who?"

"All of us. Just leave. I'll see if it's clear." He moved towards the window and peered across the street. Graham stayed in the corner out of the way.

"We're not leaving until you tell us what's going on," said Annalise. "We can help."

"You can't help," he said without turning his face from the window. "You don't understand. Now leave. Someone could be here any minute."

"No one followed us, if that's what you're worried about. Everyone thinks Graham's at work. No one saw him slip out the back."

"It's too risky." He pressed his face against the window pane and peered as far as he could up and down the street.

"We know about the parallel worlds."

He stopped looking out the window and turned towards her. He didn't say a word. He just stood there, an uncertain look in his eye.

"ParaDim scans all calls, right?" said Annalise, pulling out her mobile phone. "So what would they do if I start dropping your name into conversations—like, Kevin Alexander's meeting Graham Smith tonight or Kevin Alexander's found a way to stop the resonance wave? Or maybe I should just call Adam Sylvestrus."

"You wouldn't do that! You'd put yourself in danger."

She walked right up to him. He towered above her. A full head taller and twice as broad. She stood on tiptoe and looked him in the eye.

"Do I look like a girl who thinks things through?" She tilted her head to one side and rolled her eyes, playing the tortured psychic for all it was worth.

"Now tell me," she said. "Why is everyone so interested in Graham? Is it because he can move between worlds?"

Kevin Alexander's mouth dropped open. His head turned, he looked at Graham. "You can move between worlds?"

Graham nodded.

"We never imagined . . ." Kevin shook his head. "How?"

"We're asking the questions. Why is everyone so interested in Graham?"

"What? Sorry." He couldn't take his eyes off Graham. "Because . . . because he's everywhere. Every world we've looked at we've found him."

Annalise frowned. "Is that all? Graham exists across two hundred worlds and you think that's amazing?"

"Two hundred?" He laughed and shook his head. "More like two hundred billion. And those're just the ones we've found so far. The number could be infinite."

"Two hundred billion worlds?" It was Annalise's turn to be amazed.

"And every one of them has a Graham Smith born on the exact same date—the sixteenth of October, 1966. We thought it was just a crazy anomaly until . . . until other people started taking an interest." He glanced back towards Graham. "How do you move between worlds?"

"I'm calling," Annalise warned, waving the phone in Kevin's face.

He held up his hands. "Okay, okay."

"So what's weird about all the Grahams having the same birthday?"

"Because it just doesn't happen. Think about it. People have accidents, they die, they're never born. There's infinite variety across the parallel worlds."

He paused and stared at Graham.

"Except for you. You never change. You're everywhere. Every world we've discovered, there's a Graham Smith born on the same day of the same year in practically the same place. Harrow or Stanmore or Wembley or Edgware.

Always somewhere in North London. Even when London isn't called London, even when it's been destroyed or never evolved beyond a village. You're there. Living in the same geographic location."

He talked with a sense of wonder, his eyes never straying from Graham's.

"How? It makes no sense. People just don't exist on every parallel world. Think about it. Think of the pattern of events necessary to bring a child into the world—then factor in the uncertainty of thousands of years of social evolution, migration, wars. And then try to bring two people together at the same time in the same place to create the same child. It just doesn't happen. Parents never meet, they meet late, they meet someone else, they go to war, they move towns."

"So Graham's parents existed across all the worlds as well?"

He turned his head slowly around and looked down at Annalise. "That's where it really gets weird."

"How?"

"Graham doesn't always have the same parents."

Graham's eyes widened. His other mother—Eileen Smith—the woman he'd never seen before. Had she been one of those other parents?

"You mean he has different mothers?" asked Annalise.

"I mean he has different parents. We can't explain it. Which is why we've been collecting DNA samples. From Graham and every close relative we can find. It's"—he shrugged—"unfathomable. Somehow, and for some reason, a Mr. and Mrs. Smith, and in some cases a Miss Smith, had a child on October sixteenth, 1966. And every one of them named that child Graham."

He glanced back towards Graham.

"And then there's your job. You're always a messenger, even in the high-tech worlds you're a courier or a delivery man. In the low-tech worlds you're probably a carter. How? Do you carry a messenger gene?"

Graham didn't answer, he looked down at the floor instead.

"Me," Kevin continued, "I'm a carpenter on one world, on others I'm an accountant, a soldier, a scientist, a teacher. I have many birthdays. I have different sets of brothers and sisters, aunts and uncles. On the worlds that branched away earlier it's impossible to find my counterpart. There are people with the same name, some with similar professions, but our lineage is so different."

He began to bring his hands into the conversation—the huge lobster hands that Annalise One had first noticed. One trait that obviously had no problem crossing the dimensions.

"I can't prove that the Kevin Alexander on 015 214 363 544 is me. The link is too tenuous. But the Graham Smith on that world is a courier for His Majesty's Ministry for Trade and lives in New Wealdstone. Most of North London was levelled during the Great War, millions were killed. But he survived and moved back during the rebuilding.

"And you don't *do* anything. None of you. You don't belong to any clubs or societies. You don't vote, you don't drive, you don't marry. The only place we find any mention of you is on census returns, tax returns, medical and employee lists. Otherwise, you're invisible.

"Which again is strange. Most people have at least one famous counterpart across the billions of parallel worlds.

Even if it's only a lottery winner. But you—"

Annalise cut him off in midsentence. "Why are you so interested in lottery numbers?"

He looked confused. "I don't understand."

"Your counterpart on one of the other worlds—he wanted to know all the winning lottery numbers. Why?"

"I have no idea."

"I've got the phone," Annalise warned, waving her mobile at him for the second time. He held up his hands, showing Annalise two huge palms.

"I still have no idea. Didn't he say?"

"He said it was a test. But what kind of test? Why would he want the winning lottery numbers from one hundred and ninety worlds?"

"One hundred and ninety? I thought there were two hundred of you?"

"There are, but ten were in London."

He was silent for a while, thinking.

"What did he say the next time he contacted you?"

"Nothing. He just gave us a contact name and address. That's how I found you."

"And he did that for all one hundred and ninety of you? Gave you a contact name and address?"

"Yes."

"But the ten in London already had contacts?"

"That's right."

He shook his head. "It shouldn't be enough."

"What shouldn't be enough?"

"Six numbers. There are only six numbers in a lottery, aren't there?"

She nodded.

"You'd need more. Did he ask for . . ."

"He wanted the results from thirty-seven states. Would that be enough?"

He grinned. "More than enough. I never realized I was that clever."

Annalise rolled her eyes. "So the whole numbers thing was just a way to find out who our contacts should be?"

"Exactly. Thirty-seven sets of six two-digit numbers would easily guarantee a unique match. He could download the lottery information from the ParaDim database and match your world against it. Then he'd know where you were and who your contact should be."

He smiled to himself and then stopped. Something must have caught his eye for he suddenly glanced to his left, towards the window. Graham followed his gaze. There were two men on the steps, deep in conversation. They didn't look like workmen; both wore suits, both looked important.

"Nobody move," hissed Kevin.

Graham froze by the stack of boxes, watching the two men, their eyes thankfully locked on each other's faces. One movement from inside the room and all that could change.

One man clapped the other on the shoulder and they moved forward. They were coming inside.

"Quick! Follow me!" hissed Kevin as he bounded for the door. Graham and Annalise followed. Kevin opened the door, swift and silent, gliding through on tiptoe, his head turned towards the stairwell.

Graham heard the front door close and footsteps from the lobby above, a man's voice, a laugh. Kevin took off. Graham and Annalise snaked after him, turning right and right again, weaving around the crates and obstacles, along a narrow corridor at the back of the building.

He led them through a labyrinth—the corridor dark, no electric light or windows, a grey light feeding in from in front and behind. The corridor turned left. There was a light up ahead, bleeding through the gaps left between Kevin and the wall.

They reached an old panelled door—half glass, half wood. Kevin opened it, waved them through. There was a yard—roses, cobbled paths, high brick walls, a small gate.

"The gate opens out onto an alley at the back. Take it and keep going."

Kevin stayed in the doorway, his back to the corridor.

"What about you?" asked Annalise.

"I've got to get back."

"Why?"

"Because I have to. Just go!"

"No, not until you tell us what a resonance wave is."

Kevin glanced back inside. Graham thought he could hear someone calling.

"There's not enough time," Kevin whispered.

"Then make the time. We're not leaving."

Annalise grabbed Graham and pulled him towards her on the step. Graham looked longingly over his shoulder towards the gate.

Kevin clenched his huge fists and glanced once more into the corridor.

"Schenck's Law," he said. Just the two words. "That's all you need to know." He grabbed the door handle with one hand and pushed Annalise with the other, propelling the two of them into the yard. The door closed. A lock turned.

Graham looked up at the back of the Georgian terrace. There were windows everywhere. Someone could look out any second. A thought shared by Annalise. They turned together and ran for the gate, pulling it open and forcing themselves through.

TWENTY-SEVEN

They stopped running at the end of the alley.

"We've gotta get back to Redfern Street," Annalise said, in between breaths, "check for Schenck's Law on the net."

Graham led the way, selecting a route parallel to the way they'd come, not wanting to risk being seen by whoever might be parked outside the new ParaDim offices.

They reached Redfern Street. Graham hung back by the entrance to the cafe and let Annalise go in first. He followed her inside, scanning the faces of all the customers, looking for *that* young man—the one who'd been so helpful, the one with the ready smile. He was relieved not to find him and ashamed that he'd taken the time to look.

They took the same station as before. Annalise took the keyboard and started to type.

"How do you spell Schenck? S-C-H-E-N-C-K?"

Graham shrugged. "Can you try various spellings?"

She tried Schenck first, tapping in *Schenck's Law*. Most of the hits were to do with legal matters. She sampled a few before giving up and trying other spellings.

Fewer hits but the same legal bias and a dearth of anything remotely relevant.

"Could it be lore as in folklore?" asked Graham.

Annalise reframed the query, paging through screen after screen of folk tales and sites that seemed to bear no relation to either Schenck or lore.

She added *resonance* to the search, tried every combination of *resonance* and *wave*, *Schenck* and *Shenck*, *law* and *lore*. She found hit after hit on medical scanners and legal actions and genealogical sites. She persevered, clicking on every reference that offered even the slightest hope.

None provided the answer they were looking for.

What was a resonance wave? What had Schenck's Law got to do with it. Who or what was Schenck?

And had Kevin Alexander thrown them a red herring? Anything to get them out of the building?

"Perhaps we should try *Schenck* and *ParaDim*? Maybe he works for them?" asked Graham.

Annalise waded through another series of matches. There were passing mentions of ParaDim in articles written by people called Schenck. There were college track scholarships provided by money from ParaDim to students called Schenck—so many tenuous links that could be vitally important or nothing more than the vaguest coincidence.

Graham's attention started to wander. He was feeling hungry and thirty minutes of disappointment and furious scrolling were making his eyes hurt. Annalise hit the back button and started a new search. She typed in *Schenck* and *parallel worlds*; a new screen popped up, she started scrolling and stopped.

Halfway down the screen, there it was.

The Search for Parallel Worlds by Jacob Schenck.

Annalise let out a scream and clicked on the link.

A new page appeared. It was a book review. Graham flicked through the details, looking for any mention of resonance wave. There wasn't any. He went back to the top and started to read more thoroughly. It was the second in a series of popular science books by philosopher Jacob Schenck.

Schenck's ability to make complex subjects easy to digest remains his greatest asset. If only there was more substance to his writing. By the end of the book I was left with more questions than I had at the beginning. Schenck, as usual, is more interested in discussing why people need to believe in the existence of parallel worlds than in the science itself.

If you're looking for a book with hard facts, this is not the one for you. But if you're looking for an entertaining introduction, and occasional unsupported tangential leaps of imagination, then Schenck is always good value.

"Do we have to buy the book?" asked Graham.

"Not yet. Let's see what else we can find on him."

Annalise tapped in a new search on Jacob Schenck. The first page didn't look promising—several Jacob Schencks but no author philosopher. The next page came up. Annalise clicked on the third entry—University of North London, Philosophy Department.

They both waited for the screen to load. There was a list of faculty staff—professors, fellows, readers and lecturers—their specialities and publications. At the bottom was Jacob Schenck, a lecturer specializing in the philosophy of mathematics, free will and personal identity. His publications included *The Search for Parallel Worlds*.

They'd found him.

"Where's . . ." she scrolled back to the top of the page, "Russell Square? Is it far?"

It wasn't—one change and six stops on the tube. They stopped for a couple of hot dogs at a stall in Victoria and shared a bar of chocolate while changing trains at Green Park.

"What if he's not there?" asked Graham as they left the Russell Square station.

"Then we search his rooms."

Graham looked hard at Annalise. Was she serious?

"You don't have to look at me like that, Graham. This is the day we solve everything."

The Department of Philosophy was situated off Russell Square in a Georgian terrace—white-painted stone this time, though otherwise very similar to ParaDim's new office.

They followed a small group of students inside. A few people looked enquiringly at Annalise—probably more to do with her bright orange hair than questioning her right to be inside. Graham followed in Annalise's wake. No one gave him a second look.

They found Jacob Schenck's name on the fourth-floor notice board. He was in room 410. Graham hesitated by the door. What if Schenck wasn't in? He could be on holiday or at a lecture. Graham checked his watch—1:30—he might be at lunch. Or worse, what if he wasn't alone? What if he had people with him, a class?

Annalise didn't seem to have such thoughts, she sailed up to the door and knocked. There was a delay of a second or two.

"Enter."

They went in. Jacob Schenck was in his fifties, with greying hair that looked as though it hadn't seen a brush for a week and an eclectic choice in clothes. A gravy-stained plate sat on a pile of papers on his desk and books filled every available surface in the room. Five chairs were randomly placed around the room that, but for the clutter, could have been called spacious.

"We've come to ask you about Schenck's Law." said Annalise.

Schenck looked surprised. "Are you from the publishers? I thought we'd agreed to delay publication."

Graham glanced at Annalise, trying to read her face. What was she going to do? Bluff it out?

Annalise blinked—just the one hint of uncertainty before the confident smile returned.

"No, we're not from the publishers. Kevin Alexander gave us your name."

"Kevin Alexander?" Schenck stroked his chin. "The name's familiar."

He picked up a book from his desk and flicked through the index.

"He wrote a book on the search for parallel dimensions," said Annalise. "We're working in the same field and he suggested we talk to you."

Schenck looked up from his book. "The Canadian? I think I met him once. Didn't like the man."

"Well, he sure liked you."

"He did?"

"You bet." Annalise darted a look towards Graham, who quickly nodded in agreement.

"I'd have thought my work was too insubstantial for his type."

"No, not at all. 'Go and see Schenck,' he told us. 'Ask him about his law.'"

"I'm surprised he knew about it. I've only discussed it with a handful of people." He stopped, a sudden look of worry etched in his face. "The publishers didn't give him a copy of my manuscript to review, did they? They said they wouldn't. We agreed to keep everything under wraps until a more suitable time."

"No, I'm sure they didn't. He meets a lot of people. Conventions, you know. I expect someone mentioned your work in passing."

Schenck looked relieved. Annalise continued before he could think any further on the matter.

"Only we really need to know about your law. We really do."

Annalise smiled pleadingly, tilting her head slightly to one side, her eyes widening like a little girl's.

Graham watched in awe. She could threaten, she could cajole, she could plead. How could anyone refuse her?

"And you would be?" Schenck asked Annalise.

"Oh, sorry." Annalise held out her hand. "I'm Annalise, Annalise Svenson and this is my colleague Graham, er . . ." she hesitated, "Graham Smithsonian."

Schenck got up and leaned over the desk to shake hands, nodding to each of them in turn. "Pleased to meet you Miss Svenson, Mr. Smithsonian. You realize my 'law' is purely hypothetical, there can be no proof—at least, not for many years."

"Sure, we understand. We just wanted to hear you explain it to us. In your own words."

He leaned back in his chair, lifting the front legs slightly.

"Well, simply put, it states that once an event occurs on one world then the probability of the same event occurring on a parallel world increases."

Graham waited for Annalise to say "that's it?" and threaten Schenck with the phone. But she wasn't given the opportunity—Schenck's eyes took on a faraway look and away he went.

"It's an idea that came to me years ago. I was attending a lecture on free will and wondering if I should exercise it by leaving the room." He shook his head. "God-awful speaker, we were all bored to tears.

"And then it came to me—out of the blue—all these infinite worlds, overlaid one upon another, how could they not impact upon each other?"

"So you're saying that what happens on one parallel world affects all the others?" asked Annalise.

"In a nutshell, yes. Of course, there's no proof. How can there be? But it fits so well. Take evolution for example. We know that random mutation and natural selection alone cannot account for the entire evolutionary process. There hasn't been enough time for the process to develop. One would need billions of years to account for all the changes. There has to be another mechanism at work and my theorem provides that external influence, without the need to invoke divine intervention."

He let his chair drop back onto all four legs and leaned forward, resting his elbows on his desk until his enthusiasm for his subject wafted them back into the air.

"You see, evolution is not a process confined to a single world. It's a parallel process with each world influencing and being influenced by countless others. Once a mutation occurs on one world, the chances of that same mutation occurring elsewhere increases. And as more worlds evolve, the pressure on laggard worlds becomes all the greater, the capacity for evolutionary jumps becomes all the greater."

He held his arms out as though they supported a world of their own—an invisible globe, one meter in diameter.

"The last Earth to evolve—if there is such a planet—would find itself pulled into an evolutionary spiral. Life would feel compelled to leave the oceans. Even if land didn't exist, creatures with legs would evolve; they might die off due to natural selection but they'd keep appearing, waiting for the day when that first island pushes up from the deep."

Graham was mesmerized. He'd rarely seen anyone talk with real passion. He'd seen arguments, he'd seen heated debates but there was no anger in this man's words. It was all passion—passion for a subject, passion for an idea that you couldn't even touch.

"But, even more interesting is that it doesn't apply only to mutations. It applies to behavioral modification too.

You see, in evolutionary terms, a change in behavior always precedes adaptation. The fish, with the exception of my Last Earth example, will move to the shore before it develops legs. It doesn't develop legs and then search for a place to use them. It finds its niche first and then adapts. But why search for a niche in the first place? Why change a pattern of behavior that has succeeded for millions of years?"

"Competition? Climate change? Looking for a safer environment?" suggested Annalise.

"Sometimes, perhaps, but take the development of the amphibians, why leave an ocean teeming with food to eke out an existence on a shoreline ravaged by waves, where food's practically nonexistent and one can't even breathe?

"There has to be an impetus. An overriding influence that impels that organism to change its behavior."

"So, your law is about evolution?"

"No, it's about everything. I postulate that the law holds for any action or event, from the mutation of a fish to you deciding to visit me today. If I raise my hand now, then the chances that my counterpart on another world will raise his hand too is increased—infinitesimally, without doubt—but if enough of my counterparts raised their hands then a critical mass would be achieved."

"And then what?"

"And then we would have a resonance wave."

TWENTY-EIGHT

"**A**nd that would be bad?" asked Annalise.

Schenck shrugged. "It would depend upon the event resonating. The discovery of a cure for a debilitating disease? I can't see many people complaining about that."

"But if it was something bad?"

"Then it could be catastrophic. Once a resonance reaches a critical mass the event is practically preordained."

"Like fate?"

"One could call it that. One could say that fate is another name for resonance. Though I see it more as a series of probabilities. Every second of our lives we are bombarded with fields of resonance generated by events in our sister worlds. Most we ignore, most we can't even sense, but some resonate with the way we feel—strengthen our determination to take a certain path. Others are so strong they can make us change our minds—the gut feeling that flies in the face of every fact, the impulse that forces us to do something totally out of character."

Graham listened. The man was describing his life—his inner voice, the feelings, the certainty that one path was right and all others wrong.

"That's the power of resonance," Schenck continued. "As I envisage it, it works on instinct rather than intellect. In the same way a professional sportsman trains by repeating the same movements over and over again until they become automatic, we, too, can be trained by the actions of our alter egos. Their repetition resonates with our instinct."

"Could you stop a resonance wave?" asked Annalise.

Schenck shrugged and settled back into his chair. "One could always try. I can only speculate about the forces involved but I'd imagine them to be intense. It would be like telling one's teenage daughter to stop seeing an unsuitable boyfriend. Even if, at an intellectual level, she could appreciate the logic of the request, she'd most likely ignore it—every fiber of her body would scream at her to keep seeing the boy."

Graham nodded. He'd felt that power Monday night at the tube station. Maybe it hadn't been his fear of making a scene. Maybe it had been resonance, and the wake from two hundred billion Graham Smiths tracing their daily route home.

"What about starting a resonance wave?" asked Annalise. "Could someone intentionally create one?"

"Unlikely. They'd have to coordinate the process across

countless parallel worlds. We don't even know if there *are* parallel worlds let alone how we'd begin to communicate with them."

"But say there are parallel worlds out there that can communicate with each other. Could they get together and force some event to resonate across the dimensions?"

Schenck's eyes narrowed as he sat up. He looked at Annalise as though he was seeing her for the first time—no longer the striking girl with the orange hair but something else. Something he wasn't quite sure about.

"What event are you talking about?" he asked. "Have you something in mind?"

"No, I . . ."

Annalise's phone rang.

"Sorry," she said, turning her body away from Schenck as she lifted the phone to her ear.

"We need to meet," said Kevin Alexander. He sounded anxious.

"Where?"

"Divide the number of girls by four and add six."

"What?"

"That's the number of the place we're going to meet."

"Oh, right! Okay, done that, divide by four and add six. What's next?"

"The street is the name of the month after April."

"Got it. What time do we meet?"

"As soon as you can. And bring your friend."

The phone line clicked dead. Annalise turned to Schenck. "Sorry, we've got to go."

❀   ❀   ❀

They thanked Schenck and left, pausing on the stairs to look up May Street in Annalise's A to Z. It was in Brompton. A small street near Knightsbridge tube station—fifteen, maybe twenty minutes away.

They hurried back to Russell Square and caught the southbound train.

"I'm going to contact the girls," said Annalise, as she settled down in the seat next to Graham. "Won't be long."

Graham watched as she closed her eyes and drifted away. She looked almost regal, the way she sat with her back and head so straight—not slouched like everyone else in the compartment—an expression of benign confidence adding to the impression.

The carriage rocked from side to side as the train picked up speed. Annalise pitched forward, Graham grabbed her arm and pulled her back. She smiled and mouthed a silent "thank you," without ever opening an eye.

Graham left his hand where it was, feeling protective—at first—and then self-conscious. He wondered what the other people in the carriage were thinking. Were any of them watching? He let his eyes drift up and down the carriage, feigning indifference while he scanned every face out of the corner of his eye. Some were looking at Annalise. The woman opposite for one; her eyes flicked up and down, resting the longest on Annalise's face—or was it her hair? Whichever it was, she disapproved, and looked away.

Others were not so disapproving. Two youths by the doors elbowed each other and leered. Another man stared at her from over his newspaper.

No one looked at Graham.

Didn't they see his hand on her arm? Couldn't they imagine that he and Annalise could be together? Was it that unlikely?

He looked at their imperfect reflection in the window opposite and filled in the gaps. She was young and exotic and he wasn't. He was weird but harmless. Ten, maybe thirteen years separated them. Thirteen years and three thousand miles.

They came from different worlds—literally.

And yet?

And yet he didn't want to think about it any more. He removed his hand. Only pain and disappointment lay down that particular road.

Annalise opened her eyes. "Are we there yet?"

"Why Svenson?" asked Graham, four stops later. They'd been discussing the candidates for possible resonance waves and not getting anywhere. They'd agreed it had to be something to do with ParaDim but beyond that they were stumped. There were so many events linked to ParaDim—so many discoveries, so many ramifications. Were they all resonating? Was one resonating stronger than the others? Graham thought he'd change the subject.

"Svenson? Oh, that! First thing that came into my head. It's my mother's name, you know. She's Danish. Came to America as an au pair, met my father and never went home. That's how I got my name—Annalise. It's Danish, too. Do you know I've never met another Annalise? Ever. Except in here." She tapped her head and smiled.

The train pulled into another station, Graham watched the station name flash by the windows—Green Park. He checked their progress against the tube map over the carriage window. He knew there were two stops to go but he liked the confirmation—you never know when a new station might appear.

He froze in his seat. Why had he suddenly thought about unravelling? The world didn't unravel—he knew that now. The world stayed as it was. It was he—Graham Smith—who changed.

And her.

He swung around. Was she still there? Had he flipped? Had he lost her? Panic. Instinctively, he threw out an arm as he turned. Perhaps there was still time to grab hold and keep her with him.

Annalise smiled back. The same orange hair, the same clothes, the same easy smile. "What's the matter?" she said. "You look like you've seen a ghost."

Graham started to say something, looked down, saw his hand fastened around Annalise's, withdrew it quickly and changed the subject as best he could.

"I was thinking . . ." He broke off as he noticed his left hand flash in front of his face in an extravagant gesture—freed of Annalise's arm it appeared to be taking on a life of its own. He clamped it back down to the arm of the seat and tried to fight the rush of blood towards his face.

"How come," he tried a different tack, "how come Kevin Alexander knew about Schenck's Law?"

"You mean before Schenck published?"

Graham nodded and looked away, relieved.

"That's easy; we know that Kevin Alexander can access data from other parallel worlds, don't we? He knew all that stuff about you."

"Ye-es."

"So, what if his Schenck—the one who published

Schenck's Law—lives on some parallel world?"

"And our Schenck just happened to come up with the same idea?"

"Exactly. Our Schenck is not THE Schenck. It's one of those resonance thingys. He said himself the idea came to him out of the blue. Way I see it, you have this really brainy Schenck on planet X who comes up with the idea and writes this mega best-seller. Maybe they're more advanced on planet X. Maybe they've already discovered other parallel worlds. Who knows? Anyway, using Schenck's Law, once one Schenck has made the break-through, then the probability of other Schencks doing the same increases. There's probably millions of Schencks out there this minute with those exact same words resonating through their brains. One of them probably shouts 'Eureka' every five minutes."

"Do you really believe that?"

"Graham," she paused, catching his eye. "I'm the girl with two hundred voices in her head. I believe everything."

They turned into May Street, a wide car-lined thoroughfare edged by two lines of grey Victorian terraces, five storeys high. Number fifty-six was on the corner, hiding behind years of grime and neglect which had left its facade dirty, pockmarked and flaking. A state shared by many of its neighbors. There was a line halfway along the terrace, beyond which the houses shone freshly-painted white.

Annalise trotted up the steps to the door and reached out to turn the handle. The door opened before she got there. Kevin Alexander appeared, his eyes flicking left and right. "Quick, come inside," he said, flattening himself against the door, one hand on the doorknob, the other shepherding the two of them inside.

A dank musty smell permeated the hallway. The tiled floor was dirty and covered in recent boot prints—the only evidence that anyone had been in the building for years.

"It's another of ParaDim's new offices," said Kevin. "It's still being renovated."

He turned and led them up the stairs, their footsteps echoing through the empty building—the only sound other than the ever-present hum of traffic.

"How many new offices does ParaDim have?" asked Annalise.

"Three in London, dozens worldwide. The company's awash with money at the moment."

They reached the landing halfway between the floors.

"But why all these old buildings? Why not build something new?"

"Mr. Sylvestrus dislikes modern architecture." A woman's voice—educated, precise, American—rang out from the landing above. "He prefers a more classical style."

Graham and Annalise stopped and looked up. A black woman in her late thirties leaned against the banisters, her eyes fixed on Graham.

"This is Dr. Kent," said Kevin.

"Call me Tamisha," said the woman, "and *you* must be Graham."

Graham smiled nervously, looking towards Annalise who, in turn, looked accusingly at Kevin Alexander.

"You never said there'd be other people at this meeting," she said.

"We're not other people," interrupted Tamisha. "We're

the Resonance project. What's left of it."

Graham felt uneasy. Something was very wrong. The way the woman spoke—he wasn't sure if she'd been drinking or she was just being sarcastic, but there was a hopelessness about the way she phrased that last sentence. *What's left of it.* Had the Resonance project been disbanded? Was he a day away from being found unconscious on the street?

"What's happened?" asked Annalise.

"We'll tell you inside," said Kevin. "We're in the room at the front to your right."

TWENTY-NINE

Graham followed everyone into the room. Everyone except Tamisha Kent, who lingered on the landing. Graham didn't like the way she stared at him. Her eyes had followed him all the way up the stairs, making him feel like a freak.

It was a large room, made all the larger by the absence of any visible furniture. White sheets were draped over objects pushed back against the walls—objects that could have been tables or boxes or just about anything bulky and rectangular. Other sheets—flecked with cream paint and brick dust—protected the floor and what looked like a large fireplace.

And there was a man—he hadn't noticed him at first— a short man, thick-set with even thicker glasses. He was standing, motionless, in the recessed window, peering down at the street.

"Is it all clear outside?" Kevin asked him.

"I can't see anyone," answered the short man, his voice gravelly and heavily accented—a hint of something East European, a hint of American. "It looks clear to me."

Kevin sighed and visibly relaxed. He waved a large hand in the short man's direction and announced: "Howard Sarkissian, third and last member."

"Charmed, I'm sure," said the short man, bowing.

"Okay, so what's happened?" asked Annalise.

"Two new members joined the Resonance project today," said Kevin. "Two men we'd never heard of."

"Observers," added Howard, moving away from the window. "All they did was listen and make notes. They contributed nothing to the discussion."

"So?"

"So, they were the two men who turned up five minutes after I met you and Graham."

"They followed you?"

"They must have. They said they were in the area and wanted to see the new offices."

"You talked to them?" Annalise's eyes widened in surprise.

"I had to. They'd heard the noise in the basement and came down to investigate."

"So they said," added Tamisha. Graham hadn't noticed her enter the room. He watched her circle slowly behind him.

"Did they ask what you were doing there?" asked Annalise.

"I told them the same thing. The offices were close by

and I wanted to try my new desk for size."

"Wait," said Annalise. "These two men. Did they follow you here?"

"We're not stupid," snapped Tamisha. "Each of us came by different routes, we changed taxis, changed subway trains . . ."

"I even went into a department store and ran out the fire exit," said Howard, clearly pleased with his ingenuity.

"We're wasting time," said Tamisha, her eyes fixed on Graham. "How do you move between worlds?"

"Wait," said Annalise, holding up her hand. "I still don't get why you're all so freaked by a couple of observers turning up at your meeting? Even if they did follow you, so what?"

"Because fifteen minutes later they were taking my office apart," said Tamisha. "I came back early from lunch and saw them. Luckily before they saw me."

"We're the last of the Resonance project," added Howard. "None of the others are answering their phones. If Tamisha hadn't warned us in time, I don't know where we'd be."

A reflective silence fell on the room, broken only by Tamisha's pacing.

"Now tell us how you move between worlds," she said.

Graham looked towards Annalise.

"He doesn't know," she said.

"Why don't you let Mr. Smith answer for himself?" snapped Tamisha, glaring at Annalise.

"He doesn't like to talk."

"Well, tell him he'd better learn to like it."

"Tamisha!" Kevin intervened, holding out his right palm like a stop sign.

"I know, I know," she said, throwing her hands in the air and walking away. "I'm sorry." She hovered by the window like a tightly wound ball of elastic ready to unravel at any second.

"Graham," Kevin said softly, "how exactly do you move between worlds?"

Graham looked towards Annalise again. He felt uncomfortable. He was the center of attention, everyone was looking at him, strangers asking him questions he didn't feel qualified to answer.

Annalise stepped in.

"He doesn't know. He just flips, okay? One second he's on this world, the next he's somewhere else. He's seen his father die three times. He's had two different mothers. And anything you're going through," she looked directly at Tamisha, her voice trembling, "is nothing compared to what he's had to put up with."

The two women glared at each other. Kevin ignored them, stepping closer towards Graham, his huge hands hovering over Graham's shoulders.

"What do you mean exactly by 'flip'? Do you travel through a portal?"

Graham shook his head.

"He doesn't even notice it's happened," said Annalise, calming down. "It's like his consciousness beams out of one place and into another. Then suddenly he notices that something's different. He's had a haircut or his clothes are different or he's moved house or . . . or his father's dead."

Annalise bit her lip and Graham wished she wouldn't keep mentioning his father.

"Your consciousness can cross dimensions?" asked a startled Sarkissian.

Graham nodded.

"How many times has this happened?" he continued.

"Many times," answered Annalise, "but it's getting more frequent, isn't it, Graham?"

Graham nodded.

"How frequent?" Kevin asked.

Graham and Annalise looked at each other. "Go on, Graham, you can tell them."

He took a deep breath. "It used to be every month or so, sometimes as long as a year. Now," he paused, "now it's more frequent. Yesterday I flipped twice."

"Twice? In one day?" asked Kevin, astonished.

"And those are just the ones he knows about," interrupted Annalise. "When something around him changes. I bet there've been other times when the changes were less noticeable."

"But you have no inkling about what triggers these flips?" asked Sarkissian. "You have no warning at all?"

Graham shook his head.

"Except the last time," said Annalise. "Remember? You told me about the little girl and the headaches?"

"What headaches?" asked Kevin.

"I had to deliver a disk to the trade talks but I saw this little girl. We were caught up in the riots. They had New Tech weapons . . ."

"Who had New Tech weapons?" Tamisha shouted, moving speedily away from the window. "How do you know about New Tech weapons?"

"Because he's been there, Tamisha," said Annalise. "Haven't you been listening?"

"Where have you been, Graham? " asked Kevin. "What trade talks?"

"The London trade talks," replied Graham. "They were at St. James's Palace. They were trying to break up ParaDim but . . ." He could still see it. The riots, the smoke, the bodies. He shook his head—as though somehow that would clear the images from his brain. "They were everywhere—the rioters—they had these weapon platforms like tiny UFOs that hovered in the air and guns that whined and blew things up."

"He's seen the London riots." Howard Sarkissian shook his head in disbelief.

"He was *in* the London riots," said Annalise. "He was a courier for the Brits. This is the guy that had to walk through the middle of Hell ferrying disks between the delegations. And he didn't even know why!" Her voice began to break. "Can you believe that? He flipped into the middle of a riot, with no idea what was happening. He was shot at, chased, saw people killed all around him. And yet he keeps going. Doing a job that wasn't even his." She could hardly speak. "He's the bravest man I know."

Graham gulped and looked away. He wouldn't have described his actions as brave.

"I'm sorry," apologized a tearful Annalise, turning away from the group.

"The headaches?" said Kevin. "What about the headaches."

"I had to get this girl to safety. She'd been abandoned. The rioters were coming. People were falling. I had hold of her hand. We were running and suddenly my head felt like it was going to explode. I had to get the girl to safety but the pain was too much, she kept flickering in and out."

"You saw her image flicker?" asked Kevin.

Graham nodded. "At one stage it was like I was looking at her down a long dark tube. I tried to fight it but the pain became too great and I must have let go."

"I saw him change," said Annalise, sniffing hard. "I was in the park on the other side. He was walking along the path and suddenly started acting drunk—staggering, pitching forward, falling over, you know? He was disoriented for several minutes."

"You always materialize at the same location you flip from?" asked Kevin.

"I guess. I don't know."

"But you've never blacked out and found yourself miles away from where you thought you should be?"

Graham shook his head.

"It must be some kind of bridge," Kevin said, turning to Sarkissian.

The older man agreed. "A bridge between the dimensions activated by . . ." He paused, thinking hard. "Two Graham Smiths being in the same relative position on their respective worlds?"

The two men appeared to have forgotten everyone else in the room as they exchanged a barrage of ideas, their heads turned together conspiratorially.

"No, not that simple or else every time he climbed into bed he'd be transported to a different world. It must be something else."

"Something which is affected by the resonance wave. That would explain the recent increase in frequency."

"This is getting us nowhere," snapped Tamisha. She turned to Graham. "Can you control these flips of yours?"

Graham looked down at his feet and shook his head.

"Can you communicate with your other selves?"

"No."

She turned to Howard and Kevin. "So what use is he? What you want is a combination of him and her." She pointed at Annalise. "A telepath who exists on every world. Then you'd have someone who could make a difference. Someone who could organize a coordinated action— maybe create their own counterresonance wave."

She held up her hands. "But as it stands you've got nothing. She can only talk to two hundred worlds. That's right, isn't it, honey?" There was something patronizing about the way she emphasised the word "honey." She looked at Annalise, waiting for an answer, maybe daring her to respond in kind. But Annalise only nodded reluctantly and turned away.

"And he," Tamisha said, pointing at Graham, "doesn't even know where he's going to be tomorrow. He could flip to a world where none of us exist. All his knowledge is transient. The Graham Smith who occupies that body tomorrow might be totally ignorant of what's happened here today. You'd have to explain everything to him again from the beginning."

A resigned silence descended while Tamisha looked from face to face, challenging anyone to disagree with her assessment. A silence eventually broken by Graham.

"Can I ask a question?" he asked Kevin in a quiet voice.

"Of course."

"Did I make things worse? I had to deliver a disk to the trade talks but I tried to save the girl instead. Did the trade talks collapse? Was it my fault?"

Howard and Kevin looked at each other.

"No," said Kevin. "I don't think you could have made a difference. Sometimes the trade talks collapse, sometimes the politicians claim success. But the result is always the same. Within six months, everything breaks down. Everyone interprets the agreement differently and countries go their own way. The West moves against ParaDim, ParaDim imposes a technology ban on the West. America revokes all of ParaDim's patents and licenses, Asia retaliates against everything American."

He sighed, his face looking tired and drained.

"Anarchy, weapons proliferation, war and chaos. Every crackpot with a cause has New Tech weaponry and the world descends into a destructive spiral. Tens of millions die."

"That's the resonance wave?" asked Annalise.

"That's the result of the resonance wave. It's like there's this massive conveyor belt that nobody can get off."

"With a huge chasm at the end of it," added Sarkissian.

"And four years of decline and anarchy to wait and watch while you sit on the damn thing," said Tamisha. "With everyone powerless to get off or stop or do anything but give in to the inevitable."

"Can't you stop it?" asked Annalise.

"How?" said Kevin. "We can't even tell people what's happening. There's no proof we can give them. We can't show anyone a picture of a parallel world. We can't take anyone there or bring anyone back. All we can do is download data. Data which, to all intents and purposes, could have come from anywhere."

"That and ask people to trust us," said Tamisha, her tone becoming sarcastic. "We're scientists, we know what we're talking about. Forget the fact we've been lying to you for three years, telling you about our wonderful new AI engine that doesn't exist. Who's going to believe a word we say let alone do anything we ask them?"

"Can't you stop the weapons proliferation?" asked Annalise.

"It's not only a matter of weapons—it's everything," said Kevin. "The pace of change, the collapse of old industries, the shifts in power. It's . . ."

"Technological and economic meltdown," finished Sarkissian. "The genie will not go back into the bottle. The technology is out there and people are going to use it."

"Can't you sabotage ParaDim? Stop the new technology?"

"People have tried," answered Sarkissian. "On one world a couple of ParaDim scientists killed the entire core research team. They blew up the labs, destroyed all the data and then turned their weapons on themselves. The entire planet's knowledge and ability to access data from parallel worlds was obliterated overnight."

He paused.

"And ten months later a new start-up company appeared out of nowhere." Sarkissian took his glasses off and wiped the lenses. "A new team had spontaneously discovered the ability to access data from parallel worlds."

"Resonance?" asked Annalise.

"Resonance," he replied.

"But . . ." Annalise looked confused. "Surely the people at ParaDim—the ones in the know—they must see all the evidence from the other worlds. They must know the dangers. Why don't they slow things down? Why all this aggressive growth and marketing?"

Kevin smiled. "Because everyone thinks their world will be different. They won't make the same mistakes."

"And, anyway," added Tamisha sardonically, "they have

four years to solve the problem. A lot can happen in four years. Someone might stop the resonance wave. If there really is such a thing."

"And if they don't push for expansion," said Sarkissian, "the board will soon find someone who can—so, goodbye big fat bonus."

"How did we get on this conveyor belt?" asked Annalise.

"You mean what started the resonance wave?"

"Yes."

"Good intentions, honey. The road to Hell's paved with them."

"Is that true?" Annalise asked Kevin.

"It's true," he said. "It started out as a simple plan to learn from others' mistakes. Simple and brilliant." He shook his head and looked wistfully into space.

"They'd been trying for years," said Howard Sarkissian, "to prove the existence of parallel worlds. They had the theory, they had the technology. All they needed was a slice of luck."

"Who?" asked Annalise. "Who needed a slice of luck?"

"The original ParaDim team," said Sarkissian. "One hundred and two years ago. Not on this world, obviously, but on a parallel one."

"A very advanced parallel world," Kevin added. "They wanted to communicate with a parallel Earth. They sought to set up a dialogue and prove to the world that other Earths were out there."

"But they couldn't do it," said Sarkissian. "They found a way to access electronically-stored data from other worlds. They even found a method of determining which parallel world the data came from."

"They mapped the entire dimensional spectrum," said Kevin. "It was inspired work."

"But," said Howard, "they couldn't transmit anything back. They could receive but they couldn't send. It was a one-way gate. If they wanted to transmit they'd have to practically throw away what they already had and start again."

"And then along came Lucius Xiang," said Kevin. "He was a junior member of the team."

"A student barely out of grad school."

"And he said, 'Why not use the information downloaded from other worlds to help solve the great problems of our day?'•"

Kevin's eyes took on a distant look as he almost changed personas—presumably thinking himself into the mind of the young Lucius Xiang.

"•'Think about it,' Xiang said. 'All those billions of worlds at various stages of development. Some are certain to be more advanced than we are. If not technologically, then perhaps socially, or culturally or economically. Worlds where they'd faced and found solutions to problems that we're still wrestling with. How to live together, how to cope with ageing nuclear arsenals, which lines of research to outlaw, which drugs to avoid.'

"•'Think about the benefits,' he said. 'The ability to know if a certain drug in development today would later be found to have harmful side effects. To know which diseases can be cured and how. To learn from the successes and failures of a billion worlds. To peek into the future.'•"

"So what went wrong?" asked Annalise.

"Haven't you guessed yet, hon?" asked Tamisha in a

world-weary voice. "Haven't you been on this planet long enough to know where all the shit comes from?"

For a second, Graham thought Annalise was going to march over to the window and put Tamisha through it. She wavered visibly before turning back to face Kevin.

"Greed," he said. "That and curiosity. They were scientists, they wanted to know the answers to everything. They wanted the formulas, the theorems, the knowledge. They downloaded everything they could find. There was so much data, they couldn't keep up. They had to farm out the work, bring in more computer capacity, to scan, to sift, to search through the data from tens of billions of worlds."

"After a while," said Sarkissian, "people lost interest in the social data. They didn't want to know how worlds solved the problems of inequality, prejudice, hatred and war. That took too long. They wanted the easy stuff—they wanted the formulas, the equations, the patents, the money."

"So, Xiang was sidelined and a new project manager was brought in to put the project on a more sound commercial footing, and the ParaDim that we all know was born."

"That was enough to create a resonance wave?" asked Annalise.

"Not in itself," said Kevin. "Human nature *created* the resonance wave. As other worlds evolved technologically, they stumbled upon the same one-way gate. They downloaded the same data and came up with the same idea. Not every world had a Lucius Xiang, but every world had a scientist who saw an opportunity and grasped it with both hands. After all, if you can access all that data, what are you going to do with it? You've got to look, right? What would *you* do if you downloaded a file and found a formula for a drug that cured cancer? File it away? Or push for its development?"

Graham nodded in agreement. He could see the appeal. You couldn't turn your back on information like that.

"But why the subterfuge about the AI engine?" asked Annalise. "Why not go public and tell the world about parallel dimensions?"

"Fear of public reaction," said Kevin. "People in power have a very low opinion of the average Joe Blow. The assumption is that once people know there's a hundred billion parallel worlds out there, they're going to panic and do something stupid. And if *they* don't, then the leaders of every other country on the planet will. There'll be an arms race like you've never seen before. Each country will know that if they get their hands on the doomsday weapons of the future first they'll be top dog. So, they'll all demand their own ParaDim project, except they'll concentrate purely on weapons technology. They'll trawl the parallel worlds looking for the meanest, evillest, son-of-a-bitch killing machine they can find, and the world blows itself apart in three years."

"So ParaDim keeps quiet," said Annalise quietly to herself.

"Inventing something innocuous," said Sarkissian. "Like artificial intelligence or quantum simulation."

"But it still goes wrong?" prompted Annalise.

"It still goes wrong. They go too fast, too soon, and push the planet beyond its limits."

"And then the resonance wave kicks in."

"Exactly," said Kevin. "A resonance develops. As each

world chooses the same path, the pull of that path on future worlds strengthens. A critical mass is achieved. Worlds that shouldn't have the capacity to start a ParaDim project spontaneously develop the technology. We, on this planet, shouldn't have the ability to build a dimension discriminator. We're a century away, at least, from such technology. But two years ago, it happened. Inspired research, we thought. A mixture of genius, persistence and luck."

He shook his head.

"Resonance. The ideas were dropping too patly. The team did not make one single mistake. Not one blind alley. They went straight from idle thought to working model in a matter of months."

"And from there it develops," sighed Sarkissian. "ParaDim grows, new technology proliferates, the rate of change accelerates, old industries become obsolete, companies go under, political systems can't keep pace, a power struggle begins and anarchy descends."

"You were our last hope," Tamisha said to Graham. "A lot of good people have died trying to figure out how you fit in. There are billions of project teams researching your every move this very minute. And now," she paused, "and now I wonder if our interest in you is real or influenced by resonance."

"Shhh!" said Kevin. "What was that?"

"What—"

"Shhh!" he said again, cutting Sarkissian off. "Downstairs," he whispered, pointing at the floor. "I heard something."

No one moved. Graham could hear a police siren a long way off, a background hum of traffic, a creak from somewhere in the house.

Tamisha crept closer to the window and peered outside. A few seconds later she turned to the others and shook her head.

Another creak from inside the house—louder this time and . . . was someone on the stairs?

Tamisha stood on tiptoe and pressed her face against the window, peering down at the pavement by the front door. She drew back almost immediately, terror written all over her face.

They'd come.

THIRTY

"**Q**uick! Through here!" hissed Kevin Alexander, lifting a sheet on the wall and uncovering not a fireplace but an opening into the building next door.

They ducked through the gap, its sides toothed by jutting bricks, Graham near the back, Annalise pushing him through. The stairs creaked behind him—once, twice, three times in quick succession. People were on the stairs, probably more of them filing in from the pavement outside.

Graham came out into another room—more white sheets, musty smells—they ran to the door, onto the landing, along a short corridor into another room. The floorboards creaked and echoed as they ran. Shouts rang out from behind—"They're in here! Come on!"—barked orders and thundering feet.

Kevin threw aside another white sheet in the middle of the far wall—another unfinished doorway. They ducked through and followed the same course as before—all the buildings identical. As Graham reached the landing, Sarkissian broke away from the group and fled down the stairs. Graham hesitated. Should he follow? Were they splitting up? Annalise shoved him from behind and propelled him along the landing.

"Come on!" Tamisha hissed at them from the doorway. "This way's safer."

They crossed into the next building and the next. ParaDim had to be knocking them all into one big suite of offices, all the work was identical—the same sheets, the same stage of renovation.

Noise pursued them—shouts, threats, running feet—louder and closer and . . .

"Shit!"

Kevin Alexander stood by the far wall, tearing down white sheets. None covered an opening. Tamisha turned and pointed at the ceiling. Annalise reacted first, pushing Graham back towards the door and onto the landing. Maybe there was a way through on the next floor?

They ran upstairs, Annalise and Graham in the lead. More white sheets, more mirror-image rooms. No hole in the wall.

They tried the next floor. A shout came from below, "They're in here!" followed by more shouts and clattering feet. Their pursuers were in the building, two floors below. Graham tried to soften his tread but the stairs creaked and Kevin's boots clumped and Tamisha's heels clicked. Only Annalise seemed to glide noiselessly over the boards.

Annalise lifted the white sheet in the center of the far wall. Graham prayed. Kevin and Tamisha stood in the doorway, ready to try the next floor.

There was an opening. Annalise dived through. The others followed, swinging right then left into the next room.

No white sheets.

They ran back to the landing. Kevin took off, running down the staircase as fast as he could. Tamisha hesitated—looking up, looking down—her head jerking between the two options—up or down? A shout from below resolved the problem. Men were on the stairs, three floors down and coming up fast.

Graham, Annalise and Tamisha took the next flight, rounding the half-landing to find they'd reached the top. No more stairs. And no more white sheets or holes in the wall.

Sounds of a struggle came up from below. Shouts, a crash, several thuds. Had Kevin been caught?

Graham tried to push it all out of his head. He had to focus, find a way out, something!

They ran from room to room. Maybe there was a way back into the other buildings, maybe they could double back and slip past their pursuers?

They couldn't. But they found a door in a room at the back. A narrow staircase lay behind—steep, dimly lit. They stepped through, closing the door quietly behind them. Tamisha removed her shoes. The stairs were so steep and it was so dark that Graham had to use both hands to guide his progress. The staircase opened onto a small attic corridor. As his eyes became accustomed to the gloom, he could make out four doors, two to the left and two to the right. He opened the first one and stepped into a small attic room with a low sloping ceiling and a narrow dormer window.

Annalise pushed past. She ran to the small sash-window, looked out then beckoned the others over.

"Look," she whispered, "we can walk along the roof."

She unfastened the catch and pulled the lower pane up as far and as noiselessly as she could. Before Graham could say anything she'd wriggled through the window and pulled herself onto the roof.

"Come on, your turn," she whispered, peering through the top pane.

Graham wasn't so sure. He leaned out of the window and looked along the roof line. There was a one-foot-high brick parapet running along the entire terrace. Annalise was standing with her feet wedged in the gutter between it and the slate roof, her hands holding onto the sides of the dormer.

Annalise beckoned to him again. He could hear voices downstairs. They'd find the stairway to the attic any second.

He pulled and wriggled and crawled outside onto the gutter. Annalise helped him up and waited for Tamisha.

Tamisha stood in the window and shook her head.

"Go," she whispered. "No one's seen you. They probably don't even know you're here. I'll hide here. Heights never agreed with me."

She smiled sadly, slowly dragged the window shut and pushed the lock back into place.

"Good luck," she mouthed and turned away.

❀　　❀　　❀

Annalise led the way, walking along the roof, wedging her feet into the angle between brick and gutter, leaning into the roof and occasionally touching down with her right hand. Graham followed. There were nine, maybe ten, dormers ahead. Each dormer taking them further away from number fifty-six and the chasing pack.

Annalise tried the first window, and the next, both of them locked. Graham could see the latches through the glass securing the top and bottom windows. They continued along the roof, glancing behind them every few steps, speeding up as they became more accustomed to the terrain.

They reached the gable wall. Every dormer had been locked, every attic room empty. Could they smash their way in without being heard from the street below? Could they make sure no glass fell onto the pavement?

"We'll try the ones at the back," said Annalise. "We can climb up the gable wall."

Graham looked up at the roof. The gable wall was rough rendered and nearly two feet wide. It stood one foot proud of the roof and ran for about thirty-five feet up to the ridge. He glanced back along the roof line. Any second now a head could appear from one of the dormer windows. They were bound to search the roof.

Annalise moved upward, ascending like a caterpillar, using her knees and feet to lock either side of the gable wall, pushing off, finding a handhold, clamping her hands and forearms against the rough render.

Graham followed, glancing to his right, waiting for the first head to appear, the first shout of pursuit, and trying not to think about the huge drop to his left.

Annalise reached the top and pulled herself astride the

terra-cotta roof tiles before dropping over, feetfirst, onto the other side. She looked back at Graham and smiled, and for a brief moment Graham forgot all about gravity and being chased across rooftops. She was beautiful, captured in that moment, her face set against an azure blue sky, a gentle breeze ruffling her hair.

And then she was gone, her head dropping out of sight. Graham glanced back along the long line of dormers. Nothing stirred.

Yet.

He pulled himself to the top and swung his right leg over the slates towards the ridgeline. He hooked his leg at the second attempt and rolled his body over the ridge and down onto the other side.

By the time he reached the bottom, Annalise was standing on one leg by the first dormer, wrestling with a shoe.

"We've got to break in," she said, pulling her shoe free. "Stand back."

She smashed the upper window at her second attempt, pushed away the shards and forced open the rusted latch. The bottom sash was stiff but she tugged it free and pulled the window up as far as it would go.

She swung down feetfirst into the attic room and hopped as she struggled to avoid the broken glass and slip her shoe back on at the same time. Graham followed close behind.

It was dark, the only light coming from the one small window. Furniture appeared out of the shadows—desks and chairs piled on top of each other, filing cabinets, telephones—everything heaped together, haphazard, dusty and abandoned. Graham closed the window behind him and locked it.

Annalise had found the door and had opened it a crack. No light came in. There was a corridor outside—unlit and musty. Graham could see the outline of a door opposite—presumably to the room at the front.

They crept into the corridor and closed the door behind them. Everything went black. There was a hum of noise from somewhere below, the source difficult to place— machinery? people?

They felt their way along the corridor. The stairs should be close. Annalise started to descend, leaning back into Graham as she slowly moved down the steep staircase.

The sounds increased—a telephone rang in the distance, a snatch of conversation, a background hum of activity. A thin strip of light shone from under the door at the bottom of the stairs.

Suddenly, the stairs were bathed in light. Graham jumped in panic. Annalise hissed an apology.

She'd found a light switch. They were at the bottom of a narrow staircase. Their only line of escape lay through the door ahead of them. And neither of them knew what they'd find on the other side. A family, an office or ParaDim.

THIRTY-ONE

They had to do something. People could be on the roof by now. They were bound to find the broken window.

Annalise's hand rested on the door handle. Was she going to bluff it out? Open the door and walk straight into God knows what? A wedding reception, a ParaDim hitmans' meeting?

Maybe they should throw themselves on the mercy of whoever was on the other side of the door? Maybe get them to call the police? Or would ParaDim intercept the call and have their men run in from next door? *We're Special Branch, we'll handle this.*

There had to be another way. There had to!

"Got any matches?" whispered Annalise, pointing at a smoke alarm on the ceiling.

Graham shook his head. He'd never smoked in his life

but he patted at his pockets just in case. Who could tell what habits his alter ego had acquired?

Annalise turned off the light and opened the door a crack. The background hum of conversation rose. There had to be over a dozen people, maybe more. The door closed.

"It's an office," whispered Annalise. "Open plan from what I could see. Very busy. You could slip out."

"What about you?"

"I'm orange girl, remember? People kinda notice me."

"What do you want me to do?"

"Look confident. Pretend you work there, pretend you're a messenger. Find some matches or a lighter and bring them back here. I'll find something to burn."

Graham brushed himself down, took a deep breath and slipped through the door. After the darkness of the stairwell, everything was suddenly bright. He blinked. He was in a large open plan office—they'd removed all the internal walls and replaced them with pillars. Graham was in a walkway at the back of the office screened off at shoulder height from the rest of the room. There had to be dozens of people, he could hear them talking, he could see heads bobbing behind screens, people at the coffee machine.

He kept going, his head up and back straight. *I belong here. I'm the office messenger.* He passed an out-tray on a table by the wall and emptied it. He glanced briefly at the addresses. *I work here. I'm the office messenger.* He passed a bank of filing cabinets, a coffee machine, two men with their backs to him. The screen wall parted and he turned into an aisle. Screened compartments came off to his left and right, each cell containing a desk, a chair and a computer. No one looked up, everyone was busy—

tapping on keyboards, talking on the phone, collecting printouts.

Some stations were empty.

In one there was a packet of cigarettes on the edge of a desk. A lighter lay on top. Graham slipped in, removed the lighter and left. He retraced his steps back towards Annalise. No one stopped him or called out. He felt elated. His pulse raced. He reached the walkway at the end of the aisle and turned towards the coffee machine. The two men were still there—talking, cups in hand—one glanced in Graham's direction. Graham looked straight ahead, his fingers tightening on the envelopes.

He passed the two men. Their conversation had stopped. He could feel them looking at him. The back of his neck burned. He wanted to run but couldn't.

"Excuse me," said a deep voice a few yards behind him.

Graham kept walking, the door was ten yards away. Ten yards and he could slip the lighter to Annalise.

"I say, *you*." The voice was louder. "Who are you?"

Graham kept walking. He was nearly there. Six yards, five. The door was open a crack. He couldn't see Annalise but she had to be there.

Three yards. He could hear a commotion behind him; someone was running—hurried footsteps, the jingle of keys, the flex of the floorboards.

"Stop!"

He kept going. He switched the envelopes to his left hand, reached into his pocket with the right, closed his fingers around the lighter. One yard.

A hand grabbed his left shoulder and jerked him back. He caught a glimpse of orange through the crack in the door. The lighter was in his right hand, he opened his fingers and tried to guide the lighter through the air towards her as he was spun around almost off his feet.

"Are you deaf or something?"

Graham nodded and pointed at his ears, and tried to block the man's view of the door behind him. The man looked confused. Graham attempted sign language, banging his fist against his palm, flashing his fingers, touching his head and body. He *was* deaf, couldn't the man see?

He could. A look of embarrassment swept over his face.

"Sorry," he said, speaking loud and slow and exaggerating his lip movements. "I didn't realize."

Graham smiled.

The man looked down at the floor by Graham's feet.

"You've dropped something."

Graham's blood drained. The lighter! Hadn't Annalise managed to grab it?

The man bent down. Graham watched, moving his weight onto the balls of his feet, ready to grab the lighter and run.

"Your letters," he said, straightening up and holding out a wad of brown envelopes.

Graham mouthed a "thank you" and took them. They must have flown out of his hand when the man grabbed him.

An embarrassed silence followed. Graham wasn't sure what to do. Should he walk away or was Annalise behind him at the moment, her hand reaching out from the crack in the door, trying to grab the lighter?

A bell rang—loud and insistent—other bells on other floors chimed in. A light flashed from the ceiling. She'd done it.

"Fire alarm," the man said, pointing for some reason at the ceiling.

Graham nodded and prayed the man would leave. Why couldn't he panic and run screaming from the building? Instead it looked like his conscience was so deeply pricked he was going to take Graham by the arm and personally lead him to safety.

A sharply dressed middle-aged woman appeared from the central aisle.

"Mike, there wasn't a fire drill scheduled for today was there?" she asked looking in Graham's direction.

Mike turned and instantly forgot Graham. "If there was, Ursula, no one informed me."

"I think I can smell smoke," said a voice from behind Graham—a young woman, hurrying by, struggling to put on her coat and hold her handbag at the same time.

Others were streaming away from their desks, grabbing jackets and briefcases, phones and bags. Mike was walking towards the exit, his hand placed at the center of Ursula's back. No one was looking at Graham.

Or the door behind him.

He stepped back and opened it. Annalise slipped out.

They followed the exodus down the staircase; people streamed out from every floor, the same questions repeated—*is it a drill? anyone seen any smoke?*

The crowd spilled out onto the street—across the pavement, around the parked cars and into the road. Some people turned and shaded their eyes as they looked back at the roof of the building—no doubt expecting to see smoke billowing from every attic window. Graham and Annalise drifted amongst them, slowly moving towards the periphery and the corner—keeping as many people between them and whoever might be outside number fifty-six as they could.

A siren wailed in the distance, conversation thrummed all around them. *Where was the fire? Was it a drill, a hoax?*

They reached the corner and turned, a few steps more and they ran, crossing the street three cars down and taking every side street and turn they could find.

They leaned back against the wall and breathed hard. They'd been running for nearly five minutes without any sign of being followed.

"I'll contact the girls," said Annalise in between breaths. "There's so much to tell them."

Graham closed his eyes and tried not to panic. *The day after the Resonance project closes they find you unconscious in the street.* The Resonance project had just closed. The clock was ticking.

They had to hide, that was obvious, but where? Hotels cost money. He checked his wallet. He had twelve pounds. A room for the night would cost more than that. His checkbook was at home. All he had on him was a debit card but couldn't ParaDim trace him every time he used it?

And how long would that last with no job and no money coming in. He'd have to buy food, clothes. Everything he had was at home, probably being pulled out of drawers and thrown on the floor at this very moment.

He looked at Annalise. How much money would she have? Enough to keep them in hiding indefinitely? He doubted it. There'd be no more money from Kevin Alexander. Did she have money in America she could get hold of?

His mind raced for what seemed ages. For the first time in his life he had nowhere to go. He couldn't go home, he couldn't go to work. That was all he knew. Home, school, work—the occasional trip to the shops. That was his life.

And worse—what had he done to Annalise?

"What's the matter, Graham?" asked Annalise, stretching her arms as she reentered the world.

Graham glanced over, she looked concerned. "I'm sorry," he said.

"For what?"

"For all this. You shouldn't be here hiding. You should be out enjoying yourself."

She looked at him and shook her head.

"You don't have a clue, do you?"

"What?"

"What you've done for us, for all the girls. You've given us our lives back. We'd never have figured out this alternate reality stuff without you."

"But I didn't do anything."

She shook her head. "You did *everything*. You were the catalyst that brought the girls together. Before you came along we were all too freaked to really talk to each other. Only Annalise One made any sense out of her life— if you can call talking to the dead, sense. The rest of us had no lives at all—we were alone, confused and frightened. I used to lie awake at nights, terrified the voices would tell me to kill my dad." Her voice broke for an instant and she turned away.

"Two months ago," she said, gathering herself together, "I thought I had a brain tumor. I thought that's where the voices came from—a nasty little growth pressing on my brain. Before that I was just plain crazy, before that I was the next Joan of Arc and before that I was a schizoid psycho killer waiting to be told who to kill."

She shook her head and looked into his eyes.

"But now I'm me. I'm Annalise Mercado. And I matter in this world. Now shut up and tell me where we are on this map."

"You see," said Annalise, "Tamisha's right. We need to get the information to every world. ParaDim scans all data, right? So, we'll give them something to look at—the Graham Smith story—everything we've learned so far about you, ParaDim, resonance waves, the lot. We'll create a web page and pack it with every key word a resonance project would look for. The girls are going to do the same. By tomorrow there won't be a resonance project around that doesn't know everything we do."

Annalise folded her *Cyber Cafe Guide* away. The nearest Internet cafe was only a few blocks away.

"Are you going to tell everyone about the girls?"

Annalise thought for a while. "Don't think so. Not yet. It wouldn't be fair to the nontelepath Annalises."

Graham thought about the other Grahams. "Would it be fair to the other Grahams?"

"It's not the same. The other Grahams are already targets whether they know it or not."

They found the cafe, paid for an hour and sat down. Annalise typed, revised, deleted and typed again. Occasionally, she stopped and asked Graham to check a sentence she'd written. Had she got it right? Was that the way it happened?

He was amazed how much she knew about him. And

amazed to see his life chronicled on the screen. It all seemed so unreal.

"Could you print that out for me?" asked Graham when she'd finished typing.

"Sure." She hit the print button and looked around to see which printer they were connected to. Graham retrieved the two pages, folded them neatly into four and put them in his pocket.

Annalise watched and smiled. "That should help whoever gets your body next. A step up from name, address and job."

Graham smiled weakly. "You never know, I might not flip this time," he said, quickly looking down at his feet.

"I hope you don't."

Graham beamed and felt even more stupid.

"Give it here," she said, holding out her hand. "You've missed the most important part."

She took the note and wrote "Annalise 15" on the back. "Now you'll know which world you're on."

Annalise's phone rang just as she was uploading the finished page. It was Kevin Alexander.

"How?" It was all she could say. How could it be him? Had he escaped?

"Listen, I haven't much time. There's something you must know about the resonance wave. Meet me by the bandstand in Hyde Park at five-thirty. Bring Graham Smith with you."

"Are you sure you won't be followed?"

"Positive. No one's interested in me any more. The resonance project's finished."

The line went dead.

THIRTY-TWO

Graham waited for Annalise to say something. She put the phone down in a daze and shook her head.

"That was Kevin," she said. "He wants us to meet."

"He got away?" Graham couldn't believe it. He'd heard the struggle. Had Kevin managed to fight them off and find a way out?

"It's gotta be a trap," said Annalise. "You know how paranoid Kevin is about his calls being scanned. But this time he mentions you and the resonance wave in the same breath."

"You think someone forced him to make the call?"

"I think they were listening to every word. The only thing Kevin could do was drop a few clues to warn us off."

"So they know about you," Graham said quietly.

"Yes," said Annalise. "They know about me. Now let's get this web page loaded and get the hell out."

❀ ❀ ❀

A car pulled up as Graham and Annalise left the cafe. Two men jumped out—grey suits, thirties, well-built—two car doors slammed in quick succession. They left their car double-parked in the center of the street and ran ahead of Graham and Annalise, squeezing through the gaps between the line of parked cars to head them off.

"Graham Smith?" said the stockier of the two men.

"No," said Annalise, grabbing Graham's arm and trying to steer him past the two men.

A hand rested against Graham's chest. "I'm Detective Sergeant Tucker, Mr. Smith." He flashed his warrant card with his other hand. "We have a Miss Tamisha Kent at the station. She's told us everything. We need to get you into protective custody at once."

Annalise stared at them blankly. "Is this some kinda joke? We don't know any Tamishas."

Graham looked down at the hand on his chest and then at Annalise. What should they do? Were these real policemen or part of another trap?

Annalise pulled Graham back and led him away in the opposite direction. The two policemen hurried after them. A hand grabbed Graham's shoulder and pulled him back.

"We've got to take you in, Mr. Smith. It's for your own safety."

Annalise turned on him. "Where's the camera? We're on TV, right? Some guy gonna come out and tell us all about it?"

The two men exchanged glances, the first hint of uncertainty. At the head of the street, a truck turned in from the main road and almost scraped the paint from one of the parked cars opposite.

"This is no joke," said the man calling himself Sergeant Tucker. "We've got orders."

"Good for you. Now go and find this Mr. Smith you're looking for and leave us alone."

Annalise was getting louder. A few faces peered out from the cafe window. A woman stared from the street corner. A horn blared—a truck driver impatient at having his path blocked by a car parked in the middle of the road.

The two men exchanged glances again.

"I see our friends down there on the corner," said Annalise, waving. "Do you want to have a word with them? They'll tell you who we are."

The truck horn blared again. A head leaned out of the cab. "That your car, chief?"

Annalise pulled Graham towards the corner. "Ally!" she shouted. "Wait for us," and started to run.

Graham didn't look back. He heard the truck driver remonstrating with the two men, raised voices, two car doors slam and the squeal of tires. By the time the truck roared into life Annalise and Graham were on the main road and heading away fast.

They crossed over at the lights, took a left at the next junction, then a right, then another left. At each junction they stopped and glanced behind, looking for the car, the men, someone paying them too much attention.

Graham felt paranoid. The whole world was chasing him. He couldn't trust anyone except Annalise. Everyone else was suspect. The police, Kevin, Tamisha, Howard— all of them compromised.

Annalise's phone rang. She stopped and flicked it open, trying to listen and pant at the same time.

Graham stood beside her, doubled over and thankful for the rest. He tried to listen to whoever it was on the other end of the line but couldn't hear a word above the rush of passing traffic.

"Hello," said Annalise, clapping a hand over her other ear.

"Hello," she repeated a few seconds later.

Finally, she pressed the phone shut and looked at Graham. "No one there."

"Kevin?" asked Graham.

She shook her head. "Don't know. Whoever it was couldn't or wouldn't speak."

Graham glanced around. They were in Knightsbridge from what he could see. The streets were packed; rush hour would be starting soon. Shouldn't they be looking for a place to hide out?

Annalise agreed. They'd get out of London, take the tube, the train—anything—find a cheap room and hide out for as long as they could.

A plan that lasted less than a minute.

A car passed by and screeched to a halt twenty yards ahead. Two men jumped out. The same two men as before. Graham and Annalise turned and ran. There was a large department store on their right—two, three entrances— a sea of people pushing into and out of each exit.

"In here!" shouted Annalise. Graham followed, slowed by the press of people. Annalise bounced ahead, he could see her hair shining like a beacon through the crowd. Away from the doors the crowds thinned. Graham caught up with her as she snaked past intricate displays of handbags and scarves, gloves and belts. Did she have a plan? Were they running blind?

They found an escalator and ran along the outside, pushing past the line of stationary shoppers. Graham glanced back the way they'd come. The two men were forty yards behind and heading for the escalator.

They flew into Ladies Fashions. Annalise hesitated for an instant before turning right then left. They ran down an avenue of manikins, past circles of dresses and skirts, then turned right into a small section separated out from the rest of the floor. Tops and blouses adorned the walls on two sides and on the back wall—a line of changing rooms.

Annalise slowed to a fast walk, picked up a dress from a rack and, grabbing Graham, pushed him into the changing room on the far right. She pulled the curtain closed behind them.

An age passed. Maybe it was only a few seconds but it felt like hours to Graham. The anticipation, the fear, the certainty that any second the curtains would rip apart and two men would barge in.

Annalise hung the dress on the hook at the back of the cubicle and opened the curtains a crack. Graham held his breath.

"Can't see anyone," she whispered, letting the curtain fall back. "We'll give it five minutes then head for the nearest exit. I . . ."

She stopped and inclined her head to one side.

"What is it?" whispered Graham.

"Shhh!" said Annalise, her eyes becoming unfocused. She smiled, the smile gradually fading as her muscles relaxed.

Graham watched. It had to be important. A message from one of the girls. Maybe something to give them hope?

Strange, he thought to himself, he was being chased all over London, his life was in imminent danger and yet . . . and yet he wouldn't have swapped that moment for any other in his life. It was like he'd lived for years in a dark, airless room and suddenly the shutters had been thrown open. He felt alive and happy and, strangely, safe. As long as Annalise was with him nothing else mattered.

Annalise nodded once, twice and then frowned as her eyes refocused on the world around her.

"That was Annalise Six," she whispered. "Your DNA results are starting to come through. They've analyzed data from a thousand worlds so far and," she paused, "they're all the same."

She looked confused. Graham couldn't understand why. "So?" he whispered.

"So, a thousand Graham Smiths all have identical DNA—even when they have different parents."

"Because I'm adopted. Isn't that what you'd expect?"

"Maybe so, but Gary seems to think there's more to it. They've been cross-checking the DNA of your close relatives and they're finding similarities."

"What kind of similarities?"

"They think you're related. Annalise Six wasn't sure about the details—Gary went scientist guy on her. But it looks like your real parents might be someone in your family."

THIRTY-THREE

He tried to think who. He sifted through memories of photo albums. Was there someone in his family he resembled?

The phone rang. Graham jumped. Annalise tugged at her bag, found the phone and juggled it open.

Silence.

Annalise didn't move. The phone stayed clasped against one ear. Then her eyes widened, she switched off the phone and threw it into her bag. "It's the phone!" she hissed. "They're using it to track us."

She pushed past him, pulled the curtain back an inch and looked out. "All clear," she whispered and slipped out. Graham followed. One, two steps and then Annalise turned and bundled him back into the cubicle.

"They're outside," she whispered. "I don't think they

saw us, they were looking the other way."

Graham could hear the implied "but" on the end of the sentence. The two men knew they were close. They'd see the changing rooms and make the connection.

Annalise pulled the curtain back a fraction of an inch and peered out. Graham held his breath. She pushed the curtain forward and looked along the line of changing rooms. Suddenly she started gesticulating, beckoning someone to come over.

Graham slipped over to the near side and pressed himself out of sight against the cubicle wall. He felt the wall give slightly.

"May I help you?" asked a female voice—young, accentless, perhaps a hint of an expensive boarding school.

"I'm sorry," said Annalise. She sounded upset, close to tears. "Can you call the police? It's those two men over there. They," she took a deep breath, "they were in Selfridges earlier. They pretend to be police officers, they have these fake IDs and . . ." She hesitated. "They hang around the changing rooms. You know, spying on the girls."

The girl gave a knowing look and glanced over her shoulder.

"They . . ." Annalise looked down embarrassed. "They told this girl she had to be strip-searched and, you know, they . . ." She paused, her voice faltering. "The guy on the right had a camera."

"Leave it to me," said the girl.

Annalise turned and winked at Graham before resuming her vigil by the curtains. The assistant walked over to an older woman—probably her boss. They talked for a while, a conversation punctuated by dagger-laden glances before the older woman walked over to her station and picked up the phone.

The two men hovered in front of the leftmost changing cubicle. They shuffled from foot to foot, checked their watches. Women came and went, cubicles emptied and filled. The men stayed. Eventually one of them moved forward and tugged at a curtain that hadn't moved for some time. A woman screamed.

"Over there!" shouted the younger assistant as four uniformed security men marched onto the floor.

Graham and Annalise slipped out in the confusion. All eyes were turned towards the commotion in the other corner where two men protested their innocence and held out warrant cards which no one believed. A woman shouted abuse at them. Four men blocked their escape.

Graham didn't look back after that. They retraced their steps, found a down escalator and headed for an exit on the far side of the store. In the crush by the door, Annalise dropped her phone into a woman's shopping bag.

Graham stopped outside the store and looked around to take his bearings. The nearest tube had to be . . .

Something hard pressed into his back.

"Don't turn around, don't say a word." A man's voice—harsh and menacing. "We're going for a walk. Do as I say or I'll kill you here."

Graham froze. Annalise walked on a few steps then turned. "What's the matter?" she said and then stared over Graham's left shoulder. A look of surprise. "Who?" she started to say, and then stopped.

Graham mouthed one word, "run," but she didn't move. The gun dug into his back.

"Come on, move!"

Graham implored Annalise to run. Couldn't she read his lips? Instead, she rocked on the balls of her feet. *She's going to do something stupid.* Graham shook his head. No! Run! Save yourself. The man pushed again, hissing the word, "move!" into Graham's ear, so close he could feel the warm spittle on his neck. The gun dug further into the small of his back, grinding against his spine. The man shoved with his shoulders. Graham held fast, digging in with his feet, leaning back. He wasn't going anywhere until Annalise was safe. "Run!" he mouthed again. She didn't. She just stood there, rocking, her eyes flashing from side to side, lips parted, hands poised. She *was* going to do something stupid. He could tell.

Another shove from behind—harder this time—another hissed "move!" Graham lurched forward. Annalise stayed where she was. "Run," Graham mouthed for the last time. Why wouldn't she run? Why wouldn't she save herself?

He glanced frantically about him. Thoughts coming thick and fast. So many people, shoppers coming into and out of the store. Witnesses everywhere, store surveillance cameras—you'd have to be crazy to shoot someone in such a public place.

Or desperate.

Graham relaxed—totally—slumping to the pavement like a dead weight. He'd feign a heart attack, he'd feign death, he'd do whatever it took to make it difficult. He wasn't going to walk meekly to his death in some deserted side street.

People surged forward, faces peered down at him. *Is he all right? What's the matter? Do you want a doctor?*

Anyone know him? Graham stared blankly up at them, a wall of faces, was one of them his kidnapper? Or had he fled?

And where was Annalise?

"It's okay," said a male voice Graham recognized. "I'm his doctor. My car's round the corner."

His kidnapper hadn't given up.

Should he call out? Tell people he was being kidnapped? Or would the doctor turn into a psychiatrist? Was there an accomplice ready with a hypodermic? *He needs to be sedated, sad case, completely delusional.* Everyone would nod their heads and stand back.

Strong hands dug under his shoulders, he was being pulled up from behind. He had to speak out, he had to say something. But what? His life might depend on finding the right words.

His kidnapper's face pressed close to his. "We've got your girlfriend," he whispered. "One word out of you and she's dead."

Graham stopped struggling and let the man haul him to his feet.

"He'll be fine now," said the man. "This has happened before."

The crowd pulled back, show over, nothing more to see. Graham was led away, an arm around his back, a threat over his head.

After fifty yards, the arm was removed—his kidnapper looking left and right before dropping slightly behind Graham. A familiar feeling in the small of his back told Graham the gun had returned.

They turned a corner. Graham wondered where he was being taken—a building, an alley, a car?

And where was Annalise? Where had they taken her? There were so many people on the pavement it was difficult to see more than fifteen yards ahead.

The man steered Graham towards the roadside edge. Parked cars formed a line to his left, shoppers filed by on his right. Was he being taken to one of the cars?

A large black car was parked three spaces ahead. It became a magnet to Graham's eyes. Was it that black car? The one they'd used before? The one that Annalise Twelve had seen him bundled into the back of?

They walked closer. Black-tinted windows hid whoever was inside. Suddenly, the rear door clicked and swung open across the pavement. A hand, briefly visible, withdrew back inside. They were five yards away. Five yards from the gaping maw of the black car and . . .

She came through the crowd in a blur of orange. People stopped, stood aside and gaped. Graham couldn't believe it. It was Annalise, coming in from his right, a flaming waste bin held out in front of her, walking across his path towards the black car. There was a strong smell of petrol. Flames licked two, three feet into the air. She didn't look at him once. Her gaze was fixed on the black car. She tossed the bin and its flaming contents through the open door onto the back seat, slammed the door shut and turned towards Graham, her eyes wild.

"I'm soaked in gasoline," she said, staring beyond Graham to his kidnapper. "And I'm going to kill you all."

She held a lighter in her hand. She looked insane, her head tilted to one side, her eyes wild and staring.

A muffled scream came from inside the car, its roadside doors opened, smoke billowed out, the smell of burning, the smell of petrol everywhere. A man rolled in the street, his clothes on fire. A uniformed chauffeur tried to beat out the flames with his hands. Traffic stopped. People screamed. Flames danced inside the car.

Graham could feel the man's hold on him relax. The gun moved away from his back. Annalise advanced, the lighter held high, its flame flickering. Any second now, Graham was certain, she was going to rush forward, grab the man and immolate them all.

"Keep back!" yelled the man, his gun now pointed at Annalise. Graham could see it close to his left shoulder.

The kidnapper glanced to his left—the man rolling in the street, the driver trying to beat out the flames, the screams, the car about to explode.

Graham grabbed the gun and pushed it up and away from Annalise. They wrestled, the gun went off. Annalise came in kicking—once, twice—the man crumpled, holding his groin. The gun fell to the ground.

"Run!" shouted Annalise.

Graham hesitated. Was she really dowsed in petrol? Was she going to set light to herself?

"Go!" Annalise shouted again, bending down to pick up the gun.

Graham turned and ran. The pavement opened up in front of him. People had heard the gunshot, seen the flames, heard the screams. No one blocked his way.

His thoughts strayed behind him. Was Annalise following? Was she running too? He glanced back. She was.

A bus pulled out ahead of him, a red double-decker lumbering away from its stop. The rear platform beckoned—a few strides, a jump and he'd be safe. Annalise too. It was the logical choice. He was running back towards the department store. Who knew how many other men ParaDim had out looking for him.

He jumped, grabbed the pole and swung himself aboard. Annalise was twenty yards behind and gaining fast. A gap had opened out behind her as people moved away from the black car. Graham wasn't sure but he thought he saw a body lying on the pavement with another man leaning over it.

The bus began to accelerate. Annalise was closing but not as fast as before. She was five yards away and pumping fast.

A pain hit Graham between the eyes and dropped him to his knees. *No! Not now!* Annalise was three yards away, her right hand outstretched towards him, the bus keeping pace with her. He reached for her, one hand on the pole, one hand waving through the blur. He couldn't see. His eyes were clouded in pain and smeared in color. He was losing consciousness, the world receding . . .

No!

He tore himself back. He would not leave. Not this time or any other. He would stay or die in the attempt.

The world surged back, images rolling in like a surf up a beach. Annalise—she was there—dropping back but still running. Surely the bus had to stop sometime—a junction, a traffic jam!

Five yards away, six, seven, nine. He couldn't bear it. The pain in her eyes, the effort in her face. After all she'd done, he couldn't leave her. He couldn't . . .

His stomach contracted—it felt like he'd been punched. A stabbing pain in his side, an explosion in his head. Someone screamed. Probably him.

He'd roll off the bus, that's what he'd do. His legs might not work but he could still roll, couldn't he?

He rolled, let go of the pole and hoped gravity and centrifugal force would do the rest. He'd hurt himself but she'd find him and know what to do.

Hands grabbed him. People on the bus? He could make out vague images of faces and arms and concerned voices.

No! Let me go!

He tried to fight back. He was sure he did. But his limbs had taken on a dreamlike quality. They shimmered and moved back and forth out of time. He was losing them, he was losing everything.

No!

One last effort. All or nothing. *Concentrate! Focus! Annalise!*

He saw her—crisp and clean—twenty yards back, her hand still reaching for him.

"I'll find you," he shouted. "Whatever it takes, I'll find you."

A shot rang out. A vague image of a man in the distance, a spark flashing from his hand.

A second shot, a third. Annalise fell.

And everything went black.

THIRTY-FOUR

He came to. He was lying, twisted on a floor, people standing over him. The floor was moving. He was on a boat?

A wave of nausea overwhelmed him; he rolled onto his side and retched.

"Are you all right?" A voice out of nowhere. He unscrewed his eyes, tried to focus and failed, a blurry face swam before him.

And then it hit him.

Annalise! Where was she?

He tried to get up. An arm, somewhere, obeyed. He tried to push against the floor; he tried to slide a leg under his body.

Hands helped him up, pushed him onto a seat. He was on a bus. Now he remembered. Where was she? He looked for her, his head panning up and down the row of seats, the world lagging behind his gaze, faces blurring into their neighbors', a pain ever-present behind his eyes.

"Where's Annalise?" he asked, his voice echoing inside his head, loud and slurred.

"Who's Annalise? Your daughter?" asked a stranger close by.

He shook his head and immediately wished he hadn't as the world spun once more.

"She was running behind the bus. You must have seen her." He was talking with his eyes closed, talking to whoever would listen.

"No one was running behind the bus, dear," said the woman.

"She was! I saw her! She was . . ." He turned to the woman and grabbed her arm. "Was she shot? Did you see her fall?"

He tried to open his eyes. A woman's face appeared—concerned, middle-aged, slightly startled. He let go of her arm.

"Has he been drinking?" asked another woman.

"He looks drugged to me," said another. "Or mental."

The bus stopped and Graham slid off the seat. He had to get off. He had to find Annalise. He'd promised. She might be lying in the road. She might be waiting for him.

He lurched along the aisle towards the back of the bus, his legs half asleep. He jumped down onto the pavement, stumbled, fell into a group of people, hands pushed him back up, shoved him away, someone shouted. He walked in a daze, back the way he'd come, back the way he'd imagined he'd come. People barged into him, his

shoulders reeling from one impact to the next. *Keep going.
She's waiting. Not far.*

He was wet. Everything was wet. His hair, his clothes,
the sky. The world was melting, running down his face.

An umbrella caught him high on the cheek, nearly
taking his eye out. He lurched to the side. More umbrel-
las, so many colors, the pavement blossoming in blues
and greens.

Was it raining?

He staggered onto the road, the pavement too
crowded, too wet. He leaned against the back of a parked
car, caught his breath, retched, then started to walk. Car
horns blared, lights flashed, cars pulled alongside, people
shouted at him from wound-down windows.

He didn't care. He kept walking, falling against the
sides of cars when the ground moved unexpectedly. She
had to be here, somewhere. Lying in the street, bleeding,
waiting for him to come to her. Maybe she'd rolled underneath one of the parked cars to hide?

He bent down to look and the sky pressed hard against
his shoulders, pushing him over. He crumpled, unable to
get up. Rain fell all around him, shiny rain that danced in
headlights like a thousand fairies.

And after the rain came the tears.

He had no idea how long he lay there. Wet, cold and
confused. Alternately racked with guilt and grief but never
quite sure what it was that he'd done.

When he came to his senses, the rain had stopped. He
was lying in the road by a parked car, traffic swerving
around him. He drew in his legs and, leaning back against
the parked car for support, pulled himself up.

A motorist cursed at him, a horn blared three times. Graham staggered onto the pavement. People stared at him, moved aside to give him extra room. No one stopped or spoke.

He looked at his watch. It was five o'clock. He should be at work. Why wasn't he at work? A vague memory brushed against the back of his mind. He'd been on a bus.

Why had he been on a bus? And why were his clothes wet? He looked at the pavement—the dark grey of the paving slabs, the puddles. It had been raining. Had he taken the bus to get out of the rain? But where had he been? He checked his pockets. There was an appointment card and—his eyes widened—hundreds of pounds in cash.

He hastily replaced the money, glancing furtively to see if anyone had noticed.

He examined the card. Something familiar about the name. The Cavendish Clinic in Knightsbridge. He'd been for a medical.

Everything came flooding back—medicals, ParaDim, Annalise, the flames, the bus, the look on Annalise's face as she fell.

No!

He started to run. Where had she fallen? Was it here? Over there? He ran out between the line of parked cars and looked up and down the street. He couldn't see her. He couldn't see the black car either. Was it further along?

He ran. He searched. He stopped.

She'd gone. Everything had gone. He'd never felt so empty in his life.

❀   ❀   ❀

He walked for miles, not sure of where he was going but knowing that he had to keep moving. His jacket steamed in the sun, his trousers too. Only his socks refused to dry, his feet squelching with every stride.

He didn't have the energy to run. Or the will. If ParaDim wanted him, they could have him. He didn't care any more.

Eventually, he went home. Eventually, he cared enough to read his note and find out if anything else had changed. Nothing had. He still lived at Wealdstone Lane, he still worked at Westminster Street.

He sat at his kitchen table for hours, waiting for the energy to make a hot drink or maybe a meal. By ten o'clock he'd managed a coffee. By ten-thirty he went to bed.

He couldn't sleep. Annalise was everywhere—in his thoughts, in the shadows—he could see her face in the wallpaper, the ceiling, his dressing gown that hung on the door. If he hadn't jumped on that stupid bus she'd be with him now, safe and alive. She wouldn't have run along the road in full view, she'd have dodged in and out of the shoppers, taken side streets, melted into the background. It was his fault! Everything was his fault!

He tossed and turned and counted the intervals between gusts of wind that rattled his bedroom window pane.

And worried. Had he turned off the gas? Had he locked the doors? What time was it? What day? What . . .

He pulled on his slippers and slowly toured the house. He double-checked the gas cooker, triple-checked the doors and windows, and drew every curtain he could find.

❋　　❋　　❋

Annalise Fifteen rolled over in the street. Someone was shooting at her, the bus was getting away and Graham was flipping between worlds. The new Graham wouldn't have a clue what was happening. Wherever he went—home or work—they'd be waiting for him. He wouldn't survive the day.

She felt the gun in her hand and sprung to her feet. She'd stop a car, any car. She stood in the middle of the road, chest heaving, both hands on the gun, her arms locked straight and pointing at the driver of a car that swung and screeched to a halt a few feet in front of her.

She ran around the front to the passenger side and yanked the door open. A shot rang out, she ducked and threw herself into the car.

"Drive!" she shouted.

The driver hesitated. He had one hand raised, the other on the door handle. "You can have the car. Don't shoot!"

"I don't want the car. Just drive! Now!"

She waved the gun. The car jerked forward and stalled. The driver swallowed, started again, revved hard and pulled away.

Annalise was thrown back against the seat. The bus was now a hundred yards away—four cars filled the gap in between.

"What's your name?" Annalise asked.

"Martin," said the driver, his voice cracking.

"Well, Martin, you see that bus ahead, the red one?"

"Yes."

"Follow it. Get me to that bus and we'll all be fine."

She swivelled in her seat and checked behind. She couldn't see anyone running after her. She couldn't hear any more shots. Maybe he was no longer on foot? She checked the cars behind, expecting to see someone leaning out the passenger side with a gun pointing in her direction.

All she saw was a line of traffic—an intermittent line of traffic that snaked to avoid a flaming black car in the distance.

"The bus is stopping," Martin said.

"Pull in behind."

The car stopped.

"Congratulations, Martin," she said as she climbed out. "You've just helped save the world."

The bus started to pull away. Annalise jumped onto the back, grabbed the pole and swung herself inside. Graham was slumped in the first seat. He looked in pain and confused. People were moving away from him. "What's the matter with him?" she heard someone say.

"He'll be fine, now," said Annalise. "He's with me."

Graham awoke early the next day and immediately felt guilty. He should have lain awake all night. He didn't deserve sleep. He'd left Annalise lying in the road. How could anyone sleep after that?

He tried to make himself busy. He tried to imagine what she'd say to him if she found him wallowing in self-pity. She'd shout at him, he was sure. She'd tell him to snap out of it and climb some roofs or race through an abandoned building.

After breakfast he checked for listening devices, looking in all the usual places. The house was clean—either that or ParaDim had learned to hide them in different locations. He checked his notice board. No mention of Annalise. Perhaps he'd flipped to a world without her. Or maybe she was back at home, struggling with voices that she couldn't understand. Maybe he should find her phone number and call her? He could help her . . . and, maybe, she could help him.

He arrived at work as normal, sweeping in unnoticed behind a group of people. He presented his card and walked through to the Post Room.

He printed the staff list and checked the names—the usual mix of additions and departures. Sharmila was back and Brenda was using her maiden name again.

Graham sighed. Brenda and Bob were the happiest couple he knew. They shone in each other's company; apart they merely endured. Brenda lost her bounce and Bob . . . well, Bob was a different person. Married Bob had a twinkle in his eye and laughed as he worked. Single Bob, or married-to-someone-else Bob, worked hard, kept his head down and couldn't see the funny side of anything. Work was his life but it wasn't a life worth . . .

Graham considered his own life—the one he had before Annalise. Was that a life worth living? Go to work, come home, go to bed?

"Morning, Graham," said Sharmila from the doorway. She sighed as she heaved a heavy shopping bag onto her desk. "Did you see that note I left you?"

Graham shook his head.

"Frank dropped it by yesterday. He wants to see you this morning. Something urgent about ParaDim."

Graham closed his eyes. It was all happening again. ParaDim! He should have realized when he saw the medical appointment from the Cavendish Clinic. Would he never be free of them? He scanned his desk. Sharmila's note was stuck to his terminal. *Frank Gledwood called. Wants to see you first thing Thurs. a.m. Room 551. Urgent.*

"If he gives you any trouble, come and get me."

Graham took the lift to the fifth floor. Perhaps he deserved it? Punishment for abandoning Annalise.

He knocked on the door of 551 and went inside. Frank Gledwood was leaning back in his chair, his hands crossed behind his neck.

"About time," Frank said. "I have someone here who wants to see you." He withdrew his hands and let his chair fall back to rest with a thump. "Tamisha Kent," he said, waving an arm towards a woman in the far corner, "meet Graham Smith."

Graham turned, he hadn't noticed anyone else in the room, and instantly froze.

The woman was not Tamisha Kent.

THIRTY-FIVE

Annalise smiled back at him. An Annalise with brown hair this time—straight, cut close against the face, a slight curl at the end, a fringe at the front. And she'd discarded her jeans and trainers. She was looking smart and businesslike in skirt, blouse and heels.

"Hi," she said, holding out her hand. "I'm the ParaDim liaison for the Census project."

They shook hands. Annalise beamed. "Your family history greatly interests us, Mr. Smith. I hope I can persuade you to work with us."

Graham stared. Why was she calling herself Tamisha? Was this a prearranged plan? Something the previous Graham had omitted to document?

"I've been talking to Mr. Gledwood . . ."

"Frank. Call me Frank . . . Tamisha." He pronounced

the last word with every syllable oiled and followed it with a smile that wouldn't have looked out of place on an Argentinian gigolo.

Annalise didn't appear to notice. "I've been talking to Frank," she continued. "He thinks he can persuade the department to release you for another day or two. If that's agreeable to you."

"Of course it's agreeable to him, isn't it, Graham? Time off, a change of scenery, the beautiful Tamisha. What else could anyone want?"

Annalise coughed. "Sorry," she said, glancing in Frank's direction. "My throat's dry. Is there somewhere I can get a drink?"

Frank bounced out of his chair. "Would you like a coffee? I can get you one if you'd like?"

"That'd be great."

Frank scooped a coffee tray from Shenaz's desk. "I won't be long," he said, smiling one last time from the door before slithering away.

"You can close your mouth now, Graham. He's gone."

Graham had but one thought. "Have you heard from Annalise Fifteen? Is she okay?"

Annalise looked surprised.

"Why do you . . ." Then came the realization. "Have you just come from Fifteen's world?"

"I was with her yesterday. I think she was shot. Have you heard from her?"

"Yes . . . no." She was confused. "She was shot?"

"I think so. I was flipping worlds at the time. She was running behind the bus. There were gunshots and she fell."

"Stop. Slow down." She grasped his shoulders. "What gunshots? Who was shooting at who?"

He told her. He told her about the black car, the flaming waste bin, the smell of petrol, the gunshots, his stupid decision to jump on a passing bus. Annalise listened, shaking her head.

"I talked to her yesterday," she said, her eyes distant. "She said the two of you were hiding in a changing room. I thought she was joking."

Graham shook his head. "She wasn't."

"I'll contact her now," said Annalise. "Nudge me if anyone comes in."

She sat on the edge of Frank's desk. Graham's eyes flicked between Annalise and the door. He prayed for a long queue at the coffee machine, a gaggle of senior managers for Frank to suck up to, anything to ensure Annalise had sufficient time to get through.

Annalise looked worried. Graham stopped glancing towards the door. Her eyes were closed, her face alternating between concentration and concern.

Graham waited for her to say something—to open her eyes and tell him he'd been mistaken, she hadn't fallen, there'd been no gunshot, he'd hallucinated it all in the throes of flipping worlds.

After two minutes she opened her eyes.

"She's fine," she said. "She tripped, that's all."

A great weight fell from Graham's shoulders. He could breathe again. He felt as though he'd been holding his breath for hours.

"What happened? Where is she? Are you sure she's okay?"

"She's fine. And she wants you to know that she caught up with that bus."

"She did?" Graham was amazed.

"Yeah, she caught up with it, all right." Annalise looked away and for a brief second there was a hint of worry in her face. Then back came the smile. "Wow, you are *so* unlike the other Graham I had."

"I am?"

"Totally. Don't get me wrong. I know you've all been through a hell that none of us could even begin to imagine but you've spoken more in the last five minutes than the other Graham managed in three whole days. You're almost . . ."

She stopped and bit her lip. Graham finished the line for her. "Normal?" he suggested with a slight lift of his eyebrow.

"Yeah, and I mean that in a good way. Something only another freak can say, right?" She laughed. "I'm Annalise Six, by the way." She held out her hand. "Good to meet you, Mr. Smith."

A few seconds later, the door opened and Frank came in with two coffees on a tray.

"Thank you," said Annalise, taking a sip. "I'll take it with me."

"You're going?" Frank looked devastated.

"Yeah. There's no problem getting clearance for Graham, is there? I was told that if anyone could swing it, you could."

"You were?"

"Sure. You know they call you 'Frank the Facilitator' at ParaDim?"

"They do?"

Graham watched in awe. Annalise had barely met the man and yet she played him like an old instrument. Frank Gledwood, the mention of whose name was enough to ruin the brightest of Graham's days, was being wound around one of Annalise's perfectly formed fingers.

And Frank neither realized nor cared.

"Where are we going?" asked Graham as they left the building.

"ParaDim," said Annalise. "Didn't I say?"

Graham stopped dead. How could she even think about going to ParaDim?

"It's okay, Graham. ParaDim's different here. It's not like the other worlds. Everyone's really open and friendly."

Graham couldn't believe it. "ParaDim's the same on every world. Kevin said it was something to do with the resonance effect. They can't help it."

He looked around. He felt uncomfortable talking about ParaDim so close to work. He grasped her arm and hurried her along the pavement.

"Trust me, Graham, it's different here. Gary and Tamisha are great."

"You like Tamisha?"

"Sure, why wouldn't I?"

Graham relaxed and released her arm and thought about a girl with orange hair. "Yesterday, I thought you were going to push her through a window."

Annalise looked worried. "Annalise Fifteen tried to push Tamisha through a window?"

"She thought about it. And Tamisha had been asking for it."

Annalise looked shocked. "But Tamisha's one of the nicest persons I've met."

"You wouldn't have thought so yesterday. Pressure does strange things to people."

"Yes, it does, doesn't it?" She gazed away into the distance, her mind elsewhere for an instant. "Anyway, Tamisha loaned me her ID until Gary can sort something out. She's in the States all week recruiting for the Resonance project. So, as far as this country's concerned I'm Tamisha Kent, ParaDim liaison to the DTI. Gives me access to you while you're at work and to ParaDim when I need to see Gary. Beats those cloak and dagger phone calls."

"Isn't there a picture on the ID? You don't look anything like Tamisha."

"Don't need to. ParaDim don't use pictures. All their security over here is automatic—retinal scans and fingerprints. Gary had Tamisha's file updated with my details. I tell you, anything the Resonance project wants they get. No questions. Gary said change the file and the security guy jumped to it."

It still sounded wrong to Graham. ParaDim was like a big, bloated spider with a foot on every strand of existence—it may let you walk softly around its outer edges for a while but that didn't mean it wouldn't rush out and bite you when it felt like it.

"They're really great guys down there," said Annalise. "They've given me guided tours and this pass gives me unrestricted access. I can walk anywhere I want and, believe me, there's nothing scary going on there at all. Just a bunch of guys trying to save the world."

"So why are we going there? You've seen the building and I must have had every medical test there is yesterday."

"Didn't I say?"

He shook his head.

"It's your DNA results. You know, they started coming through yesterday? The message in the changing room?"

"I remember."

"Well, they finally worked out what was going on. Gary stayed up all night double-checking the results from nearly ten million worlds."

"And?"

"They found your parents."

THIRTY-SIX

"Gary can explain it better," she said. "Do you want to sit down?"

"No, just tell me."

"Okay. Gary says you're some kinda composite. He thinks you must have hundreds of parents, maybe more than a thousand. It's difficult to tell because so many of the donors appear related."

"Donors?"

"Gary says it's like someone took genetic information from all your parents on all the worlds and combined it into a single Graham Smith hybrid. No one has a clue how. It's way beyond anything they can do here. Gary's downloading genetics data from every advanced world he can find to see if there are any parallels."

"I'm a hybrid?"

329

"Of all your parents. Some kinda Smith soup that blended together to form two hundred billion identical Grahams."

"Smith soup?"

"Sounds kinda icky, doesn't it?" She screwed up her face. "Howard came up with it and . . . it kinda stuck. Sorry."

They took the tube to Putney Bridge. ParaDim's office was over the river—a modern tower block ten storeys high, gleaming white concrete and black tinted windows. Annalise inserted her card, placed her palm on the security panel by the front door and stared into the retinal camera. Graham stood to the side, trying to peer inside but seeing only his reflection in the black glass doors. A green light flashed and the door opened.

A lone security guard watched them walk across the foyer. "Good morning, Miss Kent," he said. "Is this the gentleman to see Mr. Mitchison?"

Annalise agreed on both counts. "It is a good morning, isn't it?"

She seemed so happy. Graham couldn't understand why. How could anyone walk into a ParaDim office and feel happy?

He swept his eyes around the marble-clad foyer—so huge, so quiet, so deserted. Where was everyone? And why the one-way glass? He could see people walking by outside—ordinary people going about their business, shopping, sightseeing, taking the dog for a walk. Not one of them glanced his way. Not one showed any interest in the strange unmarked building in their midst.

"Keep this with you at all times, Mr. Smith," said the

security guard, handing Graham a temporary pass.

"Come on," said Annalise, dragging Graham towards the lifts. "Watch this."

She placed her palm on a console panel. "Location required for Gary Mitchison."

"Gary Mitchison is in 5G, Miss Kent." A woman's voice—American, natural, not a hint of being computer-generated.

"Neat, huh? You can find anyone in the building." She held up her card. "We're tracked by these."

They took the lift to the fifth floor. The doors opened on a wide corridor that stretched nearly the entire length of the building, doors and entry consoles were dotted along both its sides.

But still no people. The corridor was deserted. There was no glass in any of the doors, no sounds from within or without save the steady hum of the overhead lights.

They found 5G, three doors down on their left. Annalise went through the motions, the green light flashed, the door opened. Graham wondered if he was supposed to do the same? Was there somewhere he should insert his pass?

Annalise flowed into the room. "Gary?" she called.

Graham followed. There were banks of desks and screens around the walls. Two men were talking by a terminal in the corner. They both looked round. Graham recognized the shorter of the two men—Howard Sarkissian. A feeling of guilt washed over him. Was the Howard that he knew dead?

"You must be Mr. Smith. Can I call you Graham?" said the other man—tall, early thirties, a hint of a Scots accent. He held out his hand and smiled as he advanced towards

Graham. "I'm Gary and my friend in the corner is the redoubtable Howard Sarkissian."

"Charmed, I'm sure," said Howard, bowing.

Graham shivered. He'd heard the exact same words barely twenty-four hours earlier. The same words, the same voice, the same craggy smile, the same twinkle in the eye behind the same thick-lensed glasses. It was unnerving.

"Have you told him?" Gary asked Annalise.

"On the way over," said Annalise, smiling up at Gary.

"So, what do you think about your remarkable family history, Mr. Smith?" asked Howard.

Graham shrugged. He didn't know what to think.

"The data's still coming in," said Gary. "At the last count you had 472 fathers and 4,487 mothers."

Graham blinked. The numbers meant nothing to him. He had one father and one mother. The others were mere strangers, as anonymous as a page of Smiths in a telephone directory.

"We'd like to perform further tests. If that's agreeable to you," asked Gary.

"We know you can exchange your consciousness," said Howard. "We're wondering if you can exchange other material as well?"

"Like genetic material," said Gary. "Could the source of your remarkable genetic make-up be in part caused by a transference of genetic material."

"We're very much in the dark," said Howard. "Unfortunately, we're not geneticists."

"Which is why Tamisha's in the States busily recruiting. We're desperately short of expertise."

"Graham flipped yesterday," Annalise told Gary. "Is that any help?"

Gary looked from Annalise to Howard to Graham. He looked as though he could barely contain himself. "Before or after the medical?" The words came out slow and precise. "This is very important."

"After, wasn't it, Graham?" prompted Annalise.

Graham nodded. He didn't like the way Annalise was looking at Gary. She had barely taken her eyes off him since entering the room. And did she have to stand so close?

Gary exchanged glances with Howard. "This is exactly what we wanted," he said. "We can do a before-and-after test and look for anomalies." He turned to Graham. "You couldn't have come to us at a better time."

Three faces smiled at Graham. Graham tried to smile back but Annalise turned and touched Gary's arm. He watched her fingers curl and caress and move away. He felt betrayed and stupid and guilty and . . .

What was the matter with him! How could he be jealous? She was Annalise and yet he knew she wasn't *his* Annalise. She wouldn't step in front of a gunman and threaten to set herself alight. She wasn't Annalise Fifteen. Annalise Fifteen was unique. There could never be anyone else like her.

And yet . . .

And yet there she was, standing right in front of him. Annalise Fifteen in a different guise—maybe the girl that Annalise Fifteen would or could have been if circumstances had been different.

It was disconcerting in the extreme.

"I'll call Shikha," said Gary, picking up a phone. "She'll want to see you anyway. And she'll need time to coordinate appointments with the Cavendish."

"Where is Shikha?" asked Howard.

"Trawling the medical databases last time I saw her. Looking for any world that has experimented with ways of measuring consciousness."

Graham drifted away from the conversation flying around him and walked over to the window. The Thames was laid out below like a vast blue snake. Small boats skidded silently like many-legged insects—their oars moving in unison. Clouds scudded across the sky, cars filed slowly over distant bridges. Everything so normal, so far removed from CAT scans, electroencephalography and submolecular analysis.

Gary replaced the phone and spoke to Howard. "Shikha's already booked the Cavendish for this afternoon. She'll catch up with us in an hour when she's finished downloading."

Graham turned away from the window. "What's any of this got to do with stopping the resonance wave?" he asked.

Gary and Howard looked at each other.

"Ah," said Gary, for the first time looking lost for words. "Unfortunately, we're not sure. If it wasn't for the interest shown in you by other Resonance projects—specifically the ones that were closed down—I'd say, very little. There is no obvious link that we can find between you and the resonance wave."

"Other than the possibility that you were the result of an earlier resonance wave," added Howard. "After all, there are two hundred billion of you. You appear identical in all respects. Could that be the result of a resonance wave that forced all your counterparts to develop the same way?"

"The truth is—we simply do not know where or if you

fit in. These Resonance projects—were they closed down because they were close to finding an answer to the resonance wave or because they were close to uncovering the truth about you?"

"We hope the former, but fear it's neither. All this could be an elaborate scheme of disinformation to send research teams down a blind alley."

"But, for the moment, you're all we've got," said Gary. "And, believe me, we've travelled the same path as every other Resonance project. We've considered creating an interference pattern to nullify the resonance wave. We've discussed the possibility of creating a counterresonance wave—something so large it could overwhelm all other resonance effects."

"But everything stumbles on one very important hurdle. We just don't know enough about resonance."

"We've tried simulations," said Gary, "but we can't find an accurate model. Schenck's Law is more idea than hard fact. There are no equations to verify. We have approximations, ideas, but there are too many holes, too many variables that we don't fully understand."

"And we've trawled the advanced worlds," said Howard, "downloaded every model we can find . . . but," he paused, "even their simulations—ones we barely comprehend—don't predict the intensity that we see in this resonance wave. ParaDim projects are being created ten times faster than predicted. There has to be a missing component."

"What do you think of our setup, Graham?" asked Gary as they waited for the lift to take them down to the ground floor. Annalise had persuaded the two men to give Graham a guided tour while they waited for Shikha to arrive.

"I thought Adam Sylvestrus didn't like modern architecture," said Graham.

"Who?" Gary looked puzzled, his brow furrowed for a few seconds. "Oh, him! He doesn't exist on this world. Kenny Zamorra runs ParaDim here."

Graham wondered what Kenny Zamorra was like. An Adam Sylvestrus clone? Worse?

"ParaDim's not evil on this world, Graham," said Annalise. "They do a lot of good. They've really made a difference in the Third World with their drug programs. They've cut through a lot of red tape. Saved a lot of lives."

"I don't think you could call ParaDim evil on any world," said Howard. "Not the company. There are a few individuals who put profit before compassion but the majority of ParaDim employees only want what's best for the world."

"Does that include New Tech weapons?" asked Graham.

"No," said Howard. "The proliferation of New Tech weaponry is an unqualified disaster. But not every world has to repeat that mistake. We haven't here. There are no plans to open a weapons research program anywhere within ParaDim."

Graham wondered if that was true. And if anyone would tell Howard if it wasn't. ParaDim was caught up in a resonance wave. If one person didn't create a New Tech weapons project, someone else would. It was inevitable. Whatever anyone's good intentions.

"ParaDim is totally committed to solving this resonance problem," added Gary. "Believe me, I should know. The Resonance project is top priority. Kenny Zamorra said so himself. Whatever we need we can have. No questions asked. If we want people, ParaDim brings them in. If we want more computer capacity, it's there the next day. Money's no object. The only thing that counts is finding a solution."

"After all, who wants to live in a world that's going down the tubes? No one benefits from that scenario—you, me or the CEO of ParaDim," Howard added.

Graham shook his head. It all sounded so reasonable—even Annalise believed it—but Kevin said that all ParaDim boards were affected by resonance. Why should this one be different? Was there a boardroom coup just around the corner?

Gary placed his palm on the entry panel to Room G and stared into the retinal camera.

"Where is everybody?" asked Graham, looking up and down the corridor. It all looked so deserted. He hadn't seen anyone else since he'd entered the building.

"It is quiet, isn't it?" said Howard. "But you get used to it. Most of the building is filled with computers and equipment. Everything's automated. I doubt there's more than twenty people in the entire building."

The door slid open. Gary stood back to let Annalise enter first. A giant dimpled sphere dominated the room. It was like a matte black golf ball twelve feet in diameter sitting on a similarly colored plinth.

"And this is where it all begins," said Gary, waving a hand in the sphere's direction. "There are only twenty of these on the planet at the moment. This is the heart of ParaDim."

Graham half expected to see it pumping. He walked around it, wondering if he was allowed to touch, wondering what it was. It was so black and strange-looking—light seemed to slide off it, there was hardly any reflection from the overhead lights or from the windows. He let his hand hover near the surface, as far as he dare go; any closer and he was sure his hand would be sucked into some deep, cloying void.

At the back of the plinth an array of pipes—ten of them, each about a hand in circumference—ran along the floor before disappearing into the wall.

"Cabling to the front-end computers," explained Gary. "Imagine this black beauty as a giant sausage machine—raw data from parallel worlds being sucked in at one end and distributed about the building in neat packages for us to translate and analyze."

"This can access parallel worlds?" Graham continued his slow circumnavigation. There were no features on the sphere at all—other than the dimpling. There were no lights or dials or switches or even a line showing where two pieces had been joined together. Had the sphere been cast in one piece? And one piece of what? Metal? Plastic? Something else?

"Isn't it just the most mind-blowing thing you ever saw?" said Annalise, joining him on the far side.

"The technology underlying this machine is phenomenal," said Gary, his hand lightly brushing the sphere's side. Graham held his breath and peered at Gary's fingers, expecting them to come away stained black.

"It's a century beyond anything we should be able to produce," continued Gary. "We're only now adapting some of this technology for use elsewhere—New Tech computers, New Tech data storage. Another year and we'll be able to speed up the process a millionfold."

"But at the moment," said Howard, "we've a bottleneck at the processing end. We're sucking down data far faster than we can process it. Most of this building is filled with mainframes and disk drives trying to keep up."

"Isn't it neat?" Annalise said to Graham. "You can see which world's being accessed from that terminal over there."

"Which world is this one?" Howard asked Gary, who was standing by the terminal.

Gary leaned over and read from the screen. "024 544 691 337."

"Which means like less than nothing to everyone on this side of the room," said Annalise, smiling. "What kind of world is it?"

Gary tapped at the keyboard and a new screen came up.

"One of the more advanced ones," he said.

"According to Gary," Annalise inclined her head towards Graham, "most worlds are more advanced than us. We're an average, could-do-better world."

"Which is what you'd expect," said Howard. "The sample will always be skewed in favor of the more advanced worlds because they're the ones with data. What are you going to find on a less-developed world? Without the technology to broadcast or store data electronically all you'll get is static."

"This one's not much better," said Gary, peering at the screen. "It's one of the Chinese worlds. Most of the interesting files are in a distant variant of Mandarin. They take ages to translate and even then I'm sure we miss many of the inflections."

"Do you get many different languages?" asked Graham.

"Do they ever," said Annalise. "Tell him about the code freaks."

"Code freaks?" asked Graham.

"There's several worlds who encrypt everything," said Gary. "Even their radio broadcasts. We're not sure if it's a commercial consideration to make their customers buy decoders or a security matter."

"Very difficult to decrypt," said Howard. "But, with help from other worlds, we did it."

"Then there are the worlds with languages we've never met before or ones that have diverged radically from our own. Some use character sets we're not familiar with. Some use octal or duodecimal numbering systems. We even have worlds where all we can access is a white noise. It's not static but we can't tell if it's data, interference or something else. There's something there but we can't even begin to ascertain what it might be."

Annalise moved away from Graham and ran an absent-minded finger along a bank of screens on the wall behind her.

"What's this?" she said, turning to Gary. "Your name's all over this screen."

Gary walked over and peered over her shoulder. "Is that still there?"

"What's still there?" asked Howard.

"I was doing a 109 search over breakfast."

"What's a 109?" asked Annalise.

"Something we do more often than we should," explained Gary. "It's fun to see if any of your counterparts are famous. One of mine won a golf tournament in Ohio last month. Made me think I should take up the game."

"It does have more serious applications," added

Howard. "It's part of the general name search against the other worlds. Developed for the Census project, though some of us"—he looked at Gary "—have found other uses for it."

"You're familiar with the Internet?" Gary asked Annalise.

"Duh!" she said, raising her eyes.

"Well, imagine the dross you pick up on an Internet query and multiply it by a thousand billion. You have to apply filters to the search to make them manageable. So we have preprogrammed filters. And Type 109 checks the media files. If any of your counterparts made the papers, a 109 scan will find them."

"Can I have a go?" asked Annalise, pulling the chair out and sitting herself down in front of the screen. "Where do I type my name?"

Gary took Annalise through the procedure.

"You can select name and date of birth, place of birth, country of birth, age range, parents. The tighter the search criteria, the tighter the match."

"I'll do it for all the girls. There can't be too many Annalise Mercados in the universe."

"I'd enter as much as you can. Some of the worlds out there have records going back several millennia."

Annalise selected U.S.A. and entered a one-week range for date of birth. The machine hung for ten seconds, twenty.

"You realize I can check how accurate this is?" she said. "If Annalise One's name doesn't come up for solving the De Santos kidnapping, you're busted."

"It'll come up," said Gary. "Don't worry."

A new screen came up. Slowly, names appeared.

Several entries appeared for Annalise One—*Psychic Saves Kimberly, Kimberly Psychic Questioned, Kimberly Psychic Gets Own Show, Psychic's Show Cancelled*.

But it wasn't one of those headlines that drew Annalise's attention.

It was the one below.

Telepathy Project Ends In Failure.

THIRTY-SEVEN

"How do I get more information? Can I click on that?" Annalise said, pointing at the entry on the screen.

Gary leaned over and clicked on the link for her. An article appeared. An extract from the *New York Times* dated fifteen years ago. There was a picture of a baby—Annalise Mercado—the first human to be born with the experimental telepathy gene.

Graham looked at the picture. Was it really Annalise? All babies looked the same to him, but was there something about the eyes?

He read on. She'd been the center of an experiment into telepathy. An attempt to access underutilized portions of the brain by a mixture of gene and drug therapy. One of the last projects before the global moratorium on human genetic engineering. But it had failed. Repeated tests on the infant Annalise failed to show any sign of telepathic ability and yesterday, on her fourth birthday, the last funding for the project had been withdrawn.

"Where is this?" said Annalise, grabbing Gary by the sleeve. "Which world? Can you find out? Is it one of the girls?"

Gary clicked and tapped, lists unfurled in windows on the screen, lists of names and numbers.

"It's not one of the two hundred," said Gary after about a minute. Everyone looked at Annalise. She stared blankly at the screen.

"Annalise Two," she said, her voice low and drained of all emotion.

"No," said Gary. "Annalise Two's address is . . ."

"Not that Annalise Two. The original."

"There was another Annalise?"

"Yeah, but I never talked to her." She continued to stare straight ahead. "No one did but Annalise One. She was Annalise One's big friend. From the age of five through to . . ." She stopped and shook her head. "Sorry, I can't remember—ten, eleven, twelve, something like that. I'll find out from Annalise One. But I remember they used to tell each other stories. The girl said she was dead. She kept repeating it. *I'm dead. Mommy told the man from the papers. My real name's Annalise too but mommy gets angry when I use it. I'm Tammy now. Tammy Marchant.*

"That's how she became known as Annalise Two—*my real name's Annalise too.*" Annalise smiled. "I used to think that was a real cool story."

Gary started tapping on the keyboard and a new screen appeared. *Census Project—Name Search.* He typed in Annalise Mercado, the twelve-digit world ID, took her date of birth from the newspaper article, ticked birth, marriages and death, and waited. The details came back. Just the one entry—the registration of her birth.

"She's still alive?" said Howard.

"Or changed her name." He transcribed Annalise's details into a search for Tammy Marchant. One entry. Her death at age twelve. A car crash.

"Do you think she changed her name again?" asked Howard.

Gary shook his head. "I don't even know why her mother changed names in the first place."

"To give her daughter a normal life," said Howard. "Away from the media spotlight."

"A bit late to think of that. She must have agreed to have the child modified in the first place."

"Have *we* been genetically engineered?" asked Annalise, looking up at Gary. "The girls, I mean? Is that why we can talk to each other?"

"I doubt it," said Gary, resting his hand on her shoulder. "I can only guess but I think that in an odd sort of way the experiment worked. But instead of bonding with someone on her own world, she found another version of herself—Annalise One. Maybe the rest came about by resonance. Maybe the ability to access greater portions of the brain is something that can be taught or triggered by extended use. Annalise Two teaches Annalise One who, in turn . . . who knows? Are the number of Annalises increasing faster than they used to?"

"Yeah," Annalise nodded, her face fixed on the screen. "I might have heard her, you know? In my head. I heard fragments of voices long before I learned how to reply. I might have heard Tammy Marchant calling to me."

She took a deep breath and turned to Gary. "I've got to contact the girls:"

Annalise Fifteen was running out of money. She'd used most of her cash on the train fare to Brighton and a hotel room for herself and Graham. Yesterday, money had been the least of her worries. Now, it was moving towards the top.

She looked at herself in the wardrobe mirror. Her clothes were stained—a mixture of slate dust, attic grime and dirt from rolling in the road. Not to mention the gasoline. She could still smell it despite soaking her top in the sink overnight. But they were all the clothes she had. Everything else was back in London, sixty miles away.

She glanced over at Graham—the new Graham, the quiet one—sat by the window, playing Solitaire. He'd been playing for hours and would probably keep on playing for days—or until she told him to stop. He was the most malleable person she'd ever met.

But he wasn't company.

She wondered what the other Graham was doing. Had he really thought he'd abandoned her? She shook her head in disbelief. He'd tried to throw himself headfirst off a moving bus rather than leave her behind. He'd barely been able to move—she could tell he was in the throes of flipping worlds—but he'd never given up. Not once. When he couldn't crawl, he'd rolled. If the passengers on the bus hadn't pulled him back, he'd have succeeded.

She flicked on the TV. Something to take her mind off money and ParaDim death squads. A news program came on. She shuffled closer along the bed for a better view. Would setting a car alight and being shot at in a London street be considered newsworthy?

She watched for several minutes. No mention of shootouts in Knightsbridge but there was one story that made her sit up. A jewelry heist from a month ago. A little girl—Tracey Minton—had been killed as the gang made their getaway. A senseless murder. The girl had been walking by with her mother when the gang ran out of the jewelers. One of the raiders had turned and shot her. Panic, reflex action, for-the-hell-of-it thuggery—no one knew why. But people wanted little Tracey's killers caught. And newspapers were willing to pay for information. With the number of leads drying up, one of the papers—*The Sketch*—had just announced their reward was to be increased to £100,000.

Annalise sat bolt upright.

And thought of Annalise Six.

And the ParaDim computers.

"Are you coming?" asked Gary, holding the door to 3C open. "Annalise?"

Annalise Six didn't appear to hear. She was leaning against the corridor wall and staring into space.

"What is it?" asked Howard from inside the room.

"Another message," whispered Gary over his shoulder.

"But I thought she just . . ."

"Shhh!" said Gary.

Graham wondered if silence made any difference. It hadn't to Annalise Fifteen. She'd conversed quite happily as a tube train rattled and shook along the tracks.

Concentration seemed to be the key—the ability to focus and blot out all extraneous sounds.

Annalise's expression changed. She shook her head. Her eyes flicked left and right, unfocused, unseeing. She looked blind and confused.

"Is this . . . normal?" Gary whispered to Graham.

Graham nodded. Emotions seemed more transparent during telepathic communication. He wondered why. Was she robbed of her ability to mask her feelings or overwhelmed by the emotional charge created by the telepathic link?

Annalise's face went slack. Her eyes refocused. She forced a nervous smile and wobbled slightly. Graham reached for her arm and held it.

"Are you all right?" asked Gary.

"Sure. I'm fine. Never better. Have you shown Graham the Census project logs yet?"

"What about the message?" asked Gary.

"Nothing important." She stepped in front of Gary and waited for him to let her pass. He paused, watching her intently before turning and letting her inside.

Graham listened as Howard explained how ParaDim had twenty black spheres placed throughout the world sucking down data at mind-boggling speeds. How the information was shared and processed and interpreted. How every ParaDim office was connected to this vast array of data. How specialist teams were dotted throughout the world, sifting through the material—analyzing, refining, passing back requests to search particular worlds or for specific topics.

"It's a huge iterative process," Howard explained. "We

discover A, become interested in B, dig about for more data, find C. Someone else discovers D, which in turn throws more light upon A. And so on. It's like being in the middle of a huge forest fire. So many flames and sparks all around, each igniting and feeding off each other."

"How up to date's everything?" asked Annalise out of the blue. It was the first time she'd spoken since walking into the room. "Twenty spheres are going to have a hard time catching up with two hundred billion worlds, right?"

"We do our best," said Howard. "Some worlds are better sources than others so we tend to concentrate on them."

"And a new sphere comes online every month," said Gary. "It's finding the computer capacity to keep up with the spheres that's the biggest problem. We're having to lease capacity wherever we can find it."

"So," said Annalise. "If I wanted to, say, find out if something happened yesterday on a particular world, when would I be able to check that newspaper database?"

"Do you have something in mind?" asked Gary.

Graham watched her carefully. She'd been unusually quiet since receiving that message in the corridor. She'd stood at the back, distracted, biting her lip.

Until now.

"Well, take what happened to Graham yesterday. The attempt to kidnap him."

"Someone tried to kidnap Graham?" Gary was shocked.

"Didn't I say?" said Annalise. "They closed the Resonance project on Annalise Fifteen's world."

She told Gary and Howard what had happened. Graham filled in the gaps.

"So, when could we see if any of that made the papers?"

she asked. "Only, she's kinda scared and can't get hold of any newspapers."

Graham looked hard at Annalise. What was she up to? Annalise Fifteen wasn't scared of anything. If she wanted a newspaper she'd get one. Nothing defeated her.

"She wondered if you could find out for her," continued Annalise, looking at Gary. "That search you were showing us earlier—can you use it to look up events as well as people? Like a shooting, say, in Knightsbridge?"

"No problem," said Gary. "We do it all the time."

"Could you show me how?" asked Annalise.

"Of course, but the data won't be available yet," explained Gary. "We have a cycle of rolling updates. It could be days, months before that world is accessed again."

"We could express the update," Howard said to Gary. "Add that world to the express list. We have the authority."

"That would be great," said Annalise. "And if you show me how to search, I won't have to bother you again."

Annalise smiled and, for the first time in over a week, Graham didn't feel warmed by the experience. He felt excluded. She was up to something, something she should have shared with him—with a look, a knowing smile, a wink. He and Annalise were a team—they'd been that way since the beginning—them against the world. Why was she pushing him away?

Was it Gary?

He watched Annalise pull up a chair and shuffle it towards Gary's until they practically touched. He watched her hand fall on his shoulder and the way she leaned all over him to get a better view of the screen.

He barely heard what Gary had to say.

"That is so clever," said Annalise. "And if I wanted to see if the same event happened on other worlds, I'd omit that world filter thingy, right?"

"Right," said Gary.

Howard checked his watch. "We'd better get on. Shikha will be finished soon and we've only shown Graham two rooms."

"Is it okay if I sit here for a while?" asked Annalise. "I don't feel too steady on my feet. I guess two telepathic sessions in ten minutes took more out of me than I realized. I'll catch up with you in five minutes."

"Sure," said Howard. "Take as much time as you need."

Graham hung back to let the others out and glanced back at Annalise. She'd turned her back towards him but over her left shoulder he saw the flash of a new screen.

Annalise Fifteen bought a copy of *The Sketch* and took it with her to the nearest phone booth. She found the piece with the contact details and tapped in the telephone number.

"Tracey Minton Information Line, how can I help you?" A woman's voice—young and eager.

"I have the names of the men you're looking for but I need money and protection. My life's in danger."

"You're American?" The girl sounded puzzled.

"What's that gotta do with anything?" said Annalise. "Look, I'm no time waster if that's what you think. I'll give you three names now, the rest you get when I see the money. I know where the stuff is, who masterminded it, the lot. Are you interested?"

"Can I have your name and a number where we can contact you?"

"Haven't you been listening?" Annalise snapped. "I'm risking my life just talking to you. Now, listen, I'm gonna give you three names, you're gonna tell the police and I'll call back at three this afternoon. Got that?"

"I've got that."

"Okay, the names are John Farmer, Marcus Roberts and Brian Sweeney. They're the guys from the heist. John Farmer's the shooter. I'll give you the rest as soon as I see some money."

She put the phone down and prayed she knew what she was doing. Annalise Six had given her the names of the three robbers, the guy who planned it, the fence and various addresses they'd used on the other worlds. But was this world the same? What if one of the names she'd been given didn't exist on this world? Would it discredit her case?

She stepped outside and shielded her eyes. White paving slabs dazzled in the glaring sun. A salty in-shore breeze played with her hair. Tourists, in a mass of flesh and primary colors, ambled along the sea front.

If she'd named the wrong man, she could always say it was an alias. Whatever the problem, she'd think of something.

"Have you ever thought of using the ParaDim database to solve crime?" Annalise Six asked Gary.

"Pardon?"

Every eye turned towards Annalise. She'd barely said a word since catching up with the guided tour.

"To solve crime," she said. "Like Annalise One did. To use information on similar worlds where the bad guys got caught to solve the cases on the worlds where they didn't? It would do a lot of good, don't you think?"

There was something about the way she looked at Gary—an almost pleading look in her eyes.

"I don't think anyone's considered the possibility."

"It *would* make an excellent project," said Howard. "Very easy to pass off as another marvel of AI wizardry. I can hear Kenny Zamorra now." Howard changed his accent, adding a nasal quality to his voice. 'Give us your most puzzling cases, gentlemen, and our AI engine will connect the unconnectable.'•"

Gary laughed. "But how would it make money?" he asked Howard. "You know how many projects there are fighting for resources. How do you choose between solving crime and curing cancer?"

"You choose both," suggested Graham quietly from the back of the room. Gary and Howard glanced his way and smiled as though noticing a small child for the first time, then turned back to their conversation.

"You could try for government funding," said Howard. "And there's always book and film deals. You could commission studies into old mysteries—Jack the Ripper, the Lindbergh baby . . ."

"But would it be right to make money out of it?" asked Annalise.

"There's no commandment that says 'Thou shalt not profit from good deeds,'•" said Gary, still smiling. "If there was, ParaDim would have been damned a long time ago."

Graham felt cold. All this talk of ParaDim as though it was a benevolent organization. The ParaDim he knew was evil. Nor could he adjust to Gary and Howard's laid-back attitude. Shouldn't they be doing something? Why were they wasting time showing him around when they should be searching for an answer to the resonance problem?

Didn't they have work to do? And why were there only two of them. If the Resonance project had such a high priority, why wasn't the building teeming with people?

A buzz came from the door. It clicked and opened.

"Sorry I'm late," said a breathless Shikha, smoothing a long strand of hair away from her face. "I lost track of the time."

She shook hands with Graham. Her hand felt small within his. Everything about her was small and slight—except for her hair, which hung long and straight and reached down to the small of her back. She was in her mid to late twenties, Indian—maybe Pakistani—and she looked so delicate, Graham thought her hand would crack if he squeezed it too hard.

He spent the middle part of the morning with Shikha, following her from room to room, experiment to experiment. He had electrodes clipped and unclipped to his chest and head, he was told to sit, to stand, to lie down. He was shown pictures, asked questions, given small puzzles to solve.

Shikha didn't say much in between. She watched the monitors, made notes, clucked and absent-mindedly twirled a long strand of hair around her pen.

Annalise came in for the last half hour. She sat quietly at the back and watched.

"Howard's updating the Resonance logs," she said to Graham when Shikha had finished. "He's in 5G if you want to watch."

Graham glanced towards Shikha. Was it okay for him to go?

"We're finished in here," said Shikha. "I'll see you in the foyer at one-thirty."

❊ ❊ ❊

Annalise accompanied Graham to 5G. She still appeared distracted. Graham wondered if he should say something but couldn't find anything appropriate. Annalise inserted her card and placed her palm on the door panel. The door opened. Annalise hesitated.

"I'll catch you later," she said, turning and heading off down the corridor.

Graham watched her go, unsure what to do next. He appeared to be marking time, being shunted from one person to the next. Wouldn't it be more productive if he kept out of everyone's way and let them get on with their work?

"Are you coming in, Graham?" asked Howard from his terminal in the corner. "I've nearly finished. Pull up a chair."

Graham walked over and sat down next to Howard.

"We upload it every day," Howard said. "The Resonance log. Our small part in helping the other teams. We may not be as technologically advanced as the other worlds but we're thorough. Everything we learn—from whatever source and however unlikely—we collate and comment on. Even if we can't see a link, someone else might."

Graham glanced at the screen and saw his name. *Graham Smith brought in for further tests today. We have the opportunity to compare results post and prior an exchange of consciousness.*

"Aren't you worried about someone seeing this and closing you down?" he said.

"No. Why should we?"

Graham shook his head in disbelief. Kevin Alexander had been terrified of discovery as soon as he'd learned of the other Resonance project closures. He'd kept all mention of Graham Smith out of his logs and he'd recruited Annalise—his secure line of communication to the other Resonance projects. Didn't Howard know all this?

"What about the other Resonance project closures?" Graham asked. "As soon as anyone gets close to an answer they're closed down."

"Not here," Howard said, shaking his head and clicking on another file. "We have the full backing of the board and everyone's committed to finding a solution."

"But what about the logs from the closed projects? Kevin said their last entries all contained references to me."

"A coincidence," said Howard. "Seventeen projects stopped reporting. Maybe they were closed down, maybe something else happened . . ."

"I was there," interrupted Graham. He couldn't believe what he was hearing. "Resonance projects *are* being closed down. People *are* being hunted. I've seen it."

"Sorry," apologized Howard. "I forgot. Make that eighteen projects. But even so, what about the ten million projects that haven't been closed down? They mention you in their recent logs. Why haven't they been closed down?"

"How do you know they haven't?"

"Because we'd know."

"How? I thought Gary said you did rolling updates that might take weeks or months to get back to certain worlds."

"We do."

"So how would you know what's happened in the meantime?"

"We have a program that searches for RPs that used to

report daily but no longer do. We run it every day. Yesterday's count was seventeen."

"But that number could be weeks out of date."

"Possibly but unlikely. It's a skewed snapshot of the data we have. Some of it's days, some of it's weeks old. But logs from the important worlds are collected daily."

"When do you run today's?"

Howard stopped what he was doing and raised his eyebrows.

"I'll do it now."

He pulled down a new menu and clicked through it until he found the program he wanted. "It'll only take a few seconds. All the RP logs are filed together."

Graham watched the screen, unsure what he was looking for. Would a number flash on the screen and, if so, where?

A box appeared in the top-left corner. The count was sixty-three.

Howard looked worried. "It could be a mistake in the program."

He ran it again.

"It assesses a project purely on whether it's filed a log entry for the most recent date. If a project used to report but stops, for whatever reason, it's counted as closed. A bank holiday could throw the figures out."

"Would you shut down a Resonance project for a bank holiday?"

Howard was silent. "Or a major computer failure. Something like that. Some of the worlds are experiencing blackouts due to the chaos."

The program stopped running and a number flashed on the screen—sixty-three.

Howard muttered to himself as he pulled down details of the sixty-three worlds and cross-checked the dates they'd last filed. Most hadn't reported for days, some for weeks.

"Damn!" he said. "I'm picking up more recent data from all these worlds. No reports of any prolonged power cuts or disturbances."

A sudden idea hit Graham.

"Can you do a cross-check on Graham Smith and hospital admissions."

He was amazed at how calm he sounded. He was asking to see a list of his counterparts—bodies he may once have lived in, faces he would have seen in the mirror every day.

Sixty-three matches appeared on the screen. Every one showed a Graham Smith admitted unconscious.

THIRTY-EIGHT

Howard put in a call for Gary and Annalise to come to 5G immediately.

"What's up?" said Gary as he entered the room.

Howard told him. Sixty-three Resonance projects closed and sixty-three comatose Grahams.

Graham stared at the screen. Line after line of Graham Smiths—all of them lying on a bed somewhere and who would care? Who would even know? He had no family or friends. Only Annalise.

He thought of Annalise Twelve and her daily vigil at the hospital, watching over his lifeless body. Was that what the future held for the girls? Daily trips to the coma ward as the only visitor to a man who'd barely lived.

He felt so useless. His life summed up as a name on a screen. That was all he was—a name. He wasn't a person.

A person had friends, people who'd notice if he was no longer there. Who'd grieve and reminisce and lift a glass in his memory? Who'd have more to say about him than "weird but harmless?"

He felt a hand on his arm and started at the touch.

"Are you okay?" asked Annalise, withdrawing her hand. She looked concerned.

Graham forced a smile. "I'll be fine."

Gary and Howard were deep in conversation.

"It was only seventeen yesterday," said Gary, throwing up his hands. "How can it have risen so fast?"

Graham waited for someone to say "resonance" but no one did. It was left unsaid, hovering over him like a blunt instrument. Seventeen yesterday, sixty-three today, how many tomorrow?

Annalise contacted the girls while Gary and Howard brainstormed in circles: Were they safe? Should they be more circumspect in their logs? Who was closing down the RPs and why? Was there a common denominator? What motive could anyone have? Greed, power? In a world tumbling towards anarchy? Anarchists? Were there still anarchists in the world? Anarchists who happen to have access to the Resonance project logs?

Graham let it all flow over his head. They were only words. Words chasing names. No substance.

"Quiet!" shouted Annalise. "I've talked to the girls. One of the Kevins says he makes it seventy-one projects closed down. Probably more. He says that none of the RPs access current logs from every world."

Gary and Howard nodded in agreement.

"He says the only thing they know for certain is that it's increasing. Fast."

"It's got to be an insider," said Howard, continuing his earlier argument. "Someone who benefits or thinks they can benefit from a society in upheaval."

"But no one benefits. We've been through all that!" said Gary.

"Can't you list all personnel with access to the ParaDim database for the worlds that have stopped reporting?" asked Annalise.

"Do we have such a list?" Howard asked Gary. "We might be able to cross-check all ParaDim employees but how could you tell which of them had access to the database."

"The number of staff who actually know about the parallel worlds is very small," Gary explained to Annalise. "Most employees think they're analyzing data from the AI engine."

"Or are working in the Admin or Finance divisions."

"Or manufacturing," added Gary. "ParaDim employs tens of thousands of people but only about thirty or forty know the truth."

Howard agreed. "Maybe more, maybe less on other worlds. Plus people at the periphery, people we've never heard of—consultants, assistants, IT personnel who might have put two and two together."

Annalise shook her head. "How do you keep the parallel worlds a secret when so many people know what's happening?"

Graham wondered that too. People loved to gossip. The greater the secret, the greater the compulsion to say something.

"Because working for ParaDim is infinitely better than not working for them," said Gary. "It's like going to work every day knowing that the Holy Grail is not only out there, but its location could be in the very next file you read. You don't get opportunities like that anywhere else."

"Plus the money," said Howard. "ParaDim pays double the going rate. Whatever the job."

"Okay," said Annalise, holding up her hands. "Why not cross-check all ParaDim employees and see who exists on all sixty-three worlds? Then you can haggle over which of them has access."

"Works for me," said Howard. "Is there one employee file or is it split by country?" he asked Gary.

The two men conferred and typed. Annalise joined Graham by the window.

"I won't let anything happen to you," she said. "None of us will."

Graham didn't know what to say. So many people risking their lives to protect him and for what? A possibility? A dream that maybe he was some sort of key who could unlock the secret of the resonance wave? What if he wasn't? What if all those people had died for no reason at all. Yes, there were sixty-three Graham Smiths lying in comas but what about the missing Resonance project members? The Kevins and the Howards and the Tamishas who were being hunted and tortured and killed at this very moment. Who was going to save them?

Several minutes passed. Graham watched the river flow slowly by, counted the boats and watched them fight against the tide. Annalise stood alongside, silent and supportive.

"The scan's running now," said Howard. "The hits should appear any second."

"It has to be someone with power," said Gary.

"Someone who can close a project down without anyone questioning them."

Graham and Annalise walked over to stand behind Howard. A cursor flashed hypnotically, counting down the seconds.

And then a name appeared.

Just the one.

Adam Sylvestrus.

Graham should have guessed. He would have if his mind hadn't been elsewhere.

"What about external consultants?" Gary asked Howard. "Are they included in the employee files or are they logged somewhere else?"

Howard wasn't sure. He pulled up one file after another.

"What are you doing?" asked Graham. "You've got your answer. It's Adam Sylvestrus."

Gary shook his head. "Sylvestrus is head of ParaDim on two-thirds of all worlds. You'd expect his name to be flagged."

"Sixty-eight percent of all worlds," added Howard, tapping on the keyboard. "I read it in an RP log this morning. Which," he paused and pulled down another screen, "if you bear with me for a few seconds, computes to a probability of . . ." He paused again and read the numbers off the screen. "Thirty-five billion to one." He turned to Gary. "I'd call that significant."

Gary shook his head again. "Did you find the external consultant files?"

"I'm adding them to the scan now," said Howard. He pressed "enter" and sat back.

Graham couldn't understand what was happening. How much more proof did anyone need?

A thought which ended abruptly when two names flashed on the screen.

Adam Sylvestrus and Maria Totorikaguena.

"Who's she?" asked Annalise.

"The name's familiar," said Gary, "Try . . ."

"Already doing it," interrupted Howard, clicking and tapping furiously on the keyboard.

Maria Totorikaguena's personnel file appeared on the screen. She was a theoretical physicist attached to the Resonance project.

"She's part of the RP?" said Annalise incredulously.

"Not on this world," said Howard. "I picked the first personnel record I could find."

"What does she do on the other sixty-two worlds?" asked Gary.

Howard flicked through file after file. Sometimes she was an employee of ParaDim, sometimes a consultant attached to the Resonance project.

"Pull down a bio," said Gary. "What's her area of expertise?"

Howard pulled down another screen and copied data across from the personnel file.

A profile came back. Maria Totorikaguena—25, Spanish, quiet, quirky sense of humor, child prodigy—gained her first degree at the age of twelve. The first of many. Published fourteen papers—including "The Twelve-Dimensional Universe" and "Schenck Revisited."

"I thought I recognized the name," said Gary, pointing at the first of her publishing credits. "Interesting theory but flawed. She proposed an extra dimension to solve anomalies with the eleven-dimensional model of the universe. But it wasn't necessary. One of the advanced worlds had already shown that the anomalies didn't really exist."

Howard accessed bios and personnel records from other worlds. The same picture emerged. Quiet, quirky, brilliant. Someone who liked to work by herself and avoided positions of responsibility.

"Not exactly the profile of someone who could close down sixty-three Resonance projects," said Howard.

"On how many other worlds does she work for ParaDim?" asked Annalise.

"I'll check on the other terminal," said Gary. "Howard, you check to see if she's working for us on this world."

Graham watched as the two men tapped and clicked through a series of screens and menus.

"She's not on any of the ParaDim files here," said Howard. "And . . ." he paused while he waited for a search to finish, "I can't find any record of her birth. Not in Spain. Not anywhere." He turned to Gary. "She doesn't exist on this world."

Gary didn't say a thing. He stared at the screen in front of him, slowly shaking his head.

"What's the matter?" asked Annalise, peering over his shoulder.

"How many RPs did Kevin say had closed?" he asked her.

"Seventy-one. Why?" She stopped, the last word trailing off on her lips. Graham followed her gaze towards the bottom left-hand corner of the screen and the two numbers that flashed.

Maria Totorikaguena only worked for ParaDim on sixty-five worlds.

THIRTY-NINE

There had to be some mistake. Maybe she'd joined the RPs in the last few days and her details hadn't reached the employee files. Maybe Kevin was wrong. Maybe . . .

Gary and Howard argued at speed while Graham listened, waiting for an opening that never came—by the time he'd thought of something constructive to add, someone had either said it, refuted it or the argument had moved elsewhere.

"Quiet!" shouted Annalise. "Kevin's double-checked. She doesn't even exist on six of the seventy-one worlds."

Gary shook his head. "It's too much of a coincidence. She works for ParaDim on only sixty-five worlds and on sixty-one of them the RP is closed down."

"Sixty-five," said Annalise. "Kevin checked. Every time she works for ParaDim, the RP closes."

"She must have stumbled upon something," said Gary. "Something to do with Graham and the resonance wave."

"If she did, she never wrote it down," said Howard. "I've been all over the closed Resonance logs. They're interested in Graham Smith but they never say why."

"We'll check again," said Gary. "There's another forty-six logs to look through."

They checked and sifted, the two men scrolling and searching for anything written by or mentioning Maria Totorikaguena. They found nothing. All sixty-three logs ended with a note saying they were downloading every file they could find on Graham Smith but none of them gave a reason.

"Maybe she didn't write anything down," said Annalise. "If she liked to work on her own, maybe she kept her ideas to herself."

"Until someone found out what she was doing," added Howard.

"Like Adam Sylvestrus," said Graham.

"It makes sense," said Howard, nodding in agreement. "Sylvestrus has to be involved. He must have seen something in Maria's work that forced him to take drastic action."

Graham could see how that could explain the sixty-five closures where Maria and Sylvestrus worked together, but the other six? Could the same action repeated in quick succession across sixty-five worlds resonate so powerfully that it influenced the decisions of the other Adam Sylvestruses? Was sixty-five enough? Wouldn't you need more?

"It's not Sylvestrus," said Gary, raising his voice. "If he *is* involved, it's as an unwitting agency. Maybe he told the wrong person about Maria's discovery."

"Who?" said Howard. "We've been through the ParaDim files. There's no one else."

"Then it's someone outside ParaDim," snapped Gary. He was becoming increasingly agitated. Graham couldn't understand his continued defense of Sylvestrus. Even Annalise looked surprised.

"Someone in government," continued Gary. "Or the intelligence community. Maybe they were bugging his office."

"Why do you keep defending Sylvestrus?" asked Graham. "You said yourself it had to be someone with power, someone who could close you down without questions being asked. Who better than Sylvestrus?"

Gary sighed and shook his head. "This is getting us nowhere. It can't be Sylvestrus."

"Why not?" asked Graham. "I've met him. He's creepy—the way he looks at you. And I saw him on TV during the middle of the London riots. He wasn't trying to stop weapons proliferation, he was defending it."

Gary still wouldn't have it. "Trust me, it won't be Adam Sylvestrus."

"Then explain it to us," said Annalise.

Gary activated his monitor and called up a search. He clicked through several pages until he came to the one he wanted.

"Because of this," he said.

The front page of the *New York Times* appeared on the screen. It was dated several months earlier. *Sylvestrus Assassinated.* Stark headlines besides an even starker picture. A man lay slumped on the pavement, a coat thrown over his head, a dark pool of liquid seeped out from under the coat.

"It's the same on every world," said Gary. "Within six months of the trade talks collapsing, the Americans move against ParaDim. Sylvestrus is the first to go. The Americans throw their hands up and deny everything, no one believes them, one of the Asian countries retaliates and suddenly everyone's mobilizing and pressing buttons."

"We call it 'the Chaos,'•" said Howard.

"Now you see why Sylvestrus has to be the last person who'd want the resonance wave to proceed unchecked. It brings about his death."

Graham was unconvinced. He'd met the man. The others hadn't.

"Besides," continued Gary. "He's the one who initiated the Resonance projects. Why start something you want to close down?"

"Maybe it took a path he wasn't expecting?" said Graham.

"You?" said Annalise, looking worried.

Graham didn't reply. Sylvestrus *had* been strangely interested in him that time they'd met. And why *had* they met? What was the CEO of a huge company like ParaDim doing trying to persuade lowly Graham Smith to take a medical. Why hadn't he left that to his Resonance team?

"Someone has to benefit from all this," said Gary. "There has to be a motive. Who gains from the resonance wave?"

"I'll set up a series of scans this afternoon on all the Chaos worlds," said Howard. "Off the top of my head, I'd say everyone loses. No one stays in power long enough to benefit. But we might have missed something."

❀　❀　❀

Graham and Shikha left at one-thirty. He felt strange walking through the revolving doors of the Cavendish Clinic. He half expected the receptionist to leap up and shout "Stop!" the moment he saw him. But he didn't. Everyone smiled and nodded and couldn't be more polite.

The medical took the rest of the afternoon. He was scanned from all angles, poked and prodded. But he didn't try to escape. He didn't even complain when they asked him to remove his clothes. For some reason he felt he deserved the indignity. It was his small sacrifice in the war against resonance.

And besides, Adam Sylvestrus didn't exist on this world.

FORTY

It was three o'clock. Annalise Fifteen picked up the phone and tapped in the numbers.

A male voice answered. "Tracey Minton Information Line, how can I help?"

"I called earlier," said Annalise. "I gave you three names. Have the police come back to you?"

"You're the American girl?"

"That's me. Do we have a deal?"

"I'm switching you through to Jenny Wilson. She wants to talk to you urgently."

Annalise waited, tapping her feet impatiently. Were they stalling? Trying to trace the call?

A woman's voice broke the silence. "Hi, my name's Jenny Wilson. I'm the senior reporter on the Tracey Minton story. Can we meet?"

"You got the money?"

"Possibly. The hundred grand's dependent on a conviction but I can authorize money for a story. Do you have a story?"

"How much money are you talking about?"

"Depends on the story. Do you know the gang? Did they talk about what happened?"

"What if I give you an even bigger story?"

"The bigger the better. Look, where are you now? I can send a car."

Annalise hesitated. She hadn't said anything to remotely interest ParaDim but did they voice-match calls?

"If I leave here I'm gonna need protection. Somewhere safe to stay for two people. Can you arrange that?"

"I can arrange that for tonight. Longer depends on the story."

Annalise closed her eyes. Once she gave their location away that was it. No going back.

"I'm in Brighton," she said. "When can you get here?"

The line went silent. Annalise held her breath. She could hear a muted conversation on the other end of the line.

"We can get a car to you in ten minutes. Where are you?"

Annalise glanced at the line of hotels across the road and picked the name of the nearest. "The Esplanade Hotel. We'll be waiting outside. The name's . . ." she paused, plucking a name out of her subconscious. "Phoenix," she said. "Tell the driver my name's Phoenix."

Annalise Fifteen rushed back to her hotel. She had five minutes to persuade Graham to accompany her back to London.

She needed less than one. She watched—amazed—as he gathered his playing cards together. He hadn't asked a single question. Never even raised an eyebrow.

The taxi was waiting for them outside the Esplanade Hotel.

"Phoenix?" said the driver. "Party of two for London?"

"That's right," said Annalise, smiling with relief. She called Graham over and they climbed in.

The journey dragged. Sixty miles of Graham staring out of the window and Annalise trying to convince herself that she hadn't made a terrible mistake.

She had a plan—of sorts—but it was more framework than fleshed out. She was going to light a fire and pray the wind was blowing in the right direction.

Jenny Wilson sat on her desk, legs crossed and cigarette in hand. Mid-thirties, thought Annalise, mid-thirties, too much makeup and eyes that said, "try to bullshit me and you're out the door."

Annalise glanced sideways at Graham. He was looking down at the floor—probably tracing patterns in the carpet. Jenny hadn't asked who he was. Not yet anyway. And Annalise hadn't ventured anything other than his name. Hopefully, that would be enough until she could think of something plausible.

Annalise passed a slip of paper to Jenny. She'd written everything down. The names of the gang, the fence, the guy who'd planned it all, a list of addresses they'd used in the past. Everything.

Jenny read it as she shuffled off the front of her desk and walked round to her chair. She stubbed out her cigarette, picked up the phone and waited as it rang.

"Dave, Jenny here. I have more info on the Tracey murder." She looked at Annalise. "That's right, two more names and," she paused while she checked the list, "five addresses."

She passed on the information, stopping every now and again to nod and smile and twine the phone cord around her fingers.

"I don't think she's ready to see you yet." She looked towards Annalise and raised an eyebrow. Annalise shook her head. "No, she's not ready." She laughed. "And you," she said and then replaced the receiver.

"You'll have to see them sometime. We can delay them for a while but not indefinitely. Now," she paused, "you said you had a story."

Annalise took a deep breath. "Have you heard of a company called ParaDim?"

"Of course," said Jenny, narrowing her eyes.

"You've heard about that AI engine of theirs that can take all kinds of unrelated data and put them together to solve all manner of problems?"

"Ye-es."

"Well, you can use it to solve crime as well."

"Is this a joke?" Jenny leaned forward, hands on desk.

"Ask Dave if he thinks it a joke," snapped Annalise. She could tell Jenny was on the verge of asking them to leave. "I'm giving you the biggest story you've ever had and I can give you proof."

"How?"

"Give me two unsolved crimes and I'll solve them for you. Any case you like as long as they're at least a month old."

Jenny shuffled in her chair. She looked uncomfortable.

She shook her head. "This is ridiculous," she said.

"Look at ParaDim's results. They create patents out of nothing. How come that's not ridiculous? It's all to do with analyzing data and finding patterns. Ask your science guys. ParaDim's making incredible breakthroughs every day."

"Why would they have data on crimes?"

"Because they have data on everything. You've heard of the Census project. It's packed with data about people."

"Do the police know about this?" She still sounded incredulous but at least she was listening.

"No one knows about it," said Annalise. "The police, the politicians, nobody. I kinda hacked in and stumbled across it. I couldn't believe they were keeping the information secret."

"Wait, let me get this straight. ParaDim has a mechanism for analyzing and solving crime but they're keeping it quiet?" She still sounded incredulous.

"Right."

"But why? They could generate fantastic publicity for the company. It would be a tremendous boon to society."

Annalise shook her head. "Not enough profit in it. ParaDim's only interested in the big bucks. *And*," she stressed the word, "there are certain crimes ParaDim doesn't want solved."

"Like what?"

"I'm coming to that. First you've gotta know the reason. ParaDim's researching weapons that make chemical and biological weapons look like children's toys. They call them New Tech weapons and they're gonna sell them to the highest bidder. Mass-produced mass terror. They don't care who they sell to as long as they can pay."

Jenny was silent and looking far from convinced.

Annalise had hoped the smell of a story would have been enough but she was losing her. She could tell.

"And anyone who speaks up against what's going on disappears," Annalise continued. "Three people yesterday. I was with them in May Street when all hell broke loose. People with guns everywhere. Me and Graham got away by climbing over a roof. The other three weren't so lucky. You can check it out. Kevin Alexander, Howard Sarkissian and Tamisha Kent. I'll write the names down for you."

Annalise searched for a slip of paper. Jenny handed her a note pad and Annalise scribbled the names down.

"There," she said, handing over the paper. "Check them out. They're all well-known scientists and they'll all appear as ParaDim employees but you won't be able to find them anywhere. They've disappeared."

"I won't be long." Jenny took the list and walked outside. Annalise tried to listen. The door to the main office was open but she couldn't isolate Jenny's voice from the surrounding buzz.

A minute later Jenny returned and closed the door. "I have someone checking those names right now." She paused and looked hard into Annalise's eyes. "If you're spinning me a line . . ."

She left the rest of the sentence unsaid.

"Have you any proof at all? Documents?" asked Jenny, lighting up another cigarette.

"No, that's why I was meeting Kevin yesterday. He had papers, disks, the lot. But ParaDim must have been on to him and had him followed."

Annalise prayed she wasn't going to have to repeat this story word for word later on. It was all she could do to keep her story afloat. She had to convince Jenny to open an investigation. The dirt was there. All it needed was someone to point the press in the right direction. Once that was done, Annalise could disappear.

That was the plan—discredit ParaDim, mire them in investigations before they became too powerful to stop. If she could delay the development of New Tech weapons maybe there'd be hope.

"How did you meet this," Jenny looked down and read the name from the paper, "Kevin Alexander? I can't see how you progressed from hacker to . . . to whatever you are now."

Annalise opened her mouth with no idea how the next sentence would end. If needs be, it wouldn't. She'd keep talking until she found something to say.

"His name was with the New Tech weapon files. He'd written a whole bunch of letters warning against their development. I contacted him and he introduced me to the others."

"Why? You say he's a respected scientist. Why should he put his trust in you?"

"Because he needed to trust someone and I was there. He knew what ParaDim would do to him if he went public so he was looking for a third party. Someone who could front his story to the press without his name getting back to ParaDim."

Jenny shook her head. "Why a third party? He'd have to know that reporters go to jail rather than reveal their sources—"

"Because," interrupted Annalise, "ParaDim scans all calls. They've been doing it for months. That's one of the first things he told me. They have these search algorithms scanning all communications looking for certain keywords. The technology they have is generations ahead of everything else. He couldn't risk his name being dropped in an unguarded phone call or email. That's why I used the Tracey Minton story over the phone. To get an intro to you so I could tell you in person what was really happening."

Jenny looked worried. "The information you gave me on Tracey . . ."

"Totally legit," interrupted Annalise. "Don't worry. Test me again. Like I said. Give me another two murders and I'll prove it to you."

Annalise looked Jenny in the eye—half pleading, half challenging. Jenny returned the look, her face impassive. Annalise couldn't tell which way she was going to decide.

The reporter smiled. "What have I got to lose?" she said. "I'll find you two murders."

Jenny returned with two files which she handed to Annalise. Two murder investigations that were going nowhere.

Annalise memorized the information she'd need— names, dates, addresses—then turned to Jenny and asked, "Do you have a washroom? I need to freshen up."

A minute later she closed the stall door, sat down and sent her mind in search of Annalise Six.

"Where have you been?" asked Six. *"I've been trying to contact you for ages."*

"Busy," said Fifteen. "Listen, I need you to solve another two murders for me."

"What!" She could tell that Six was upset. A telepathic shout didn't have the volume of a vocal shout but it had an intensity—an almost echoing quality as though the

receiver's head had expanded to the size of a cathedral and someone had all the organ stops pulled out.

"Have you lost your mind?" Six continued. *"We're trying to stop a resonance wave . . ."*

"So I'd heard," Fifteen projected sarcastically. "But stopping the resonance wave isn't going to help people like me. We're already on the conveyor belt."

"What conveyor belt?"

"ParaDim's conveyor belt. The four-year slide into New Tech chaos and destruction. Way I see it, stopping the resonance wave's great for all those worlds without a ParaDim but what about the rest of us? Zap the wave and the conveyor belt might slow down but it's not gonna stop. You're still gonna have people at ParaDim looking at blueprints of New Tech weapons and seeing a big fat profit. The only way to stop that is to stop ParaDim. Now, before it's too late."

"Why does everyone hate ParaDim so much? They're curing cancer!"

"Check your files, Annalise. The bad outweighs the good. In four years' time we'll all be too busy killing each other to worry about who's sick. ParaDim has to be broken up. Now."

"How? By solving murders?"

"No, by an old proverb—my enemy's enemy."

"What?"

"My enemy's enemy is my friend. Don't they teach you that on your world? Find out who hates ParaDim the most and give them something to hurt ParaDim with. Email the Pentagon, tell them about New Tech weapons and the plan to keep the Pentagon out of the loop. Feed scandals to the press. You don't need to tell anyone about parallel worlds. No one'd believe that anyway. Tell them about greed and conspiracies and things they'd understand. ParaDim gets away with murder because no one takes them seriously until it's too late. No one believes a company can grow that big that quick. They succeed by stealth and they can be beaten by publicity."

"Are you being paid to solve these murders?" Six's words came across clipped and accusatory.

"Only the first one. I need to eat and I need a change of clothes. I'm still wearing the same gasoline-soaked clothes from yesterday. And I need money to fund the attack on ParaDim. Now, are you gonna help me or not?"

"Give me the names. I'll see what I can do," Six said resignedly.

"I'm really desperate, Six. If I can't convince this reporter I'm for real then me and Graham are on the streets tonight. No money, no place to go and a city full of big black cars and guys with guns. I need names and I need them in the next thirty minutes."

"I'll fetch a pen," said Six.

Annalise Fifteen returned to find an empty office. Empty except for Graham. He looked up as she came in and promptly looked down again.

"Where's Jenny?" she asked.

Graham shrugged. She envied him his implacability. She had taken him off a bus, dragged him across the country and back, sat him in a strange woman's office and spent the last half hour making up stories in front of him. Yet, he hadn't turned a hair.

Which, looking at it another way, was utterly sad. The fact that he could put up with it—probably had put up with it all his life. *Strange things happen. Endure and they go away.* Was that his credo? She shook her head. That was no way to live.

Jenny returned. "Is there anything else you need?" she asked Annalise.

"A laptop and a phone line out. And somewhere private for an hour. The AI program takes forever to process the data."

"I'd like to watch."

Annalise shook her head. "Sorry. Trade secret. I made a promise to the guy who showed me the back door in. It's not a problem, is it?"

"No," said Jenny, looking hard at Annalise. "Not for the moment."

Jenny showed Graham and Annalise into a small room on the other side of the office. A minute later, a young man came in with a laptop and connected it to a phone socket for her. A girl dropped off a notepad and pen.

Thirty minutes went by. Graham played Solitaire. Annalise paced the room. How long would Annalise Six take? What if the murders hadn't been solved? Not anywhere. What if they were one-offs—a chance meeting between two strangers who didn't exist on any other world?

"Annalise? Fifteen, are you there?"

Annalise jumped as the words entered her head. "Yes, I'm here. Is that you, Six? Did you get it?"

She scrambled back to her chair, grabbed the pen and notepad.

"Victoria Pitt's murder's weird," said Six. *"I've found three different killers. Either she really pisses people off or it's the husband hiring different guys. I'd go with the*

husband. He was convicted on five of the worlds. I've got a list of the men and the evidence that put them away."

She gave Annalise the details. Names, addresses, witnesses.

"This is amazing," Fifteen said, as she tried to keep pace, writing the details down as fast as she could.

"The little girl was killed by a man called Stephen Landcroft. He killed two other girls—Naomi Barnes and Karen Greenhill. They're all buried in his basement." She paused. *"He kept mementoes in the attic. A real piece of work."*

"You have just saved my life," said Annalise Fifteen as she copied down the last line.

She'd filled three pages.

Time raced after that. Jenny was pleased. Warmth began to replace suspicion in her eyes. She loved the amount of detail Annalise had provided. The police loved it even more. Especially the link to Naomi Barnes. It was a connection they'd made a month earlier but hadn't made public.

It was a similar story when Jenny rang her contact on the Victoria Pitt murder. They'd suspected the husband but couldn't find a motive. Now they had their first real lead.

A succession of people filed in to meet Annalise. The editor shook her hand and told her how much the paper valued her assistance. Then came the paper's science correspondent. He'd heard of Howard Sarkissian and had met Tamisha Kent.

"Striking blonde girl," he said, looking straight into Annalise's eyes.

"Funny, she was an African-American yesterday," corrected Annalise, staring straight back until he looked away.

Others questioned her about ParaDim. They'd heard about New Tech weapons research—shield technology and side arms—innovative and profitable but hardly weapons of mass destruction.

"That's what ParaDim wants you to think," Annalise told them. "They don't want the Pentagon sniffing around. New Tech weapons make other weapons obsolete. They're cheap, easy to produce and ParaDim doesn't care who they sell them to."

As the evening wore on, Annalise felt better and better. People were listening to her. Really listening.

Then Jenny's phone rang. It was Dave. They'd recovered the jewelry in the Tracey Minton murder and the fence had confirmed Annalise's story.

"No, Dave, she's not a witness," said Jenny, turning back to her phone. "She . . . she hears things." Dave said something and Jenny laughed. "No, she's not a bloody psychic. She's a well-placed source." She looked over at Annalise and smiled. "One that you and I can't afford to lose."

She put the phone down. "How would you and Graham like to stay with me tonight? I have a spare room . . . or two," she said, glancing over at Graham.

"That'll be great. Two rooms'll be fine."

"I'll send out for food. My kitchen's more ornament than workplace." She laughed as she tossed her cigarettes and lighter into her bag and pulled out her car keys. "It'll be nice to have company for a change."

They left. Jenny pulled her coat on as they walked through the vast open plan office. Graham followed a few paces behind. Jenny leaned in towards Annalise.

"What's his story?" she whispered, nodding back towards Graham. "Where does he fit in?"

"He's someone who needs to hide even more than me."

FORTY-ONE

Graham sat in the foyer of the Cavendish Clinic. Shikha was upstairs processing results and Annalise was on her way to fetch him. In the meantime, he'd found a comfortable leather chair and was drifting inexorably towards sleep.

The door spun furiously and Annalise tumbled through.

"Sorry I'm late," she said as she saw Graham. "Something came up."

Graham could guess what. Something to do with Gary. He stretched and changed the subject.

"Did Howard find anything in his search through the Chaos?"

"Not a thing," said Annalise, flinging herself down into the chair next to Graham. "Everyone loses. It's like someone sticks a giant hand in the pot and stirs everything up.

People rise to the top, last a few months, then sink without trace."

"No one benefits at all?"

"A few people on the sidelines, maybe. But it's different guys on each world and Howard can't find any link between them and ParaDim."

"So it has to be Sylvestrus."

"Not according to Gary," she said, raising her eyebrows.

Graham's heart leapt. Was she disparaging Gary? Was there a rift? Was there . . .

He looked away. What was the matter with him? He was being ridiculous. Lives were in danger and all he could think about was Annalise and Gary.

"And the guy really does die. Howard thought . . ." She paused. "Graham? You okay?"

"What?" He turned. "I'm a bit tired that's all. Who did you say died?"

"Sylvestrus. Howard thought he might have switched bodies somehow but he didn't. The guy shot dead in the street was definitely Adam Sylvestrus."

"What about the Spanish girl? Has anyone found out any more about her?"

"Not much. Gary and Howard are sifting through every word she's ever written. Every article and dissertation from every world. Just in case there's something there."

She smiled and, suddenly, his breath was taken away. The tilt of her head, the smile, the sparkle in her eyes. It could have been Annalise Fifteen—different hair, different background—but the expression was the same. The same look she'd given him yesterday on the roof, the moment before she'd dropped behind the ridge.

"Are you sure you're okay? You look like you've seen a ghost," said Annalise.

He had. And he'd keep on seeing ghosts. Was that what hurt the most about Six and Gary? Was he projecting his feelings for Fifteen upon her? Was it Fifteen's hand he saw on Gary's arm? Or was he attracted to all the girls? Would his life be forever miserable until every Annalise had joined a convent?

He forced a yawn. "I'm just tired," he said. "I didn't sleep too well last night." He let the sentence trail off and looked down at his hands. He had to get away. Proximity was making things worse. The way she looked at him, her voice. She only had to smile and he could feel his IQ plummet. If he didn't say something stupid, he was going to do something stupid. It was only a matter of time.

"Have you decided where you're staying tonight?" asked Annalise. "Gary says you can stay at the Putney office if you want. There'll be a night shift there and they have beds."

Graham shook his head. Spending a night at a ParaDim office was never an option.

"What about a hotel?" She dipped into her bag and produced a wad of notes. "Gary gave me this for you. There'll be rooms at the hotel I'm staying at."

He shook his head. Being in the same hotel as Annalise was not an option either. Not the way he felt. He'd be convinced any voice or footstep he heard was Gary's. Best to stay away from her, push her out of his mind, go home, take out a jigsaw.

"I think I'll go home," he said, placing his hands on the armrest and pushing himself unsteadily to his feet.

"Do you want to eat first?"

"No," he said, stretching his arms. The thought of sitting opposite Annalise for an hour, tying himself in knots trying to read her feelings towards him from every nuance of her voice or tilt of her head . . .

He shook his head. He'd eat at home. His Thursday meal. Macaroni and cheese, sausages and baked beans. He could almost taste it. His mouth watered at the thought.

"Are you sure you'll be okay on your own?"

He was. Now. Now he could see a way out of the constant emotional turmoil. He'd ground himself in ritual. Forget about futures he could never have and embrace the discipline of the past. Familiar surroundings, old routines. Something to fill up his day and take his mind away from the exotic and the unattainable.

He looked around for something to count.

Annalise refused to let him go home alone. She'd see him to his door and make sure everything was okay. Graham acquiesced and spent a nervous ten minutes walking to the tube station. However much he tried to blot her out, he could feel her presence alongside him. It was like walking next to an emotional furnace.

It was worse on the tube. He could feel the warmth of her body, the two of them pressed close in the crush of a packed carriage, their bodies swaying and bumping together as the train rocked and rattled through the tunnels.

Harrow Station couldn't come soon enough.

As he stepped onto the platform, her hand settled on his shoulder.

"Graham," she said, "there's something I've got to ask you."

He closed his eyes and swallowed. She sounded serious, embarrassed even. This was not a conversation he wanted to have.

"You've spent time with Annalise Fifteen," she said as they walked slowly along the platform. "Is she . . . is she liable to do anything stupid?"

Graham stopped dead. "Has something happened to Fifteen?"

She told him everything. How Fifteen had hijacked a car at gunpoint, her plan to bring down ParaDim, her involvement with the press, her use of ParaDim data to solve crime, the reward money. Graham listened, no longer caring about Six's proximity.

"So, what do you think?" she asked. "Has she lost it?"

He shook his head. Annalise Fifteen hadn't lost anything. That was *her*. She did what she had to do and used what she had at hand. He could feel his eyes filling up. He'd only been away a day and already she was taking the fight to ParaDim.

"She hasn't lost a thing," he told her. "Whatever Gary or Howard says, ParaDim has got to be destroyed. On this world and every world." His voice quivered. "And if anyone can find a way, it's Fifteen."

He said goodbye to Annalise at the front step, closed the door and slumped back against it. He was home. The world of ParaDim, resonance and the unattainable was on the other side of the door.

He clothed himself in routine; his Thursday meal, his after-dinner vacuum, a game of cards. He didn't even feel tired any more. Ritual had given him a second wind.

He could even put his feelings towards Annalise in

perspective. It was obvious now. He'd misinterpreted excitement as love. Annalise Fifteen was an exciting person to be around. They'd been thrown together, chased, threatened, shot at. No one could have gone through that without feeling something for the other person involved. But love?

What did he know about love? He'd been dazzled by the attentions of a beautiful, young girl, that's all. He'd allowed himself to believe that maybe—just maybe—he was the same as other people. When all along he was just plain Graham Smith, weird but harmless, and hopelessly out of his depth.

He went to bed happy, secure in his own unimportance. He'd take a back seat from now on. Gary and Howard could work far quicker without having to look after him all the time. He only got in people's way.

Graham's happiness lasted until nine o'clock the next morning when Ray arrived with the early morning van.

Graham felt like banging his head on the desk. He should have checked the roster! He'd assumed Ray was on midmorning delivery.

"Hiya, Sharmy," said Ray. Graham had his back to him but he could still see Ray sauntering through the delivery bay door. He didn't need eyes—it was an image etched into memory. The swagger, the darting eyes, the hands-in-pocket naughty schoolboy charm.

And the nasty schoolboy humor.

"On a flying visit are you, Graham?" Ray said in the loud voice he reserved for long-distance repartee. "The doctors found your brain, did they?"

Ray laughed, Sharmila tried to shush him and Graham

hunched deeper over his desk. He could have been fifteen again. He could have been any age from his childhood—any age, any playground. The same taunts, the same baiting, the same juvenile humiliation.

Why did he put up with it? He was thirty-three! He wasn't a kid any more.

"Ray, don't," hissed Sharmila.

Graham heard footsteps behind him and braced himself.

"Don't what? Me and Graham are old mates, ain't we, Graham?"

Ray ruffled Graham's hair—hard. Graham's head shook under the pressure. He could feel Ray's nails digging into his scalp. He could imagine the smug, mocking look on his face.

The ruffling stopped. Ray rapped on Graham's head twice. "Anyone home?"

"Ray!" snapped Sharmila. "Come and move these boxes!"

"Anything for you, princess," said Ray, turning away.

Graham closed his eyes and let out a deep breath. He'd wait ten seconds then leave. He glanced towards the door and immediately stopped counting. Annalise stood in the doorway. She looked stunned. Graham looked down and turned away.

She was waiting for him outside. The moment Graham emerged from the Post Room, Annalise grabbed his arm and pulled him along the back corridor. She didn't say a word. Neither did Graham.

When they reached the back stairs, she turned on him.

"Why did you let him get away with that shit?" She was angry. Her hands clawed at the air.

Graham shrugged. "It's what you do," he said in a quiet voice.

"It's what you do?" She sounded incredulous.

"I've met hundreds of Rays," he said. "If you react, it makes it worse. If you ignore them, they go away."

"Has *this* Ray gone away?"

"No," he said quietly, looking down at his feet.

"Doesn't that tell you something?"

Graham shrugged and fingered the stair handrail.

"I'll sort him out," she said, turning towards the door. Graham reached out, caught her arm and swung her back.

"It'll only make things worse."

"How?" she said, jerking her arm free.

"He might be dangerous. He . . . I think . . ." The words wouldn't come.

"You think what?"

Graham took a deep breath. "I think he might have attacked some little girls on another world."

Annalise was shocked. "He's a pedophile?"

"I don't know. I heard rumors that he attacked a girl in his van. Someone said there were others. The police were involved but I never heard any more about it. It might have been a mistake."

"I'll find out. What's his full name?"

The first-floor door swished open and a man hurried down the stairs. Graham waited for him to pass. The man smiled at Annalise before pushing through the door onto the ground floor.

"What are you going to do with the information?" asked Graham. "He might be innocent in this world."

"And he might have an attic full of trophies. Relax, I'm

not going to call the cops. I just want his name."

"Ray Benskin," he said reluctantly.

Annalise left immediately afterwards.

Graham pushed the incident behind him, filling his head with tasks and the revised staff list. He was not going to get involved. With involvement came pain. He'd get on with his job and she could do whatever she wanted.

A ploy that lasted until lunchtime. He walked to Green Park and found himself looking for her everywhere—on the grass, on the benches, walking towards him. He was torn. A safe half wanting to be left alone and another half—a half he didn't even know he had—craving the excitement, the uncertainty that followed in her wake.

He returned to work, disappointed and guilty. Disappointed that he hadn't seen her and guilty about practically everything. Guilty that he'd looked for her when he'd made up his mind not to. Guilty that he hadn't asked her about Gary and Howard. Guilty that another sixty Resonance projects had probably closed. Guilty, guilty, guilty.

He grabbed the mail trolley and swung it through a wild 180 degrees towards the Post Room door. Ray's van was due at two and in his current mood he didn't trust himself being in the same room as Ray.

He'd calmed down by the time he reached the fifth floor. He stopped outside 502 and stood back to allow a woman through—Phoebe from the Nigerian desk. Stephen Leyland came running out, barging past and nearly knocking her over.

"Stephen!" Phoebe said angrily.

The man didn't respond. He ran for the lift, his coat half pulled over one shoulder, a briefcase slapping against his thigh. He punched the lift button—three, four times—swore and then ran for the stairs.

Graham watched, stunned. Stephen Leyland was one of the most polite people he knew.

"What's got into Stephen?" said Phoebe from inside 502.

"Janie just called," answered a woman's voice. "They've found Jason."

"No!" said Phoebe. "Is he?" She left the question hanging and Graham suddenly remembered—Stephen's son, Jason, the boy who'd gone missing.

"No, he's alive, thank God. It sounds like he's been staying at some hostel in Camberwell. Stephen's running over there now."

"That *is* good news."

Graham agreed, nodding to himself as he emptied Stephen's out-tray. He remembered how cut up Stephen had been when he'd seen him last. The day that Adam Sylvestrus had first appeared in Graham's life.

"Graham?" said a familiar voice. He turned and saw Annalise pulling Frank's door closed.

"Sharmila wants you in the Post Room," she said. "Something about the two o'clock van breaking down. Ray's stuck in traffic." She paused and smiled. "I'm sure it couldn't happen to a nicer person."

Graham looked down at his feet and shuffled nervously. Annalise swung the mail trolley around for him. "I'll come with you," she said. "I need to talk to Sharmila. It seems dragging you away has been disrupting her routines."

Two other people were waiting for the lift. Graham and Annalise settled in behind them. Time dragged. Annalise asked about his lunch, which park he went to on Fridays, the weather.

Graham nodded and shrugged and prayed for the lift to arrive. He couldn't talk. Not here.

He followed Annalise out of the lift and into the Post Room.

"Hi," said Annalise, holding out her hand as soon as she walked through the door. "You must be Sharmila. I'm Tamisha, Tamisha Kent, from the ParaDim Census Project."

Graham waited to hear Sharmila's answering greeting. But heard something else instead.

A wolf whistle.

"Ray!" admonished Sharmila. "You'll have to forgive him, Miss Kent. He's never grown up."

Graham shrank behind the mail trolley. He had a bad feeling about this.

"Was that for me?" Annalise asked Ray. She sounded both surprised and amused.

Ray adjusted his shoulders and sauntered over, half smiling, half leering.

Annalise laughed. "Sorry," she said, placing her hand on his arm. "I thought you were the pedophile."

Graham wasn't sure whose face drained the quickest— his or Ray's. Only Annalise appeared unaffected, looking from Sharmila to Ray, her face a picture of confused innocence.

"You know . . . the other Ray?" she said. "What's his name? Benskin? The van driver?"

Ray looked terrified. Sharmila's eyes extended on stalks and Graham hoped the floor would open up. This was not going to help. This was going to make things twenty times worse.

Annalise clasped her hand to her mouth in feigned embarrassment.

"Me and my big mouth," she said. "You're him, aren't you!" She looked him up and down. "I should have realized." She turned to Sharmila. "Does he flirt as much as the files say he does?"

Sharmila nodded.

"Overcompensation," said Annalise. "Due to his many inadequacies. He can't handle a real woman so he picks on thirteen- and fourteen-year-olds. Easier to control."

Ray stabbed an angry finger in her direction. His mouth moved like a fish. He wanted to say something but nothing came out.

"That's my specialty on the Census Project," Annalise told Sharmila. "Trying to map degenerate tendencies to specific genes. But where do you start with something like that?" She waved a dismissive hand in Ray's direction.

"You lying bitch!" shouted Ray, his face coloring.

"Ray," Annalise said, turning towards him, a hint of admonition in her tone. "No one here appreciates the b-word. I know you have mental problems but . . ."

"I don't have mental problems!" Ray's face completed its transition from white to red.

Annalise smiled sadly towards Sharmila and shook her head. "Classic symptoms of pedophiliac denial. Red face, small penis—telltale signs."

Graham had to turn away. He didn't know how she could keep a straight face. Behind him he heard Annalise's voice. "He has got very small feet, hasn't he?"

Graham left the room. He had so many contradictory feelings. He marvelled at Annalise's ability to find the right words. He was grateful, he knew she meant well but . . .

He was angry at her too. How could she! Humiliate the bully and the bully came back looking for someone to humiliate even worse. Playground rules. The boy at the bottom of the chain suffers for all.

Didn't Annalise know that?

And then he felt guilty. Guilty for being angry at someone who only wanted to help.

But she'd tricked him! She could walk away from Ray tomorrow but he'd have to live with the consequences for years. Years and years of spiteful revenge.

The delivery bay door slammed shut; Graham heard it from his hiding place halfway down the corridor. Ray had obviously given up and run.

Annalise must have stayed and chatted with Sharmila. He could pick out their voices but not the words. It seemed friendly enough.

Annalise emerged two minutes later.

"What happened to you?" she said as she saw Graham.

"You've made things worse," he said dejectedly.

Annalise was taken aback. "How?"

"He'll come looking for me."

"Graham," she said, hands on hips. "You can hurt him far more than he can hurt you. Remember that. He picks on you because he can. Give him a reason to stop and he will."

Graham looked down at his feet. Annalise did *not* understand bullies.

She touched his arm. "Graham," she said softly. "Do you know what people here think of you?"

He could guess.

"They," she hesitated, "they think you're either deaf, retarded or both."

Graham looked up, hurt. "You think I don't know that? I . . ."

Two women turned into the corridor from the lobby. Graham stopped speaking immediately and lowered his head until they'd passed.

"I'm worried about you, Graham," said Annalise after the two women had moved out of earshot. "Away from this place you're the real Graham. You talk, you hold your head up, you do stuff. But here"—she shook her head—"here, you drop back into the old Graham. You don't say a word, you look at the floor, you let everyone walk right over you. It's not healthy. You're not that Graham any more. He's gone. But as long as you keep coming back here, so does he. You've either got to leave this place for good or find a way of introducing everyone to the new Graham."

He shrugged. He knew what she was saying but . . .

"Don't think I don't know how hard it is," she continued. "I was the oddball at school. I know what it's like to be shunned and laughed at. And I know what I'd be like if I went to a school reunion. I'd regress. I'd become her again—the self-conscious little girl that everyone laughed at. But then I'd tell myself I'm not that girl any more. I've changed and so have you. We matter in this world. More than anyone else in this building. Maybe more than anyone else in this world . . ."

Annalise let go of his arm and jumped back.

"What's the matter?" Graham said.

She didn't say a word. Her eyes were unfocused, her breathing slowed.

"Is it Fifteen?" he asked, realizing as soon as he'd said it that she probably wasn't listening, her mind focused elsewhere.

Her face lit up, a broad smile—a flash of teeth. Her legs flexed, almost a bounce. She clapped her hands.

Graham could hardly breathe, the anticipation was stifling. What was the message? Who was it from?

Annalise exploded into life. "It's Annalise One," she said. "Something's happened. Something amazing."

FORTY-TWO

Annalise Six scrambled through her bag for her phone. "Gary, it's me," she said. "This is urgent. Tune to 001 574 121 357 immediately. Express it. Do whatever it is you've got to do to it. But read it. Kevin says it's incredible. He thinks it's the breakthrough we've all been waiting for."

Graham held his breath and tried to hear Gary's reply.

"He didn't say," Annalise continued. "Annalise One says he's barely coherent at the moment."

She repeated the numbers and folded the phone away. "Come on, Graham. We're off to Putney."

Graham was little wiser by the time they arrived at the ParaDim office. Annalise One had conveyed Kevin's message as soon as he'd stumbled on the download from 001

403

574 121 357. What the download contained she didn't know. Repeated attempts to get back to Annalise One had been met with a rushed "Not now, later."

They found everyone clustered around the far terminal in Room G—the black sphere room. Howard had the chair while Gary and Shikha hovered over his left and right shoulders respectively. Only Shikha glanced towards the opening door. She smiled and beckoned them over.

"It's starting to come through," she said.

"What kind of world is it?" asked Gary, his hand drifting towards the keyboard.

Howard batted it away. "I've got to enable it first," he said curtly. Graham smiled; they looked like two children fighting over a new toy.

"It's one of the white noise worlds," said Howard.

"That's impossible," said Gary. He turned to Annalise. "Are you sure Kevin said they were receiving a message?"

"That's what Annalise One told me."

They rechecked the coordinates. All twelve digits were correct.

"Is anything coming out?" asked Annalise, peering over Shikha's shoulder.

"Too early to say," said Gary. "There's a delay before anything comes through on the terminal."

No one spoke for thirty seconds. Ten eyes fixed on the screen. A cursor blinked.

Then the screen filled. Words and numbers scrolled past too fast to be read. Howard hit a button. The screen froze and everyone at the back leaned forward.

"What language is that?" asked Shikha.

Graham wasn't sure it was a language. Numbers and words were intermingled with symbols and foreign-looking letters—Greek, Russian, something like that. But there was an order to it. It wasn't random. And some of the words were repeated further down the screen.

"It's stopped," said Gary, glancing at the small window at the top right of the screen. "That's all there was. A few seconds' data and now it's moved on to the next world."

"I've seen this language before," said Howard, his eyes fixed on the text in front of him. "One of the advanced worlds. Maybe not the same, but similar. We might be able to run a translation."

"What's that there?" said Gary, pointing at the bottom right of the screen. "Those symbols. I've seen that combination recently. It's part of an equation. It's . . ." He fought to remember. "It's something to do with Schenck. Can you scroll to the next page?"

Howard flipped to the next page.

Embedded in the text were two words that everyone understood. Two words that appeared again and again.

Graham Smith.

Everything moved into overdrive after that. Howard and Gary moved from terminal to terminal, pulling down lists, conducting searches, running programs. They had to find a match for the language. Was there more than one language? What other files had been downloaded from that world? Were the symbols mathematical inserts, format characters or part of the language's alphabet?

And why had they suddenly been able to extract data from a world that a week ago had presented nothing but white noise?

The two men barely talked and when they did the content flew over Graham's head. He stood back, out of the way, and watched alongside Annalise and Shikha.

"This is outside my area of expertise," Shikha told them. She leaned closer to the screen on the left for a few seconds before shaking her head. "I keep thinking I see gene sequences but they're not."

Annalise asked her about Graham's tests. "Did they show anything?"

"Unfortunately not," she said, still watching the screen as Gary flipped from sample to sample. "There were no measurable changes compared to the previous tests." She paused and looked at Annalise. "I would like to run some tests on you though. If that would be acceptable? Maybe next week?"

"Why me?" asked Annalise.

"The telepathy experiment. I'd love to see a map of your brain activity during a telepathic episode. If that's all right with you, of course."

"Sure."

"Got it!" shouted Howard. "Not an exact match but close."

Everyone crowded around his terminal. The screen was divided into two halves of similar-looking text.

"The one on the left's today's sample, the one on the right is Etxamendi."

"Is there a translator?" asked Gary.

Howard grimaced. "Of sorts," he said. "Etxamendi's a difficult language to translate." He pulled down another screen and flipped through a series of pages before finding the one he wanted.

"This'll take awhile," he said. "Many of the words are untranslatable and others are approximations. It might not make much sense."

A translation progress bar appeared at the top left of the screen.

Graham felt the anticipation as everyone waited? What

was it going to say? Was it going to be the breakthrough that Kevin had said it was? And why hadn't Annalise One been back in contact?

The progress bar barely moved. It had been stuck on six percent for nearly a minute.

Howard filled in the silence. "It must be one of the very advanced worlds. Etxamendi's only found in civilizations that survived the post-glacial flood. The nearest we have to it is Euskara—the Basque language."

The progress bar ticked to seven percent. Howard checked his watch.

"Anyone want a coffee?" asked Shikha. "I think we're going to be here some time."

They weren't. When Shikha returned with the drinks, the process had finished.

Howard pulled up the translated file and displayed the first page.

It was a strange mix of English, untranslated Etxamendi and embedded mathematical formulae. Even the passages in English were hard to understand. The sentences were long and technical and the verbs were in unexpected places. It read like a scientific treatise by an author with no gift for communication.

But there was one passage that everyone understood. The title.

The Conjunction of the Worlds.

Gary and Howard picked their way through it, guessing the meanings of the untranslated passages, shouting them out to each other in their excitement, refining those guesses as they understood more. It was astounding. And unexpected.

According to the file, there had been a conjunction of the worlds. For a few hours in one tiny corner of North London, all the dimensions had touched.

"See this section here?" said Gary, pointing to the screen. "This is a modified proof of Schenck's Law. If you use this in conjunction—no pun intended—with the text above, it starts to make sense."

Not for Graham, it didn't. He was still waiting to hear what happened to the tiny corner of North London.

"I don't see it," said Howard.

"Here," said Gary, pulling out an envelope and writing on it. "If you replace that expression with this one, change all the alphas to that wiggly character there and let the dimensional constants cancel each other out."

"My God!" said Howard.

"Anyone care to translate for the stupid kids at the back?" asked Annalise.

"Not yet," said Gary. "This needs more work. The mathematics and the text are bound together inextricably. Anything I say now could be disproved totally five minutes later."

"How long will it take to find an answer?" asked Annalise.

Gary and Howard exchanged looks. "Ten? Twenty minutes?" suggested Gary.

"Any more than fifteen and I start screaming," said Annalise.

"Okay," said Gary, fifteen minutes later. "We have most of it but some of the proofs don't make sense."

"Yet," added Howard.

Graham didn't care if none of the proofs made sense.

He wanted to know what the file said.

"Imagine that all the parallel worlds," said Gary, "for some reason as yet undefined, begin to move closer together. According to this paper, that happened in 1966."

"The year Graham was born," said Annalise.

"Exactly," said Gary. "As the worlds moved closer they began to exert an increased influence over each other— not widespread, but localized, very localized, touching down in North London."

"Like a tornado," added Howard. "But without the destruction."

"And much more focused," said Gary. "It's difficult to make out from the text but it appears to say that as the worlds moved closer, an attraction developed and a bridge was formed."

"What kind of a bridge?" asked Annalise.

"We're not sure. The word could mean 'bridge' or 'field' or just about anything else implying a connection of some sort. But what we do know," Gary paused as he turned to look at Graham, "was that Graham's father was touched by that bridge."

Everyone turned to look at Graham. Which made him annoyed as well as impatient. What did they expect to see—a look of recognition? Oh, that bridge! I remember my dad telling me about it?

Gary continued. "We're not sure if it was the person closest to the phenomenon or the person most susceptible, or maybe when the first two worlds touched, Graham's father was standing in the exact same spot as his counterpart on that other world."

"The text is unclear on that point," said Howard. "It may be that the presence of two or more counterparts at the exact same location drew the phenomenon to that point rather than, say, two or three miles further away."

"Exactly," said Gary. "And once the link was made it spread out into the other worlds, finding all his other selves. Where it couldn't find his other self, it followed his genetic path to a brother, a sister, a father, a mother. Spreading out until all the worlds were joined and, suddenly, for a few hours, all the worlds were one."

"Why would it choose a genetic path?" asked Shikha.

Gary shrugged. "There appears to be a proof associated with the text but . . ."

"It's not one we've encountered before," finished Howard. "The genetic link makes sense because of what happens later. Perhaps it was characteristic of the type of connection?"

"Anyway," said Gary. "At this point of connection, it was as though all the worlds were overlaid, one on top of another." He used his hands to illustrate the point, bringing them together slowly. "And a massive resonance developed for Graham's father. An idea on one world would bleed through to the next. It would have been overpowering. He would have felt driven as his head filled with ideas, desires and feelings. All the thoughts of his other selves, all the people he was linked to across billions of Earths would percolate through his mind. Some would be drowned out while others would resonate and build until they became imperatives."

"And they all ended up having sex?" said Annalise, raising her eyebrows.

"It's a strong emotion," said Gary. "Perhaps the strongest."

"And one of the commonest," added Howard.

"Exactly," said Gary. "And what happened on one world, happened on all. A child was conceived—Graham—a child that belonged not to one world but to all worlds, genetically fused with the DNA of all his parents across all the worlds. A hybrid with over five hundred fathers and almost five thousand mothers."

"Why ten times as many mothers?" asked Annalise.

"That's why we think the link followed the father's line," said Howard. "His fathers averaged ten different wives. If it had followed the mother's line, most likely we'd never have noticed. Graham would have had different surnames. It's sheer fluke the link formed around a male and not a female."

"Then the worlds separated," said Gary. "But the resonance lingered, there was a link—the unborn Graham—between the worlds. Hence his name. I expect many names were put forward over those next nine months, but gradually one name became dominant, and the more dominant it became the greater the resonance until no other name could have been chosen.

"Each couple would think they'd come upon the name by accident. A name that suddenly entered their head and wouldn't go away."

"And look where Graham was born," said Howard. "Always in North London. Even when his parents lived elsewhere, they appear to have been drawn to Harrow and Stanmore and Pinner. It's a resonance of place and genetics. Maybe, as we think, they were drawn there because that's where the bridge first developed or, maybe, the resonance created by all those unborn Grahams was too powerful for them to resist."

"And that resonance is still strong today," said Gary,

pointing at Graham. "Not for Graham's family, but for himself. Notice how he chooses the same career path and he still lives in North London."

Graham felt uncomfortable—being pointed at, being talked about, having his conception talked about. It made his parents sound like rutting animals.

"Does any of this tell us how to stop the resonance wave?" asked Annalise.

Howard and Gary looked at each other.

"We're closer than we were before," said Gary, a little too noncommittal for Graham's liking.

"And there's so much else in that file," said Howard. "There are equations that, once we understand them, are certain to revolutionize our resonance wave models."

Gary nodded. "We've barely scratched the surface. And I can't believe a world would go to the trouble of giving us a file we can download, if it doesn't contain the answer we're looking for."

FORTY-THREE

Gary and Shikha phoned the other Resonance project members and brought them up to speed. They needed to bring in a linguist, they all agreed on that. Tamisha said she'd arrange it. ParaDim had several linguists who'd worked on Etxamendi.

Howard pulled together all the formulae on resonance he could find, hoping that one of them might provide an insight—a stepping stone—to the thinking behind the Etxamendi formulae.

And paused.

There was something familiar about one of the Etxamendi equations. He couldn't put his finger on it. It might even be an error introduced by the translation program. But . . .

He looked harder at the screen, turning his head to

the left and right. There was something about the pattern of letters in the right-hand expression. A familiarity of form, something he'd seen quite recently, different symbols but . . .

Maria Totorikaguena!

He searched for her files, dragged them onto the screen, flipped through them—articles, theses, dissertations—there it was! He split the screen in two. The Etxamendi file above, Maria's model for a twelve-dimensional universe below. There *was* a similarity. Not an exact match, the Etxamendi equation had extra components, but once you substituted the Etxamendi symbols for Maria's . . .

It couldn't be coincidence.

He must have called out. Annalise appeared at his shoulder asking him what was the matter.

He told her.

And then he phoned Gary.

Graham stood in the background, trying to feel as excited as everyone else but lacking the conviction. He barely understood half of what Howard had said even after Annalise had asked him to slow down and explain.

And now even she was busy, tapping away at a keyboard, running searches and programs.

"Graham," said Annalise, swivelling round in her chair, "you'd better take a look at this."

Graham pushed away from the wall. He could tell by her tone that it wasn't going to be good news.

"I've just run the Resonance project closure program," she said, glancing up at him.

The number had grown to 172.

Graham shrugged and wished he could feel more. But he couldn't. It was as if everything was happening to someone else. Ever since he'd heard his life explained and dissected, he'd felt numb. He wasn't sure if he was even human.

He noticed Annalise watching him out of the corner of his eye. Even that didn't affect him. He'd become immune to all feeling.

She turned away. "Howard?" she called. "How can you tell if Adam Sylvestrus is linked to all these worlds?"

"What?" said Howard distractedly from the other side of the room.

"I've run the closure program. There's 172 now. How can I see if Sylvestrus is linked to ParaDim on all these worlds?"

"I'll come over."

He leaned over Annalise's shoulder and flipped through a series of submenus. "Run that," he said, highlighting a file.

She did. Adam Sylvestrus's name flashed onto the screen. He worked for ParaDim on all 172 worlds where the Resonance projects had been closed.

"I'll tell Gary," said Howard. "Even he can't argue with the math this time."

The afternoon passed by in a blur. Everyone was busy except Graham who alternated between sitting and watching and standing and watching. He had nothing to contribute. Except his peculiarity. And even that couldn't be measured—at least not by any instrument that Shikha had at hand. He was unique and, at the same time, the commonest man in the universe.

Something that frightened and bewildered him. What was he? One man fragmented over two hundred billion worlds or two hundred billion men trapped inside a single life—a life bound together by fields of resonance. A life so constricted it was barely worth living.

He dwelt on that question for a long time. Picking at it until it hurt. Why him? Why not someone else? Why did all the worlds have to come together in the first place? Was he the victim of a resonance wave or the key to its destruction? Was he solution or distraction?

He raged at his plight and he raged at himself. And then he raged at his rage. What was the matter with him? One minute he was numb, the next he was raving. Where had all this anger and self-pity come from? It was so unlike him. Was he caught up in a surge of resonance from billions of slowly awakening Grahams? Or was it something else? Was he overdosing on thirty-three years of repressed emotions, learning for the first time what it was like to be a real person, a person who could be hurt and angry and feel things?

Like guilt.

That was the other thing. He was consumed with guilt. Guilt that he was alive and safe while 172 other Grahams were lying unconscious in hospital beds. Guilt that he was a fraud. That all the attention was unwarranted. He wasn't a key. He was an anomaly. A distraction that had cost countless lives and hours. Guilt that he was so useless. That all he could do was stand and watch while others worked so hard. Guilt about the way he'd treated his mother—his other mother. The poor woman who was as much a parent as the one of his memories, but whom he'd treated as a stranger. Worse, he'd treated her with contempt.

He even felt guilty about Ray. Guilty that a part of him had enjoyed his humiliation. A darker side of himself that he'd never seen and didn't like. The old Graham wasn't like that. The old Graham didn't have strong feelings about anything. He ignored, endured, looked the other way.

Was he losing the old Graham? Was he losing the tolerance and the patience and the stability? He wasn't sure. He wasn't sure about anything.

As afternoon turned into evening, Annalise found Graham and took him up to the lounge area on the sixth floor—a room devoid of terminals, black spheres and anything work-related.

Howard was already there, holding his glasses in one hand while he rubbed his eyes with the other. He looked tired.

"What happens after the resonance wave collapses?" Annalise asked him as she poured herself a drink.

A question that had haunted her ever since Annalise Fifteen had first raised it.

"How do you mean?" asked Howard, pushing his glasses back over his nose.

"I mean . . . does everything go back to normal? We stop the resonance wave and everyone lives happily ever after."

"I wouldn't go that far," said Howard, smiling. "There's always work to do."

"I know that but," she paused, "I can see how it works for the pre-ParaDim worlds. They're left to develop normally. But what about the ParaDim worlds? Haven't the seeds of chaos already been sown."

Howard shook his head. "Remove the impetus of resonance and all worlds will have the chance of developing normally. Humans are a highly adaptive species. We can adapt to change."

Annalise sank down in the sofa opposite Howard. "But what about the pace of change and weapons proliferation and the greed?"

"There'll always be problems. On some worlds they might be insurmountable. But what else can we do?"

"Disband ParaDim?" suggested Annalise. "Break up all those black spheres and let worlds evolve at their own pace."

Howard looked horrified. He sat up. "Destroy knowledge? Would you burn books? Would you deny hope to the sick and suffering? We're on the verge of eliminating disease; of finding cheap, clean, renewable energy; of finding solutions to our deepest problems. Would you throw away all that?"

Annalise looked away, uncertain. "What if the price was too high? What if you couldn't have the cures without the weapons? What if you cured the sick only to have them wiped out in a war or a genetically engineered plague?"

Howard waved a large weathered hand in a dismissive gesture. "We could talk about this for days. It all depends on whether you're an optimist or a pessimist, whether you think people are inherently good or evil."

Was she a pessimist? Two days ago, she'd have classified herself as an optimist. ParaDim was good. They were curing cancer. Now she wasn't so sure. She'd spent most of the afternoon reading the Chaos files, scrolling through the historical accounts of thousands of worlds. All of them following the same slow path to hell. Knowledge proliferation, trickle-down technology, weapons for all. The ability to construct weapons of mass destruction made available to the zealots, the bigots, the maniacs, the vindictive and the power-hungry—people with little idea of responsibility and an overriding belief in their own destiny. It was like showering sparks over a tinder-dry forest.

"Don't forget," continued Howard, "stopping the resonance wave will allow other voices to be heard and other paths to be taken. We can't save everyone. No one can. All we can hope for is to save those we can and pray for those we can't."

Graham listened from the back of the room, his little voice telling him to stay out of the conversation, that nothing good ever came from arguing, while all the time he felt like railing against ParaDim, injustice and the human race. Why was it that every good idea had to be corrupted? Why couldn't everyone be saved? Why couldn't all weapons be decommissioned? Why couldn't people live together?

He gripped his wrist. Left over right. Took a deep breath.

And spoke. As calm as he could manage. "What about Lucius Xiang and the original ParaDim project?"

Howard looked surprised. "You know about Lucius Xiang?"

"Graham knows a lot more than people think," said Annalise, smiling in Graham's direction.

"Did they ever find what they were looking for?" said Graham, swallowing hard. He was talking too fast, his heart racing, he felt every word so strongly. "Did they find a world where they'd solved the problem of how everyone could live together?"

"LifeSim," Howard said, his face broadening into a grin.

"What's LifeSim?" asked Annalise.

"They found it on one of the very advanced worlds. Part of every child's education—spending a simulated year in the body of another person. From another race, religion, country, sex, social background, age—the list was endless. One year of someone's life compressed into a day, so that each child would know what it was like to be black, white, male, female, straight, gay, Christian, Muslim, poor, old, blind, sick. Brilliant, don't you think?"

"Did it work?" asked Annalise.

"For the majority it did. A few didn't take to it. But most learned to appreciate from an early age that everyone is an individual with their own history, beliefs and needs. To see strangers as living people and not stereotypes or threats."

"Why didn't anyone at ParaDim develop LifeSim?" asked Annalise.

"They do," said Howard. "Eventually. Usually in Phase Three or Four. And after the marketing men have 'improved' the product." Howard's fingers provided the quotes. "They repackage LifeSim as entertainment. Take out all the ordinary people and replace them with the extraordinary." He stressed the "extra" part of the word. "The sports heroes, the killers, the porn stars, the psychos—people with interesting lives."

"Is that going to happen here?" asked Annalise.

He shook his head. "LifeSim is one of our priorities. We're moving the development up. Kenny's assured us.

After resonance and disease, LifeSim's the top priority.

"And there'll be no psychos or porn stars," he added. "We're going to do it right."

Graham went home shortly after that. He didn't trust himself to be around people. Howard meant well, he knew that. And he had enough to worry about with the resonance wave but . . .

Didn't he realize that this world was the same as all the others? The same people, the same high ideals, the same grubby compromises. ParaDim would sell out. Kenny Zamorra would sell out. LifeSim would be shelved or repackaged and everyone would throw up their hands and say, "What else could we have done? We're curing cancer. We're the good guys. We only produce weapons for our friends."

He slipped out while Annalise was busy elsewhere.

It was an unsettling journey home.

He was on an emotional roller coaster. He was starting to feel things—intensely—all the time. He felt attracted to girls on the tube, frightened by groups of youths, enraged by newspaper headlines, frustrated by trains that sat for minutes outside empty stations with no word as to why or when they'd ever move. Things that never used to bother him, things that used to belong to the outside world—that world, the world that barely touched him. It was like he'd been moved from audience to stage. Life was no longer something he watched from afar but something he experienced in the round.

It was not a pleasant experience.

Walking home from the station, he had to fight to keep himself in check, force himself to count, subordinate himself to the abstract world of numbers and checker-board pavements—let the imperfect world slide by overhead.

It wasn't easy.

A group of children made faces at him from the back of a bus. He wanted to make faces back. He wanted to taunt them like they were taunting him. He wanted to run onto the bus and drag them outside. He wanted . . .

He grabbed his right wrist, clasped it with his left hand—tight. Calm. He'd stay calm. He wouldn't look, he wouldn't feel, he wouldn't get involved.

Annalise Fifteen surveyed her new flat—a three-bedroom apartment in Kensington, courtesy of the newspaper. Jenny had shown it to her that morning and she'd moved in after lunch.

Things were looking up. She had new clothes, a credit card, a thousand pounds in cash and a laptop. And Graham had three five-thousand-piece jigsaws. He'd cleared a six-foot-square area in his bedroom and she'd barely seen him since. Give him a coffee machine and an en suite bathroom and he'd never come out.

Annalise deleted another paragraph of her email and started again. She'd been trying all evening to get it just right, to give it the feel that it came from a ParaDim insider—a whistle-blower—without sounding like a deranged conspiracy theorist. As much as she liked the guys at the paper, she didn't trust them to run with the ParaDim story if the going got tough. She needed other avenues of pressure. If needs be, she'd email every government, every news organization, every ParaDim competitor. She'd tell them ParaDim's plans, their strengths and their weaknesses. Even if most of the recipients deleted the file unread, someone would notice.

And if they didn't, she'd keep on until someone did.

Jenny arrived just before ten with a bottle of champagne. She was bubbling with news. The Tracey Minton gang had been arrested, Stephen Landcroft had confessed to three murders and the evidence implicating Victoria Pitt's husband had been found just where Annalise had told them it would be.

Everything was great and everybody loved Annalise. The police, the paper, Jenny.

"What about the ParaDim story?" asked Annalise as the bubbles settled.

"Great story. We're really keen. Though it's going to take longer to research without documentary proof."

"What about the disappearance of Kevin and the two scientists?"

"ParaDim says they know nothing about it." Jenny shrugged and took another sip of champagne. "It's going to be difficult to prove otherwise without more evidence. Can't you hack in and download evidence of ParaDim's activities?"

"No," said Annalise, thinking quickly. "They've blocked all their internal files."

"But you do have access to the crime files?"

"Census files," corrected Annalise. "Why?"

"Nothing. Have you seen the papers today?"

Was she changing the subject?

"No," said Annalise.

"There's a big political scandal. It's been going on for days. A government minister accused of corruption. You know, the usual story—did he, didn't he?"

Annalise waited for the question.

"But you'd know, wouldn't you? If he did or not? You could look it up on the crime . . . sorry," she corrected herself, "the Census database."

She looked so innocent—Jenny—even her eyes appeared to hold nothing back. An innocent question between friends over a glass of wine.

"You want me to find out?"

"Only if you have no objections. We'd make it worth your while, of course."

Was this how it started? The slippery slope into temptation. New Tech weapons are a good story but here's a bunch of better ones. Next, someone'll say—"Hey, why bust ParaDim's ass when they're the ones with the golden database that solves crime and boosts our circulation?"

"Perhaps next week," said Annalise. "The files need time to be updated. Anything I did now would only uncover half the story."

The doorbell rang.

Both women looked over their shoulders.

"Were you expecting anyone?" Jenny asked.

"No," said Annalise, darting a look towards Jenny. "Who else knows we're here?"

"I've told no one, I swear."

Annalise put down her glass and leaned forward to stand up. Jenny stopped her. "I'll handle this. You hide in the bedroom."

Annalise pulled the bedroom door open and peered across the lounge towards the front door.

Jenny slid the chain into place and opened the front door a crack.

"Dave?" she said, taken aback. "What are you doing here?"

"What are *you* doing here?" came the policeman's muffled reply. "I was told *this* girl lives here."

There was a pause. Annalise could see Jenny looking at something—a picture, a photograph—something small that Dave pushed through the gap in the door.

"It's late, Dave," Jenny said, returning the picture. "I told you earlier. She'll talk to you when she's ready and only through a lawyer."

"*This* girl? She's your source?" He sounded shocked.

"Dave, whatever it is, it can wait. Now go. She's not talking and that's final."

"I'm sorry, Jenny, but I'm not here to interview her. I'm here to arrest her."

Annalise almost fell through the door in surprise.

"What for?" said Jenny, her voice rising.

"For the attempted murder of Adam Sylvestrus."

FORTY-FOUR

Annalise felt like she'd been hit by a truck. She didn't see the front door open or the two policemen walk in. She was somewhere else, suspended in disbelief, trying to figure out how her crazy world could have possibly become any crazier.

"Miss Mercado?" said a male voice.

Annalise's eyes refocused to find two men standing a few feet away from her.

"Don't say a word," said Jenny from the middle of the room. She had a phone in her hand. "I'm calling a lawyer."

"Miss Mercado?" repeated the taller of the two men, though looking at them both there was little to choose between them—both were tall, thick-set and wearing suits that looked as though they'd been slept in for days.

"What?" she said.

"Annalise Mercado, I'm arresting you in connection with the attempted murder of Adam Sylvestrus . . ."

The preprepared statement droned on. The policeman's voice monotonous and barely punctuated with a breath let alone emotion. In the background, she could hear Jenny remonstrating with a lawyer, telling him to put his dinner in the oven and get the hell over to Ladbroke Road. She'd meet him there.

It all seemed so unreal.

"I didn't do anything," Annalise said to no one in particular.

"I know you didn't," said Jenny, appearing magically at her side and supporting her arm. She turned on the taller of the two men, presumably Dave, and asked him. "Who put you up to this?"

"No one put anyone up to anything," he replied. "This case is as cast iron as they come."

"I've never even met the man," said Annalise.

"We have twenty witnesses who disagree with you, miss."

"That's ridiculous. I've been here all day."

"But not Wednesday. On Wednesday you filled a waste bin with petrol, set light to it, threw it in Mr. Sylvestrus's car and slammed the door shut."

Annalise sat in the back seat of the police car. Numbed. They'd known her name. She hadn't told anyone her name. Not the paper, not the hotel, no one. She was Phoenix, she was Lisa Brown, she was anyone but Annalise Mercado.

Yet the police had both her name and address. An address she'd only moved to a few hours earlier. How? She'd covered her tracks so well.

She groaned when it came to her. She'd given Jenny three names to prove her story—Kevin, Howard and Tamisha. A reporter would have rung ParaDim and asked questions. Even a harmless request for confirmation of employment would have rung alarm bells. Those three names linked together in a single enquiry. A newspaper asking questions before they'd even been declared missing.

She held her head in her hands. How could she have been so stupid!

But how had that led anyone to her flat? Were they tracing all calls made by *Sketch* reporters? Were they having them followed?

Graham!

Panic! Was her arrest a ploy to isolate Graham? Get her out of the way so they could get to him unhindered? She'd asked Jenny to stay with him and not to open the door to anyone but would that be enough?

Had she now put Jenny at risk?

"You have to put a police guard on the flat," she shouted at the two men in the front of the car.

Neither of them so much as looked round.

"Jenny's in danger," she implored. "If you're a friend, Dave, you'll help her. The least you can do is call and warn her. Tell her not to open the door to anyone. Not to a doctor, not to anyone. Tell her they'll be plausible. Tell her to check the windows . . ."

"Tell her yourself," Dave said, handing her his cell phone. "Just do it quietly."

She grabbed the phone. If ParaDim was scanning the call she'd give them something to think about. She'd make sure they knew that Jenny was a high-profile reporter who'd not only be missed if anything happened to her, but had been warned that same night in front of police witnesses that ParaDim was after her.

And she'd tell Jenny to look in the top drawer of her dresser. She might not be able to mention the gun over the phone but she'd make damn sure Jenny had some protection.

Annalise sat at a battered table in a police interview room. Waiting. Counting the minutes as they ticked relentlessly towards Saturday. A bare light burned into her eyes and glared off the stark white walls. Everything was so quiet. The woman police constable by the door stared into space, not saying a word.

The door opened. A dapper middle-aged man in a suit and what looked like a paisley waistcoat came in, his broad red face showing advanced signs of five o'clock shadow.

"Miss Mercado?" he said, holding out his hand. "Jerry Saddler. I'll be representing you."

He placed his briefcase on the table and released the catches. "I'll have you out of here within the hour."

He took her briefly through the charges and the procedures.

"Let them know you have nothing to say and the interview will proceed the quicker for it. Remember, do not volunteer information. It's up to them to make their case; you don't have to help them."

Advice Annalise ignored within five seconds of the interview starting.

"I'm the victim, not Adam Sylvestrus," she said, stabbing her index finger against the table.

"You threw a burning waste bin into his car," said the

younger of the two policemen—a Sergeant Davis? Something like that. Annalise's thoughts had been elsewhere when they'd introduced themselves.

"To stop them pushing Graham into the back of their car!"

Her lawyer leaned over and whispered in her ear, "I really think . . ."

She brushed him away and continued without pausing. "I had to stop them getting Graham into the car. Once he was inside, they'd have killed him. Didn't your witnesses tell you about the guy with the gun stuck in Graham's back?"

She looked from face to face. Didn't they believe her? Hadn't they interviewed the other witnesses?

"Can I have a moment alone with my client?" asked Jerry.

"I don't need a moment alone. I'm innocent and can prove it."

"You're saying that Adam Sylvestrus was attempting to kidnap your friend?" asked Dave.

"That's right."

"Why?"

"Because he's obsessed with him. You ask at the DTI, where Graham works." She paused and leaned over the table, tapping on the piece of paper the sergeant was making notes on. "Graham Smith," she said slowly. "He's a messenger at the DTI in Westminster Street. Sylvestrus wanted him to take medical tests. Wouldn't take no for an answer."

"So, if we talk to this Graham Smith he'll corroborate your story?"

Annalise stopped dead. She hadn't thought of that. The

only Graham Smith who could corroborate her story was worlds away. The Graham Smith back at the flat had no recollection of the kidnap, the black car or the men. His Wednesday had been spent having a medical in Knightsbridge.

"Sure," she said, playing for time—nodding her head and smiling as she tried to think of a plausible reason for excusing Graham. "But at the moment he's terrified and doesn't trust anyone. He can barely talk." She looked at Jerry. "I'm sure the paper would want you to look after his interests as well as mine. You'll do that, won't you?"

Jerry agreed and made a note of Graham's name.

Annalise turned to Dave. "Can't you confirm events without his testimony? I can pick out the guys, the car, and there must be camera evidence. I can tell you everything you need."

She told them about Kevin, Howard and Tamisha. The meeting they'd had in May Street. How it had been broken up by men with guns. How she and Graham had barely escaped with their lives.

"Check the attic window at the back of the house on the corner of May Street. It's broken, from the outside. We had to break it to get in. Ask the company there about the fire alarm they had that afternoon. We set it off. Ask them about Graham; they'll recognize him."

She told them about the two fake policemen.

"Ask at the store. They had them arrested. They were working for Sylvestrus. They had fake IDs. Check the store cameras and you'll see them chasing us. Check the cameras outside and you'll see where the guy kidnaps Graham. Ask people about the guy who collapsed in the doorway and the other guy who said he was his doctor."

"Have you checked the CCTV cameras in the area, Chief Inspector?" asked Jerry.

"Not yet," said Dave curtly.

"What about the guy shooting at me? People must have seen that."

"The driver's already admitted to that," said the sergeant.

"For which he will be prosecuted," added Dave. "He says he overreacted when you tried to kill his employer." He paused and steepled his fingers. "His associate claims you also took his gun. Do you still have that gun, Miss Mercado?"

"It's at the flat," she said softly. "I didn't know what else to do with it."

But she hoped Jenny did.

FORTY-FIVE

Graham was on his knees, weeding the front garden, when Annalise Six arrived.

He'd calmed down since the night before. He'd thrown himself into every ritual he could think of. He'd played Patience for hours, filling every inch of his mind with red jacks and black queens. He'd sat on every disconcerting thought or emotion the moment they'd bubbled up. His little voice had helped. The other Grahams too. And the house.

"What are you doing here?" asked Annalise, leaning against the front gate. "Aren't you coming in today?"

He didn't look round. "I'd only be in the way," he said, pulling at the thin line of weeds protruding between the patio slabs.

"You'd never be in the way. We need you."

He looked up, suddenly concerned. "Has something happened?"

"No," she said, her lips coming together in the suggestion of a pout. "Not yet, but something will soon. Gary's sure of it."

Graham looked down at the mention of Gary's name and searched for another weed. It was happening again. He could feel it. His self-control eroding. The supporting strength of 200 billion Graham Smiths blown away by one pretty face.

But what a face.

He could see it beneath him, overlaid from his memory onto the white patio slab. Even as it faded he felt a tug on his neck muscles—involuntary, insistent—a desire to turn and refresh his memory, to fill his mind with the way she looked and smelled and moved and . . .

"Are you okay?" she said.

"I'm fine," he lied, swallowing hard. He felt awkward and stupid. He wanted to disappear, he wanted *her* to disappear, he wanted her to be next to him, to feel the warmth of her . . .

"Do you want a hand?" she asked. "Never had a garden myself but I'm a quick study. Tell me what you want me to do and I'll do it."

Why did she have to say that? Did she know? Could she read his thoughts?

He felt like banging his head on the paving slabs. His resolve had deserted him. He took a deep breath and tried to think of something else. Something neutral and calming. He felt a spot of rain, then another. His washing!

"Could you help me get the washing in?" he said, not looking at her as he pushed himself to his feet.

"Sure."

They stripped the washing line together. Occasionally their hands touched as they reached up to unpeg an item. Each time, Graham withdrew further away. What could a girl like Annalise ever see in someone like him? A grown man who made a beeline for his underpants. Boring, white, unfashionably old underpants that he had to take off the line first, had to wrap up in a shirt before throwing them in the basket in case Annalise saw them. Or worse . . . had the misfortune to touch them.

Shortly after that, he decided that an afternoon in Putney wasn't such a bad idea after all. He couldn't face being alone with Annalise. She'd already invited herself for lunch and showed every intention of staying all day.

They found Gary in the black sphere room, staring into space and looking like he hadn't slept. He acknowledged the two of them briefly, forced a smile, then faded from the conversation.

Howard was only slightly more communicative. They were near to a breakthrough, he was sure. So close it was frustrating. Several times during the night they thought they'd cracked it but—he shrugged, nodding his head as it tracked from shoulder to shoulder—they hadn't.

Tamisha was having more luck, he said. She was working through the Etxamendi with the linguists and they were refining the translation every hour. If only they could make more headway with the math. So much of it was unfathomable—the terminology, the symbols, the structure. Maybe they weren't equations, maybe it was another language altogether.

"What about the Spanish woman's work?" asked

Annalise. "I thought you said it was a stepping stone."

He grimaced and shook his head. "Not as much as I'd hoped. There are similarities but . . ." He shrugged again.

They found Shikha on the third floor, scanning resonance logs.

"I don't read them all," Shikha said, pointing at the list of logs on screen. "I scan for phrases like 'amazing discovery,' and 'breakthrough.' It's preferable to wading through a million files every day."

"Have there been any amazing discoveries?" asked Annalise.

Shikha shook her head and flicked a strand of hair away from her face. "Only the Etxamendi file. Most of the other worlds haven't seen it yet. The few that have are as baffled as us."

"Isn't there any way you can ask the Etxamendi for clarification?" asked Annalise.

"We've asked but so far they haven't answered. The only readable file on their world is the one we found yesterday. You're the only two-way communication we have between the worlds."

The two women talked and Graham traced patterns in their hair with his eyes. He was fascinated with the length of Shikha's hair, its blackness, the way it tumbled over her shoulders and back. And the precision of Annalise's hair, the way each strand stayed in place, the shine, the way it followed the contours of her face.

Gary's name came up in conversation and Graham switched from Annalise's hair to her face. Was she looking happier at the mention of Gary's name? Had her heart skipped a beat?

He looked away, feeling embarrassed and stupid.

What was the matter with him? Feelings surged within him, coming and going like tides. He was up, down, happy, sad, hopeful and crestfallen. All within minutes of each other. The world was falling apart and all he cared about was whether Annalise liked him. And which Annalise? There were so many of them. Two hundred telepaths and thousands, maybe millions of others. Was he attracted to all of them? Were they all the same? Was the only difference between them one of hair color and experience?

He looked at Annalise Six and wondered who it was he saw. Annalise Six or Annalise in her sixth manifestation? How much of a person's character was determined by experience? How much by genetics? Or did none of that matter? Were love and attraction entirely random, a product of time and space?

A line of thought which came to an abrupt end.

Annalise's face had just blanked out.

"Annalise!" The name shrieked inside her brain. Her head jerked back in shock.

"Don't say a thing. I haven't got time," the voice continued. *"This is Annalise 141."* The voice sounded out of breath; it jerked as though she was running. *"We've been closed down. Kevin and the team have been taken. There are men all over the office, carrying stuff away. I'm going for Graham. He should be at home. I'll talk later."*

"Are you okay?" Shikha asked Annalise. "You look like you've seen a ghost."

Annalise swayed unsteadily and blinked. "They've closed down another RP. Annalise 141 is looking for Graham."

She sat down. "Have you run the closure program today?"

Shikha shrugged. "Howard normally . . ."

"I'll do it," said Annalise.

She ran the program. The number had risen to 383. She ran the hospital check for Graham Smiths—382. Just the one discrepancy—thanks to Annalise Fifteen.

"Annalise!" Another voice in her head. This time it was Annalise One. *"Spread the word,"* she said. *"We're going underground. All the Sylvestrus worlds. It's too risky not to. Kevin says he can work off-line. They're going to keep moving, use dial-up lines to access ParaDim, download what they need and post their progress. He's advising everyone else to do the same. Someone's gonna stay behind in London with me and Graham. We're gonna keep the link to the other two hundred worlds open."*

Graham listened and felt progressively guilt-ridden. People were running for their lives and all he could think about was Annalise. He had to become more focused. He had to start contributing. He had to regain control.

Gary and Howard arrived soon after Annalise called them. They both looked drawn. Now, they had more pressure—the Sylvestrus teams were scattering, the baton had been passed.

It was up to them.

"I still can't see a motive for Sylvestrus," said Gary, shaking his head.

Graham wondered what it would take to convince the man. "You don't need a motive if you're mad," he said.

"You can't run a successful high-profile business and

be crazy," said Gary, pushing his hands through his unkempt hair. "Someone would notice."

"People see what they want to see," said Graham. "No one's going to complain about Sylvestrus while ParaDim's doing well."

"Graham's right," said Annalise. "I've seen the Chaos files. Sylvestrus is seen as this mythic figure with the golden touch. Everything he tries, succeeds. People don't realize he's picking winners from races that finished years ago. They think he's a genius. Maybe it goes to his head?"

"And selling weapons of mass destruction to the general public has got to be madness," said Graham.

"ParaDim never sells weapons of mass destruction to the public," snapped Gary. "They make the technology available. They share knowledge. They," he paused, looking caught between two minds. "It's difficult to defend, I know, and with hindsight it was wrong but . . . the ethos of ParaDim is all about sharing—making knowledge available, advancing through cooperation."

"They made powerful weapons cheap and easy to get hold of," said Annalise softly.

"Governments could have banned the weapons," said Gary, his voice rising. "They didn't have to let their civilians own them. ParaDim was doing nothing different than any other weapons manufacturer."

"Except do it better," said Annalise.

Gary looked spent. He waved a dismissive arm in Annalise's direction and the effort seemed to take all his strength. "Anyway," he said, stretching and rotating his neck, "it won't happen here. Kenny Zamorra has banned all research on New Tech weapons."

"And I'm banning you," said Shikha, taking Gary by the arm. "You too, Howard. The pair of you can barely stand up. You need sleep and you need it now."

Annalise Fifteen was still in police custody. It was early Saturday morning and the argument over her release raged unabated.

"My client has cooperated with you fully," said Jerry Saddler, her lawyer. "Furthermore, she's provided you with information leading to the arrest of seven individuals and the solution of five murders. She can hardly be considered a danger to the public."

"She threw a firebomb into someone's car! She admits it," said the sergeant.

"She regrets any injury caused to Mr. Sylvestrus, which was entirely accidental, and resulted from her efforts to protect the life of her friend."

"The man has second-degree burns to his face and hands."

"Which he received in the course of committing an offense."

"She's a flight risk."

"My client will willingly surrender her passport."

"And the gun?"

"Naturally."

Annalise had belatedly accepted her lawyer's advice and let him do the talking. She had other things on her mind. What had happened at the flat? Were Graham and Jenny safe?

A phone call from Jenny answered that question. They'd survived a fretful night. A man had knocked on the flat door about two a.m. claiming to be a neighbor locked out of his flat. Jenny hadn't said a word. She'd stood ten feet away from the door, shaking like a leaf while holding Annalise's gun trained on the front door.

Graham had slept through everything.

Annalise was released at 9:15 in the morning. She took the police to her B and B in Harrow where she collected her clothes and handed over her passport. The room didn't look like it had been searched.

They went to the flat next. Annalise called out to Jenny before knocking on the door.

"Thank God," came the muffled cry from inside. Annalise heard the chain slip back before the door opened and the smell of stale cigarette smoke wafted into the corridor.

"Has anyone got a cigarette?" said Jenny, looking desperate. "I ran out two hours ago."

The police left as soon as they'd recovered the gun.

"Why don't you want the police to interview Graham Smith?" asked Jerry Saddler, settling into an armchair and using his briefcase to slide two empty packs of cigarettes and a very full ashtray along the coffee table. "He's your key witness."

Annalise wasn't sure what to say. She looked at Jenny. Jenny raised both eyebrows. She wanted to know too.

"Graham's . . ." Annalise paused, searching for something plausible. "He . . . he wouldn't make a good witness. He doesn't like to speak. Sometimes he doesn't speak for days."

She looked at the closed bedroom door and wondered if he was listening.

"He'll have to talk to the police sometime," said Jerry.

"Then you'll have to make sure it's not anytime soon. He's had a hard time. Harder than anyone can imagine."

Annalise was torn about what to do next. ParaDim knew where she was. If she stayed, she was in danger. If she ran, she'd be followed. Either way, she was going to be looking over her shoulder and starting at every noise.

"The police would have to be informed of any change of address," said Jerry.

Which meant that ParaDim would know within the hour. They'd monitor every phone at the police station, they'd scan all London traffic for the words "Annalise" and "Mercado."

"We'll turn this flat into a fortress," said Jenny. "We'll bring in round-the-clock surveillance—a car outside, someone in the flat, video surveillance of the hall and windows. I'll stay as well, if you want?"

By early afternoon, the flat was full of people. Men running cables, unpacking boxes, drilling into walls.

Annalise stood by Graham's door watching, checking every face, looking for anyone acting suspicious. This was the ideal time for ParaDim to smuggle someone into the flat, however reputable Jenny said the security firm was.

She checked on Graham. He was halfway through his first jigsaw. His bed was pushed well away from the window to make room for the mountain landscape taking shape on the carpet.

She asked if he wanted anything—a drink, a book, something to eat. He shook his head without looking up.

She wondered what was going on inside his head. Was he really blocking everything out? Did he have any conception of the danger around him, the attempts on his life?

Did he wonder why two men had fixed a camera outside his window?

She shook her head and closed the door behind her. Perhaps it was better he didn't know. Innocence was a warm blanket to snuggle under.

The flat started to empty around seven. Annalise was introduced to Mark, a twenty-something wall of muscle who was going to stay with her until morning. He grunted something which passed for a greeting and settled in behind a bank of monitors that had grown behind the breakfast bar.

Annalise said goodbye to Jenny and the last of the day shift and watched them file along the corridor in the left-hand monitor. There were four screens: hallway east, hallway west and two covering the windows—one looking down onto the street, one looking up to the roof. The flat was on the fourth floor and no one could approach without being seen.

Jenny called a few minutes after ten. She'd just got off the phone with Dave. He'd reviewed the CCTV footage and agreed it could support Annalise's account of what had happened. He'd again asked to talk to Graham and Jenny had stalled as best she could.

"Would it help if I arranged a session with a counsellor?" she asked. "Maybe if Graham could talk to a professional?"

Annalise said she'd talk to Graham about it and hung up.

Annalise awoke with a start. It was the middle of the night and something was wrong.

Very wrong.

A bell was ringing. Loud and incessant.

She threw off the covers and stumbled to her feet. Everything was black and was that a fire alarm? She opened the bedroom door and ran to the living room.

"What's happening?" she shouted to Mark.

"Fire alarm," he said, the first hint of emotion creeping into his voice.

Annalise's eyes flicked from monitor to monitor. No sign of smoke, no sign of people. Was there really a fire?

She ran back to her bedroom, pulled on a pair of jeans, a coat, shoes. Then ran to Graham's room, opened the door and peered in. Everything was quiet. She flicked the light switch. Graham stirred, his eyes blinking towards her.

"It's all right," she lied. "Fire alarm—probably a mistake. Get dressed just in case."

She switched off the light and shut the door. Mark was on the phone, reporting the incident. Annalise knelt down and laced her shoes. The room was in darkness except for the steady flicker of grey light from the monitors. It gave the room a ghostly feel. She shivered.

Movement appeared on one of the screens—the hallway. A front door opened—one of the flats—a head popped out, an elderly man, looking worried, unsure, glancing left and right.

Other doors opened, more confused residents, some in nightclothes, some hurriedly dressed. They gathered in groups, peered towards the stairwells, shook their heads, asked the same questions. Annalise heard them on the loudspeaker. What's happening? Is there a fire? What should we do?

Some began to head for the stairs; others went back

inside to collect belongings. A woman appeared with two large cats in her arms.

A siren sounded softly in the distance.

Mark was still on the phone. He covered the mouthpiece. "They've confirmed a call has been sent to the emergency services. One of the residents reported a fire."

"It's a trick to get us out," said Annalise instinctively. "There's no fire. We stay here until the police arrive."

Mark looked less sure. "I'm here to see to your safety."

"Then keep the door locked. I'm not moving 'til I see a flame."

A fire engine pulled up outside. Annalise saw it in the camera pointing at the ground. The siren stopped wailing, men jumped out and ran towards the building.

Then everything went dead.

The screens, the loudspeakers, the light from under the front door.

A residual bleed of light radiated from the screens as they crackled into inactivity. A muffled scream came from the corridor. Annalise held her breath.

Mark shouted into the phone. He was like a shadow standing next to her. A shadow losing his cool. Annalise guessed he was talking to the two men outside in the car.

"The whole building's out?" she heard him say. "Could a fire have cut the power lines? Can you see a fire?"

She listened for a reply, attuning her ears to the quiet of the room.

There was a muffled crash from nearby. Breaking glass. Graham's room!

"The window!" Annalise screamed and ran blindly towards the bedroom door.

FORTY-SIX

Annalise flew into Graham's room. Everything dark, a hint of grey from the window, a shape climbing in, feet crunching over glass and jigsaw pieces. Another shadow in the corner, hunched over, it had to be Graham.

Annalise moved instinctively, fast and low, her hands pushed out in front of her. One thought, intercept and stop. She launched herself, hit something hard, something that moved with her and thudded against something even harder.

There was a sharp intake of breath.

Not from Annalise.

"Run, Graham!" she shouted as she grappled with the body she'd pressed up against the far wall. Sound all around her, running feet, ragged breaths. She hung on with her hands while she thrust up with her knees. Then she was flying across the room, tossed like a rag doll onto the bed.

She rolled with the momentum, off the bed, onto the floor, found her feet and ran towards the door. Graham would be out by now, he'd be in the lounge, maybe at the front door. She'd given him time to escape.

A series of grunts and sickening crunches sounded behind her. Mark and the intruder. A second later she was in the lounge. A shape was fiddling with the door chain, the door was opening. She reached Graham in the doorway, bundled him through, grabbed his hand.

"Follow me."

Noise all around them—from the stairwell, the corridors, above, below. Doors slamming all over the building, running feet from the floor above, shouts, questions— "What's happening?" "Should we evacuate?"

She pulled Graham towards the back stairs. Hand in hand, they ran through the darkness, pushed through the fire doors into the window-lit stairwell. And froze, listening to the echoes—the shouts, the cries, the click and clatter of feet on the stairs.

Up or down? Which way? All logic said "down," down towards the exit and safety. If there was a fire, it was the only way out. Her heart said "up." There was no fire. ParaDim would have people watching all exits. They'd grab her and Graham the moment they emerged. Hit them a few times, call them hysterical, carry them off to their big black cars and no one would lift a hand to stop them.

That was not going to happen.

They'd hide upstairs. Stay in the building until the

police arrived. "Come on!" she hissed and pulled Graham up the next flight.

Heavy feet clattered on the stairs above. Someone large coming down fast. Another turn and they'd meet.

She pushed Graham through the fire doors on the fifth floor, held the door as it swung back, cushioned it and let it close gently—no noise, no hint of someone having just run through.

They were back in a windowless void, moving swift and silent along the corridor. They had to find somewhere to hide. Someone must have left their front door open in the panic.

Annalise tried every door they passed. A gentle turn, a push. Locked, locked, locked . . . open!

They fell inside. Closed the door behind them. Annalise leaned against the door, listening, her ear pressed against the wood. The landing door crashed back against the wall, footsteps vibrated along the hallway, a fist banged on doors.

Annalise stepped back, felt for the lock, found a catch, pushed it; the lock clicked home far louder than she'd hoped. She froze. The footsteps stopped.

She closed her eyes and took a deep breath.

A fist hammered on the door. "Anyone in there?" a male voice boomed. "You have to evacuate the building. There's a fire."

Annalise waited—silent, immobile—unsure if the man outside was a fireman or a kidnapper.

The man hammered on the door again. Louder.

"Stand away from the door!" Annalise shouted. "I've got a gun."

The hammering stopped.

"Tell your boss I'm not coming out until I see Graham Smith on the other side of this door," she yelled. "Understand?"

"There's a fire . . ."

"There's no fire!" interrupted Annalise. "And I'm not coming out until you show me Graham. Show me he's unharmed and we can talk. Until then I'm staying here. And shooting anyone who tries to get me out."

The hallway went silent. She closed her eyes and prayed. He had to believe that Graham wasn't with her. He had to!

Graham awoke. Someone was banging on his front door. He looked at his alarm clock—8:15.

The banging continued. He thought he heard someone call his name. A woman's voice. Annalise?

He pulled his dressing gown around him and trudged downstairs. The doorbell rang continuously.

"Graham!" shouted Annalise through the letter box.

He slipped the chain and opened the door. Annalise Six charged through.

"Come on, get dressed," she said. "Gary's found out how you flip."

He blinked into the early morning sun flooding through the doorway. What had she said? Her words hit him on a time delay. *Gary's found out how you flip*.

"How?" he said as she turned him around and pointed him back towards the stairs.

"He didn't go into detail. All he said was, 'Fetch Graham and don't let him make any choices.'"

"Choices?"

"Exactly. Choice bad. And in this house it's even worse.

Way I see it, every time you make a choice you risk flipping worlds. And if you stand in a spot where millions of other Graham Smiths are standing the risk is increased."

She pushed him gently in the back. "Come on, Gary's waiting. Do you want me to choose your clothes? No! Don't answer that. Point me at your wardrobe and I'll choose everything."

He started to protest but was brushed aside. Annalise selected everything, flicking through his shirts and ties, sorting through his socks and dwelling far too long on his underpants.

"I'll be downstairs," she said when she'd finished. "Remember, no choice. If you need any help, shout."

He washed and dressed as quickly as he could, his mind alive with potential choices. He'd never felt so indecisive. As soon as Annalise had warned him of the danger of choice, he'd been inundated. Should he put his left sock on before the right? Which shoelace should he tie first?

He asked Annalise.

"What do you normally do?"

He stopped and thought. It was Sunday. Sundays were right-handed days. Why hadn't he remembered that? Was he starting to forget his rituals?

A taxi was waiting outside. Graham sat in the back and tried not to think. He gazed out the window and let the journey wash over him.

Gary and Howard were waiting for them in 5G. Both were smiling; gone were the haggard, drawn faces of the day before.

"It's activated by choice," said Gary, launching into an

explanation as soon as Graham entered the room.

"Or interaction," corrected Howard. "We're not sure of the exact translation. Tamisha says the word can mean both."

"Choice, interaction—call it what you like," said Gary, impatiently waving Howard's intervention aside. "Whenever you make a choice, the potential for forming a bridge to another world is created. If another Graham Smith on another world makes a choice at the same time in the same place, then that potential can be realized and your consciousness exchanged."

"Every time I make a choice?"

"Or interact," said Howard. "It's the impact you make on the world. The bigger the choice, the bigger the potential for creating a bridge."

"The mathematics behind the explanation is mind-boggling," said Gary. "It blurs the boundary between thought and energy and introduces a twelfth dimension where . . ." He ended the sentence in a shrug.

"His mind is boggled," said Howard, pointing a finger at Gary and adding a raspy laugh. "With good reason. The twelfth dimension is a place where nothing is certain."

"And Maria Totorikaguena was right all along," said Gary. "Though for all the wrong reasons. Her theory was flawed, her proofs incorrect . . . but she was right. There *are* significant holes in the eleven-dimensional model. Once you know where to look."

Graham was losing touch with the conversation. Gary and Howard may enjoy the intricacies of a well-turned equation but what did any of this actually mean?

A thought echoed by Annalise.

"Are you saying that if Graham got up tomorrow morning and decided to put his socks on in a different order, he'd flip?" she asked.

"Could flip," corrected Gary. "From what we can deduce, every time you"—he nodded towards Graham—"make a choice, a filament of charged particles is formed in this twelfth-dimensional space. The greater the choice, the longer the filament. The greater the effect on other people's lives, the greater the charge."

"And if it connects with a filament from another Graham Smith then," Howard clasped his hands together. "Contact. A bridge is formed."

"But it doesn't always connect," said Gary. "You have to be in the same place at the same time."

"And even then," said Howard, "there's no guarantee that the two filaments will touch. There's a chance they miss each other altogether."

Graham followed the conversation like a spectator at a tennis match, turning from Gary to Howard then back again.

"How long do these filaments last?" asked Annalise. "Could Graham flip because of a choice he made yesterday?"

"From what we can calculate," said Gary, "they last from a fraction of a second to several minutes. The greater the charge, the longer they last."

"What if more than two Grahams make a choice at the same time?" asked Annalise. "Do they all flip?"

"No. The first two that connect form the bridge," said Gary. "The third filament gradually dissipates. It's like the formation of lightning. The ground emits many strands of negatively charged ions." He wiggled his fingers as he slowly raised his hand. "Some rise higher than others—like the tall tree on the top of a hill or the metal pole on a church tower. But only one will ever connect with the line of positively charged ions descending from the thundercloud. It's more likely to be the tree or the church but sometimes it's neither, sometimes it's the short blade of grass in the field next door."

He pointed at an imaginary blade of grass on the carpet.

"And then they meet," he continued. "Positive and negative. And zap." He clapped his hands. "The lightning flashes up from the ground and back down again. It's the same with Graham. The two strands connect and one consciousness is fired up the bridge and another one is fired down."

"You see," said Howard, "nothing is ever certain. Graham can flip if he selects a different shirt or if he decides to blow up the Houses of Parliament. Both would generate the possibility, though the latter would send such a filament of such a charge that it might exist for hours."

"But why me?" said Graham. "Why my choices, why not someone else's?"

"It's a residual effect of the conjunction," said Gary.

"Although we haven't totally worked out how," said Howard. "Tamisha's still cleaning up the translation and some of the math appears contradictory. One appears to posit no residual effect, another implies there has to be."

"Can I stop a bridge from being formed? I've tried twice and both times been beaten by the pain. Could I stop it if I hung on long enough?"

The two scientists looked at each other.

"I can't see how," said Gary.

"I can't see how you even fought it," said Howard.

"Transfer should be instantaneous. Are you sure you weren't feeling a side effect of the transference?"

He shook his head. "I know what I saw," he said softly. And he had seen the world shimmer before his eyes. He knew he had. Maybe if next time he was stronger?

"So," said Annalise, "the most dangerous places for Graham to be—flipwise—are the places where the other Grahams are. His home, his work, the park at lunchtime."

"Exactly," said Gary. "Which is why he's probably safe here. The number of Grahams on other worlds with access to this building will be extremely low. On most worlds, ParaDim doesn't even own this building."

"So if Graham stays out of his usual places, he won't flip."

"Exactly."

Everything suddenly became clear. In a strange way, he'd been right all the time. His routines, his rituals, his daily repetitions. They *had* stopped the world from unravelling. By limiting choice he'd reduced the opportunities for flipping worlds. He'd kept himself sane by obeying his internal laws of repetition and ritual; he'd removed choice from his world and, in so doing, had saved himself from a life of constant flipping.

Which was why the frequency of flips had increased over the last two weeks. He was making more choices. His routine had been upset. It was all so clear to him now.

His stomach rumbled. And something else became clear.

He'd missed breakfast.

❀　　❀　　❀

Gary told him about a small cafe off the High Street.

"A bit of a greasy spoon but their bacon sandwiches are to die for."

Graham didn't need more of a recommendation than that. He left the building with a bounce in his step. He was beginning to understand things that had confused and terrified him for years. The world wasn't such a frightening place. There were reasons behind everything. Strange reasons, but reasons he could understand and control.

Even having Annalise walk beside him didn't faze him. For the first time in days he could walk alongside her without feeling overpowered by her proximity. He could appreciate other sensations: the beauty of a brilliant white cloud against a deep blue sky, the soft touch of a warm summer breeze, the smell of a full English breakfast.

Graham salivated as he stood outside the cafe, reading the menu by the door.

"Should you be choosing from a menu?" asked Annalise.

"Just checking they have it," he said. "I always have the same Sunday breakfast—two pork sausages, three rashers of bacon, one slice of fried bread."

"Neat," said Annalise, far from convinced.

They went inside. Formica tables and red-checked tablecloths. Bacon sizzled, tea steamed and the smell of fried food hung over everything like a dripping fog bank.

"What is this place?" asked Annalise. "Cholesterol Central?"

Graham smiled and ordered his breakfast. Annalise had an espresso.

As he sipped at his coffee, a newspaper headline caught

Graham's eye. Something about ParaDim. He screwed up his eyes and peered across the tables.

America and ParaDim sign deal on New Tech weapons development.

FORTY-SEVEN

Graham charged into the room and threw the newspaper towards Gary.

"I thought you said it would never happen here!"

Gary looked startled. He glanced at Annalise, at Graham and, finally, at the paper.

"What does it say?" asked Howard, hurrying over from the far end of the room.

"ParaDim's developing New Tech weapons," said Annalise, her voice as angry as Graham's.

"I don't understand," said Gary, his eyes flicking from side to side as he read the article.

"It's easy," said Annalise. "ParaDim's climbed into bed with the Pentagon to develop New Tech weapons."

Howard looked shocked. "That's not possible," he said, shaking his head.

461

"Wait," said Gary, holding up a hand. "It says here the project is to develop shield technology. There's nothing about offensive weapons. Defensive weapons only, it says."

Annalise leaned over and pointed to a paragraph at the bottom right of the page. "Have you seen the list of defensive weapons? Antimissile missiles, New Tech pulse cannons. I've read the Chaos files. It's the same technology— defensive, offensive—once you've produced one, you can produce the other."

"No," Gary continued to shake his head. "This has to be a mistake. Kenny wouldn't do something like this . . ." He paused. "Unless . . ."

"Unless what?" asked Howard.

Gary exhaled deeply and nodded to himself. "It could make sense."

Graham wondered if he was ever going to come to the point.

"How?" said Annalise, sounding as exasperated as Graham.

"One of the major problems leading to the Chaos was the animosity between America and ParaDim. This could be a clever move. Building bridges with the Americans could help prevent the Chaos and maybe keep New Tech weapons out of the hands of terrorists."

Gary looked from face to face, looking for support. Annalise bit her lip. Howard rubbed his chin.

Graham sighed. Couldn't Gary see what was happening? New Tech weapons research was starting. Shields first, then what? Good intentions, curiosity, and resonance. How had the other Howard put it? The genie was loose and no amount of shoving would force him back in.

❋　　❋　　❋

Graham wasn't the only one to become agitated by a news story. Annalise 141 made contact midmorning.

"It's all over the news," she fumed. *"Internal ParaDim investigation uncovers massive fraud. They're framing the Resonance guys. Making out they've been stealing money and have skipped the country. No one's gonna look for their bodies now, they're gonna think they're all living it up with new identities."*

"Did you find Graham?" asked Six.

"Yeah, didn't I say? He's with me now. Anyway, tell the guys to check their bank accounts. Looks like ParaDim's clearing the way to explain their disappearance. They planted millions on the guys over here."

"At least we don't have to worry about that here," said Gary after Annalise had told him.

Annalise was about to make some snide comment about having enough to worry about with New Tech weapons but thought better if it. Gary's complacency was becoming annoying. His world was perfect. Kenny Zamorra was perfect. He even defended Adam Sylvestrus. Was he naive or a crazy optimist?

She stopped. When had Annalise Mercado become a cynic?

A question she didn't have time to consider.

Gary's phone rang. It was Tamisha. She was speaking so loud Annalise could make out every word. She was downloading the latest translation. She'd cleaned up the problems with the contradictory equations and was feeding everything she had into the resonance models.

"It all makes sense," she shouted. "It really does."

A strange crackling sounded over the phone, like rain falling on a plastic sheet. Were people clapping?

Gary laughed and folded his fingers over the mouthpiece. "Get the others," he said to Annalise. "Tell them Tamisha's done it. Tell them to get the simulation tests ready."

Annalise Fifteen waited behind the door. She hadn't heard anything for thirty minutes. A fireman would have gone for help, wouldn't he? The crazy lady would have been reported to the police and someone would be hollering up at her from the other end of a megaphone.

Which meant?

Which meant her gamble had worked.

Again.

The hall light flickered on. A bead of light at the foot of the door. Voices. Had she spoken too soon?

She pressed her face up against the peephole in the door. People were walking by. One dressed in his pajamas. Residents returning to their apartments. She opened the door, grabbed Graham and slipped out.

She held her breath as they walked along the corridor. She felt conspicuous, nervous, distrustful. Everyone looked so normal, ordinary people displaced in the middle of the night—dishevelled, weary, chatty, quiet.

But any one of them could be an agent for ParaDim.

She kept going, avoiding eye contact, took the main staircase down to her floor, hovered by the fire doors, held out a hand, steeled herself, and pushed.

Two men were standing outside her apartment, their backs toward her. One was on the phone. He turned. It was Mark.

❋   ❋   ❋

Two hours later her apartment was full of people. Police, security men, strangers. All wandering around, poking into this and that, asking questions. Annalise fended them off, told them most of what had happened and shielded Graham.

"He's traumatized," she told them. "Can't you see? He won't say a word."

"He doesn't look traumatized to me," said the policeman in charge.

"And you're an expert, I suppose?"

"No, but I know a man who is."

"And I know a lawyer," she snapped, balling her fists and glaring at the man until he smiled, closed his notebook and turned away.

The police left soon after that. No fire and no intruder—he'd apparently run off after knocking Mark to the ground. And no mention of the crazy woman with the gun on the fifth floor.

Jenny arrived as soon as it was light. She'd brought a photographer, who flitted around the apartment, taking pictures of Annalise, the broken window, Mark's bloodied face and Annalise again. He appeared captivated by her, taking pictures of her from all angles.

"You ever done any modelling work?" he asked.

"You ever been pushed out a fourth floor window?"

Gradually, the apartment cleared. Graham's window was repaired and the steady stream of people was reduced to four. Annalise, Graham, Jenny and Jermaine—the latest bodyguard.

The two women talked, closeted on the sofa.

"Adam Sylvestrus has a lot of friends," said Jenny. "And

deep pockets. His lawyers are lining up government ministers to lobby on his behalf."

Typical, thought Annalise, running her hands through her hair.

"Everything the police do is going to be scrutinized," continued Jenny. "Everything they do against Sylvestrus that is. Dave has the Met Police Commissioner on the phone to him every hour."

"But they'll back off once they see Sylvestrus is guilty, won't they?"

"Faster than fleas off a drowning rabbit but until then he's whiter than white."

"So who broke in here last night?"

"You did."

"What!"

"That's what they're saying. I've been on the phone all morning. Sylvestrus's people are lobbying like crazy. They say you have no defense so you invent a conspiracy and when that doesn't work you invent a break-in. And because you're getting paid by a newspaper, we're in on it as well. They're briefing all the media, trying to get our rivals to take the bait—evil newspaper in league with deranged psycho."

"They're calling me a psycho?"

"They're calling you everything they can think of. They're even saying you're a threat to peoples' jobs because ParaDim's thinking of pulling out of the UK."

Annalise shook her head. "But that's crazy."

"Not as crazy as you, apparently. Sylvestrus's lawyers want you locked up. They've already applied for an injunction against you. They're painting you as a deranged stalker obsessed with Sylvestrus. You're not allowed within four hundred yards of the man."

"I don't even know where he is!" she said, waving her arms in exasperation.

"The Cavendish Clinic, Knightsbridge," said Jenny. "He's supposedly undergoing treatment."

"You don't believe he's injured?"

"I'm a journalist, dear. I distrust everybody."

Annalise wondered if she should feel remorse for what she'd done to Sylvestrus. She knew she should—if she were a good person—but she found it hard to feel anything for the man. He'd been in the car. He was going to harm Graham, put him in a coma. And all for what? Some motive that no one could fathom.

And had she actually seen him? That instant before she'd thrown the bin, had she registered a presence in the back of the car?

She tried to tell herself that she hadn't. That the inside of the car had been a black void, that she hadn't seen anyone, couldn't have seen anyone through the flaming heat haze of the burning bin.

But she must have known—somewhere, deep inside, that people had to be inside that car. Someone had opened the back door; she'd seen it swing open. She must have known that someone could get hurt.

She shook her head. *People* had not been in that car, kidnappers and murderers had been in that car. People who would kill and torture and lie and probably laugh about it afterwards. She'd done what she had to do. No more, no less. And that was an end to it.

Jenny left, came back and left again. Pressure was being applied at the paper as well. Questions about the wisdom of bankrolling a dangerous psycho were being raised and Jenny was having to reassure her editor—and the legal department and various members of the board.

Jerry Saddler stopped by just after twelve.

"Ignore the flummery," he told Annalise. "Sylvestrus's people are worried and becoming desperate. The police have warrants out for the arrest of four men, the two with Sylvestrus's car and the two men posing as police officers. They're picking them up now. The police will probably want you and Graham to attend an identity parade later today."

Annalise's spirits sank. "Does Graham have to go to this line-up thing?"

"Of course. Without him it's your word against theirs. If you want, I can go through the procedure with him. He won't have to meet these men and no pressure will be placed upon him at all."

As soon as Jerry left, Annalise pushed open the door to Graham's room. He was kneeling on the floor by the window, picking through the tiny pieces of jigsaw. He looked so peaceful, so controlled. Less than twelve hours ago, someone had abseiled down from the roof and smashed their way into his bedroom. And now he was back in front of the same window as though nothing had happened.

She walked over to the window and ran a finger along the base of the new pane. You could hardly tell it had been replaced.

"Strange things happen," said Graham, unexpectedly reaching out and squeezing her hand.

The words came out so matter-of-factly, so unexpectedly, it took her by surprise. They were the first words she'd heard this Graham say. He smiled up at her, fixing his eyes somewhere to the left of her shoulder. She felt like crying. Stupid, stupid emotions. She choked back the tears and squeezed his hand.

"They do," was all she could say.

Sunday afternoon flew. A video conference link had been quickly thrown together to link London with New York, Boston and Kyoto. The images of Tamisha and various people Graham had never seen before flickered from wall screens, their voices slightly out of sync with the stuttering video.

"Hopelessly outdated Old Tech equipment," apologized Howard. "It was all we had on hand."

Together, they tested their new resonance model. Discussing the failures, refining, revising and interpreting. Sometimes heatedly, sometimes with everyone talking at once but always with an underlying sense that success was close at hand.

Graham and Annalise kept to the periphery. Graham, terrified of making a choice and flipping just when an answer appeared imminent. And Annalise? Graham wasn't sure. She'd been quiet ever since they'd both confronted Gary over the New Tech article.

After two hours of standing and leaning up against a wall, Graham's back stiffened and he left to stretch his legs. When he came back, a silence fell on the room and all eyes turned towards him.

He swallowed hard. He'd seen that look before—on the face of a doctor seconds before being told his mother was dead.

"What's happened?" he asked, not sure if he wanted to

know the answer. He looked at Annalise. She looked away. Her eyes were red.

"It's you," said Gary. "You've made things worse."

FORTY-EIGHT

Graham rocked slowly, almost imperceptibly, back and forth in the silence that followed. Each sway in time to the ebb and flow of his breath.

"How?" he said, his voice so quiet it came out more breath than sound.

No one answered. People looked away.

"You haven't"—Gary paused and inhaled deeply—"you haven't broken the link with your other selves."

Graham didn't understand. He waited for Gary to continue; he looked from face to face. "What link?" he asked.

Tamisha's voice cut in. "It's a by-product of the conjunction, Graham. When the worlds move apart, a residual link remains in the twelfth dimension. It's not a physical link—it's difficult to describe—but think of it as a thread of potential that links all the worlds together and specifically links you to all your counterparts on all the other worlds."

"It's the mechanism behind your flipping," added Howard. "Without the existence of the link you wouldn't be able to flip."

Graham shook his head. "So what's the problem?"

"The link accentuates the resonance effect," said Tamisha. "Without the link, the resonance wave would have a fraction of its power."

"You don't know that!" cried Annalise. "You said it would be reduced, you didn't say it would be a fraction. You're making it sound like the resonance wave was all Graham's fault."

Gary moved to comfort Annalise, placing a hand on her shoulder. She shrugged it off angrily. "And you're just as bad," she told him. "Tell Graham your idea for breaking the link."

"It wasn't a serious suggestion. We were brainstorming ideas."

Graham swallowed. He could think of one very sure way of severing the link.

"Is that why Adam Sylvestrus has been attacking all the Grahams?" he asked.

"We don't know," said Tamisha. "It could be, but," she paused, "this is difficult to say and I apologize for my bluntness but . . . it would be easier if he killed you. Killing you breaks the link; putting you in a coma does not."

"But it does stop you flipping," said Howard. "It's like he sees your flipping as a threat and so he places you in a state where you can't interact or make a choice that impacts on the world."

"How could my flipping be a threat?"

"Because accelerated flipping can burn out the link," said Tamisha.

Graham's heart leapt. "I can break the link by flipping?"

As soon as he saw Annalise turn and look away, he knew the answer.

"You could have," Tamisha said, "when you were a child."

He didn't understand. What had it to do with being a child? Why couldn't he try now? He could flip all day, all year if needs be. He'd go home, make choices, interact with the world. Whatever it took.

"From what the Etxamendi file has told us," said Tamisha, "the link is broken in childhood. As the linked children start to interact with their worlds, they flip constantly and this flipping increases until the charge becomes so great that the thread is burned away and the link destroyed."

"This has happened before?" said Annalise.

"Yes," said Tamisha. "We found four this morning."

"How?" asked Shikha, surprised. "We've checked the Census files. Graham's the only person who occurs on every world."

"The Census files are incomplete. Most only go back to the 1850s and only for those countries that collect the data. We checked the advanced worlds. Their data go back millennia. We looked for children with the same first name, date of birth and location. We found four. A girl and three boys, roughly three to four hundred years between each event."

"And they lived normal lives?" asked Annalise.

"They appeared to. All of them had problems during early childhood. We found entries pointing to medical and psychological problems. Their school grades were low. Many were diagnosed as problem children."

"But they recovered?" asked Shikha.

"So it seems. After the age of six, their grades picked up and their psych visits tailed off. As adults they had a variety of jobs, they married, divorced, had kids and led a normal varied life."

"Whereas you," said Howard looking directly at Graham, "developed differently. You found a way of managing your situation. You learned—subconsciously, instinctively, maybe by resonance—who knows?" He shrugged and spread his gnarled fingers out wide. "But, somehow, you learned and adapted. You withdrew into yourself, stopped interacting, stopped making choices and resonance did the rest."

"Which has left you trapped," said Tamisha. "The link is stronger and more difficult to break and the Grahams . . ." She paused again, a slight grimace forming on her lips. "Pardon my bluntness again, Graham, but from what I've read and with the exception of yourself, the Grahams have neither the will nor the capacity to break the link."

He didn't understand. Why didn't they have the will or capacity? He waited for Tamisha to explain. He looked to Gary, to Howard, to Annalise.

"She thinks all the Grahams are too withdrawn to be reached," Annalise told him, her eyes flashing angrily. "They all do. They're just like your colleagues at work. They think you're all mute retards."

"We don't think that," said Shikha. "But you can't underestimate the effect that consciousness exchange has had on their lives. I couldn't begin to imagine how I'd cope under similar circumstances. Not knowing from day to day if the house I left in the morning would be there when I came home. Having a stranger call herself my mother. Having history change just before a history test."

She walked over to Graham and took hold of his hand. "You have my profound respect," she said. "I couldn't have lasted one month in your shoes."

Annalise's hand flew to her mouth. She looked away.

"Mine too," said Tamisha. "But that doesn't alter the fact that it'll take years of therapy to reach all the Grahams. Some may be too traumatized ever to be reached. And time is something we don't have."

"Are the other Grahams traumatized?" Graham asked Annalise a few minutes later when they left to fetch coffees.

Annalise didn't reply immediately. "They're quiet," she said, "but I wouldn't call them traumatized." She thought for a few more strides. "Calm, I'd say. Like they have an inner peace. Somewhere safe they can live and look out on the rest of the world. The other girls say the same." She smiled. "Annalise Ten says it's like being around this real cool monk. My Trappist guy, she calls you."

Graham reflected on Annalise's answer while they waited for the lift.

"Do you think we could coordinate a synchronized flip?" he asked. "Get all the Grahams together in one place and make them interact?"

The lift bell sounded and the doors opened. They stepped inside.

"I don't know," she said. "Some of them definitely. Some of the Grahams will do anything you tell them.

Others are more stubborn. Some of them deliberately ignore everything you say. They pretend they didn't hear but the girls say they can hear fine when it suits them."

Graham looked down at his feet. He'd hoped that all the Grahams would be the same as him. Big children learning to take their first steps in an alien world. Shy, quiet and hopeful. Overwhelmed by what they saw but thankful to be freed from the uncertainty of an unravelling world. But then he remembered that only two hundred Grahams had been told the truth. Two hundred billion still lived in that old unstable world.

How could he ever reach them?

Graham and Annalise carried the drinks back to 5G. Graham waited for the discussion to stop the second he opened the door. It didn't. He sighed with relief and helped hand out the coffees.

"How can we coordinate anything across two hundred billion worlds when we don't have two-way communication?" said a man Graham didn't recognize—someone on the Kyoto screen.

"We include it in the Resonance log," said Gary. "Detail the plan and give a date, time and place. Get all the Grahams together and force them to make a choice."

"Who reads all the Resonance logs?" asked Tamisha. "I sure as hell don't. And some worlds won't schedule us for a month."

"We could fill the Resonance log with key words to make sure it's picked up on a search," suggested Shikha.

"And I could coordinate the date and time thing with two hundred worlds right now," said Annalise. "If two hundred RPs put the same details in their logs, someone's got to read them."

"If there are any Resonance projects left to read them," said Tamisha.

The discussion continued in circles. So many things were possible but nothing was certain. Even if they did manage to bring every Graham Smith to the same place at the same time there was no guarantee the Grahams would cooperate. They might dig in their heels and refuse or sink even deeper inside their shells.

And worse. Breaking the link would not stop the resonance wave. It would weaken it—maybe buy themselves a couple of years—but it would still be there.

Graham thought about his own experience. If everyone was right about the other Grahams—that they were withdrawn and never spoke—how had he broken out? According to Schenck, he should be beset by resonance, incapable of doing anything other than follow the collective will of all the Grahams. And yet, *he* could talk. Not to everyone and not in all places, but he *could* talk.

Did that mean that the resonance effect could be beaten? Was he somehow stronger than the rest? Or were the other Grahams not as withdrawn as people thought?

"Quiet!" shouted Annalise, clapping her hands over her ears. "It's one of the girls." She closed her eyes, swayed slightly. No one made a sound.

"There's a new file from the Etxamendi world," she said, her eyes still closed, the words coming out unevenly. "It contains a message . . ."

She opened her eyes wide in surprise.

"A message from Maria Totorikaguena."

FORTY-NINE

Kevin's running the translation program," Annalise said, her eyes closed, her head tilted to one side, her right index finger pressed against her ear.

The tension was unbearable. Annalise's lips moved as though she was reciting lines in her head. The silence extending to twenty, thirty, forty seconds.

"Express the Etxamendi world now!" shouted Tamisha over her shoulder.

"Shhh!" said Gary and Howard in unison.

Ten more seconds. Annalise nodded, started to smile, the smile broadened into a grin.

"Break the link and the strength of the resonance wave is diminished," she said, the words coming out in a rush. "Break the link with enough energy and the resonance wave is destroyed. You can set off a shock wave that'll purge the twelfth dimension!"

Everyone spoke after that, bombarding Annalise with questions. Graham watched in awe as she relayed messages back and forth between the worlds. It was like watching someone speaking in tongues. The mathematical formulae, the strange unfathomable words that came out of her mouth. It wasn't her speaking and yet it was.

Then Tamisha broke in. They'd downloaded the Etxamendi file from the New York sphere. They had their own translation. And a new set of proofs. It confirmed Kevin's interpretation. If they could generate enough energy, they could break both the link and the resonance wave.

Howard was next. He'd pulled up Maria Totorikaguena's personnel files. She wasn't only Spanish, she was Basque.

"Etxamendi," said Gary, smiling to himself. "We should have noticed. Etxamendi is related to the Basque language."

"Which probably explains her interest in Schenck and twelve-dimensional models of the universe," added Howard. "She was accessing the knowledge of her counterparts in the Etxamendi Diaspora. Knowledge centuries ahead of her understanding. No wonder she made mistakes."

"Who said she made mistakes," said Tamisha. "I've been rereading her work. She published solidly for six years; then four years ago, she stopped. If you ask me, the girl took her work off-line. *And* she knew exactly how to break the link. How else would Sylvestrus know the significance of keeping Graham in a coma?"

"You don't think he could have been trying to stop the resonance wave?" asked Gary.

"By closing all the Resonance projects? Gee, I hadn't thought of that," said Tamisha.

Graham smiled. She'd lost none of her edge.

Thirty minutes later Graham had to leave the room. The flow of conversation had been interesting for a while—the excitement of a solution in sight, the optimism, the rush of ideas. Brilliant minds brainstorming in unison all the different ways to increase the charge of a flip, how to intensify the interaction, how to ensure the maximum impact.

But then it had become unsettling.

They were talking about the Grahams as objects—pawns to be moved and sacrificed. No more asking the Grahams to cooperate—that was too uncertain. They'd trick them, shock them. Every now and then someone would glance Graham's way and apologize. "We're only brainstorming," they'd say, "throwing ideas around, saying the first things that come into our heads. We don't mean any of this."

They'd smile, their consciences assuaged, and leave Graham wondering why so many first thoughts involved his death.

When the man from Kyoto suggested placing explosives on the Grahams and making them unwitting delivery devices in political assassinations, Graham decided he'd heard enough.

Annalise followed him into the corridor.

"They really don't mean it," she said, pulling the door closed. "It's the way they work. They think in abstracts.

They throw ideas up in the air and sort them out later. No one's going to make the Grahams do anything they don't want to."

Graham nodded. He didn't want to talk. Not even to Annalise. He felt distanced by events as though the universe had been split into two camps—the Grahams and the not-Grahams, the expendable and the non-expendable. Why *not* kill all the Grahams? They'd never be missed.

"I'm only going to the bathroom," he lied, knowing that any other statement would give Annalise an excuse to tag along. Company was not something he wanted.

He paused by the cloakroom door and glanced back. Annalise was watching so he went inside. When he came out, she'd gone.

He pushed through the doors to the stairs before she had time to reappear. He needed to be alone, he needed time to think.

He trudged slowly down the concrete steps. He knew everyone meant well but he also knew that desperate people embraced desperate measures. If only he were cleverer. If only he didn't have to depend so much on others.

He reached the stair door to the ground floor and stopped. The stairs continued down. He peered over the metal handrail. There was a basement level? He'd never been shown a basement level on his tour of the building. And he was sure the buttons in the lift stopped at "Ground."

He followed the steps down. Why would they have a floor you could only access from the stairwell?

At the bottom, there was a sign above the doors—

Lower Ground. He pushed through into a corridor, a mirror image of all the other corridors in the building. Doors dotted along its length, each door with an entry panel.

He walked along the empty corridor, wondering what each room contained. There was a low rumble in the distance, becoming louder the further he walked. Machinery of some sort? A generator?

A green light shone above one of the doors, two rooms ahead on the right. As he moved closer he could see that the door hadn't closed properly, it was resting against the lock. He walked over, placed a hand in the center of the door and pushed ever so slightly.

The door opened a crack and he peered in. There was a notice board on the side wall, four words written across the top: *New Tech Weapons Research*.

He blinked and read the words again. Gary had sworn he knew nothing about New Tech weapons on this world. He'd acted surprised at the newspaper headline. Had it all been an act?

He pushed the door wider, slid inside and peered around the edge of the door. The room looked empty. There was a row of head-height metal cabinets running left to right across the room. He couldn't see anyone on the other side and if he kept low they wouldn't be able to see him either.

He slipped silently inside, crouching low and moving cautiously. He had to read what it said on that board. If Gary couldn't be trusted, he needed to know. Now.

He reached the edge of the cabinets; the notice board was only a few feet away. There were brochures, memos, lists and timetables. He started to read. One memo indicated that weapons research had been running for fifteen months. There were . . .

The door behind him clicked shut.

Graham turned in surprise.

Adam Sylvestrus was standing by the door, his fingers tapping numbers on the entry console. The green light above the door flashed to red. He turned and smiled.

"Delighted to at last meet you, Mr. Smith. I have been following your progress with great interest."

FIFTY

Graham froze. Sylvestrus blocked the door—he'd probably locked it, probably entered some code that Graham couldn't crack in a million years. They were in the basement—no windows, no exits. Solid concrete and a hardwood door between him and any way out.

He'd charge Sylvestrus, that's what he'd do. He'd knock him over, force him to open the doors. Sylvestrus had to be in his sixties, he was no threat.

Sylvestrus produced a gun. He didn't point it at Graham, he let it rest in his hands, fondling it, letting Graham know it was there.

"A wonder of technology," said Sylvestrus, looking down at the gun in his hands. "The first of our New Tech and weapons."

Graham recognized it. He'd seen one before. He'd

heard it whine; he'd seen it arc terror into a crowd of screaming people.

"I expect you're wondering why I sent for you."

Graham thought he'd misheard. *Sent for you? How . . .*

The realization made him feel slow and stupid. He'd flipped again. He checked his clothes. He wasn't wearing the shirt that Annalise had picked out for him. He'd been so blind. He'd been so wrapped up in his own thoughts he'd forgotten about the dangers of making choices.

"Have you lost something?" asked Sylvestrus.

Graham ignored him. When had he flipped? Which choice had it been? His decision to leave the others, to hide in the gents, to take the stairs, to investigate the basement?

And what was Sylvestrus doing here? Gary had said he'd be safe in Putney; it wasn't one of ParaDim's usual offices. And hadn't Tamisha said that Sylvestrus didn't like modern architecture?

"I thought you didn't like modern buildings?" The words came out of Graham's mouth before he'd had time to think.

"You *can* speak," said Sylvestrus in a mixture of surprise and amusement. "I suspected as much but," he paused, "however did you know about my dislike of modern architecture?"

"I know a lot of things." Graham wasn't sure what he was doing. He kept thinking about Annalise Fifteen and what she'd do. Somehow, she'd think of a way to turn the situation to her advantage.

"Indeed?" Sylvestrus smiled as if amused at the presumption of a young child. "Enlighten me, what else do you know?"

"I know about the resonance wave."

Sylvestrus blinked. Graham saw the surprise—shock even—that flashed across his face. It only lasted for a fraction of a second, but it had been there. He'd rattled Sylvestrus.

"You're a different Graham, aren't you?" he said, smiling once more as he looked Graham up and down.

Graham rocked slowly from side to side, shifting his weight slightly from foot to foot. If only he had Annalise's speed of thought. And her ingenuity: she'd do whatever it took, use whatever was at hand. What did *he* have?

He racked his brain. He had knowledge. He knew Sylvestrus's future from the other worlds. He knew the man was going to die.

"I know what's going to happen to you," he said, faster than he meant to, the words rushing out in a breathless stream. "You'll never have the time to enjoy your power. The money won't last. I've seen the pictures of your death."

"Is that what you think this is all about? Money and power?" Sylvestrus smiled and slowly shook his head. "You *really* think I need more money? You think I haven't amassed all the wealth a man could possible require?"

He advanced slowly towards Graham. There was something about his presence that awed Graham. The smug self-assurance, the way his eyes seemed to look right through you. Graham felt pinned by them, he felt opened up and exposed.

And the gun didn't help.

Graham backed off until he felt the frame of the notice board digging into his back.

"When one approaches my age, Mr. Smith, it's not

money one craves, nor power. But one's place in history, one's legacy to future generations." He paused and ran a finger along the barrel of the gun. "Do you believe in natural selection, Mr. Smith?"

Graham shrugged and nodded at the same time. And kicked himself for being so easily silenced. He was supposed to be grabbing the initiative, not Sylvestrus. But he couldn't think straight with Sylvestrus talking.

"Survival of the fittest. Market forces," continued Sylvestrus, slow and unruffled. He could have been talking to his favorite grandson. There was no hint of nerves or malice.

"The human race is at a crossroad. We've thrived under natural selection. The best and the bravest have prospered and passed on their genes. But now what happens? Who's most likely to pass on their genes today? The clever, the successful, the people who have something to offer future generations? Or the couldn't-care-less, the bored, the irresponsible, the 'whatever' generation?"

He paused, his eyes staring directly into Graham's. Graham looked away.

"You've met Miss Kent?" Sylvestrus said, raising an eyebrow. "A brilliant mind, a healthy body. Wouldn't you say that she has everything to offer future generations?"

There was a passion to Sylvestrus's voice now. The detached amusement had gone.

"But she's decided against children. Her gene line ends with her. As does Mr. Sarkissian's. Professional people are having fewer children, Mr. Smith. Talented people are having fewer children."

"What has that got to do with anything?" said Graham.

"You still don't see?" Sylvestrus looked surprised.

"Who's having children these days?" He changed his tone, introducing a hard sarcastic edge, a hint of parody. "The bored, fifteen-year-old girl—lonely, low self-esteem—who thinks that having a baby will be the answer to all her problems. She'll get respect, she'll get love. She'll be a mother. Won't it be neat?

"No thought as to how she would look after her child or whether she was fit to be a mother. Hell, no, it was her right! The state would look after both her and her baby— that's what other people paid their taxes for, right?"

Graham stayed wedged against the wall as Sylvestrus ranted.

"Natural selection would have slapped her across the face. But natural selection ain't around no more. This is a no-fault society. Trip over in the street—ain't your fault, the road was poorly maintained—sue the local authority. Trip over in life—ain't your fault—you can't be expected to think ahead. Sue the government, big business, anyone with a wallet. It's gotta be someone else's fault 'cause it sure as hell can't be yours."

He paused, breathing hard.

"Is that it?" said Graham.

"Haven't you been listening, Mr. Smith? The weak survive these days. Tomorrow's gene pool comes from them." He waved an arm in the general direction of the door. "Natural selection is being reversed. We are sowing the seeds of our own destruction."

Graham was confused. "What has any of that to do with the resonance wave?"

"Natural selection *is* the resonance wave. Can't you see that? It's nature's way of restoring the balance. Of weeding out the weak and clearing the path for the strong."

"By plunging the world into war and chaos?"

Sylvestrus shook his head. "Your mind is too small to appreciate the bigger picture. You think in individuals, I think in species. The human race will exit the Chaos leaner and stronger. *That* will be my legacy."

"You're mad."

"People of vision frequently are . . . to the small-minded. Only history can judge a man's sanity. You're a gardener, Mr. Smith. Do you let every weed grow? Do you prune and thin out?"

Graham didn't bother to reply. Suddenly, Sylvestrus seemed less formidable. The man was mad. He saw the resonance wave as nature's revenge. Something quasi-religious, to be celebrated and protected at all costs.

Perhaps that was his weakness? His need to sustain the wave. His fear of the Resonance projects discovering an answer.

"We know how to stop the resonance wave," Graham said.

Graham saw the flicker of panic flash across Sylvestrus's face.

And he saw the light above the door flash from red to green.

Sylvestrus didn't. His back was to the door. There'd been no sound. Any second now the door would open.

"We've cracked the equation," said Graham, trying to keep Sylvestrus's attention and watch the door at the same time. He'd time his move. It might be his only chance.

The door clicked. Sylvestrus began to turn his head. Graham barged forward and grabbed the gun with both hands. They struggled, for a second; Graham wrenched the gun free, turned round and ran behind the bank of filing cabinets.

"Stop him," yelled Sylvestrus.

Graham ducked down and ran the length of the cabinets. If he could swing back to the door . . .

An armed security guard suddenly blocked his way. The man crouched low, arms extended, both hands on his gun. Graham stopped, spun round. Sylvestrus and another guard appeared at the other end of the cabinet line. He was trapped. He looked at the gun. He looked at Sylvestrus. And he thought of Annalise Fifteen.

"You can't escape," said Sylvestrus.

"I don't need to escape," said Graham. "I can stop you now."

He flicked a switch on the gun, a red light came on, it started to whine.

"Killing me won't stop anything," said Sylvestrus. "Whatever happens to me, you're not leaving this room."

"Who said anything about killing you?" Graham turned the gun on himself. "I'm going to stop the resonance wave."

Sylvestrus's eyes widened in panic. Not for a fraction of a second this time but for two slow heartbeats. Graham took a deep breath. He felt remarkably calm. He felt exhilarated and composed at the same time. Maybe this was what it felt like when death became an inevitability. No more panic, no more fear of what might happen. Indecision replaced by a clarity of purpose. Just you, the gun and destiny.

"Put the gun down," said Sylvestrus. "I'm sure we can work something out." He motioned for the guards to back off. They did.

"Nothing to work out," said Graham. "I've seen the projections. Kill all the Grahams and the resonance wave stops dead. A small price to pay, don't you think?"

"You're only one Graham. Your death will have no effect," said Sylvestrus, his voice regaining some of its former equilibrium.

"Who said anything about just one Graham? Haven't you seen the latest Resonance logs? We're all earmarked for slaughter. It's the only way to collapse the wave."

"They'd never do it," said Sylvestrus, shaking his head.

"They don't have to," said Graham. "We're doing it. The Grahams. We're men of vision. Maybe your mind's too small to appreciate that. But we . . ."

Graham stopped. He felt strange, the light in the room was flickering. He felt . . .

No! Not that! Not now, he couldn't flip now!

A pain exploded in the back of his head. He reeled forward, men were all around him, grabbing his arms, the gun. The whining sound increased. It might have been the gun, it might have been him, everything was moving and coalescing—ceilings, floors, sounds. He felt like he was being stretched and pulled. There was an explosion. He was falling, flying, rolling.

No! A thought burrowed into the back of his head. He was flipping out of danger. He was going to wake up in a new world. Someone else was going to wake up with a gun pressed against his head.

No! He fought. He concentrated. He summoned whatever will he possessed and then dug deeper. He was not going to put someone else in jeopardy. He couldn't. He wouldn't.

He dragged the world back to him. Sylvestrus, the

guards, a smoking hole in the ceiling. He was on the floor, writhing, his arms and legs pinned, the gun nowhere to be seen, debris everywhere.

"Hold him down," shouted Sylvestrus, removing something from his breast pocket. A syringe. Graham struggled, the pain and nausea building. Sylvestrus's face loomed towards him. The needle, the prick, the burning sensation in his arm.

No! He fought, he struggled, he screamed. And then he was flying again, everything so hazy, he was being pulled and squeezed and stretched. The world had lost its cohesion. He wasn't sure if he was dying, losing consciousness or flying.

He awoke, lying on the floor. No Sylvestrus, no debris, no hole in the ceiling.

Only pain.

He retched.

When one pain eased, another hit him harder. Guilt. He'd exchanged lives. He'd dragged someone to a slow, lingering death.

He jumped to his feet and immediately fell down again. His legs had buckled beneath him. His head felt like it was going to explode.

He looked around the room. It looked identical to the one he'd left. Except the filing cabinets were gone. He could see the door. He crawled towards it, used the handle to pull himself up, pressed the release button. The door clicked. It hadn't been locked. He pulled it towards him and squeezed through, keeping a foot in the door to stop it from closing. The corridor was empty. Did that mean he was safe?

He prayed for his head to clear. He couldn't think through the pain. How could he determine if he was safe or not?

The notice board! He swung round. The notice board was there but no mention of New Tech weapons. He staggered towards it. Memos about joint ventures and procurement, something about the Census project and accommodation. Nothing about Sylvestrus or weapons.

Was that proof?

And did that matter? He'd left someone to die on the other side. He'd made a choice and someone else had suffered the consequences. They wouldn't even have a chance! They'd materialize in a drugged body, pinned to the ground by two armed guards.

He'd go back! He'd make things right. He'd make a choice, ten choices, and lie in the exact same spot.

"I choose to go back," he said, tilting his head back and shouting at the ceiling. He ran to the spot where he'd struggled and threw himself on the floor.

Nothing happened.

How long did it take, he wondered? Should he make another choice? Should he make a larger choice? What if the other Graham was in no condition to reciprocate?

He dismissed the thought. He had to try. He jumped. He filled his head with decisions. He chose to walk to the wall, to hop back, to use his left foot, his right. He picked up a pencil and snapped it. He took the stub and marched over to the notice board. He started writing. Telling everyone about Sylvestrus and the resonance wave and how to stop it.

Nothing happened.

Maybe the other Graham was no longer in the room? Maybe he'd been moved?

He left the room. He ran down the corridor towards the stairs. Would this be the way they'd bring him? He banged on every door he passed. He chose to run, he chose to walk, he chose to shout at the top of his voice.

Nothing happened. Not one door opened, not one person came out to investigate. Was the building empty?

He reached the stairs. Would they have taken the other Graham this way? He took the first flight. He ran back. He thought of every possible meal he'd cook for dinner that evening—choosing each in turn and then changing his mind.

He chose until he had no choices left. And then he collapsed. On the cold concrete steps by the basement doors. The other Graham could be anywhere now. He'd failed him. He'd failed everyone.

He stayed on the stairs for hours. Or maybe only a few minutes. Time lost all meaning in the wallowing landscape of guilt and what-might-have-beens.

A voice called out to him from above.

"Mr. Smith? Graham, are you all right?"

Graham looked up and saw a face peering down at him from the railings above. It wasn't a face he recognized. Or could talk to. He pulled himself slowly to his feet and trudged up the stairs.

The man came down to offer him a hand. A middle-aged man in shorts and a T-shirt that failed to encompass his bulging stomach. Graham shrugged away his offer of a hand. He wasn't deserving of any help this day. Graham pushed through the doors to the ground floor lobby and strode out. He didn't care if Sylvestrus and all his henchmen were waiting for him. Let them do their worst. He'd already done his.

FIFTY-ONE

Annalise Fifteen refused for the third time. There was no way anyone was going to interview Graham. He needed time.

"The guy's been chased, kidnapped, shot at and terrorized," she told Jerry Saddler. "He's traumatized."

"The police are not going to wait forever, Annalise," said the lawyer. "Let me at least have a doctor see him. If we can provide the police with a medical report, it will strengthen our hand. At the moment it looks like we're stalling."

And so the conversation continued. As it had most of Sunday afternoon. The same conversation—different venues, different combatants. When could the police see Graham? Why won't he attend an identification parade? What exactly is the matter with him?

Annalise stalled them all. Graham was going nowhere, seeing no one and talking to no one. Not until he was ready. Maybe tomorrow, maybe the next day.

"We can't hold these men forever," Dave had told her, minutes after she'd identified the two phoney policemen from their respective lineups. "Twenty-four hours and then we have to charge them or let them go."

"Then charge them," Annalise had said.

"Without Mr. Smith's evidence we don't have enough. We're under extreme pressure as it is. My phone's backed up with lawyers and VIPs. All of them want these men released and you locked up."

"You owe me," she'd snapped. "I've given you three murderers. The least you can give me is a lousy twenty-four hours."

He'd relented. "One o'clock tomorrow afternoon," he'd said. "The twenty-four hours runs out then. Make sure Graham's here before that."

Jenny ran through the options again. Stay in the flat or move to a house outside London.

Neither appealed.

Security at the flat was being tightened. Three men would stay the night, another two would watch the roof, another four on the ground outside. But there was still the memory of the previous night. The ease with which the intruder had broken in.

"That won't happen again," Jenny said. "There's more men and all the cameras have an independent power supply. Plus Dave has promised to have a car come by every half hour. Sylvestrus would have to be mad to try anything again."

Annalise wondered how crazy Sylvestrus was. And how desperate. She could imagine him firing one of his New Tech rockets into the building and waiting for the two of them to run out.

And moving to another house wasn't an option. Sylvestrus would have the building watched. He'd follow them wherever they went.

"Another option," said Jenny, "is to do both. We can hire some look-alikes—with your hair, it'll be easy. We can bring them here in disguise, dress them up, and then you choose where you want to spend the night. The decoys take the option you turn down."

"Won't it be dangerous for the decoys?"

"We'll look after them. If you want, we'll spread the risk. Have ten addresses, ten cars and ten sets of decoys. Sylvestrus won't be able to keep track of them all."

Annalise agreed. She liked that idea. She liked that idea a lot.

Graham wandered through Putney in a cloud. Why was it sometimes he flipped without knowing and other times he felt like he'd been pulled through a mangle? It made no sense.

Maybe it wasn't supposed to, maybe it was punishment for not breaking the link as a child.

Or maybe there was something different about the flips themselves. He thought back. The girl in the park, jumping on the bus, holding a gun to his head. Was there a common denominator? Fear, guns, something tightly grasped in his hand—the girl, the pole, the gun. Was there something about that type of situation—the flow of adrenaline, the overpowering desire not to flip, the

physical connection to some kind of restraining anchor—
that interfered with the flipping mechanism?

And was it something he could use?

A thought that lasted less than a block. What good was
he at using anything. He'd tried to flip and failed and
tried not to flip and failed. That was the only thing he
was good at. Failure.

It wasn't until he reached the tube station that he
thought to check his pockets.

He'd moved house. He was back at Oakhurst Drive.
And he had a ParaDim key card.

He rotated the green and gold card between his fingers.
Did having a key card signify anything? Did it mean he was
safe in this world? Was he helping the Resonance team?

Or had Adam Sylvestrus given it to him? Was that his
way of ensnaring Graham, making him welcome, bringing
all the eggs into one basket so he could crush him and the
Resonance team in one go?

Graham went home, not caring if his house was bugged
or full of assassins. Let them all come, he said to himself,
what do I care?

He ate late and sat in silence, reflecting on his failures.

He was *not* Annalise Fifteen. He couldn't think on his
feet the way she did. When she'd threatened to kill herself, it had been part of a plan—a way to knock her
opponent off balance. When Graham had threatened to
kill himself, it had been *the* plan. He hadn't thought any
further. Even now, he wasn't sure what he'd have done
next. Pull the trigger, negotiate, bluff? He'd expected
something to pop into his head. He hadn't expected it to
be another Graham.

❀   ❀   ❀

The next day dawned under the same cloud. Graham settled into his familiar routine—wash, breakfast, catch the usual train. He didn't want to think, he didn't want to choose, he just wanted to forget.

At work, he printed off the staff list and watched the familiar names roll by. Brenda was married again, back with Bob. He felt a flicker of vicarious happiness. At least someone was having a good time.

"Good morning, Graham," said Sharmila from the doorway.

Graham grunted a greeting as he flicked through the list of names.

"I saw Brenda outside," she said. "She asked me to remind you about her birthday."

Graham swivelled round. It was Brenda's birthday? He'd forgotten. He usually bought her something.

"She's inviting everyone for drinks in her room at twelve."

Graham glanced down at the staff list. Brenda, Brenda, Brenda . . . room 501. Same as always.

Graham smiled and nodded a thank you to Sharmila. If he took an early lunch he could buy something at that little shop by the lights.

He sorted through the morning post, loaded up the mail trolley and set off on the first of his rounds.

Five minutes later, he pushed the mail trolley past the second-floor coffee machine and pressed the up button for the lift. Two women behind him were locked in an earnest conversation. Liz and Steph, from the sound of their voices.

"Is Brenda going to cancel the party?" asked Liz.

Graham's ears pricked at the mention of Brenda's name. Had something happened?

"No, she said Holly wouldn't hear of it," said Steph.

Graham leaned further into the conversation. He knew Holly well. She often worked in the same room as Brenda.

"How old's Holly's mother? She must be getting on," asked Liz.

"Sixty-five. Still, that's no age, is it? Not these days."

Had Holly's mother died? Graham had seen pictures of her once. Holiday snaps that Brenda and Holly had passed around one year. Rhyll. Or had it been Tenby?

"At least it's operable," said Liz. "Holly says she's just thankful they caught it in time. If it hadn't been for the headaches, no one would have known."

"Ugh!" said Steph. "The thought of having something like that growing in your brain . . ."

The lift bell drew the two women's conversation to a close. They filed past Graham, who was suddenly lost in thought.

"Do you want the lift, Graham?" Liz asked, holding the door open.

Graham wasn't sure if he answered. He meant to shake his head but couldn't remember if he had or not.

He did remember the two women laughing.

But none of that mattered. He could see a plan forming in his head. It was so simple. Probably too simple to work. But if it did?

He pressed the down button. He had to find Annalise. He had to plan. And he needed somewhere he could think and make choices without the risk of flipping. He needed to be elsewhere. Fast.

He left the trolley by the Post Room door and hurried outside. He turned left instead of his usual right and started to run. He had to get far enough away. Flipping now would only complicate matters.

He stopped a block away and took a deep breath. For his plan to work he had to find Annalise. But how? She could be anywhere. She could be back in the building he'd just left or at home in America.

Or she might not exist on this world at all.

Think! He slapped his head. A passerby gave him a wide berth. Graham didn't care. Nothing mattered other than finding Annalise.

Should he flip until he found her? Run back to work and cycle through a series of choices and interactions until she appeared? How long would that take? There were 200 billion worlds and only 200 telepathic Annalises. And every day he wasted, another hundred, maybe another thousand, Resonance teams would disappear. The Grahams too—hundreds of them collapsing into comas.

He had to narrow the options. Find some place where he and Annalise would be together.

Like the ParaDim office at Putney!

He checked his pockets. He still had the key card.

He ran, dodging past the crowds, stopping only for roads and then only for the minimum amount of time. He pushed to the front of queues, something the old Graham would never have done. He crossed roads on red. He stepped on cracks.

Occasionally, doubt pushed inside his mind. He'd tried to flip last night. He'd spent ages in the basement, why should today be any different? Wouldn't it be better to go back to work and try Frank Gledwood's office?

He threw the idea aside. Annalise spent as little time as possible with Frank. If one of the girls were on this world, she'd be with the Resonance team.

The spectre of Sylvestrus appeared to Graham as the tube rattled through the tunnels outside Earl's Court. What if Sylvestrus was with the Resonance team? What if there was no Resonance team?

What if, what if? He slapped his head again. The woman opposite scowled, two boys by the door giggled.

He arrived out of breath at the ParaDim building. The same white concrete and black-tinted windows, the same key card entry system. He inserted his key card, placed his right hand on the scanner and looked directly into the camera.

The door opened.

He composed himself, took a deep breath and walked to the reception desk.

"Is Mr. Sylvestrus in?" he said, trying to keep his voice calm.

"Mister who?" said the puzzled guard.

Graham almost collapsed in relief. "How about Miss Mercado?"

The guard ran a finger down a screenful of names and shook his head. "No Mercado listed here. Have you tried the Victoria office?"

"How about Miss Kent?" Was Annalise still using Tamisha's name and ID?

"Miss Kent is in 5G."

Graham slid the last three yards to the lift and slapped the button hard with his palm. He was so close. The lift arrived and Graham jumped in. He turned and stood close to the doors. And wondered. How close did he have to be to create a bridge to another world? Standing on the exact same spot or in the same room? Was standing by the lift doors instead of his usual place at the back protection enough? Or didn't it matter? Would resonance step in and force the two ends of the bridge together? Would his two selves be compelled to meet in the center of the lift? Was that how it worked?

The lift doors opened on the fifth floor. He stepped out and reined in his imagination. He couldn't risk flipping. Not when he was this close. Annalise might be on the other side of that door.

He inserted his key card, placed his hand on the panel and waited for the light above 5G to flash green. The door clicked, he went inside, his heart thumping, her name on his lips.

"Ann—"

He stopped.

The woman was not Annalise.

FIFTY-TWO

"Tamisha?"

Tamisha swivelled in her chair. She looked almost as surprised as Graham.

"Where's Annalise?" he said.

"Who?"

"No time to explain. I've got to get to a world where Annalise is in this building. You know who I am?"

"Graham Smith on speed?" she said, raising one eyebrow.

Graham's mind filled with a thousand things to do. He had to make choices, interact, force himself to flip until he found her. She had to be in this building. Annalise Six practically lived here.

He paced around the room, spontaneously changing

direction, staring at Tamisha, waiting for her face to morph into someone else.

"What the hell is the matter with you, boy?" said Tamisha, standing up. She looked confused, a hint of anger. Graham felt stupid. It wasn't working. He was making choices but nothing was happening.

Maybe his choices were too small to have any impact? Hadn't Gary said as much? The greater the choice, the greater the chance of forming a bridge.

"Sit down, Tamisha," he said. "I'm going to tell you something huge."

He told her everything he knew. The Etxamendi file, Sylvestrus and natural selection, the link across the twelfth dimension, how the resonance wave could be blown away if the Grahams broke the link with enough energy.

She listened and took notes, told him to slow down and go back. She'd heard of the Etxamendi file. She'd seen it referenced in a log she was reading barely twenty minutes ago. She'd been wrestling with the math when Graham had burst in.

Graham waited to flip. With every new fact he divulged, he imagined the charge building.

Nothing happened.

"I don't understand," he said. "I should be flipping now, shouldn't I? Doesn't this count as a major interaction? I've given you information you're going to pass on to countless others and change the lives of thousands, maybe millions of people, right? You are going to pass this on?"

"Oh, I'm passing this on, all right," she said nodding. "I'm calling Kevin and Shikha now."

She leaned over and pulled the phone towards her.

"Then why aren't I flipping? With the charge I've just

set off, I should be attracting every other Graham Smith in the building."

"It doesn't work like that," said Tamisha, as she waited for someone to pick up. "Hi, Kevin, get the others and come down to 5G immediately."

She put the phone down. "From what I read this morning, you have to be in the exact same spot or the bridge won't form. Doesn't matter how powerful the charge is."

"I thought it increased the chances of connection?"

"It does." She turned and flicked through a series of screens. "There," she said, pointing to a line of text on the screen. "The greater the charge, the longer the filament's life." She turned back to Graham. "You should be trailing a filament right now. But if you sit here, you'll waste it. Run around the building, visit all the places you think other Grahams might be . . ."

Graham had the door open before she'd finished.

He ran, he visited every room he'd frequented before. Even the one in the basement. He circled each room, quartered each room, covered every inch he could think of. He took the lift from top to bottom. Ran the stairs from bottom to top. Every few seconds he checked his clothes or the note in his pocket to see if it had worked.

And every few seconds he was disappointed.

He returned to 5G, despondent. What else could he try? Go back to work and flip through 200 billion worlds? Or keep trying here?

He opened the door to find Kevin, Shikha and two other men he'd never seen before closeted around Tamisha. Not one of them turned to see who'd come in.

Tamisha was talking about bridges and the twelfth dimension.

"I need help," said Graham. "I need to get an urgent message to another world this morning. Is there any way of doing that?"

Kevin answered. "The only gate we have is one-way. We can receive but we can't transmit."

Graham felt stupid for asking a question he already knew the answer to. He was failing again. The pressure was on and he was floundering. Without Annalise, he was nothing. Even when he had a plan, he couldn't manoeuvre himself into the right place. Everything hinged on him being in the right place at the right time and he couldn't even manage that!

"Are you okay?" asked Shikha.

He turned away, embarrassed and angry.

"Graham, are you okay?" repeated Shikha.

Maybe he'd given up too early? Maybe it was a matter of perseverance, keep making choices, keep interacting, keep circling the building?

He turned and froze. Everyone had left. Except Shikha, who was sat at Tamisha's terminal looking at him quizzically.

He'd flipped. He must have.

"Are you all right?" Shikha said again, an element of concern in her voice.

Graham was about to respond when a thought stopped him dead. Was replying a choice? Would a yes or no send him back where he'd come from?

"I don't know," he said as impartially as he could. His eyes flicked across the room. Should he move? Stand somewhere else. Was the filament still active? Could he be sucked back if he made the wrong move?

He shuffled his feet. Shikha was staring at him, concern turning to worry. How could he ask her if she knew Annalise? Wouldn't that be interacting? Should he leave the building and call from a public phone?

"Graham?"

Graham took a deep breath. He was undoubtedly being stupid. Ten minutes ago he was trying everything he could to flip and failing, why should it be any different now? His little voice provided the answer—Murphy's Law, more powerful than Schenck: if anything can go wrong, it will.

He tried something else.

"Annalise," he said in a voice devoid of inflection.

"You want Annalise?" asked Shikha.

Graham's brain felt like it was seizing up. He couldn't think straight. He was terrified of flipping, he was terrified of thinking, he was terrified of doing anything that might precipitate a flip.

"Shall I call Annalise?" asked Shikha.

Graham closed his eyes, relief flooding over him. She was here! She had to be. Shikha wouldn't have said that otherwise.

"Do *you* think I should talk to Annalise?" he asked.

"Graham, you're worrying me. Why are you talking like that?"

"Annalise," he repeated and pointed to the corridor. "Do you think I should wait in the corridor?"

Shikha stared at him and Graham felt like the stupidest robot ever conceived.

"I'll call her," Shikha said.

Graham hurried into the corridor. Was he any safer out here? Was there a place he'd be safer still?

There was. It came to him just as Annalise stepped out of the lift. An Annalise with brown hair. Annalise Six? He grabbed her and pushed her into the Ladies.

"Graham!" she shouted.

He threw himself against the far stall, as far away from the door and the corridor wall as he could.

"It's all right. We'll be safe here," he said, breathing hard.

"Safe from what?"

"Flipping," he said, unable to stop smiling. "It's me. I'm back."

"Graham?" She blinked twice. "Is it really you?"

"It's really me."

She fell on him and hugged him so hard he thought his ribs were going to crack.

"I think I know how to stop the resonance wave," he said when he got his breath back. "Fetch the others. I want to make sure I'm right."

"Bring them here?" asked Annalise.

"It's the only place I feel safe."

He told them everything that had happened. How he'd flipped, Sylvestrus, natural selection and how he'd returned.

Then he told them his plan.

They were sceptical at first but he won them over. He knew the Grahams, they didn't. All he wanted from Gary and Howard was confirmation that his theory was correct.

"It'll take time to confirm," said Howard.

"How long?"

"An hour?" said Howard glancing at Gary for confirmation.

Graham checked his watch—10:15 a.m. He was forty minutes away from Westminster Street. He'd need five, ten minutes contingency.

"You've got fifty-five minutes," he said. "I leave at 11:10 whatever happens."

Annalise stayed after the others had left.

"I'll start contacting the girls," she said. "It's not going to be easy—this plan of yours. Most of the girls have taken their Grahams into hiding. And only five of us have security passes to Westminster Street."

"I know," he said. "But I also know how resourceful the girls are. They'll get passes from ParaDim, they'll set up dummy interviews, they'll get Graham to open the delivery bay doors. They'll do whatever it takes. They always do. And I know that come twelve o'clock, when I start things off," he paused, his voice quivering, "there'll be two hundred Annalises with me to keep it going."

Annalise's eyes suddenly widened in horror.

"What's the matter?" he said, swallowing hard. Had she just received a message?

"Graham," she said. "There's something you ought to know."

"What?"

"It's Annalise Fifteen."

FIFTY-THREE

Annalise Fifteen spent a restless night at the flat. Several times she awoke convinced she wasn't alone in her room. Each time she had to check, each time she had to search the built-in wardrobes and look under the bed.

And once awake, she had to check on Graham.

She thought the night would never end. But it did.

She rose at seven, forced herself to eat something and drank far too much coffee. She was nursing her fourth cup when Jenny burst in.

"Sylvestrus is running," Jenny announced. "I heard the news on the way over."

Annalise spilt her coffee in her rush to sit up. "Why? What's happened?"

"Ostensibly he's flying to Geneva to consult a plastic surgeon but I'm sure he's fleeing the country. I'm having the facts checked now but I can't see him receiving better treatment in Geneva than at the Cavendish. It's one of the world's top hospitals."

"Can he leave just like that? Doesn't he have to report to the police like I do?"

"Rich men obey a different set of laws than you and me, dear," she said, reaching into her handbag and pulling out her cigarettes and a lighter. "Once he's out of the country, he's not coming back."

"Does Dave know he's skipping the country?"

"He will in five minutes when I tell him."

Annalise felt like a huge weight had been taken off her. "So, the case against me collapses?"

Jenny screwed up her face. "Not exactly. Jerry thinks Sylvestrus will try to distance himself from proceedings while his legal team try to rip you to shreds. If they can nullify you, then the case against Sylvestrus goes away. If they can't, they'll sacrifice the four men in custody—two overzealous employees and two strangers with no links to Sylvestrus. Whatever happens Mr. S. will be out of the country and denying everything behind a wall of lawyers."

Annalise had a worrying thought. ParaDim did not leave loose ends. Any one of those men in custody could cut a deal. Would Sylvestrus risk his future on the lives of four men?

She didn't think so.

Without Graham's testimony, four men would be released at one o'clock. How many would be alive at one-thirty?

Or were they booked on the plane as well?

"What time's Sylvestrus's plane due to leave?" asked Annalise.

"Two, why?"

"How long does it take to drive from Ladbroke Road to the airport?"

Jenny looked hard at Annalise then shook her head. "Sylvestrus would never do that. He needs an element of deniability. If he takes any of those men with him, he's pushing himself closer to the crime."

"Then someone's going to kill four men very soon."

Annalise paced the room. She had to *do* something. She checked her watch. Ten o'clock. The men would be released in three hours, Sylvestrus would be out of the country in four. Could she coach Graham? Would he lie for her? Was there a way she could persuade him that in this world it was the truth? Would there be a bruise in the middle of his back from where the gun had dug in or cuts from the struggle?

The phone rang.

It was Jerry. The police wanted to know when Graham was arriving. They were prepared to send a car. They were prepared to do anything.

Except extend the deadline.

Dave's career was on the line as it was. And if Annalise didn't produce Graham by 12:45 at the latest, a warrant would be sought for her immediate arrest.

"On what charges?" Annalise shouted down the phone.

"Attempted murder—"

"But the kidnapping," Annalise interrupted. "The witnesses. They must have found other witnesses by now. The cameras." She was too angry to be coherent. She thought all this had been settled. Sylvestrus was on the run. Didn't that count for anything?

Jerry attempted to calm her down. There were witnesses. *One* thought she might have seen a gun in Graham's back; *some* saw the struggle between Annalise and the gunman. But *everyone* recalled how the orange-haired girl had thrown the flaming waste bin into the big, black car.

"What about the man shooting at me? You can't tell me no one remembers that."

"That's not a point of contention. The man claims to have overreacted. You'd attacked his boss. He thought you were terrorists and opened fire."

And the CCTV cameras hadn't been much help either. The resolution was poor. Several cameras showed Graham and one of the gunmen walking together, but without Graham's testimony there was nothing to suggest anything criminal was taking place.

Annalise put the phone down and slumped onto the sofa. She had less than three hours to coach Graham. Somehow she had to describe the faces of four men in such detail that Graham could pick them out from a line of similar-looking men.

She held her face in her hands.

"*Annalise,*" said a voice in her head.

"I'll go to her," said Graham. He'd made up his mind before Annalise Six had finished explaining. "I can testify."

"How can you get there?" asked Annalise.

"I'll find a way."

She shook her head. "What about your plan? Do you want me to contact the girls or not?"

Graham felt like he'd been kicked in the stomach by a

herd of wild horses. Was Fate conspiring against him? Was his plan so abhorrent to the nature of the universe that it had to be thwarted? Or was he being forced to choose? Was there some malevolent deity out there testing him—okay, Mr. Smith, you wanted choice, here's the biggest choice you'll ever have to make. Who do you save? Millions of strangers or the love of your life?

He looked at Annalise, and all he could see was Fifteen. She looked so sad. How could he not go to her? His plan could be postponed. There'd be another opportunity.

Not like today. Three words that cut him like the sharpest knife. There wouldn't be another opportunity like today. Not for a long time. He knew where everyone would be at twelve o'clock. The longer he waited, the less chance of success. Every day there would be fewer Grahams and maybe fewer Annalises too. How long could the girls stay hidden?

And how long could Fifteen stay alive? Sylvestrus would hunt her down. As long as she remained a threat to his plan, she'd be a target. And Fifteen would always be a threat. She wouldn't stop until she brought down ParaDim. A chance she had now. If Graham testified.

He had to go to her. He owed her, he loved her. He realized that now.

And he realized something else. Once the resonance wave was stopped, there'd be no more flipping. Fifteen would be left to fend for herself on a world he could never reach. He'd never know what became of her, he'd never see her again, he'd never know what might have been.

He had to go to her.

But if he did, thousands more people would die.

He couldn't save one without dooming the other.

Unless . . .

"Tell the girls," he told Six. "Then send this message to Fifteen."

Graham checked his watch for the seventh time in as many minutes.

"It's eight minutes past," he told Annalise. "I've got to go."

The door to the Ladies slammed back against its hinges. Howard burst in.

"It works," he said, out of breath and wheezing. "Simulations confirm a . . . ninety-seven percent probability . . . but you must keep it going."

Graham took a deep breath and looked at Annalise. "Ready?" he asked.

"Always," she replied.

Graham closed his mind to anything resembling a choice. He couldn't afford to flip now. He and Annalise had to arrive together. One mistake and everything would be lost.

They didn't exchange a word on the tube. Graham shut himself off from the outside world and let Annalise guide him.

The train stopped in the tunnels outside Earl's Court. Seconds ticked away. Why had it stopped? Graham tried to keep calm and detached. He wouldn't check his watch, he wouldn't open his mind to doubt. All his energy had to be focused on the one room and the one time. Twelve o'clock. He had to plan, he had to run through the sequence of events; once there he couldn't afford to freeze or be deflected.

The train jerked forward, accompanied by creaking

metal and carriage lights that weren't sure if they were supposed to be on or off. Graham closed his eyes and sank deeper within himself. He wasn't on a train, he was in Brenda's room, it was twelve o'clock and everything was going according to plan. He held onto that thought, breathed life into it, gave it form and substance. The train wouldn't be late, couldn't be late, because he was already there, his foot wedged in time's door pulling the two realities together.

An age later, he felt a tug on his arm. A disembodied voice. Annalise. The train had arrived.

He walked; one foot in reality, one squelching half-asleep through a liquid realm of fear and possibility. The closer he came, the more nervous he became. There was so much at stake. So much that could go wrong. How could any plan of his have any credibility?

They left the station, walking arm in arm down streets that barely registered in his mind. He couldn't concentrate. His mind was cycling though his plan, replaying strategies, recasting roles.

He shivered outside the door to the DTI. He stretched, he took a deep breath. He felt terrible. Nerves, stress, emotion, the feeling that everything was about to unravel any second.

They went in, produced their passes, waited for the lift. Annalise forced a smile, her face looked strained. He could only guess what his looked like.

Graham started to count. The lift took forever.

A bell sounded, the lift arrived, people tumbled out. Graham stood back, staring at his shoes while the lift emptied.

He stepped inside, his legs feeling heavy, the lift doors

refusing to close, Annalise pressing the button for the fifth floor over and over again.

They ascended in silence, taking it in turns to check their watches, their arms rising and falling like a conjoined slow-motion drummer. Graham counted the floors, timed the intervals between each light flickering on and off.

The fifth floor. Nearly there. People trickling into 501. The sound of laughter and conversation from inside.

Graham and Annalise waited outside—two, three yards away from the entrance. Graham knelt down to tie a shoelace—anything to make him feel less visible.

He stood up and adjusted his tie.

"Are you okay?" Annalise asked and immediately put her hand to her mouth. "Don't answer that!" she hissed through her fingers. "Sorry."

Graham swallowed hard. His hands were starting to shake, his stomach churned. Every fiber of his being screamed at him to turn and flee.

He took a deep breath, turned to Annalise and whispered, "Are the girls all here?"

She closed her eyes. Graham checked his watch—11:56—could he survive four more minutes? More people arrived. Graham avoided eye contact, keeping his head lowered and his mind counting down the seconds.

"They're all here," whispered Annalise. "Except Twelve and Fifteen."

Graham could guess where Twelve was—watching over her sleeping Graham. He hoped he knew where Fifteen was.

Graham took a deep breath and tried to steady his nerves. *You don't have to do this,* his little voice said. *Wait until tomorrow or the next day. Work on the plan, don't rush it.*

He turned in the doorway and whispered to Annalise.

"Remember, it's up to you and the girls to keep this going. Stay in contact the entire time. Impress upon the Grahams that this is the only way to stop the world unravelling. Tell them that the world changes because they let it. Tell them to interact and choose and talk and do whatever they have to do. The world will spin for a while, maybe an hour, maybe a day, but when it stops, it stops for good. Tell them that. They'll listen, they know what's happening."

"You're crying, Graham."

"Am I?"

She wiped a tear from his face with her finger and wished him luck. He took a deep breath, checked his watch for the final time and stepped into the room.

FIFTY-FOUR

He slipped in unnoticed as he'd slipped in so many times before. There were twenty, maybe thirty people in the room. Not a crowd but enough to make it difficult to walk between the desks. Brenda was in the far corner, thanking people for coming. It was a typical birthday drink. Good-natured heckling, friendly banter, alcohol in plastic cups.

Graham pushed his way close to the front. Holly was at her desk, a party hat on her head and a cup in her hand. Red wine, thought Graham as he pushed closer. Holly always drank red wine.

It was time. He was in place, he was ready. He . . . he couldn't do it. Not here, not now, not with these people! He had a history with them. Seventeen years of silence. He was Graham Smith, weird but harmless. He couldn't break that spell. The weight of time was too great, too powerful. In this building he'd never be anyone other than the old, silent, invisible Graham.

He felt a hand rest gently on his right shoulder. He felt Annalise's breath against his neck.

"You can do it, Graham," she whispered. "We believe in you."

He closed his eyes and thought of another Annalise, the one from Boston, the one without a number. She'd believed in him. She'd dragged him out of his silent world. Could she do it again? He tried to imagine the entire room in their underwear. And quickly released the thought—Brenda was like a sister and Annalise . . .

He summoned other images instead. Annalise Seven and her cardboard box. Annalise One by the fridge, Fifteen on the roof, Tamisha's face in the attic window. So many sacrifices by so many people. People he'd barely known, people he'd never know. All of them working towards this one moment.

He couldn't let them down, he couldn't let anyone down. He was the key.

"Holly," he said, his voice shaking and throat tightening. He coughed and tried again, louder, his voice rising to a shout. "Holly, listen to me. Holly!"

Holly glanced towards him, her face smiling, not a care in the world.

Graham swallowed hard. Holly's eyes widened in surprise. Other faces turned towards him. People close by stopped talking.

"How's your mother, Holly?" Graham said, maintaining the level of his voice—one notch down from a shout, several notches above that of every other voice in the room.

"She's fine, Graham," Holly said, regaining her composure and waving a plastic cup. "Do you want a drink?"

"You have to ring her now, Holly. It's important."

All conversation in the room ceased immediately.

Holly looked confused. "Did she give you a message for me?" She looked towards Brenda. "She didn't ring earlier, did she, Bren?"

Brenda shook her head. She looked stunned.

"Ring her now," Graham continued. "Ask about her headaches."

Holly's face dropped. She started to speak and then grabbed the phone.

Graham waited. He had to be right. And even if he wasn't, Holly's mother had to have a checkup. She had to be made aware of the risk.

A few giggles from the back of the room broke the silence. A silence reimposed the moment Holly spoke.

"Mum, is everything okay?" Holly's voice rose half an octave. There was a gap while her mother replied. Graham strained to make sense of the low buzz of conversation. He could feel the entire room lean collectively towards Holly's desk.

"What headaches, mum?" Holly's voice took on a growing panic. "You never said anything about headaches before."

"She needs a brain scan," said Graham, keeping his voice as loud as he dare. "Tell her she'll be fine. It's operable. You've caught it in time."

"Mum, stay where you are! I'm coming home now!"

It had begun.

He shut out the gasps and the rush of confused conversation and focused on Brenda. It was her turn now. He walked towards her, slow and purposeful, not glancing left or right, blinkered, her face filling his vision. She stared back, her eyes wide, her lips slightly parted.

People moved out of his way, a desk scraped along the floor. Holly grabbed her belongings and fled. Graham held out his hands and laid them gently on Brenda's shoulders. She didn't move. He looked into her eyes.

"Bren," he said softly. "Your future is with Bob. I've seen the two of you together. I've seen your children. You complete each other. Go to him."

She dropped her cup. Someone at the back gasped. Brenda swayed for a second and then rushed forward, pushing past Graham. He turned and watched. Brenda was in the middle of the room, her eyes darting from face to face.

"Bob!" she cried. "Bob!"

A nervous Bob appeared in the center of the aisle at the back, half-pushed by his neighbor. Brenda walked up to him. The two of them stood a foot or so apart, looking at each other. Seconds passed and then they fell into each other's arms, locked together, rocking from side to side.

Graham scanned every face in the room. They were all people he'd known for years—some for five, some for ten, some for seventeen. He knew them all. Their lives, their histories, their likes and dislikes. He'd seen them on a thousand worlds. He'd observed, he'd listened. He'd overheard their lives—snippets of conversation from rooms and corridors, from queues and lifts. Regurgitated stories from Sharmila and Michael, from Brenda and others.

He'd seen them when they were happy and seen them when they were sad. He knew which relationships worked and which never could.

He knew them better than they knew themselves.

Because he'd been there. He'd seen their "what ifs." The lives they could have led. Their befores and afters. He'd seen the triumph and the tragedy and all that lay in between.

And he could tell them.

He went amongst them. A strange mixture of silence and tumult, awe and expectation. What was he going to do next? He could see it in their eyes. The pleading looks, the shake of the head—no, not me, go to someone else.

He noticed a middle-aged man standing near the back, his head down, trying to be invisible. A state of mind Graham knew all to well.

"Colin," Graham said. The man's head snapped up as though he'd been stung. A path opened up in front of him as people moved aside. Someone fell over a desk in their haste to get out of his way.

No one laughed.

"How's Terry?" Graham asked, part of him hoping that Colin had reconciled his differences with his estranged son.

Colin shrugged, sadness mingling with fear in his eyes. And then panic. "He's not ill, is he?" he shouted, his hands flying to Graham's lapels.

"No," said Graham as soothingly as he could. "I've seen the two of you together. The problems between you can be bridged. It takes time but I've seen it happen. Ring him now. He's waiting."

"Thank you," said Colin, his eyes misting up. He hugged Graham, almost rocking him off his feet, he thanked him again, broke down and then hurried out of the room.

More people appeared in the doorway. Shouts came from the corridor.

Graham spun in the center of the room, looking for the next person to help. Annalise came up to him, tears streaming down her face.

She placed a hand on his shoulder. "Are you still here?" she whispered.

He was. A fact that worried him. He was changing people's lives. He should have flipped by now. Perhaps he wasn't in the right place? He started spreading out from the center of the room. People stepped out of his way.

Except one. Frank Gledwood. He walked over and placed a hand against Graham's chest.

"Are you drunk?" sneered Frank, looking into Graham's eyes, imparting his usual mix of ridicule and contempt. "Just what the hell do you think you're playing at."

"Leave him alone, Frank," said a voice from the back. "He's got messages for us. He's seen the future."

"Ah, the future, is it?" said Frank, his eyes sparkling, looking like a cat with a fat paw on the tail of a struggling mouse. "And what message have you got for me?"

Graham looked him in the eyes, held him there for two seconds, and said, "Take an AIDS test."

There was a collective gasp. Frank spluttered, shaking his head. His hand fell from Graham's chest. "It's a mistake," he said. No one listened. Graham moved on and a wall of people moved with him.

Annalise pushed her way alongside Graham. "Frank has AIDS?" she hissed into his ear.

Graham shrugged and threw her a smile. "No harm being careful."

The room changed in that instant. People were spread out. They were laughing, talking, drinking. He'd flipped.

He pushed through to the front, looking for Holly. She was talking to Brenda in the corner.

"Holly," he began, "how's your mother?"

Deja vu. The same tearful phone call home, the same headaches, the same shocked silence.

But no matchmaking for Brenda this time—Graham saw Bob's arm wrap around Brenda as soon as Holly rang home.

Graham moved from person to person, asking questions about their lives, their partners, looking for the ones he could help.

"Don't get back with that man, Rosie. I've seen what he does to you."

"Kath, have your son tested. He may be allergic to nuts."

"Jo, he never leaves his wife."

He flipped again.

Annalise One appeared in front of him, unmistakable with her long black hair.

"You can stop the world unravelling, Graham," she said. "It's not easy but you can do it. We believe in you. Look at all these people around . . ."

Graham put a finger to her lips and smiled. "I know," he said. "Thank you for everything, Annalise."

They hugged, a brief interlude before he went in search of Holly.

Within a minute he'd flipped again.

And then again and again.

Sometimes he saw Annalise, sometimes he didn't. Sometimes she had red hair, sometimes black, blonde, orange or blue.

He hugged them all. And moved on.

He checked his watch. Fourteen minutes gone. Many more to go. He had to keep the momentum going to generate the charge. Continued flipping in the same spot. Starting with the one Graham and spiralling out. Two hundred Annalises keeping it going. Persuading each new Graham to take up the challenge. The two hundred Grahams becoming three then five then a thousand.

Keep it going, he'd begged the Annalises. The Grahams will help and if they don't—ask them a question, force them to make a choice. And with each flip the choices will come easier. A resonance would develop. A resonance that would accord with the Grahams' desire to end the unravelling. A resonance greater than their desire to hide and retreat and withdraw from the world.

One came from hope, the other from fear.

He flipped again.

A sea of faces; expectant, reticent, hopeful, terrified. Was it his imagination or were they growing in number? He moved amongst them, darting in and out of the crowd, selecting people, changing their lives.

What did *they* see? These people, his colleagues. An idiot savant, a prophet, a miracle? A nobody who'd walked in their midst for seventeen years, silent, deaf and retarded? But who could now speak, who came to them with visions of the future, with messages from God?

Were they frightened of him? They moved back whenever he walked towards them. But they didn't run. The room was filling up, more were outside in the corridor. The phones were ringing continuously.

Were they in awe of him? Frightened and attracted in equal measures? Not sure what he'd do next?

He moved to the other side of the room. So many faces. Some he hadn't seen for years. A girl's face caught his eye. Her face so familiar but not from this building. He'd seen her somewhere else. In another context. He stared. She stared back. More deja vu. He'd seen that face staring back at him before.

From the side of a bus.

She was an actress. Josie someone . . . Josie Nelson? She was in a West End play. Her face was everywhere.

He beckoned her over. She obeyed instantly.

"Josie?" he said. "Josie Nelson?"

She nodded.

He laid his hand on the top of her head. "You don't belong here. You're a talented actress. Go."

He removed his hand. She left. Without a word, she spun towards the door and kept walking.

Someone at the back applauded.

He flipped and continued flipping. The interval between the flips diminishing with each exchange. Most times he materialized at a party. Most times he began by finding Holly. But sometimes he flipped to worlds where the party spirit had been replaced by a religious fervor.

Sometimes he didn't even have time to deliver a message. Sometimes the mere fact of selecting a person was enough to send his consciousness streaming from one world to the next. Or his touch on their head enough to send them crashing to the floor. It was like a religious revivalist meeting; he'd touch someone and they'd faint. Overcome by the anticipation, the moment, the belief that something miraculous was about to happen.

The room flashed before him, at times stroboscopic in the speed of change. He closed his eyes, tried to step back and remove himself from the furious pace of change.

He checked his watch—12:28—and blinked. Where had the time gone? He'd barely started. His hand changed before his eyes. A different watch.

He had to leave! He had to run! He had two minutes to get to the third floor. He headed for the door, the crowd so dense, he could barely move.

"Give him some room," someone shouted. "He's coming out."

A man struggled through the door towards him. "Graham," he shouted. "Have you got a message for me?"

The crowd parted and Stephen Leyland threw himself on his knees before Graham.

"Help me," he begged. "My son Jason. Do you know where he is?"

Graham tried to focus on the door, tried to push past but Stephen grabbed his legs. The man was desperate. Graham understood loss and he understood the pain of not knowing whether a loved one was alive or dead. He looked at the door, he looked at Stephen, he looked at the door again.

He couldn't leave.

He pulled Stephen to his feet. "There's a hostel in Camberwell," he said quickly. "I've seen him there before."

"Thank you, thank you so much. Thank . . ." Stephen broke down. Graham caught him before he fell and pulled him towards him.

He flipped again, Stephen Leyland morphing into an Annalise with braided, honey blonde hair.

"One Eight Seven?" he said, leaning back.

She tilted her head to one side. "How do you . . . ?"

"No time," he said. "I have to find Fifteen." He pulled himself away and pushed through the crowd by the door.

Guilt hit him before he'd reached the door. He hadn't even thanked One Eight Seven. And there was so much left undone. All those people. He wanted to talk to all the Stephens and the Hollys and the Colins. He wanted to give them hope, spare them pain, end their torment. He wanted to stay and thank all the Annalises. He wanted to see the flips through to the end.

But he *needed* to save Fifteen.

Someone shoved him hard from behind and kept shoving. "Go," said Annalise. "You're needed elsewhere."

He started to walk, pushing towards the back stairs.

"Give him room," shouted Annalise. "He needs a break. Wait here and he'll be back in five minutes."

The crowd parted. He checked his watch. Twelve-thirty. He was late. He should have been there already. He started to run, faster and faster. Had he blown it? Would the other Graham have left by now? He sent the stair door flying, panic and frustration smashing it back against the wall. He launched himself through, took the steps two at time, three at the landing, pushing off from the handrail, swinging down. Flight after flight. The staircase resonating to the sound of his clattering feet.

He leapt onto the third floor landing, clearing four steps, landed heavily, almost driving his knee up into his chin as he folded and sprang back up again. He reached out, found the stair door, pushed and drove through, sliding on the polished tile as he tried to turn right. The door to the Ladies beckoned. His meeting place. His goal. The place he should have been a minute ago.

He ducked inside, not caring if it was occupied or not.

He ran to the first stall, locked himself inside and waited.

He checked his watch. Two minutes late. Would the other Graham have waited? Was his watch right? He gave it a shake. And then wondered what he'd expected to happen? The digits to roll back to half past?

He dug in his pockets, hoping to find the two pages from his web site that Fifteen had given him, but they weren't there. He went through his wallet, maybe he'd put them in there instead. He hadn't.

He looked at his note. Name, job and address. His whole life summed up in so few words. But not any more. He took out a pen. The other Graham would need far more than this.

He pressed the note flat against the wall and started to write.

Go to room 501. Annalise is there. She's blonde this time. She'll tell you what to do.

He checked his watch again. 12:33. He stood up, sat down, climbed on the seat. He made choice after choice. He wrote on the cubicle door, "If Jason Leyland goes missing, check hostel in Camberwell."

He checked his clothing, he prayed, he waited. He switched the contents of all his pockets. He should have flipped by now. He was in the first stall on the third floor. Exactly as agreed. Hadn't the other Graham made it in time? Had there been trouble? Had the stall been occupied?

He'd try the other stalls, he reached for the door, he . . .

His hand froze in midair. The writing on the door had disappeared. He'd flipped. He threw life back into his hand, reached for the stall door, opened it, dived through, ran to the far corner and pressed himself flat against the wall. He couldn't flip again. He had to stay in this world.

He fumbled in his pockets. If he was in the right world, there'd be a note to prove it. He found three pieces of paper, his fingers growing three sizes as he tried to unfold the first one. They shook, they moved independently of his thought. He fumbled, he tore, he . . . stopped.

It wasn't his web page.

t was a list of instructions.

> *IMPORTANT—DO NOT read until 12:30 EX-ACTLY.*
>
> *You have to make as many choices as you can in five minutes. Act on those choices. Choose to untie your shoes, empty your pockets, stand up. Anything you can think of. The only rule is you have to STAY IN THE STALL until 12:35.*
>
> *Do this and the world will unravel but DON'T be afraid. It's the only way to make the world settle down. If you make the world unravel enough in a short space of time it will STOP unravelling FOR-EVER.*

This is the TRUTH.

GOOD LUCK
Annalise

He clutched the note to his chest. He'd done it! And then he was running. *She* was outside. Annalise Fifteen. He'd found her. He'd told her he would.

He raced down the stairs, bounding onto the landings. Two people pressed themselves flat against the wall as he clattered past.

"What's the matter with him?" one said to the other.

Couldn't they see? Didn't they recognize true happiness when it nearly knocked them over on the stairs? He started laughing, laughing and running. He felt like he could do anything. He felt like he could run and run forever.

He reached the ground floor, a grinning, giggling idiot running along the back corridor, past the Post Room, not caring who saw him or what they thought. He dodged past the lunchtime stragglers in the entrance lobby, fixed his eyes on the pavement and exploded into the light.

Where was she? He was on the pavement outside the DTI, spinning, his hand shielding his eyes. She had to be here, she had to!

Had he flipped again?

"Graham! Over here!"

He turned. She was leaning out of a car window, the car double-parked, Annalise waving, her hair shining in the sun. He started to run, the car door opened. They met by the curb. Graham kept going, sweeping her up and swinging her around so fast they toppled against the boot of a car.

"It's really you, isn't it?" she said as they untangled themselves.

"It's really me. I told you I'd find you."

"Come on!" shouted a woman from the car. "We're late as it is."

Annalise and Graham piled into the back of the car. Graham pulled the door shut behind him and was immediately thrown against the rear seat as the car accelerated away.

"Time to get changed, Graham," said Annalise, handing him a police helmet and uniform. "Disguise," she said. "There are twenty Graham and Annalise look-alikes heading for Ladbroke Road. We're going to be the ones who don't look like us."

Annalise pulled what looked like a long black dress over her head. "I've converted to Islam," she said as her head reappeared. "It was either this or become a nun."

"You could have dyed your hair," said the woman driver.

"That's Jenny," said Annalise, "She's our fairy godmother."

Graham stared at Annalise. She was amazing. Ninety minutes ago, she hadn't known he was coming. Now she had twenty look-alikes and two fancy dress costumes.

"How did you find time to get these costumes?" he asked.

"They're not costumes," said Annalise. "They're the real thing. Thanks to Jenny and her horde of contacts."

The car stop-started through the London midday traffic, switching lanes and accelerating whenever it could. Graham slid in the back seat, trying to get changed and wishing his arms were articulated differently.

He noticed Jenny watching him in the mirror. He wondered how much she knew. And how much she'd guessed.

"Doesn't seem to be anyone following us," said Jenny. "The look-alike convoy at the flat must have worked."

"Trouble is they don't need to follow us," said Annalise. "They know where we're going."

Jenny pulled the car over two blocks from the police station. Graham grabbed his helmet and followed Annalise onto the pavement. Jenny leaned out the driver's window, gave last-minute directions and wished them luck. "See you in five minutes," she said, pulling back into traffic.

Annalise clipped her veil over her face. He wouldn't have recognized her, covered head to toe in black.

"Graham," she said. "I'm a married woman, you shouldn't be staring."

They split up as arranged—Graham walking on ahead, Annalise following slowly behind, letting the gap between them grow to forty, fifty yards.

As soon as they separated, he kicked himself for not asking her how the other Grahams were doing. He checked his watch. It had been nearly twenty minutes since he'd left the room. How was everyone coping? Were the girls keeping it going? Were the Grahams running out of choices? Were they . . .

More guilt. He'd been so busy worrying about himself and how to stop the resonance wave he hadn't stopped to consider the other Grahams. What was this doing to them? Some would see a room unravel before their eyes. One second they'd be an anonymous guest at a party, next they'd be the center of attention, people asking them for help, people in tears.

What had he done? Had he made things worse? Was he going to prosper at the expense of others? They might be scarred for life—even more scarred than they already were. Freaks to be pointed at—"That's Graham, the one with the visions. Where's my message, freak, why'd you leave me out?"

An orange-haired Annalise look-alike appeared ahead of him, briefly pulling him out of his despondency. He'd have to make amends. Whatever it took. He had to make sure the Grahams were okay.

Other look-alikes appeared, on both sides of the road, each with a look-alike Graham in tow. He wondered if that was an omen. Fate parading anonymous Grahams in front of him, every one of them a target whose sole purpose was to allow him—the one Graham—to arrive unmolested at his destination. The one Graham, the selfish Graham, the unexpendable Graham.

He suppressed the desire to rip off his uniform and shout his name to the rooftops. He'd make amends. But not now.

He increased his pace, moving up to a brisk march, took a deep breath, two. He had to concentrate. He saw the entrance on his right, a flight of steps. Two look-alikes were already there. They jogged up the steps. Graham followed. He was inside. Jenny was waiting, she was waving him over. He slipped off his helmet, ran to her and, suddenly, everything slipped into dream time. Three, four men appeared alongside, their hands supporting him, guiding him through labyrinthine twists and turns. A door opened, he was led inside, a large window, six men lined up against a wall, he recognized one, picked him out.

"Are you sure?" someone said.

"Yes," he heard himself say. "That's him."

A scene repeated four times.

A gaggle of lawyers and detectives huddled in the corner. Graham used the opportunity to drag Annalise away from Jenny. "What's happening with the Grahams?" he whispered, praying that he would have the strength to cope with the answer.

"It's working," she said. "Some of the Grahams are freaking out but we're getting through to them. Even if they can't talk, they're making choices. And the girls are prompting like crazy. Passing on details of everyone you helped."

"It's still going on?" He wasn't sure if that was a good sign or not. He'd hoped it would be over in an hour.

"Do you think I should . . ."

She grabbed his arm. "You're not going anywhere," she said. "You've done your bit."

"But . . ."

"No buts. The girls have it under control." She tilted her head to one side. "I'm listening to them now."

"You can hear them all? At the same time?"

She smiled. "If I wanted to go insane I could. I tune them in and out, though they're not at their most lucid at the moment. It's one crazy circus out there."

He wondered how long they could keep it going. And how many Grahams they'd reached. Was it just the same Grahams cycling back and forth or had they reached out to the billions as he'd hoped? And did it matter? Was it the strength and number of flips or the breadth across the worlds? If he'd been a scientist, maybe he'd have stopped and run more simulations beforehand.

He looked at his watch. 1:31. The party would be finishing soon. Maybe it already had? Maybe most Grahams had only stopped by for the first ten minutes?

Jenny came over.

"They've charged the four men and grounded Sylvestrus's plane."

Graham forced a smile. Annalise and Jenny embraced.

"They'll need to take your statement next, Graham," Jenny said. "Jerry'll be with you. if you have any questions . . . Graham?"

Something strange was happening. Jenny's voice had receded.

"Graham!"

Annalise's face ballooned into view, strangely elongated as though a giant hand had stretched it apart.

"No, Graham. You can't!"

FIFTY-SIX

Graham's head spun. He needed fresh air. The world was closing in on him, he felt disorientated. He couldn't trust his eyes and ears.

Panic! He was flipping. He reached out. His hand tapered away twenty yards distant and receding. Annalise was at the end of a long dark tube, a ray of golden orange in a night sky of starless black. He grabbed with distant fingers, felt them close around something soft, something warm. He tightened his grip and hung on. Someone screamed, the sound reverberating slow and deep, a painful scream stretched out and drawn.

Annalise sprung back into vision, the tube receding, lengthening, Annalise dancing back and forth on the end of his arm. Never in focus, always painted on a stretched canvas. Voices speeding and slowing, everything out of kilter.

Annalise disappeared. Jenny too. The room stayed. The same decor, the same sparse furniture, different people. Then no people. Then a different room. Open plan. No police. An office. A police station. An office again.

Images cycled faster and faster. He was outside. Rain was falling on his face. He was standing on a pavement, a field, a road. The sky was blue, white, black. The buildings opposite flickered with the sky. They rose and fell, gave way to green fields, castle walls, tower blocks, space ports, a forest.

Faster and faster. His head spinning. All noise compressed into a single hum. All images into one confused blur.

And then blackness.

Silence.

And pain.

He was lying in a bed. White ceiling, white walls, a clear plastic pouch hanging above his head.

He was in a hospital? A pain hit him behind the eyes when he tried to move. He opened his mouth to speak but nothing appeared to happen. Was he badly injured?

He tried to recall what had happened. He remembered the birthday party and the police station and . . .

No! He couldn't have. After everything he'd done, the preparation, he couldn't have flipped. There couldn't have been another Graham in the police station.

Could there?

A monitor somewhere in the room beeped.

And what was he doing in a hospital?

And why couldn't he move? His muscles felt nonexistent. They . . .

Was he in a coma?

Was he paralyzed?

Had he flipped into the body of a comatose Graham?

"Graham?"

Annalise's voice! Had he flipped into Annalise Twelve's world?

He tried to speak. Maybe he was coming out of the coma? Maybe there was hope?

His mouth refused to cooperate.

Annalise's face loomed over his. Twelve had orange hair. The same as Fifteen and Seven.

He moved his eyes, flicked them left and right to show her he was alive.

"He's coming round," shouted Annalise over her shoulder.

Another face appeared. A doctor. She looked like Shikha but she couldn't be. Her hair was shorter and . . .

Jenny? What was Jenny doing in this world. He could see her at the foot of the bed.

"Graham," whispered Annalise, leaning over close to his ear. "You did it. The link's broken. All the Grahams collapsed at the same time. The girls got theirs to hospitals. I'm sure the others are okay too."

He struggled to say something. Was he going to live? Was she really Annalise Fifteen? Was it over? Was Sylvestrus in custody?

"You're going to be fine. The drugs will wear off soon. All the Grahams will be fine. Sylvestrus is on his way to South America, on the run and discredited. His driver and bodyguard have agreed to testify against him."

He fell asleep sometime after that.

FIFTY-SEVEN

Graham returned to work the next day. To clear out his desk and appease his conscience. He had to find all the people he could have helped the day before if he hadn't been in such a rush to free Annalise.

He scrolled through the staff list, ticking off the names in his head—Holly, Stephen, Colin—and wondered how they'd react. Yesterday he'd been the idiot savant touched by God, every word he'd uttered had been gospel. But today? Today, his name was all over the papers. The mysterious victim in the ParaDim scandal. The friend of the Flame-Haired Firestarter. The Annaliscious babe's not-so-photogenic sidekick.

"Graham?" A voice from the doorway made him turn. Sharmila was standing there, her eyes wide open with surprise. "What are you doing here? I thought you were in a hospital. Are you all right?"

"I'm fine now, Sharmila," he said. "Thank you for asking. How are you?"

They chatted—uneasily at first—words clicking against his dry pallet. He told her he was leaving, taking a holiday until he worked out what to do with the rest of his life. He probed her about Holly and the others. She asked him about Annalise and the newspapers.

The delivery bay doors swung open.

"Well, if it isn't Mr. Post-it," said Ray. "On a flying visit, are we? Girlfriend kicked you out?"

"Shut up, Ray," said Graham.

"It speaks?" said Ray, his eyes beginning to sparkle.

"It bites too," said Graham, amazed at how easily the words came. And at how small Ray really was. What was he? Five and a half feet? Five and a half feet of swagger and mean-spirited pettiness.

"So, the big man's gonna bite me, is he?" said Ray, opening his mouth and spreading his arms wide in mock fear as he sauntered towards Graham.

"Ray!" warned Sharmila. "Leave him alone."

Graham stood up and looked Ray straight in the eyes. The shorter man kept coming, not stopping until their chests almost touched.

"Do you really want to do this?" Graham asked.

"What?" said Ray, defiant, contemptuous.

"Be an idiot all your life."

Ray stiffened. "Who you calling an idiot?" he snapped.

"You," Graham said. "You pick on people for fun. You delight in other people's embarrassment and . . ."

"And what? Do tell?" A finger poked Graham hard in the chest. The finger turned into a hand, the poke into a shove. "Come on, Graham, what's the matter? Cat got your tongue again?"

Graham shoved back. Hard. Then stopped. "This is ridiculous," he said, shaking his head. "I'm not going to fight you."

"There's a surprise," said Ray, revelling in the sarcasm.

"Ray!" said Sharmila. "Back off or I call security."

"Why?" said Ray throwing up his hands. "The fun's just starting. Graham's learned English. Come on, Graham. You hadn't finished. And what?"

"And if you don't stop, someone's going to get hurt," said Graham. "Either you or one of the girls."

"What girls?" said Ray, looking genuinely surprised for the first time.

"You know," said Graham. "And so do I." He looked hard into Ray's eyes. Did he see a flicker of guilt? Fear, maybe. Was the Ray on this world the same as the Ray on the others. And could he be saved? Could he be warned off before he crossed any line?

Graham didn't know. Maybe he'd already crossed several lines, but he had to try. If he could frighten Ray enough, maybe it wasn't too late.

"Come on then. What do you know?" said Ray, sneering.

"I know that if my friend ever sees you so much as speak to an underage girl, you'll regret it."

Ray swallowed. Graham *had* hit a nerve. He could see doubt, maybe a hint of panic in the man's eyes.

"What friend?" said Ray. "The crazy bint in the papers?"

Graham slowly shook his head. "I wouldn't call her that if I were you. The last man who called her crazy had his face set alight. Don't you read the papers?"

"Not too happy about being called a bint either," said Annalise, leaning against the delivery bay door. She tilted her head to one side, widened her eyes and waved a petrol can in Ray's direction. "Anyone got a light?"

They laughed about it over lunch. The speed with which Ray had left, the ease with which Annalise could convince people she was insane.

"Years of practice," she joked. "You think I should show up at his home a few times to keep him on the straight and narrow?"

Graham didn't know. He wasn't sure if they'd put Ray on the straight and narrow or just had a joke at his expense. He hoped the former and feared the latter. At least they'd tried. And without any evidence what else could they do?

The sun came out. St. James's Park in bloom. So many memories trapped between the trees, so many lives touched. What were they all doing now?

"Did Six get back to you about counselling the Grahams?" he asked Annalise.

"Didn't I tell you?" she said. "They've all agreed. All the Resonance projects they've contacted so far. And they're leaving messages for the others, telling them about the part the Grahams played. ParaDim will provide all the counselling support the Grahams need."

"Do I get counselling?"

"You get personal counselling," she said smiling. "From the Annaliscious one."

"And the resonance wave?"

"According to Six it's too early to tell for sure. But everyone's talking as though it's a done deal. Gary says they'll know by the end of the week. If it's worked, the

number of new ParaDim projects should slow down to a
trickle, then stop."

"And in the meantime, the RPs are still closing," said
Graham wanly.

Annalise grimaced. "Only until Sylvestrus is stopped.
The other RPs are moving against him. They're filling
their logs with warnings to the others. And they're leaking
information like crazy to their boards, the Federal autho-
rities, the EU, anyone who can slip a leash around
Sylvestrus's neck."

"They're all following your example," he said, a warm
feeling spreading over him. He felt so proud of her. The
speed with which she'd toppled Sylvestrus. The ingenuity,
the persistence . . .

"And they're gonna share information like crazy. As
soon as Sylvestrus slips up on one world, the information's
gonna get passed to the others. Every body that's found,
every gunman that rolls over—people are gonna be told.
Unless the guy changes his MO on every world, he's
busted."

Another of Fifteen's innovations, using parallel worlds
to solve crime.

"There's one thing that still doesn't make sense,
though," she said. "I can see how the Sylvestruses that
worked with the Spanish woman discovered they had to
put you in a coma. But what about the others? They never
met the Maria person, so how did they know? Do you
think he was a telepath?"

Something Graham had been wondering about. It
hadn't made sense. At first. Until he realized it didn't need
to.

"Think of Sylvestrus," said Graham, "as someone who

becomes caught up in his own mythology. He's the miracle worker, the great Adam Sylvestrus. He holds the future of the human race in his hands. And then one day he takes a long hard look at the human race and doesn't like what he sees. Suddenly, the resonance wave isn't so bad after all. It's the ideal opportunity to purge the world. He notices the spate of RP closures and the idea resonates with how he feels. He *wants* the RPs to close. He reads their reports. They all thought they were on the verge of a breakthrough and they all mentioned me. Then he reads how the day after each RP closes they find me unconscious in the street.

"He doesn't need any more than that. He doesn't need to know why I had to be rendered unconscious. All he has to know is that whoever closed the original RPs saw me as a risk that had to be neutralized."

"And so he copycats."

"Exactly."

"So what now?" she said. "How do we reverse this technological conveyor belt toward chaos?"

"That's easy," he said. "We start learning all we can about LifeSim."

"What's LifeSim?"

"Another word for hope."

The following is an excerpt from:

SHIFT

BY

CHRIS DOLLEY

Available from Baen Books

July 2007

hardcover

CHAPTER ONE

He came out of the darkness in a rush; lights appearing—above, below, to the side—sweeping past him in streaky blurs. He was flying—fast—racing across fields and hedgerows a few feet above the grass. No wind in his hair, no sound, no car beneath him, no plane. Nothing between him and the ground except the blur of speed.

What was happening? Where . . .

A building appeared. A white speck ballooning in size. He was flying straight towards it. Turn! Stop! Pull up!

He couldn't! The walls, the concrete, growing and beckoning. Impact imminent. He tried to raise his hands to protect his face. But he had no hands.

Panic. Time-stretching, gut-wrenching terror. A flash of white as he hit the wall then . . .

He passed straight through, into a corridor, a room, another corridor. Still flying, disorientated by the speed,

he blurs, the impossibility. He was flying a few inches
above the floor tiles, zigzagging along corridors, a tumbling eyeball with no limbs, no body, no . . .

A sound! Far off and muted but the first sound he'd
heard since what seemed like forever. A voice, strange
and elongated, slowed down and slurred. And light, suddenly all around him, bright and dazzling. He was falling,
falling and then . . .

"Now, Peter, tell me what you see."

A room crystallized around him, needle sharp in its
clarity: stark white walls, concrete floor, no door that he
could see. A solitary light shone from a featureless ceiling.
A face stared back at him, questioning. A face haloed in
light. A man he'd never seen before.

"It's Christmas," said the stranger, his voice soft and
emotionless, his accent unexpectedly English. "You're four
years old, sitting beneath a Christmas tree, opening presents. What do you see?"

"What do I see?"

Was the man crazy? And who the hell was Peter? He
tried to move but felt the immediate tug of restraints.
Straps? He was strapped to a chair. His arms and legs
bound. His head too. He could hardly move.

"What's the matter, Peter? What can you see?"

He strained at his ties, pulling, arching his body,
pushing with his feet against the bare concrete floor.

"What have you done to me? Why am I tied up like
this?"

"It's for your own safety, Peter. You know that."

"I am not Peter! What's the matter with you?" He spat
the words out. Disbelief and anger. "My name's John, John
Bruce. Don't you recognise me?"

His interrogator didn't reply. He just watched—impassive, unconcerned—looking down at a clipboard every few seconds to jot down a note.

"Who's in charge around here? I want to see someone in authority. Now!"

He was shouting, desperation welling up inside. What were they doing to him? He was John Bruce. The astronaut. The first man chosen to fly to the stars. His last real memory, strapped inside the Pegasus, waiting for the countdown to stop, for the dimension shift engine to engage and send him hurtling into the unknown, spiralling into the higher dimensions. And then? What had happened to him after that? Dim recollections of an all-encompassing blackness, timeless drifting, that weird flight along fields and floor tiles and now here; strapped into another chair. But where? He'd never seen this room before in his life.

And who the hell was Peter?

"It's all right, Peter. Calm down."

"I am not Peter! How many times do I have to tell you? I'm John Bruce, the astronaut."

He was very close to losing control; arms, head and legs straining against the ties. Like a four-year-old denied a treat, caught in the throes of a temper tantrum, he thrashed and screamed.

"It's okay, John. I'll get the nurse to untie you. You can watch HV if you like. Everything's going to be fine. We'll talk again tomorrow."

Doctor Paul Bazley, senior psychologist at the Upper Heywood Secure Psychiatric Unit, was not a happy man. But unlike most unhappy men, Paul Bazley knew both the reason and the remedy for his state of mind: Peter

endennis and the killing of Peter Pendennis. Unfortu-
ately, the Hippocratic Oath frowned upon murdering
ne's patients—however justifiable.

He sighed, leaned back in his chair, and tried to relax.
Iis office stared back at him, sparse and impersonal, like
verything else at Upper Heywood—institutionally fur-
ished by a distant bureaucrat on a tight budget;
vhite-painted walls, generic prints, cheap furniture.

The door opened and Anders Ziegler, Bazley's young
olleague, bounced into the room. "You'll never believe
!" he said. "Peter's found a new personality."

Peter. It was always Peter. You'd think he was the only
atient in the unit. Peter this, Peter that. Why didn't
.iegler see he was being used? Anything Pendennis said
vas suspect from the moment it left his twisted little brain.
Ie was a liar, a manipulator, a fantasist.

And a killer. As sick as they come.

But to Ziegler—young, enthusiastic Ziegler—he was
till a challenge. Something new and exciting, an enigma
vho hid behind madness and layers of multiple person-
lities, peeling off one after the other but never showing
nything but a glimpse of the monster that dwelt inside.

"I said, Peter's found a new personality."

"I heard you the first time," snapped Bazley, watching
is colleague walk over to the small table in the far corner
nd pour himself a coffee. A conversation was imminent.
\ long conversation if Ziegler had his way.

Bazley felt the tic above his left eye flicker into over-
lrive.

"Yes," said Ziegler, stirring in the last of the milk substi-
ute. "Personality number thirteen. John Bruce. *The* John
3ruce."

"Who's John Bruce?"

"You know. The astronaut running for President."
Ziegler pulled up a chair and placed his coffee on the
edge of Bazley's desk. "If Peter thinks he's someone else,
is that a delusion or another personality?"

Ziegler smiled. Bazley did not. Pendennis was not a
subject to be joked about.

"I wonder if any of his other personalities are based
upon real people? An interesting line of research, don't
you think? But why suddenly latch onto Bruce? You'd have
thought that if he were going to, he would have done so
two years ago when Bruce first hit the headlines. So why
now?"

"Probably fed up inventing his own."

Ziegler took a few tentative sips of coffee. "You don't
believe a word he says, do you?"

"Not one."

"Even though he passes every test there is? Hypnosis,
drugs, every lie detector we can find. His stories always
check out and they're always consistent."

"He's clever."

"Clever enough to keep twelve or thirteen personalities on the go? Separate family histories, separate
memories, mannerisms, ways of talking. He even sounded
like an American this morning."

"I told you, he's clever."

"But he's not! Look at his old school reports, his IQ
tests. He's average to below average. He shouldn't know
half the things he does. Let alone express himself the way
he can at times."

Bazley was ready to explode. Didn't Ziegler ever listen? He'd told him so many times. Pendennis had never

been interested in school or tests. And as for lie detection, that assumed you had some concept of truth. Pendennis didn't. He had no heart, no conscience, no concept of right or wrong. Just a hollow core wrapped in layers of sham multiple personalities. An empty box in a shiny package, reflecting whatever it was he wanted you to see.

That was Pendennis. A manipulator who craved to be at the centre of every universe, pushing and prodding until he achieved a reaction. Provoking warders—what did he care if he spent a few weeks in hospital recovering from a beating? He'd won, hadn't he? Sent a warder over the edge, a warder who'd have to be disciplined, a warder who'd never forget the man responsible.

And there might be an inquiry—a chance to widen Peter's circle, suck in a few more people into his expanding world. Social workers, liberal lawyers, nurses at the hospital. Sympathetic ears to soak up harrowing stories, he'd feed them whatever they wanted to hear. Beatings, victimization, a hint that he might be innocent.

He'd crawl inside their heads, pushing everything else aside like a cuckoo in a man's soul. He'd be a puzzle, a victim, a friend. A source of stories that insinuated into your dreams. Stories that beguiled, terrified, made you search beneath your bed before you could sleep, made you stare at shadows in the middle of the night.

And if he got bored, he'd attack—without warning, without reason—130 pounds of feral energy, clawing, biting, gouging with whatever came to hand.

And back Peter would go into solitary confinement and a month or two later it would start all over again. Different victim, different story. The man was so plausible, so persistent, he could cry wolf a dozen times and still find a receptive ear. He had a personality for every occasion, one that he could hide behind later and shout—it wasn't me! I don't even know what you're talking about!

"You all right?"

"What?" Bazley looked up to see Ziegler staring at him across the desk, concern in his eyes. "I'm fine," lied Bazley, uncurling whitened fingers from the arms of his chair.

"Anyway," continued Ziegler, "I was regressing him back to that Christmas when he was four years old. To the time before the first manifestation of multiple personalities. You remember the story he told me of how he found the knives—the set of kitchen knives—meant for his mother and thought they were his?"

Bazley bit his lip. He'd told Ziegler . . .

"I thought it would be interesting to pursue that line. A four-year-old associates brightly wrapped packages with presents for himself. He can't discriminate between gifts for himself and gifts for the rest of the family. He finds a pile of presents and begins to open them all. One of the presents contains a set of kitchen knives, all bright and shiny. Later he believes it to be a sign, a message from God instructing him to use the knives."

Unbelievable! "Can't you see he's playing you?"

"He might be. But if he is, isn't it better to draw him out? The more he talks the more likely he is to reveal something that's actually true. It's got to be better than ignoring him."

Bazley shook his head. Ignoring him was the *only* answer. If it wasn't for the EU and prisoner's rights, he'd have had Pendennis locked away in permanent isolation. Bricked up in a wall cavity, if he could have gotten away with it.

A knock on the door interrupted their conversation. A head peered around the door.

"Sorry to disturb you, Doctor Bazley, Doctor Ziegler, but it's Peter. I think you'd better take a look."

"Why, what's happened?"

"He caught sight of himself in the mirror and went berserk. He's shouting and screaming for a whole bunch of people I've never heard of and we don't know what to do with him."

"He went berserk at his mirror?"

"Yeah. He totally lost it."

Bazley couldn't believe it. His mirror? The one calming influence in Peter's life. The only reason they allowed one in his cell. He'd spend hours staring into it, smiling, nodding, carrying on strange one-sided conversations with his reflection.

Why the sudden change?

Bazley could feel the curiosity surge inside him, just like old times, the rush, the desire to know. Was that what Peter had planned? The whole episode designed to lure him back into Peter's world?

"No." He shook his head. Not again. He'd stayed clear of Pendennis for four months. He couldn't get involved again now.

The warder looked confused. "Doc?"

Ziegler stood up. "I'll come immediately," he said.

Bazley didn't move. He looked down at his desk and tightened his grip on the arms of his chair.

Peter stood in front of the cell mirror clutching his face.

"What's happened to me! My face! What have you done to my face?"

"We haven't done anything to you, Peter," said Ziegler, standing in the doorway.

"I told you! My name isn't Peter, it's John Bruce. Get SHIFT control in here. I want to talk to Harrington. I want explanations."

"Okay, John. Calm down. Let's start from the beginning. What's SHIFT control?"

"You know!" His anger burned. Then turned to surprise. "Isn't this SHIFT medical center?"

"No. This is the Upper Heywood Secure Psychiatric Unit."

A long pause in which Peter's—or John's—eyes traced the small, sparsely furnished cell as if seeing it for the first time.

"A prison?"

"We prefer to call it a psychiatric unit."

Peter looked away, opened his mouth as if to speak then shook his head. He took a deep breath. "In England? Upper Heywood's near Oxford, right? Where the old air base was?"

"That's right."

"Then what am I doing here?"

Ziegler paused. What should he say? Confront Peter with the truth and risk a negative reaction or let the scene play out? Both had their dangers.

He tried a middle way. "You were committed eight years ago."

"What!" Peter's mouth opened and closed in confusion. "But ... What year's this?"

"2056."

"2056! But that's . . ." He shook his head, turned away, the fingers of both hands flexing then balling into fists.

"No," he said, swinging back to face Ziegler, spitting out the words as he fought to keep control. "I can remember August '54 like it was yesterday. And I sure as hell wasn't here. What the *hell* is going on?"

Ziegler didn't answer. He didn't want to guide the conversation.

"You must have seen me on HV." Peter waved his arms in exasperation. "Everyone did. The space launch, John Bruce the astronaut, the SHIFT project, you must know who I am!"

There was a pleading look in his eye.

"We've heard of John Bruce," said Ziegler. "And the space launch, but that was eighteen months ago and you've been here eight years. How do you explain that?"

"I . . .

I don't know." He looked confused. And increasingly desperate. He looked from Ziegler to the warders and back again.

"But I can prove I'm John Bruce. Ask me a question, any question. I was born on September 28th, 2024, in Denver, Colorado. My father's Daniel John, my mother's Michelle. Bring them here, they'll recognize me!"

The words came out in a rush and then trailed off as he glanced at the face in the mirror. Ziegler could imagine what he saw. John Bruce had the face and physique of a chisel-jawed superhero. Peter Pendennis did not. Even in his mid-twenties, he still looked like a slightly built adolescent. Sallow complexion, large childlike eyes, scrawny limbs.

"What have you done to my face? Plastic surgery? Was there a fire? Is that it? The launch went wrong and I got burned up bad?"

Ziegler was unsure how to proceed. Peter was becoming agitated again. Was this the moment to tell him the truth? That John Bruce was alive and well and running for the Republican nomination? Or could he deflect him with questions about the SHIFT mission? Test Peter's knowledge, maybe find a reason for Peter's sudden interest.

"Well?"

Ziegler still wasn't sure. Peter was unpredictable and capable of extreme violence in all his guises. And at the moment he wasn't restrained.

And Ziegler was between Peter and the warders.

Ziegler shuffled—imperceptibly, he hoped—back towards the cell door.

Peter advanced towards him, his hands rising towards Ziegler's shoulders. A pleading look in his eye. Or was that an act?

"Tell me!" he shouted.

And then froze. His arms locked in space, stretching towards Ziegler's collar. His face rigid. His lower jaw . . . slowly beginning to twitch. Then his head shot back, his back arched, and his chest pitched forward.

Ziegler threw himself back against the door. He'd seen this before. So had the warders. They rushed past him into the room.

Peter staggered in front of them, legs buckling, eyes bulging, a gurgling sound bubbling up from his throat.

Experienced hands grabbed hold of his shoulders, took his weight. After a few seconds the straining body relaxed and Peter smiled.

"You don't wanna believe a word that Yank says. He's madder than I am."

Then came the laugh. A forced laugh that gradually increased in energy, building and surging until it took control of his entire body, shaking it, shaking the arms of the warders who struggled to keep their grip. Jack was back. Jack enjoyed a good laugh. Trouble was he couldn't stop. Laugh himself into a convulsion would our Jack. And then they'd have to tie him down again. Until Peter, or one of his friends, returned and Jack could go home.

Wherever that was.

—end excerpt—

from *Shift*
available in hardcover,
July 2007, from Baen Books